"FIR

PRAISE FOR *NEON TOUGH* AND TONY KENRICK

"Brilliantly conceived, marvelous insanity."

—*The Pittsburgh Press*

"Vivid! . . . Provocative. . . . Kenrick introduces us to powerful money men, hired killers, elegant women, and a cast of unique characters . . . the suspense level is high."

—*The Herald* (Statesboro, Ga.)

"Drugs are only part of the plot. The bonus is the lively portrait of Hong Kong."

—*City Limits*

"Kenrick is an accomplished storyteller, who carefully hones his narrative to produce a gripping tale."

—*Publishers Weekly*

QUANTITY SALES

Most Dell books are available at special quantity discounts when purchased in bulk by corporations, organizations, and special-interest groups. Custom imprinting or excerpting can also be done to fit special needs. For details write: Dell Publishing, 666 Fifth Avenue, New York, NY 10103. Attn.: Special Sales Department.

INDIVIDUAL SALES

Are there any Dell books you want but cannot find in your local stores? If so, you can order them directly from us. You can get any Dell book in print. Simply include the book's title, author, and ISBN number if you have it, along with a check or money order (no cash can be accepted) for the full retail price plus $2.00 to cover shipping and handling. Mail to: Dell Readers Service, P.O. Box 5057, Des Plaines, IL 60017.

NEON
TOUGH

Tony Kenrick

A DELL BOOK

Published by
Dell Publishing
a division of
Bantam Doubleday Dell Publishing Group, Inc.
666 Fifth Avenue
New York, New York 10103

ISBN: 0-440-20475-5

Reprinted by arrangement with G. P. Putnam's Sons

Printed in the United States of America
Printed simultaneously in Canada

October 1989

10 9 8 7 6 5 4 3 2 1

KRI

For Melanie and Tim,
two of my all-time favorite people.

ACKNOWLEDGMENTS

I had enormous help in the preparation of this book from a lot of people, most notably agents and ex-agents of the DEA in London, Washington, Tokyo and Hong Kong, and many members, past and present, of the Royal Hong Kong Police. My sincere thanks to all of them.

I
DECKER

1

The green Chrysler, a seized car a Grade 7 gofer had driven up
from the South the day before, glided in to the curb outside the
Sun Yan Tun Beauty Parlor, killed its headlights, flashed them on
again, then cut them with the engine.

A man came out of the dark doorway of the Chinese Conservative Baptist Church, hurried along the sidewalk, and climbed into
the rear of the car.

He sat back against the seat, unmindful of the plush comfort, a
scrawny thirty-five-year-old Chinese with stringy, neck-length hair,
work pants, a plaid shirt, scuffed high-top basketball shoes, and a
brown double-breasted jacket which was the top half of a suit.
Turning around from behind the wheel, Hugh Decker said, "How
are you, Eddie?"

"Fine."

The man in the passenger seat, a man named Schweitzer, who
was Decker's junior partner, said, "You don't sound too fine." He
got out of the car, got into the rear.

"I'm okay," the Chinese insisted.

Decker peered at Eddie Fong, the man's thin, nervous face illuminated by the weak light struggling in from the sidewalk. Decker
watched his partner go to work on him, going in under the man's
plaid shirt, taping the Kel to his washboard ribs. A sour smell of
anxiety, released from the open shirt, began to fill the car.

Decker saw something in Eddie Fong's eyes which he took for
uncertainty.

"You're not gonna choke on me, are you, sport?"

The Chinese swallowed.

"Because," Decker went on, "I can't do much for you if you

choke. I want you to know that. You got a room reserved in the steel hotel, Eddie, and you're looking at about ten gallons of time. You go limp on me, you'll do every drop. You understand that?"

Eddie Fong swallowed again, nodded, winced at the feel of cold plastic and plaster tape against his skin.

Decker looked at him hard, trying to read him. Decker was generally very good with street folk; he had the music, an ability to get behind their eyes and separate what they were saying from what they were thinking. It wasn't an infallible talent, and Decker wasn't one hundred percent sure about Eddie Fong. He hesitated, making up his mind, then decided to go with it. Hell, he'd put a lot of work into this one.

He reached into a pocket and handed over an envelope.

"Ten thousand bucks, Eddie. If I don't get that back, they'll have me washing cars for two years."

Eddie Fong took the envelope, slipping it inside his suit coat jacket as Schweitzer finished the wire job.

Decker continued his little pep talk.

"Just do it like I told you, and we'll all come out of this at the nice end. You give the man the money, chat to him, get him to say a few things. He gives you the two and a half. Get him to talk about that. Then you say, loud and clear, 'Ho ga chien, a fair bargain.' Then you get out of there, leave the room immediately. Don't hang around because we'll be coming in heavy, kicking down doors. All right?"

The Chinese grunted, a not very confident sound. As he leaned forward, reaching for the door handle, a sliver of exterior light sparkled on the moisture beaded across his brow.

"Eddie?"

"I got it. Don't worry, I got it."

Eddie Fong stepped out of the car and started walking.

"I don't know, Deck," Schweitzer said, getting back into the front seat. "He looks a little shaky."

"He's facing his future. Wouldn't you be nervous?"

"I'm already nervous. How come the busts are always in weird fucking places like this? Always at night?"

"Because," Decker said, starting the engine, "the bad guys live in weird fucking places like this. And they're all rich enough to sleep late."

Decker took the Chrysler slowly away, following the figure up ahead. Yellow light falling from a first-floor window landed briefly on Eddie Fong's narrow shoulders as he turned the corner into Henry Street.

Decker stretched for a switch that controlled the radio mike tucked out of sight under the dash.

"Cupcake?"

A voice answered, the low receiver volume muffling its cheekiness.

"Yes, ma'am?"

"You get where you going yet?"

"We're sittin' and a-rockin'."

"What's the green word?"

"Gates."

"Don't leave home without it, okay?"

"You bet your balls."

Decker clicked off the mike. The green word he'd referred to was the signal to move, in this case the phrase "The gates are open."

The Chrysler, with very little traffic around this late, had the street to itself as it eased by the Chinese Evangelical Mission, then a dark, unpaved private ear park big enough to squeeze in six or seven automobiles, barbed-wire spirals topping its busted Cyclone fence.

A few yards farther on and the smell of fish drifted through the Chrysler's windows, and Decker caught a glimpse of men in white aprons and black watch caps sweeping down a shiny wet cement floor, the sound of snapped Cantonese clashing with the scrunch of stiff brooms.

Three men standing outside of the New Taiwan Barber Shop turned to watch the car glide by, saw only a couple of uptown gweilos cruising around looking for a little chow mein, or maybe something with a bit more kick to it. Apart from its obvious luxury, the Chrysler didn't look anything special; the radio antenna had been worked along the top of the windshield and was invisible.

At the corner of Catherine Street, looking south, the towers of Wall Street burned with a rich, fiery brightness, cleaners and clerks versus the paper mountain thrown up by the day's trading, getting things in shape for another day's frenzy. To the north the skyline was bulky and flat, the soaring heights of midtown unseen from this location. From East Chinatown, Decker thought, if you faced north, New York could have doubled for Cincinnati.

It was a brief observation; his eyes were on Eddie Fong up ahead, the Chrysler following him under the smash and chatter of the

Manhattan Bridge, then out the other side to the arrow-sharp conjunction of Forsythe and Eldridge. On the point of the corner a grungy-looking body shop featured a collection of mangled cars scrunched up like used Kleenex.

They were well into the old Jewish East Side now, what had since become the new Chinese East Side when Chinatown had burst the seedy constraints of the Bowery which had hemmed it in for one hundred years.

It was not yet a total takeover; the Eldridge Street synagogue, unlike the one a block over on Allen Street, which was a boarded-up wreck, was in beautiful condition, with polished stone arches and immaculate windows, and was crowded on holy days. A number of jewelry polishers had hung on in the old neighborhood, and were still in business. Their small, conservative signs, lettered in black Hebrew script, fought a losing battle with the florid red-and-gold signs of their Chinese neighbors, giving the street the appearance of a ghetto in Peking.

"Danish? This is Sweet Roll." Decker only had to talk softly; the mike beneath the dash was sensitive enough to pick up a whisper. "How you doing?"

A couple of blocks south, near Madison Street, two men in the third radio car, a blue Buick, shifted in their seats.

"In place with big boots on."

"What's the commercial?"

"The bit with the gates."

"Hold tight, hear?"

Eddie Fong had stopped outside of a tenement, was standing beneath the black fire escape that zigzagged down the shabby exterior. A single light was on in a second-story window, diffused by a pulled shade. Some tired plants, potted in rusty forty-ounce tomato cans, leaned against each other behind the broken wrought-iron grille of the window ledge.

The green Chrysler slid into a space on the opposite curb, a ghost of its long shiny image haunting a window full of sequins and glitter for the fur trade. There were steps beneath the storefront, leading down to a blacked-out basement entrance.

The engine died, and the headlights died.

The street was quiet.

Poorly lit.

Eddie Fong was just standing there, looking up at the tenement as if he wasn't sure he had the right address.

"The hell's he waiting for?" Schweitzer murmured in the dark of the Chrysler.

He got an answer, but not from Decker.

A sound, faint at first, then growing in volume until it became the low, angry burble of a big-bore motor.

Tires squealed around a corner. A flashy Oldsmobile, low suspension and pounds of chrome, barreled down the street, wheeled in to a skidding stop level with Eddie Fong.

Schweitzer licked his lips. "Hey, this ain't in the script."

Decker said nothing. With a tightness starting up behind his belly button, he watched the Chinese youths getting out of the car. He knew who they were by the way they were dressed: flak jackets over patterned silk shirts, dirty sneakers, and designer jeans with knife-edge creases. They'd each spent about fifty bucks on their pompadoured hair, shiny and full and black as bats' wings.

Schweitzer recognized them too. "Jesus." He had hollows in his voice. "It's the fucking Shadows."

Decker snapped on the mike, gabbled instructions. *"It's mud! It's mud! Eldridge and Forsythe. Quick!"*

Across the street the gang was talking to Eddie Fong, and shooting hot angry glances at the Chrysler. One of their number, partly obscured by the others, was fumbling with something in his hands, something that Decker and his partner caught a glimpse of at the same time: a short, fat tube, the sights springing up.

They moved at the same instant.

Like sprinters they bolted out of the car doors, Decker hurling himself across the hood, shoulder-rolling, hitting the sidewalk, and vaulting over the iron railing of the open stairs.

Both men collided, tumbled together down the steps, somersaulting over, crashing into garbage cans stacked outside the basement door. The clash of the cans went unheard, overpowered by a roaring, tearing explosion that ripped a huge hole in the night and stuffed it with a roiling ball of searing white incandescence.

The roar expanded as the Chrysler was flipped over and hurled sideways into the storefront, glass smashing, wood splintering, the car buckling into a ruptured hunk of torn and burning metal. A concussive wave of heat and sound leaned on Decker, holding him down like a giant hand trying to drown him in the hard cement of the basement landing.

Then the ink seeped back into the night, and vision returned, and hearing, bringing with it the crash of gunfire, bullets chunking into the ruined Chrysler, spanging off the iron railing, cracking whatever was left of the plate-glass jeweler's window.

The street gang was blazing away with absurd handguns—41's and .44's, with eight- and ten-inch barrels—firing repeatedly, mindlessly; kids with expensive and deadly toys loving the loud, explosive power that kicked in their hands and jarred their fingers.

Another sound climbed over the top of the pounding guns, and Decker caught it: the high screech of a burning skid; another right behind it—a Buick and a Ford LTD coming hard and fast.

The gunfire stopped; doors banged.

Decker pushed himself up, jumped over his stunned partner, made it to the top of the steps.

The Oldsmobile was smoking the street as it shot away.

Decker kept right on going in the opposite direction because the gang hadn't offered Eddie Fong a ride. He was racing back down Eldridge, back the way he'd come.

The two cars, the Buick and the LTD, both slammed to a swerving stop when their drivers spotted Decker sprinting down the sidewalk. He was flinging his finger at the running man ahead.

"Get him! Get him!"

Transmissions chunked, rubber crunched over busted glass as the two cars screamed back down the street in a tandem reverse. The lead car, the LTD, immediately ran into trouble. A triangular shard from a shattered window speared into a rear tire, slashed it apart. The spinning tire twisted and warped off its rim, and the Ford, still charging backward, lunged sideways across the street, blocking off the Buick.

Decker kept going; ran through the shouts and the cries, ran beneath heads shoved out of a hundred tenement windows, through the shrill, insistent clang of fire and burglar alarms. Behind him the Chrysler's gas tank, somehow intact till now, went up with a whumpfff! of brilliant red flame that flashed a reflection off two men ahead of him. One was Eddie Fong, fleeing across Division Street, heading for the pools of darkness that spilt from the arched supports of the enormous, thundering bridge. The other man, big and heavy, had to be Bateman, who'd been in the stricken LTD.

Decker pumped arms and legs, his topcoat flapping around his knees, inhibiting his sprint.

He dashed into the bridge arch, ran into blackness, out again, saw Bateman clearly now as a streetlight yellowed his running figure, sixty feet behind Eddie Fong, Eddie in his brown suit jacket and flying hightop basketball shoes. Eddie was really moving, running from ten years in jail.

Ahead, the Bowery lay spread wide like a state line promising freedom, freedom for Eddie Fong. A zillion Chinese tenement flats huddled west of the avenue, into any one of which a New York Chinese could vanish like a fish darting into a coral reef.

Decker lengthened his stride, tight strings in his thighs, his lungs beginning to feel the pain.

He gained on Bateman, took a couple of yards out of Eddie Fong's lead, put his head down, his shoes stamping into the sidewalk.

He looked up, and got a surprise.

Way short of the Bowery, Eddie Fong pulled up, jumped off his left foot, and scampered through the door of a restaurant.

There was no mistaking it; Decker saw him clearly for a moment, painted pink and gold by a gaudy neon sign. Yee Yat Szechwan, the sign proclaimed, its lively glow welcoming the newcomer, a starving man rushing for a table.

It took Bateman maybe ten seconds to make the restaurant, and he did the right thing: knowing Decker was on his heels, he ignored the entrance and swung his big frame into the alley in order to cover the rear.

Decker ran, wheeled, burst through the front door.

A counter ahead, tables on the right, chopsticks frozen in front of surprised faces, all heads turned, staring at a man in a topcoat, out of breath and with a gun in his hand.

Behind the counter an elderly Chinese stopped in the middle of making change as if he were uncertain whether to give the money to the departing customer or hand it over to this sudden bandit.

Decker checked the room.

No Eddie.

He trotted down a short corridor into a steamy kitchen. A cook with a box full of something collided with him.

The cook did a good job of making it look like an accident: a quick exclamation, red chilies and green broccoli jerked into the air. Fat white onions thumped to the grubby floor and rolled beneath a hissing stove.

Decker shoved the man away, quickly took in the kitchen: two cooks had left off stirring woks, another had paused in the middle of hacking up a chicken. There was a rear door, a toilet off to the right, and what was probably a storeroom off to the left.

The rear door banged open, and Bateman came in fast. Grabbing at breath, he shook his head at Decker. "No way." He gulped at the garlic scented kitchen air. "He woulda had to go by me."

Decker had kept his eye on the front door, even when the cook had barged into him. Nobody had gone out of it.

He ran to it now, slammed it closed, grabbed up a chair and jammed it under the knob. Bateman was doing the same thing at the rear door. There'd be no swift exit from the Yee Yat Szechwan restaurant. They started their search.

Bateman anchored himself in the corridor, watching both doors. Decker took the front room first: two waiters, standard New York dyspeptics, in stained white jackets. Eight tables, six of them occupied; all of the customers Orientals except for a couple of scowling NYU kids on a budget.

None of the diners was Eddie Fong. And there was no place to hide beneath the aluminum/Formica tables. And nobody crouched under the glass-fronted counter with its clogged toothpick dispenser and ancient baroque cash register.

Decker checked the diners once more. His eyes rested on a group of men at a table, four of them, all about Eddie Fong's age, and dressed somewhat similarly, as if they'd bought four suits and shared the pants and jackets between them. They stared back at Decker. One of them, in a striped shirt like a football referee's, had the beginning of a grin on his pockmarked face.

Decker left the room, strode into the kitchen.

The cooks, in their jeans and two-sizes-too-big T-shirts, were back at work. Being Chinese, nothing was allowed to interfere with the preparation of food, and the business of eating it, for very long.

There was no place for a man to hide here; everything sizzled or spat or bubbled over blue flame; everything hot to the touch. Nor was there anything to get into or hide behind, the chopping blocks too low, the preparation tables too open; nothing beneath them but bits of old food and mouse droppings.

The toilet in back was the usual tiny room with a water-stained toilet bowl, a broken plastic seat, and a triangular washbasin big enough for only one hand at a time. There was no window, no ventilation at all.

So that only left the storeroom.

Decker crossed to it, opened the door on a small room stacked with boxes of soy sauce, cans of water chestnuts, packs of MSG, strings of garlic. A low cupboard against the wall, big enough for a man to squeeze into, held nothing but plastic bottles of cooking oil. The walls were solid; blank except for a calendar opened to last month's page and its picture: an overloaded container ship carving a white path through a blue ocean.

He came out of the storeroom, looked over at Bateman, slowly checked the kitchen a second time. Eddie Fong had run into this place. He hadn't had time to run out the back way, climb over a fence, not without Bateman spotting him. Bateman was a good man. All that, and yet Eddie Fong was not here.

But he had to be.

There were no trapdoors in any of the ceilings, and none in the floors.

Decker backtracked in his mind.

When he'd run into the joint, run out here into the hot and noisy kitchen, one of those cooks had hindered him, slowed him down; done it on purpose.

What had the cook been carrying?

A box of vegetables.

So he'd been coming from the storeroom, the storeroom in which there was nothing but food, a cupboard full of cooking oil, and a calendar from a shipping line.

Decker went back into the room, searched it again.

And, this time, spotted something; something that made his stomach loop, and his throat feel hot.

The cupboard against the wall stood on four tiny wheels. It took about two seconds to shove the cupboard aside, another second to make out the outline of a low door set into the wall.

Decker jerked it open.

Blackness.

And a sour, musty smell.

The kind of smell you got in an uncared-for tenement hallway.

Bateman, watching from the corridor, seeing Decker's frozen stance, left his position quickly, hurried into the room. When he got a whiff of the smell, he knew there was no point in guarding the doors anymore.

"Fucking Chinatown," he said, squinting into the darkness of the tunnel. "It's just one big goddamn rabbit warren."

Decker didn't answer.

Eddie Fong, with ten thousand dollars, ten grand that he, Hugh C. Decker, had signed for, was on his way to another Chinatown somewhere: Toronto or Vancouver or San Francisco, who knew?

Decker brushed by Bateman, went out into the steaming kitchen. The cook who'd bumped into him caught the look in his eye, dropped the can of cashews he was opening, picked up a heavy chopper, and went to work on some roast pork, his fingers firm on the handle of the cleaver.

Decker kept going, walked into the front room.

Everybody had resumed their late-night dinner, chopsticks stabbing at rice and greens, bottles of Bud and Johnnie Walker rapidly emptying.

The man in the referee's shirt, eating at the table with his three pals, looked up at Decker, worked his chopsticks, and mailed a fat piece of duck into the slot of his mouth. Then he grinned. It was the grin he'd started before, only now it had become a gold-plated leer.

Decker had seen a grin like that, on a face like that, some time back. It was the same kind of expression the junk captain had shown him in the harbor at Stanley.

Mocking.

Jeering.

Triumphant.

Decker felt the pressure building, his jaw getting tight; a tingling current beginning to vibrate through his bones.

He tried to do something about it, tried to imagine the anger as a baseball made of soft clay. In his mind he reached for the ball, grasped it, squeezed it in his hands, felt the clay turn to soft powder and begin to sprinkle through his fingers.

Pieces of duck were stuck in the golden smile, the black eyes almost closed off, bright with mirth. The man made a sound in the back of his throat that emerged as a snigger.

Decker's hands stopped squeezing. Fuck it!

The clay baseball vanished from his fingers, vanished from his mind. He knew he was blowing it, could feel the rage, like a pushy, physical thing, elbowing everything aside.

It got loose and rocketed up. Took over.

He reached the table in two strides, grabbed the edge of the stained tablecloth with both hands, and heaved it savagely toward him. A tureen of soup, bowls of rice and meat and vegetables, a half-empty bottle of Scotch crashed to the tiled floor, glass shattering, food blotching down.

Decker scrunched up the tablecloth, wrapped it into a furious ball, hurled it at the suddenly shrunken gold-toothed grin.

"Bock meng sic le siew jia!" Decker shouted at him, which meant, "Eat hearty, fuckhead!"

"Deck!"

Bateman was behind him, a heavy hand on his arm.

Decker whirled, the anger stamped into his face, flattening his mouth, rounding his nostrils. It bunched his hands at his sides. Somebody else might have taken a step backward, but Bateman didn't do that. Instead he said, quietly, a temperate appeal, "It's time to go, Deck."

Decker stayed on the other side of the brink for a moment more, then sucked in breath, let his shoulders go, exhaled, slumped. "Yeah," he said. He wiped the palm of his hand over his mouth, covering another deep breath. "Sure. Why not?"

2

The headquarters of the United States Drug Enforcement Administration, a division of the Justice Department, is located, as many people might suspect, in Washington, D.C.

However, the DEA is not, as many people might suspect, housed in a forbidding fortress such as the FBI calls home. The DEA is one of the poorer members of the law-enforcement fraternity, and leases space in the Northwestern Federal Buildings, a reasonably modern eleven-story steel-and-glass office block on the corner of I street and Fourteenth, an area which was once the heart of the city's grind section, long since gone respectable.

Walking through the doors, his plastic ID dangling from a doggie chain around his neck, Decker saw that the same two businesses were still in place each side of the entrance: on the right-hand side, the Jacobs Gardner Office and Party Supplies; on the left-hand side, the Blue Mirror Take-Out Restaurant, Burgers and Fries a Specialty. Nobody could ever accuse his employers of being a bunch of snobs. Another thought occurred to him as he entered the unimpressive lobby: the last time he'd visited Washington on official business he'd been summoned to the Shoreham Building on Vermont Street, hauled up before two inspectors at the Office of Professional Responsibility, and asked to account for his extraordinary behavior and would he mind putting it in writing for the Board of Conduct for Disciplinary Action.

Which he had.

And the Board had promptly taken disciplinary action, and that had lasted for one and a half swell years.

He wondered why it was HQ he'd been summoned to this time, and not Vermont Street again. Probably, he decided, because you didn't have to bother with the Pro. Respon. boys if Administration had decided to trash you for good.

Decker held up his plastic for the large black man behind the sign-in desk, accepted a nod from one of the uniformed security men looking up from his monitor, stepped into a crowded elevator, and rode up with a bunch of guys carrying Styrofoam cups. The conversation was standard basketball talk, the aroma an evocative blend of Old Spice and Nescafé.

The sixth floor looked a lot like a moderately successful ad agency, although one without much pizazz: green contract broadloom, plain off-white walls, rows of small offices, each with a mid-price wood-and-metal desk and matching vinyl-covered chair. There was only one picture in the outer office, a pen-and-ink illustration of the original DEA headquarters on Connecticut Avenue. There was no receptionist; visitors wouldn't be on this floor unless they were escorted, or knew where they were going, and whom they had to see. And Decker knew all too well whom he had to see: Paul Johnson, the AAO, Assistant Administrator of Operations.

Decker walked along a corridor dividing exterior and interior offices. The interior ones were mainly reference rooms containing gray steel filing cabinets whose drawers were closed by heavy combination padlocks. Most of the window offices were empty. At a bend in the corridor Decker stopped in front of some framed sepia-color photographs. In the first one, circa 1929, some serious-looking agents stood with their feet on a sack of seized contraband, as if it were a rhino they'd shot. They held shovels in their hands; behind them was an ominous-looking furnace. Another photograph showed four different agents brandishing medals they'd been awarded; decorated heroes of some early dope bust. Decker wondered what a big score was back then in the late twenties—ten pounds of marijuana? If you could have told any of those men that, sixty years into the future, ships and aircraft would be freighting ninety-percent-pure heroin into the country like it was flour or sugar, would they have believed you?

Of course not.

A little farther along the corridor was a notice board. The pieces of paper attached to it brought a touch of prosaic Americana into a building concerned with international villains and killer drugs. A 1985 Mercury Cougar for sale, only 36,000 miles. A brown-bag party for a soon-to-be-married typist. A 10K run sponsored by the Law Enforcement Association.

Beyond the notice board, in a corner office, Paul Johnson sat behind a cluttered desk, watching Decker's slow approach with what appeared to be tolerant patience. Or the quietude of a man content to wait for a long-savored pleasure.

"Think you'll make it before lunch, Decker?"

With his face set in neutral, Decker walked into Paul Johnson's office.

Johnson, nudging fifty-five now, with an ungainly body that was getting away from him, had been a hell of an agent in his day. He'd once walked for sixteen hours through a Burmese jungle with a .38 bullet in his chest, and grabbed the guy who'd put it there. Another time, in Naples, he'd flattened a Comora lieutenant who'd carelessly insulted his lineage; coldcocked the guy and lived to tell the tale. He'd always been a hard man, Paul Johnson—Old Blood and Guns, as he was called—but now that he was doing a nine-to-five at Headquarters, out of the action, he'd become as irascible as an old firehorse removed from the traces, and tended to snap and act mean.

He sat immobile behind his desk, as if he were made of the same solid piece of wood, looking at Decker, his toughness displayed like those photographs outside in the corridor. He pointed a stumpy finger at a chair and, with very little movement in a mouth that was starched with a low-degree anger, rolled out words in a solid bass note.

"Sit down, buddy. Sit down there where I can see you."

Decker obeyed the directive, crossed his feet at the ankles, and calmly waited for the tidal wave to break.

It began with a few mild ripples.

"Did it ever strike you," Paul Johnson asked, leaning back in his chair and clasping his hands behind his old-fashioned crew cut, "just how many initials a guy has to deal with in this business? For example, there's the OH, the Heroin Desk. And the OF, the Foreign Desk. There's the OCOA, Organized Crime of Asian Origin. There's an ASAC, Assistant Agent in Charge. A DAAO, Deputy Assistant Administrator Operations, who drives an OGV, Official Government Vehicle. And, of course, there are all kinds of initials in the clerical line." Johnson leaned forward and picked up a green-covered folder from his desk. There was a red-covered one there, and a yellow one too. Decker had no doubt that his name figured prominently in all three.

"There's an IR, for instance, an Incident Report. And a CR, a case report. And let's not forget an OPF, an Official Personnel File." Johnson let the green-covered folder fall as if he were glad to have its slim weight off his hands. "Yeah," he said ponderously, "we're up to our asses in initials. And we certainly don't need any more. And yet, funnily enough, I just thought up a whole new set. Wanna hear 'em?"

Decker didn't reply.

"HHGFU," Johnson said. "Know what they stand for, boy? Hmmm? Do you?"

Decker said, "No, sir," and fixed his eyes on the large map of the world attached to the wall behind Johnson's head. It was a standard Rand McNally school map with no colored pins stuck in it, no felt-tip notations written anywhere. It was up there strictly for geographical reference.

"Well, I'll tell you," Johnson offered. He got up, crossed to the door, closed it, returned to his chair, and delivered the information at the top of his voice. *"Hothead Goddamn Fuck-Up!"* That's what you are, Decker. What did I say?"

Decker looked at Paul Johnson's boiling face, and looked back at the map. The theory of continental drift was certainly borne out by the shapes of the east coast of Africa and the west coast of South America: they could fit together like pieces of a jigsaw puzzle.

"A Hothead Goddamn Fuck-Up!" Johnson insisted at high volume. He snatched up the Incident Report, rapped it with the back of his right hand as if it were Decker's face he was slapping, and went on yelling. "You let a lightweight Chinaman steal the fucking front money. Ten thousand dollars made in the USA. Plus you put a Kel on him, a sophisticated piece of electronics worth at least two grand, and he runs away with that too. Twelve grand of the taxpayers' money lost down a rat hole in a dinky little wonton parlor. That would be a hard night's work for most agents, Decker, but not for you. You also manage to go a couple of rounds with a street gang who fire off a goddamn rocket and burn down half a block of real estate belonging to some poor slumlord. Finally, when it's all over, and any sensible person would've gone home and slashed his wrists, you take it a step further." Johnson bent his chunky body, and brought his tirade a foot closer to Decker. "A Chinese business-man, enjoying a quiet little dinner with three friends. The guy's just sitting there peacefully knitting up noodles, and for some weird reason only you and your shrink would know about, you clear his table like a gorilla on his first day as a busboy." Johnson glowered at

Decker, his face a hot shade of pink. There were agents who swore that, when Old Blood and Guns reamed you out, hot rays came out of his forehead.

He went on.

"So what do you think happens? The guy calls the Spring Roll Benevolent Society, the society calls the mayor's office and threatens to switch the Chinese vote to Fiorello La Guardia or somebody if the incident isn't reported. The mayor's office calls somebody in this town, and the shit starts to roll downhill. And guess whose Florsheims it sticks to, Decker?" Paul Johnson thumped his chest like a penitent. "Mine, you goddamn stupe. You stumbling moron. Hugh C. Decker, the hothead kid. King of the big-boots brigade. Why bother to knock when you can kick the fucking door in?"

Decker was looking straight ahead now, watching the day through the louvered blinds on the big window, concentrating on the tops of the foliage in Franklin Square. It wasn't quite late enough in the year for Washington's famous spring blossoms, but the trees were definitely thinking about it, tightening up, their juices stirring, getting ready to pop.

Paul Johnson, in direct contrast to Decker's bland demeanor, rocked forward in his chair, propped up his thick body on his desk, and glared at Decker as if he were trying to mark him with his eyes. When he spoke again, his voice still had good volume, but he'd come off the boil.

"What happened? Tell me."

Decker switched his glance to his boss. It was a genuine question he'd been asked this time, and some kind of reply was expected. "It's all in the CR. I don't have anything to add."

Johnson snatched up the yellow-covered folder and slammed it down. "Don't tell me what's in the CR. I know what's in the CR. I want to hear it from you, you dumb-ass cretin."

Decker had prepared his strategy on the plane from New York. Knowing what to expect, the chewing-out, the insults, he'd made up his mind to go with it, to bend like a reed and not be provoked into an outburst. Think nothing, and say little. And if he had to talk at any length, feed Paul Johnson blooper balls; don't give him any speed to hit off.

"Around about Christmas," Decker said in a controlled and level voice, "I went undercover and connected with a Puerto Rican. I arranged a buy. When he came up with the stuff I flashed my plastic and told him he was looking at seven long ones, but if he cooperated, and took me up the chain, I'd stand right alongside him in court and—"

"Tell the judge he was instrumental in the apprehension of blah, blah, et cetera, et cetera," Johnson said impatiently. "Get on with it."

"He took me to a black guy. Same thing. I set up a buy, then ID'd myself, and flipped him too. He gave me the Chinese, Eddie Fong, and I did the same number on Eddie. Deal was, he'd lead me to the control guy. I gave him the front roll, and he was supposed to use it to buy two and a half of pure. The minute he did that we'd go in and grab Eddie's associates. Only it didn't work out that way."

"Do tell," Johnson said sourly. "You flipped, he flopped."

Normally, Decker might have said something like, "What should I have done, asked for references?" But he stuck to his strategy and merely moved his hands in a shrug. Then he asked a question he knew could bring a scalding reply, but it was a point that had been bugging him.

"Who were those kids? The Ghost Shadows?"

"The White Tigers. It make any difference?"

"Where the hell did they get a Law rocket from?"

"The fucking Yakuza," Johnson said, quieter now, but still smoldering. "There's a gang war going on in Tokyo. The Semiyoshi Rengo's sticking it to the Yamaguchi Gumi. The Guchi's buying dope in Burma, shipping it to Manila, and trading it for Laws. The fucking Tigers pried a couple loose for services rendered on the local scene in New York." Johnson shifted position, put an unpolished size-eleven shoe against his desk, swung back in his chair, and regarded Decker like a doctor with a positive lab report. "Tell me if I'm wrong, fella. Eighteen months back, in Hong Kong, you did your hothead bit, flew off the handle, and embarrassed the hell out of this department. They booted your ass back to New York, and we assigned you to Administrative Duty. You walked the halls for a year. Ran the typing pool, made sure the pencils were nice and sharp and the coffee hot. Do you remember all that?"

Decker looked back at his boss, and didn't have to reply. Yes, he remembered that; the most frustrating, humiliating time of his life. He'd hated every second, and each week he'd been tempted to go in and quit. It was a punishment designed to humble him, but he'd been determined not to let that happen. So he'd done his time; walked the halls for a year, run the pool with not even an office to hang his hat in. And he'd come out unhumble. And they hadn't liked that, his bosses in New York.

Too fucking bad.

Paul Johnson leaned a little farther back, his jacket falling open and revealing the compact handgun snuggled in its neat hip holster. A .380 auto, Decker saw; Decker's choice too.

"You went back on the street and you did okay," Johnson continued. "Stayed cool. We thought, fine, the kid's straightened out. No more steam coming out his ears. A year doing nothing got rid of his problem. And now this. Another little temper tantrum. And I have to eat a second slice of crap pie. What have you got to say about it, huh? Speak to me, kid."

Decker told him the truth. Why not? He didn't care what Paul Johnson thought.

"I've been trying for a more Zen-like approach to life. It was working up to three nights back."

"Zen-like," Johnson said, as if the words were producing some noxious growth on his tongue. "Decker, you should be fucked up the ass like a chicken. I should rip the plastic off your neck, break it over my knee, and drum you out for good." Johnson paused, his mouth surly, brooding about it. "But that's not what's gonna happen."

Decker waited to hear his fate. If he wasn't going to get the bullet, what did they have in mind? A couple of months on the bricks? Great. If he lost eight weeks' pay he could say good-bye to that ski vacation, and a few other items besides.

"You're going back to Hong Kong on TDY," Johnson told him.

So sudden, so out-of-the-blue, the news shook Decker. Temporary duty in *Hong Kong*?

He was amazed.

"We got a call yesterday," Johnson said. "A guy named"—he broke off to consult a typed page on his desk—"Lee Yuen Chee flew into Hong Kong on a United flight from L.A. Hong Kong passport. A boxtop made right there in Kowloon. An immigration girl spotted the name on her list. Whoever churned out the passport made money both ends."

Decker knew what his boss was talking about: some of the printers in Hong Kong double their income when they faked documents by selling the real names of their customers to the local police.

"This guy's real name, this Lee Yuen," Paul Johnson, said, as if the matter bored him, "is Eddie Fong."

For the first time in three days Decker began to feel okay. "Immigration let him in?"

"You bet. Made sure he got the right cabdriver, too. Then they put his arrival on the wire, see if anybody was interested. We got men camped on his doorstep. Twenty-four-hour surveil. So when you get to meet him again, you won't forget to hand him a bill, will you?"

Decker, letting the jibe slide by, jumped ahead a week or two. It was going to be extremely satisfying to walk up to the guy in the street, tap him on the shoulder, and say, "Eddie, old pal. How the hell you doing?" And watch his lying, cheating mouth drop open, the damn thief. It was going to be something to savor for a long, long time.

"However," Paul Johnson said, with a change of tone that swung Decker's attention back, "Eddie Fong is only part of the reason why you're going to Hong Kong. Eddie's only a convenient excuse. This is the main reason." From a drawer Johnson pulled out yet another file which Decker recognized, as he caught it in the air, as an Action Crime File. If this was the reason why he was being sent to Hong Kong, Decker thought, then the crime the file would describe would almost certainly be a homicide.

Paul Johnson confirmed his guess.

"Four days back a DEA employee was murdered in Hong Kong. A woman named Angela Waters. One of the secretaries. Somebody cracked her skull. We know she'd had sex with a guy. Probably the guy who killed her."

"Why do you say that?' Decker was beginning to turn pages.

"Because somebody took a carving knife to her. Tits-and-cunt job. Which makes me wonder if the guy who screwed her wasn't disappointed with her performance. Anyway, the Hong Kong fuzz is on top of it. Their CID is damned good. Good homicide group, excellent forensic people. They'll get the guy, no question about it. And they'll give us a full report. But we're DEA, right?" Johnson asked superfluously. "If an Italian grandmother swears she knows how to make spaghetti sauce, we'd still give her a polygraph test. We don't take nobody's word for nothing."

"I know," Decker said, head down, speed-reading the file. "You don't have to tell me that."

It was the first cocky thing he'd said so far, and his boss seemed to welcome it. His eyes sparked, then went flat, and his voice strengthened again.

"There are a lot of things I don't have to tell you, kiddo. Like, for instance, we'll be setting up a war room here to monitor the thing. And we'll want regular reports till the file's closed. You'll run down every lead. Concerted action with the local office. And here's another thing I don't have to tell you," Johnson said, pressing weight onto his words. "You'll have no jurisdiction to investigate a homicide in Hong Kong. If the local cops catch you at it, they'll kick your butt right outta there, just like they did before. Eddie Fong's your cover. You're officially there to help interdict a known drug trafficker. The Hong Kong fuzz won't believe it, but they'll have to buy it just as long as you don't step on their cocks. Got it? Nod once for yes."

Decker remained silent, but he didn't nod either. The interview had been a victory of sorts for Paul Johnson, but Decker wasn't about to give him a complete walkover. Johnson recognized that, and threw in one last parting shot.

"You've got a little break, Decker. There's a new CA in our Hong Kong office. Kelly's been transferred to Tokyo. The new guy don't know what an idiot you are. Try to keep it a secret from him as long as you can."

Decker was no longer interested in his boss's attempt to wound him. In his mind, he'd already escaped the office. He was thousands of miles away in Hong Kong.

"You're damned lucky, Decker. You're getting a second bite of the cherry. Hell, a third bite. You're going because you know the territory, you speak the lingo, and because the New York office is deliriously happy to be able to spare you for a couple of weeks."

Decker closed the file, ran his fingers around its neat edges, and waited for some more scathing observations. But Paul Johnson seemed to have run out of invective for the moment.

"Is that it, sir?"

"That's it. You may leave when ready."

Decker rose, moved toward the door.

"Wait," Johnson called, perhaps annoyed that Decker had handled himself so well. "There's one more thing you know that I don't have to tell you. If you fuck up in Hong Kong again, stay there. Take a job packing kitty litter or something. Believe me, it'll pay better than anything you'll be able to get back here."

"Kitty litter," Decker said with no particular emphasis. "Yes, sir. I'll remember that."

"You do that, sonny boy," Johnson growled. "You do that."

3

The fact that Kai Tak is ranked by the International Federation of Airline Pilots as the second-most-dangerous airport in the world—Los Angeles gets the nod for the number-one spot—didn't trouble Decker as he snapped his belt into place for the landing. During his four years in Hong Kong he'd flown in and out of the place so many times he'd ceased to think about the dangers involved in arriving there. In a place like Hong Kong a diligent DEA agent could easily rack up 100,000 miles a year: New York, San Francisco, Bangkok, Amsterdam, Sydney; when you were involved in the dope business you went where the players were.

A swatch of green rose into the aircraft's starboard windows as it banked for the turn into the western flight path. This was the approach which bothered the pilots most; it meant a visual approach over Cheung Chau, the old pirate stronghold reputed to be riddled by treasure caves, then a steep right-hand turn in order to miss Kowloon Peak. three thousand hulking feet of exposed granite and bushy scrub, then into the glide path that ran not only over but eventually between a morass of high-rise real estate around Sham Shui Po. In fact, at night, a passenger with a window seat could look out, as the plane threaded the apartment blocks, and see, right there at eye level, people cooking in kitchens, feeding children, watching TV; the same kind of view that an elevated train presented passing through a city.

When the high-rises had been negotiated, the thrills still weren't over because a short landing on the one and only runway would fetch a plane up on Junction Road in Kowloon City, while an overshoot could plop a jet into the industrial murk of Kowloon Bay.

For all these reasons Kai Tak was known as an airport for expert fliers only.

A stewardess, going down the aisle checking belts, smiled at Decker but said nothing this time. She'd tried several times to get him interested in her, but without success. A shame because she was free tonight, and she liked men who looked like this one: slim-built, with no excess to them; easy action types who could always be counted on to bring their athleticism into bed. This guy was no Magnum, true; the jawline was strong and firm, but the rest of the features were too delineated to give him the rugged good looks that were in these days: the nose too slim and straight, the bones above the eyes unpronounced. Nice hair, though; California hair, sandy-colored and thick-textured.

Nice eyes, too: interesting; a soft brown if you just glanced at them quickly, but take a longer look and there was a stronger quality down deeper. She'd seen the same thing before, having gone to a college where football had been big; the running backs got that look in their eyes when they were handed the ball and expected to make the down. The good ones expected to make it, too, and defied anybody to stop them.

Too bad; he was definitely a dishy guy, specially with that mark on his cheek, a scar shaped like an asterisk. She would have enjoyed running her tongue over that, exploring the sharp grooves in the clear, grainy skin. But that wasn't going to happen. He probably had a girl waiting for him in Hong Kong, she concluded, dropping into a vacant seat as the aircraft settled itself for the touchdown.

In actual fact, the stewardess was half-right about the last point. Decker did have a girl in Hong Kong.

That is, the day he'd left she'd still been his girl.

They'd traded letters for several months, but then the correspondence had petered out, the written word proving a poor substitute for the whispered one.

Kate, her name was.

Decker had started thinking about her as he'd left Paul Johnson's office on I Street, and since then he'd hardly stopped. His feeling for her, which he admitted to himself, had been considerable—hell, he'd been in love with the woman—had been diluted by time and geography, diffused by other arms, hazed by a more familiar culture. But as the plane had crossed the endless day of the Pacific, traveling in tandem with the sun, his yearning for her had come back hot and stronger than ever.

Kate Yu Sung.

The name had been dancing though his brain for the past thirty-six hours now. That name, and another woman's name: Angela Waters. Plus a man's name: Eddie Fong.

Three people: three big reasons why he was excited about coming back to Hong Kong. And yet it was going to be a weird kind of welcome: one person he'd never met, and never would on account of she was dead. The second hadn't heard from him in months, and might not be glad to see him after so long a silence. And the third would be so put out by his unexpected presence that he might just try to have him killed.

Kai Tak stayed lucky; the plane made a soap-bubble landing. Twenty minutes later, Decker had cleared formalities and was walking through a terminal that was an accurate reflection of certain parts of the city it served: it was noisy, sweaty, crowded and decidedly smelly, and seemed to have been designed by a subway architect.

John Rizzo had come out to meet Decker, was waiting for him outside the pickup area, dabbing at his plump face in the slow heat of the late afternoon. Rizzo was the RAC at the local office, Resident Agent in Charge. Decker had worked with him during his time in Hong Kong, and they'd gotten on extremely well. Decker seldom had trouble being liked and accepted by his peers; it was just his superiors he rubbed the wrong way.

"Deck, you sonofabitch," Rizzo said. The hand he held out could have crushed two beer cans. "I would've hired a band but I remembered how much you hate Chinese music."

"Good to see you, Johnny. God, look at you. Back on your diet again, huh? You must've lost at least four ounces since I saw you last."

Rizzo patted his ample stomach. "Maybe more."

John Rizzo was known as Johnny Risotto because of his fondness for the table. He looked like a forty-five-year-old Italian poppa: slow, benign, and too docile to be anything but harmless. There were dealers in several cities around the world who'd formed a similar opinion of him initially, but had had their minds quickly changed when they'd been lifted off the ground and shaken like rag dolls. Basically, Johnny was the quiet, pensive type of agent who put a lot of late-night thinking into actions he'd take weeks later. It was the direct opposite to Decker's approach to the job. Decker was great on the street, and could slip in and out of roles like a fine actor. He'd think hard about a job, plan strategy; but if nothing was breaking after a while he'd invariably try to move things along by going out on the sidewalks and doing something about it. Johnny Risotto's strength lay in his aptitude for what was known in the trade as smart patience: something which Decker didn't have, and didn't seem to be able to learn.

Driving into town they did some catching up; talked about what they'd been doing since they'd last worked together.

"Penang," Johnny Risotto said. "I been spending a lot of time down there running down dope money. I traced it to a house not much more than a mud hut. Looked like a magpie built it. But you want to know something? A hundred million cash was flowing through that dump every six weeks. Coming in over the Thai border. They had couriers taking it to banks in Singapore. From there they had it wired to shell companies in Chicago, LA, and New Orleans. It was a lot of work putting all the ends together, but at least it got me outta this town. Place has gone crazy on account of the visit."

"What visit?"

"The royal visit. Prince Charles, Princess Di. Believe me, you'd know what visit if you'd been living here the past few weeks. They're cleaning up the town. The Council's hired about two million road sweepers, and they're trying to get the Chinese to spit into the litter bins. Plus they're a little nervous about security. Pick up a paintbrush you're liable to be arrested for carrying a deadly weapon." The big man took a half-empty pack of potato chips from the glove compartment, steered with one hand, and fed himself with the other. "So that's me," he said through crunching teeth. "What've you been doing, Deck? I mean, after the humbling was over."

Decker was taking in the highway, the huge familiar signs, the slightly wacky way the natives still drove their Japanese cars. As usual, the cabbies were the worst offenders; maybe because a lot of them drove, not Datsuns, but Mercedeses, and assumed that a superior car granted them license to ignore everybody else.

"Well," Decker said, "my biggest bust was a pregnant woman I caught smoking a nonfilter."

"They wouldn't let you loose, huh?"

"Not on anything big. But I showed 'em. I let a Chinese wise guy beat me for ten grand." He looked over at Johnny. "I don't see why the office was worried, do you?"

Johnny Risotto, a pal and a diplomat, kept his eyes straight ahead as he slowed for the traffic buildup at the Cross Harbor Tunnel. He said lightly, "Eddie Fong? Don't feel bad, Deck. He would've been damned tough to grab in New York, with the setup they got there. But he's candy now. I put him to bed myself last night. And we got guys in jeans and T-shirts eating noodles outside his front door. You can pop him anytime you like."

Decker appreciated Johnny's tact; the guy knew all about his gaffe with Eddie Fong because Eddie had turned up in Johnny Risotto's bailiwick. But even if Eddie had never surfaced again, the Hong Kong office would still have heard about the shambles back on Eldridge Street. The DEA had a worldwide network but it was staffed by surprisingly few people, most of whom either knew each other, or had met each other, or had heard about each other. So if an agent scored big in Jakarta, or fell on his face in New York, the news got around fast.

"I think I'll let him run for a while," Decker said. "He's got ten grand burning a hole in his jeans, so you can bet the first thing he'll do is start cutting a deal. We'll let him get into it, then we'll drop by." Decker switched the subject away from his Chinatown error by catching up on current events at the local office. "How's Bumpy? Still got a terminal case of the hots?"

"Bumpy? He's worse than ever." Folds in Johnny Risotto's throat bobbed when he started to chuckle. "Miriam bought him a life-size rubber doll for his birthday. Bumpy said it was the best lay he'd ever had, but he had to get rid of it because it turned out to be the marrying kind."

Decker laughed, not so much at the anecdote as at the remembered ribald interplay between the two other agents in the office.

"How is Miriam? Still making marines blush?"

"She's worse than ever too. Miriam the Mouth," Johnny said, going into the glove compartment for some Chinese beef jerky.

"I've missed them both. You too, tubby. The guys I've been working with in New York only eat three times a day."

Johnny smiled, pleased by the sentiment. He'd always liked Decker a lot, admired him for his Screw Everybody attitude. He also liked his penchant for action, which, although sometimes ill-advised, certainly demonstrated enthusiasm for the job, something not every agent had. As for his big negative, his blowup temper, it was a millstone around his neck. If he could shake it, he could go a long way in the Administration. And, what's more, live to get there; because if an agent blew his cool on the street, as Decker was capable of doing, the bad guys could turn around and lash back.

As the car crept forward, Johnny bumped the air conditioning up another notch and said, "We got a new CA. Maybe you heard. Name's Ralph Dobrinski."

"You rate him?"

"Yes, sir. He knows what he wants you to do, and leaves you alone to do it. The folks at I Street like him. He's got a good jacket, a good rep, and that makes it easier for all of us."

"Sounds okay."

"As you might imagine, things have been pretty glum lately, Angie getting it like that."

"The secretary? Angela Waters?"

"Uh-huh. She joined us about six months after you left. A real good kid. A swinger. Full of juice. Loved men. But she went home with the wrong one this time."

"Any progress?"

"Not so far."

"Well," Decker said a little flatly, "the rippers usually give themselves away. Make sure they're caught. Not that it'll do Angela Waters much good."

"Not that it will," Johnny agreed.

They were silent as they drove through the black-and-yellow flash of the tunnel, the weight of the water above them and the murder having a doubly depressing effect. The mood fled when they emerged on Hong Kong side, bursting out into cheery daylight, the heaviness whipped away by the dazzling city sweeping into view. It was different from that other famous tunnel-to-city introduction, coming into Manhattan from Queens; the buildings of New York instantly gobbled you up, and a first-time visitor could get no idea of the scale of the place. But when you drove into Hong Kong, and popped up from the tunnel in Causeway Bay, a magnificent vista stretched away to the right, a clean, clear half-mile alley which presented, at its far end, the Central District and its shiny white forest of skyscrapers. And because of these skyscrapers, a Manhattan comparison was again inevitable for a tourist. Architecturally, Hong Kong was a little like the west side of Sixth Avenue, only instead of that austere line of steel and glass running ruler-straight from midtown to the park, the buildings of Hong Kong faced every which way in a delightfully haphazard arrangement; and yet the majority still somehow managed to view the same section of the spectacular harbor.

Now, late in the afternoon, the buildings were side-lit by a westering sun, their rocketlike outlines edged with a pale pink fire. Decker was glad he'd arrived at this time of day, when the city looked softer and prettier than any he'd ever seen. It was the Hong Kong he'd pictured in his mind when he'd first arrived back in New York and had been missing the place.

Missing Kate.

Missing the good people he'd worked with.

He raised his eyes to the section above Central, the Mid Levels, as it was known. Its towering apartment blocks, bunched together like bound wheatstalks, were already being devoured by the shadow thrown by the Peak, the long, green backdrop that soared over everything else on the island.

Behind Decker—he swiveled in his seat to look—North Point was an entire second city, its huge neon signs not yet lit but giving the impression of pumping themselves up, getting ready to overpower the night.

"Jesus," Decker said, turning back. "Will you look at all the new construction. They're still going at it."

"They're like kids with an Erector set," Johnny said. "Ten years' time it'll all belong to Peking, but it's like the locals don't believe the takeover's gonna happen. Property prices are through the roof, the Hang Seng's heading for the clouds again . . . I don't know. I can't decide whether the investors are ignoring the whole business, or whether they know something." He stopped for a red light, and asked Decker where he was planning to stay. "You could bunk in with us," Johnny offered, "only we don't have the room. June's sister's over here for a couple of weeks."

"Thanks anyway, Johnny. But I got a reservation at the Kok Nan."

Johnny Risotto winced as the light turned green. "The Kok Nan? In Wanchai? What, did Old Blood and Guns put you on the bricks?"

"It could happen. So I'll save where I can. The place isn't that bad. I've stayed there before."

"Are the sheets clean?"

"Sure, if you pick your spot and lie very still."

A few minutes later the car broke from the crush of traffic on

Gloucester Road and turned down a narrow street lined with noisy, one-car-at-a-time body shops. The Kok Nan, rising an unimpressive six stories from the littered sidewalk, had a facade faced with chipped tiles the color of lima beans, and windows clouded by grit and dust. There was no marquee; just a pair of aluminum-framed glass doors propped open by a broken chair.

Johnny pulled Decker's bag from the car and looked up doubtfully at the old hotel. Air conditioners had been mortised into the bedrooms in a staggered, uneven pattern, and the runoff water had wept moist streaks down the grubby tilework. A hand-painted sign bragged about international specialties available in the hotel restaurant.

"At least you won't find any roaches in your room," Johnny said. "They'll all be on the menu."

Decker offered his hand. "Thanks for the ride, Johnny. Will I see you in the morning?"

"Bright and early. There's a meeting at nine-thirty. All resident agents, plus you, the Bureau guy, and the consulate RSO." The big man slapped Decker's shoulder. It hurt. "Good to have you back, Deck."

Decker looked at the grimy entrance of the decrepit hotel, took in the shoddy street which was going to be his new neighborhood for a while. The day's heat, trapped by the narrow avenue, thumped upward from the sidewalk, releasing a smell of hot cement and gutter water. Several doors along, tonguing out of the remains of a building, a wooden demolition chute puffed billows of heavy gray rubble dust into the air. The noise from the chute mixed in thickly with the clash and bang issuing from the tiny panel shops and the popping crescendo of several small and bustling delivery vans, their exposed two-stroke engines burping noxious blue clouds.

"It's good to be back," Decker said to Johnny Risotto.

Amazingly, he meant it.

Decker woke to the gentle return of senses.

The room had darkened enough to admit an edge of pink that splattered against the wall, the residue of some exterior neon sign. He heard the whine of a pump switch on, audible only because the body shops down in the street had closed for the day. Indeed, the noises sifting in through the thin panes of his third-floor window had a nighttime flavor to them: voices and laughter and upbeat music. The throbbing air conditioner, another sound that was louder now, had its control stuck between Cool and Vent, and was sucking in cooking aromas that smelt okay.

Decker went down the hall to the bathroom, peed, showered, shaved, then returned to his room and unpacked. The three-hour sleep, plus the hot water on his skin, had taken a large bite out of his jet lag, and he was beginning to feel good.

And more than a little excited.

In less than forty minutes, he'd be seeing her.

Kate.

He'd called the Furama first thing after he'd checked in. Yes, he'd been told, Miss Sung was still assistant night manager, and yes, she'd be in this evening around eight-thirty.

Decker, who normally didn't care about clothes as long as they were comfortable, changed a fresh white shirt for a fresh red one—Kate had the Chinese love of vivid solid colors—shoved his legs into chinos, his feet into dark tan slip-ons, and went out into the warm night.

His hotel was just around the corner from Lockhardt Road, the main drag of Wanchai, a street Decker had walked down a million times, although never in its heyday. He'd always been sorry he'd missed that, but he'd arrived in Hong Kong too late. Since the U.S. Seventh Fleet had stopped visiting the colony, the bars, the discos, the topless clubs had had a very thin time of it. Most had now closed their doors, leaving only their colossal signs to mark their passing. Even as they were, unlit, broken and weather-beaten, the signs still managed a garish and vulgar cheerfulness. Mounted on heavy, rusting scaffolding, which jutted out at right angles twenty feet above the street, the signs reached all the way to the middle of the thoroughfare and spread over it, bunched indiscriminately in a frozen midair collision of metal and glass tubing.

The nightspots themselves looked wrecked, bombed-out, as if a residue of the drunken, riotous life which had once gone on inside had eventually seeped through the walls and left its hung-over memory exposed on the flaking exterior brick.

Wanchai, before the Fleet and the clubs came, had been one of the old sections of Hong Kong, and some of the looping sidewalk stone arcades, which had once sheltered highborn Ch'in mandarins from the vagaries of the local weather, were still in place. Under one of these arches, crumbling and poster-plastered now, Decker found a display which was an old favorite of his: photographs advertising the Wo Li Tattoo Parlor, One Flight Up. The management

was still using some he remembered: a young blond girl, smiling
blearily as ever from behind the cracked glass of the smeared display case, proudly showed off a furious red-eyed cobra, rampant and
green-fanged, which was strangling her very large and very naked
left breast. The legend tattooed around her plump pink nipple said,
"If snake bit, suck here."

Another color shot revealed a young lady's crotch, freshly shaved.
There was no illustration, just words tattooed on her smooth, bald
mound with a superfluous arrow pointing in a southward direction.
"Taste that crunchy goodness," it said.

And there was a new one, one that went a long way toward
proving that skin illustration was still alive and well in Hong Kong:
a full-length shot of a naked man, photographed from behind. Red-
coated riders, white cravats flying, galloped charging horses up both
his calves and leapt the crease of his knees. On the backs of his
thighs a slathering pack of spotted hounds bayed in pursuit of their
traditional quarry. And across the left cheek of the man's bottom, a
large bushy red tail taunted the pursuers, the tail's owner having
apparently taken grateful refuge in the safe haven of the man's
anus.

Decker shook his head in amused wonder. "Only in Hong
Kong," he said.

He went a short block north, and plunged into the broad, clanging jumble of Hennessy Road with its biting, riotous traffic and
jammed sidewalks. Ninety-nine percent of the jammers were Chinese, although everybody wore Western clothes. The young dressed
like the young everywhere, the older males wore nondescript shirts
and jeans, the women opting for bright sleeveless sweaters or floral
blouses with dark pants and comfortable low-heeled shoes. Everybody was going somewhere, moving in a slow and ordered shamble,
a two-way crush on both sidewalks. Decker positioned himself at
the tram stop outside a flatiron-shaped building wedged into the
sharp-angled corner of Johnson Street. It was a local landmark, the
Methodist church, an embarrassing example of the cunning and
resilience of the nineteenth-century Christian missionaries. It was
solid, no-nonsense Edinburgh brick for ten grim stories, then,
mindful of the culture it was trying to attract, reluctantly blossomed into a pagoda roof resplendent with curling gables and fanci-
fully carved dragons.

When a tram arrived, entirely covered with painted ads for
stereo sets and ginseng root, rattling and whining like a monster

from a Chinese opera, Decker boarded it. He climbed a flight of circling stairs which were so steep he'd have skinned his forehead on them had he leaned forward as much as an inch.

On the upper deck he sat on a slatted wooden seat next to a man deep in a scratch sheet, the clash and din of the city washing through the wide-open windows, soaking Decker in well-remembered noise. The tram, which seemed dangerously high for its skimpy width, bucked and reared, then lumbered forward, its steel wheels screeching on the metal track, bell clanging angrily at a couple of slow pedestrians. Decker sat there, an aromatic breeze blowing over him, savoring the ride. It was something he'd missed very much: Hong Kong from the top of a Whitty Street tram. For the past eighteen months he'd tried to conjure up the city as he saw it now, staring out at Manhattan from his rented studio apartment. He'd tried to jell Hong Kong in his mind, tried to induce his olfactory memory to get close to the city's distinctive smell, and failed miserably. It was in his nostrils at this very moment, but what the hell were the constituents?

A thick base of taxi diesel for a start, and slim, not-so-subtle layers of a lot of other things: nose-wrinkling, eye-watering medicines from the druggists' shops certainly. And from the pepper shops cassia, cinnamon, cloves, fennel, and star anise. Sure, herbs and spices were a big part of it, contributing the high, pungent part of the mix, but also there, in direct opposition, were the various stomach-rumbling food aromas: grilled pigeon, steamed chicken, air-dried sausages, and fat, roasted, red and gold ducks dripping juice in restaurant windows. Great silver clumps of dried fish suspended from grocers' ceilings; the sweet addition from the exhaust fans of bakeries with coconut-cream sponge and Ma Lu vanilla cakes rising in the oven.

Hot metal took some credit, too, and tarred sidewalk not long finished frying in the sun. Plus you had to factor in the tangy, jutey, hessian smell given off by bulging sacks stacked in their multitudes in the countless rice shops.

And food again, always that in Hong Kong. This time a whiff of wheat noodles and plump green bok choy popping and sizzling in the busy woks of the sidewalk eateries, the Tai Pai Tong stalls, their fronts festooned with edible chandeliers of roast pork and barbecued beef, and unimaginable innards hanging in hot and glistening loops.

No other city in the world smelt like it.

No other city looked like it.

No other town compacted half as many shops into a single block. They butted up against each other as if part of the same chain. And when a cross street forced them to momentarily separate, they immediately bunched together again, once the intrusion was over. Their jumbled and multicolored merchandise spilled onto the sidewalks as if the pressure from the neighboring stall had caused a rupture.

And with the shops came the signs: neon gas, electricity, and coarse-cut sections of riveted metal, Hong Kong's favorite combination. Red, green, yellow, blue, pink, the avenue was a visual smash, each sign bolder, more strident than the last, the English and/or Chinese characters belting out their swaggering messages with an urgent and dazzling vitality.

As the tram rattled toward Fenwick Street, Decker looked for a particular favorite, and found it, still in place, and shining forth proudly in blue: Lee Kee Boots.

There were many well-loved signs in Hong Kong; one which Decker had always admired was a brass shingle belonging to a man from Delhi who dealt in curries and spices. It read, "S. Veriswami. Very Pure Indian Merchant." Although his all-time favorite belonged to a custom dressmaker on Ashley Road: "Ladies Tailor Shop. Ladies Have Fits Upstairs."

Before Decker's time, but living on in legend, there had been signs for Great Leap Forward Shoe Polish, Front Gate Trouser Company, and the much-treasured, but short-lived, Thumbs Up Toilet Paper.

The tram broke out of the confines of Hennessy Road and rattled swiftly down the long wide stretch of the Queensway into the highrise blaze of Central.

Decker got off at Statue Square, hurried beneath the venerable arches of the old courthouse, and crossed to the Chater Road entrance of the Furama Hotel, an impressive porte cochere sheltering several Mercedeses and Jaguars, and a late-fifties pink Rolls-Royce.

He bounded up the escalator in tingling excitement, knowing what he'd see when he reached the top. He'd seen it three, four times a week for how long? Ten months, at least, driving down from his apartment in the Mid Levels, or walking down the hill from the office in St. John's House, running up these same escalators, coming out into the lobby, and seeing the newsstand on his immediate right, the long reception desk on his left, the deep floral-patterned armchairs of the Lau Ling bar on the other side of the lobby. And, directly ahead, at the very end of the lush expanse of the enormous pink-and-blue rug, the assistant manager's desk, Miss Kate Su Yung in attendance; straight-backed, serene, gorgeous.

The escalator began to flatten as Decker neared the top, lowering the lobby into his plane of vision.

She was seated behind the desk, head down, hair so black it looked blue. She was writing something.

He covered the distance to her, his step muffled by the plush carpet.

"Hello, Kate."

When she looked up, recognition registered a moment before the reaction reached her face as a blink and the slight opening of her mouth.

How many times had he kissed that mouth, Decker wondered, explored the silky corners, probed the soft moistness of the under-lip, accepted the playful damage of her white even teeth on his tongue? The mouth was as luscious as he remembered. So was the rest of her; a black-and-gold woman: honey-gold skin, black page-boy hair, eyes like black almonds.

Staring at her, smiling at her, taking in her fresh loveliness, he began to realize just how much he'd missed her.

And how much he wanted her back.

And, aware of the jut of her breasts pushing at the wide lapels of her red blazer, how much he just plain wanted her.

"Deck." She let out breath with his name. "When did you get in?"

"Couple of hours ago. You're looking great, Kate. Terrific."

"You too. You look well."

She still wasn't over her surprise. There was a stiffness to her body, her expression too; almost as if he'd brought disturbing news.

"I would've called, Kate, let you know I was coming, but I only had time to step on a plane."

"Business, then   ?"

"As usual."

There was a pause, Decker still smiling at her, Kate not yet relaxed enough to return it.

"What time's your break?" he asked. "Can we grab a bean down-stairs?" There'd been a lot of those too: a fast snack in the coffee shop, after she was through for the evening, then straight up to his apartment to make love till the sun came up; staying there all day, sometimes till the moon rose, too.

"Sure," she said after a moment. "I'm off for an hour at eleven."

She was looking at him in a way he didn't remember, the angle of her shoulders different, and something in her face that wasn't caused by the suddenness of his unannounced appearance.

"Okay, then. I'll swing on by," Decker said.

Then his smile began to fade.

There'd been a tremendously strong affinity between them, and it still seemed to be working, because he caught a mental flash from her, and knew then what the problem was.

It was like taking a punch in the throat.

"Kate . . . you're married . . ."

She got up from her chair, unwinding with the liquid grace he remembered. The desk which separated them had suddenly become much broader than the width of its polished hardwood.

"Since August. I know I should have written and told you, but we seemed to have stopped writing by then." Her eyes moved in their delicate slashes, dropped to the long red paint of her tapered fingernails. "I'm sorry, Deck."

"Listen, I'm happy for you, Kate," Decker heard himself say. "I mean that."

He stopped speaking to let her news get a hold of him. It was even worse this time than the first rocking stab of intuition.

"Is it anybody I"— He aborted the question. He didn't want to know the name of the guy who now owned what was rightfully— He cut off that line of thinking too. "Well," he said at last, and found that he had actually shuffled his feet, lapsing into body cliches, and verbal ones too. "I wish you all the best."

"Deck . . . look . . ." Although English was her second language, Kate had always had a perfect command of it, but it seemed to be giving her trouble now. Decker wondered why; there was nothing more to say, anyway.

"Rain check on the coffee, okay, Kate?"

"Sure, Deck."

"I'll see you before I go."

"How long are you here for?"

The conversation flowing, now that it was about to be ended for all time.

"Not long." Decker gave her a half-salute. Kate tried for a smile, and failed. Then Decker was crossing the carpet heading for the escalator, which seemed to have been moved about a hundred feet farther away.

He hit two bars, Hong Kong-side, before he ended up across the harbor in a third, in Tsim-Sha-Tsui. He went through the three classic stages: from a morose, sorry-for-himself depression, to a dull, hurt anger, then moving on to a what-the-hell outlook. When he'd left Hong Kong, no understanding had been voiced, no arrangements made between them for any kind of future together; they'd just let it hang vaguely.

His fault, of course. He'd been on the verge of asking her to go back to the States with him; although, when you're in disgrace, is it fair to ask somebody to share it with you? Or was that a cop-out? It was a question he'd never been able to resolve.

Anyway, none of it applied now. I Street was mad at him, but he was no longer in disgrace.

And Kate was no longer available.

Hell, she was twenty-eight years old, and beautiful, and she hadn't heard from him for seven or eight months. What was she supposed to do, wait for him to fly over from New York when he felt the cold weather coming on?

Decker had another drink, and paused to take stock of his emotions. He called up damage control to assess the injuries.

How did he really feel? Hungry, he thought bravely.

Starving.

He took a cab up Nathan Road, the broad avenue which begins at the southern tip of Kowloon, threads neatly and sedately between the Peninsula and the Sheraton, then, freed of the conservative restraints of those two erstwhile hostelries, explodes into a color-crazed, sign-choked, people-infested riot of shops, restaurants, and picture palaces.

The colony's movie houses are famous for their sheer size and neon effrontery, but even they can be dwarfed by some of the Nathan Road eateries, which boast larger seating capacity, signs of greater candle-power, and a clientele far more enthusiastic and regular in attendance.

The one Decker chose was called The Great Treasure, an apt name for a place that had a Dai-see fu in the kitchen, a "great master" stir-fry chef, this one a champion of the subtle glories of Peking cooking.

It had an elevator which served three floors, each floor catering to different elements and appetites. The street-level restaurant was for the more itinerant diners, those in a hurry, and tourists who'd found the name starred in their guidebooks. The second floor was reserved for parties, weddings, anniversaries, and other drunken celebrations. While the third floor, guarded by a team of charming young hostesses in cheongsams split to the hip, was exclusively for the use of knowing gourmets, shipping and rag-trade tycoons, and ordinary customers who'd paid the appropriate number of visits.

In Hong Kong a visit to the same restaurant five times accords the diner no more than a polite reception and normal service. But should the same diner appear for the sixth time, even if it's months later, he or she is welcomed warmly and effusively, having become a valued person.

Getting out on the top floor, Decker was immediately recognized and fawned over by two of the hostesses, who shepherded him to a choice table.

The owner wasn't long in arriving.

"Mr. Deck," he said, showing teeth clad with precious metals. The Chinese had given up bowing and, as they disliked shaking hands, a wide grin was their way of demonstrating an effusive greeting. "Long time, Mr.Deck. Good to see."

"Hello, Lee. How are you?"

"In health. You look health, too."

To take the pressure off Mr. Lee's English, Decker switched to Cantonese, a great kitchen language, rich and hearty in expression and, therefore, particularly well-suited to any discussion of food.

"I bring you an empty belly, patron."

Mr. Lee, a slim, middle-aged, blue-suited figure, said, "The sign of a very poor man, or a very wise one."

"I fear I'll be the first before I'm the last," Decker replied, an answer which the proprietor rewarded with a second display of silver and platinum. He fanned open the oversize menu, but Decker waved it away.

"I leave the selection to you, patron."

"My choice, compared to yours, would be as poor as a Hakka fishwife," Mr. Lee confessed.

"Not true," Decker objected, then added in his floweriest Cantonese, knowing it was required now that they'd reached the mutually complimentary stage, "With you as my guide, my tongue and all my organs will have cause to rejoice."

Mr. Lee snapped the giant menu closed and tucked it disdainfully under his arm, a cumbersome thing required only by tourists and the gastronomically stupid.

"I suggest a meal leaning toward stimulating, heating, and yang foods, but balanced by the inclusion of calming, cooling, and yin foods, and with a touch of a powerful neutral to unite the two opposing forces."

"Harmony is all," Decker responded.

"Therefore I recommend cucumber sautéed in ginger and vinegar, to stimulate the liver and act as an appetizer. Then something calming to prepare the stomach for the feast ahead. Perhaps Tientsin cabbage in creamy bean sauce."

"A masterly choice," Decker allowed.

"Then a yang dish to follow," Mr. Lee said thoughtfully. "Perhaps roast carp with a plum-and-onion sauce. Then yam soup with pork buns, followed by deep-fired taro cakes to neutralize the wetness of the soup and avoid humidity in the body."

Decker nodded knowingly. "A fine and worthy idea."

"At that point," Mr. Lee continued, frowning slightly, putting himself in the diner's place, "I would recommend a yin dish. Perhaps braised duck with scallions and coriander to cleanse the blood and refresh the spleen."

"And for dessert?" Decker asked eagerly. He never ate when he flew, so he hadn't had anything solid for over twenty-four hours.

Mr. Lee proposed Luk Tau Ko, mashed green peas in gelatin.

"Done!" Decker pronounced. "Bring it all."

Mr. Lee waved a finger, and a busboy arrived with a tiny dish of shredded turnip in garlic just to get things going. Mr. Lee placed the dish in front of Decker, and switched, in his mind, from the formal tongue of Canton to what was known as Barefoot Cantonese, then translated that freely into English.

"Fuck hunger," he said, and headed for the kitchen.

Decker ordered an icy San Miguel and, cheered by the prospect of his first authentic Chinese meal in a year and a half, sipped his beer and delighted in the yammering bustle of the restaurant. There must have been fifty tables, with anything from five to twelve people at each, talking loud, drinking hard, eating with stupendous flair. Chopsticks, held in the Hong Kong four-finger position, darted, shoveled, hovered like hummingbirds, while left hands reached for brimming tumblers of Cognac and Scotch.

The general noise level, built in like the red latticework and dragon motifs on the walls, rose like a swelling tide, augmented by the shouts of crisscrossing waiters, brows sweating, muscles braced against the weight of deep wooden trays loaded to the edges with sizzling plates and bubbling tureens snatched from the kitchen.

The Great Treasure was a sensational restaurant; sometimes too much so. A few years previously, during Decker's time in Hong Kong, six members of the Tung Luen Sh'e, a triad lodge which smuggled in illegal immigrants and then lived off them, had gathered at the restaurant for a big, splashy dinner. When the meal was almost finished, the leader had turned his wine cup upside down—a prearranged signal—and there'd been a quick flurry of action which had upended half a bottle of brandy and a huge bowl of tripe soup. Five members had then walked out of the restaurant, leaving the waiters to clean up the mess on the tablecloth, as well as the mess slumped in one of the chairs, a traitorous official who'd been sliced up like the restaurant's famous three-day duck.

When Decker's copious order arrived, he fell hungrily on the food, and drank Siu Hing with it, yellow wine served warm in a teapot. With the strange but wonderful dessert he tossed off a thimbleful of Mooi Kwai Lo, rose-dew wine as strong as a liqueur.

His bill paid, and the ritual compliments exchanged, Decker went down to the street, replete but stimulated by the fine cooking, and nicely lit up from the alcohol.

A different mood was on him now.

He was thinking about Kate again. But not Kate as loved one. Kate as woman.

Glamorous, sinuous, sexy woman. He'd half-thought he was going to find himself in bed with her tonight, plunging into that marvelous golden body with its breathtaking moves and exquisite responses; but now that there was no possibility of that happening, it had left a large itch in his libido, an itch which he was now very much inclined to scratch.

A cab took him up the street to the Jordan Road Market—meat, fish, shoes, clothes, wire, rope, pots, pans, street dentists, sidewalk pharmacists, amateur opera—to a crooked lane too narrow for vehicular traffic. Strolling down its poorly lit confines, Decker felt funny to be moving through a shadowy nighttime alley without the familiar pressure of a holster against his hip. Or the slight tightness at his ankle where he carried his backup piece when he was on a job. But guns were a no-no in Hong Kong; they were fanatic about them. Projectiles of any kind were banned: bows and arrows, slingshots, even a kid's catapult was against the law. The police were armed, of course, and bank guards, but nobody else, not legally; not the DEA, not the CIA, not even the Secret Service when they came to town. In fact, in all of Hong Kong, the only private person licensed to carry a gun was a woman who sold sporting arms abroad and needed the protection.

As he walked through a spooky pool of darkness, Decker reflected, not for the first time, that it was a damned awkward law. Here he was, a member of a U.S. government agency which worked closely with the Hong Kong police helping them run down traffickers, just about all of whom were triad-connected and would snuff you out like a candle if they got the chance. Yet if he'd been caught carrying a gun, he'd have been thrown out of the colony immediately.

Decker wasn't a freak about guns, but there was a lot of crap walking the streets, and when you were about to interfere with their moneymaking enterprises, as he intended to do with Eddie Fong and whatever pals he'd made, not to mention go after a psychopathic slicer, it was comforting to have something more than just your shirt tucked into your waistband.

A dim light swam out of the blackness, a pale purple sign that said "Little Gladys." Below it was the entrance to what was officially described as a bar and grill. Inside, beyond the protective heaviness of red plush curtains, the room was standard, dumpy, back-alley Hong Kong: a small bar at one end, tables and chairs, banquettes around the walls, the splits in their vinyl coverings repaired by yellowing Scotch tape.

The lighting, which could have been mistaken for a power failure, fluttered fitfully on several men of various ages and nationalities, all of whom were drinking with either quick and nervous expectation or with satiated melancholy.

"Mr.Deck!" a husky voice said; surprise in it, and warmth too.

"Hello, Gladys."

"What you doing here? You back here now?"

"For a while."

The woman came out of the gloom, the mamasan who ran the place: fifty looking sixty, seams hemming in her face like compass lines, and an absurdly frizzy home permanent. She was baggy and slack now, but in her day she'd been Jordan Road royalty, a hooker queen. She'd been born Lin Yee Chow but had dropped the name at age seventeen in favor of a new one which now, incredibly, was her legal English name: Little Gladys Goodlay. It was a legacy of her Jordan Road career. Back then, most of the street girls had called themselves Suzie after the huge success of *The World of Suzie Wong*. But Lin Yee, being an individualist, had chosen the name Gladys instead. She was called Little because she was diminutive, even for a southern Chinese. And she'd earned her last name from the come-on she'd reserved for the hordes of British and American sailors: "Hey, Joe! You go with Little Gladys? Little Gladys good lay."

The name had stuck, and Little Gladys had never used another. She signed all her English correspondence in the same way: "Yours faithfully, Miss L. Gladys Goodlay."

"How you been, Glad?" Decker asked, his question coming to an abrupt halt as he saw her more clearly.

"Pretty good. Took off some weight since I see you last." Gladys grinned and pointed.

She'd lost her right arm.

"Own damn fault," she said brightly. "Talked too much."

"Jesus," Decker breathed. "Gladys . . ."

"Naw, naw, naw. Nothing to do with you, Mr. Deck. This happen long time after you leave. Nothing to do with dope. Something else. Come on back."

She turned and led the way into a small room at the rear, Little Gladys' domain, an office of a kind: suppliers' invoices tacked to the walls, a calculator, ledger books, a couple of chairs, a bottle of twelve-year-old Ballantine's, and some rice-wine cups.

Decker accepted a drink, downed it quickly, greatly relieved to hear that what had happened to Gladys was not because of their former relationship. Before he'd met Kate, Decker had hung out at Little Gladys' quite a bit, partly for her girls, and partly for her information. A lot of deals went down in the bar, and Little Gladys had good ears.

But her ears had cost her an arm.

"They took me to a hog butcher's. Six of them from the Wo On Lok. Held me down on the block," Gladys said as cheerily as if she were describing a picnic with friends. "Whack!" She chopped the arm they'd left her through the air. "Next time we take a leg, they said." Gladys slapped the thigh of the limb under threat. "They mean it, too. So, these days, I don't hear nothing but the bed springs, Mr. Deck. I don't sell information no more. I just sell fucks."

"I'm sorry, Gladys. About what those bastards did to you."

The woman dismissed the sentiment with a toss of her fingers, then cupped her hand around the stump at her shoulder. "I only miss it 'cause I haven't got it. You know what they call me now, guys who don't like my prices? The one-arm bandit."

She cackled at the joke and, pleased to play hostess, picked up the bottle and refilled Decker's cup.

It looked like a robot arm doing all the work, the movements neat and precise, and dead on target.

"Anyway," Decker said, accepting his second drink, "I'm not here for info, so your leg's safe."

Gladys brought her lined face into the thin gleam of a floor lamp, her lidded eyes bright and amused. "You wanna ride the merry-go-round?"

"I thought I might go for a spin, yeah."

"Boy, you come at right time. Got a new girl." Gladys tapped her finger against the frizz at her temple. "Not much up here, but got a twat went to Harvard."

Chinese?"

"Hawaiian."

"I'd prefer Chinese."

The mamasan nodded, and Decker saw quick understanding in the tilt of her head. Gladys knew about Kate, knew she was the reason he'd stopped being a customer. It wouldn't have been hard for her to put two and two together.

"Chinese no problem round here. You want a Kowloon Sandwich?"

This was two girls, one on top, one on the bottom, with the client in between.

"I just want a lovely Chinese girl. And I don't want a kid. A woman."

"You got her."

Gladys left to make the arrangements.

Decker went upstairs a few minutes later. Gladys had given him the Yellow Room, a color the Chinese associate with luck, virility, and sexual happiness. Gladys had only a small string of girls but she chose them with good taste, and an eye for more than just sexiness.

The woman who stood in the center of the room, a yellow robe reaching to her knees, had hair as long and shiny as a horse's tail, high-angled facial bones, and eyes like sharp dark pieces of flint. She held herself straight, as if her back was against a wall, a stance which accentuated her good slim height.

From the north, Decker decided; smuggled down to the Po On District, at the cost of five years' savings, around the rat fence to the Starling Inlet, then into the river and across the street at Sha Tau Kok.

"Yea meng?" Decker asked. What's your name?

"Kate," the woman said. And Decker had to admire Little Gladys for her perceptiveness. And for her consideration.

The woman undressed Decker, sponged him down in the little hip bath in the corner. She'd already bathed; her skin smelt like lilies.

The sheet on the king-size bed was fresh-ironed cotton, and yellow as a sunflower. Lying on it, the woman's body was gold upon gold, fingers of shadow and light playing on her flesh sent there by the bunched candles burning in pots at the four corners of the bed. Candlewax, lilies, the clean, starched smell of the sheet, sunshine in the folded yellow towels, and the high, sweet scent of sandalwood and patchouli chips smoking in a brass bowl near the door.

The woman began by disappointing Decker, taking his cock in her mouth and doing something Gladys taught all her girls: Peeling the Banana, it was called. It was slick and practiced, and on the edge of thrilling, but Decker didn't want professionalism.

He brought her back up the bed to him, began to kiss her face, her opening lips. Her breast seemed to jump into his hand like a firm, warm-blooded fish.

The woman groaned and whispered around the tongue she sank into his ear. "Sic tong. Sic tong." Eat candy. Eat candy.

Gladys had guessed wrong there; that was what a lot of Chinese girls said to their lovers, but Kate had never had to ask.

Decker brushed his fingers along the inside of her leg just above her knee, and the woman's legs sprang apart, inviting his touch. His fingers moved into moist plumpness, disciplined muscles sucking at him.

He mounted her in a single fast movement, and was home, all the way, with a quick assist from her hips. Her nails fishhooked into his buttocks, the woman pulling herself into the slam of his drive. She moaned and yipped little cries, then said distinctly, in a breathy outburst, "Deck! Deck!"

Decker almost stopped; wanted to stop.

Damn you, Gladys.

Wanted to stop but couldn't, the woman's captive now, locked in by her python legs. A clutching surge, the mindless moments of release, and Decker was allowed to go free.

He disengaged, rolled away.

After she'd attended to him, and helped him dress, he thanked her for the service, and went back downstairs.

"What did you think of her?" Gladys asked, accepting Decker's money.

"Kate?"

So as not to look at Decker, Little Gladys counted the money. "Yes."

"That wasn't her." Decker smiled to show he appreciated the effort all the same. "I'll never find another woman like Kate," he told her, and was immediately sorry he'd said it, hating the note of self-pity.

Little Gladys tossed the money into a well-stuffed cashbox and turned the key in the lock. "Pray to the right gods. You never know."

Decker told her he'd give it a try, left her, and walked through the dim little bar toward the exit.

As he brushed by the curtains, a heavy hand stopped him. A big man grinned pleasantly at him and said in a crunching Australian accent, "Hang on there, mate. You jumped your turn."

"I did? Sorry about that," Decker answered just as equably. He recognized the type: the drunken Aussie whose night isn't complete unless he's knocked somebody down, or somebody's knocked him down. Hong Kong had always been full of them.

"Yair, well, I'm goin' have fight to you for that," the man said, his lopsided grin getting friendlier.

"Look. What do you say we forget it. I'm feeling too good to fight."

"Yair? Well, I'm feelin' too good not to," the Australian said, and swung."

Decker could have stopped the punch at its beginning, its middle, or its end, but, feeling a touch slow, and more than a little enervated now, he settled for the amateur's defense and simply ducked the blow.

When the punch swished by, and the other man's momentum carried him forward, Decker gave him a rigid right-arm shot in the belly. The Australian sucked air, and went down.

Decker winced, swore, held his hand. His fist had landed on a heavy belt buckle which had gouged his skin.

Pressing a tissue to his knuckles, he walked back down the alley, found a cab, and set off down Nathan Road.

He got only a few blocks: the long flight from the States, the emotional jolt of Kate's news, the exotic food, the booze, the quick, strenuous sex, and the adrenaline rush brought on by the brief fight all ganged up on him. He only just had time to stop the taxi, jump out, and lean over a drain.

The night clerk was on duty when he got back to the hotel, a young Chinese anxious to please.

"Good evening, sir." He ushered Decker into the old-fashioned elevator, and moved the lever which closed the door. "First time in Hong Kong?" he asked breezily.

"No, I was here a year and a half back," Decker answered. He dabbed his knuckles with the bloody piece of Kleenex, and shifted on his feet to relieve the dull ache in his loins, a heritage of the expert enthusiasms of the woman at Little Gladys'.

"A year and a half," the night clerk said, as if it were a lifetime. "I bet you hardly recognize the place now."

"As a matter of fact," Decker said, getting out unsteadily at his floor, one hand on his tender, empty tummy, "I don't think it's changed much at all."

4

The structure which houses the DEA office in Hong Kong is a lot more impressive than the one that's home for the Washington headquarters.

St. John's House is a relatively new, thirty-story, high-tech building with large, round-cornered windows set flush with the building's dimpled, gray-plastic cladding: an architectural standout in a city of award winners. And as its location gives it few competing high-rise neighbors, St. John's House is allowed to show off its fine height and slim, uncluttered lines, as its designers intended. Its setting, too, is far more attractive than I Street's workaday environment, being perched on the edge of Garden Road as it begins its sweep toward the clumps of white apartment blocks salting the steep green rise of the Peak.

Across Garden Road, the U.S. consulate sits squatly behind its high steel fence, its backdrop the leafy tree-planted park which screens the governor's nineteenth-century wedding-cake residence, the finest abode, and the best address, in Hong Kong.

Squinting into the bright morning gleam, Decker climbed the steps of St. John's House and watched his reflection distort in the building's mirrored pillars. The image pretty much reflected the way he felt.

When he arrived at the eighth floor and went through the doors at the end of the quiet corridor, Johnny Risotto was the first person he saw. "Morning," the big man said. He noticed the strip of plaster on Decker's knuckles, and the faint red badge of alcohol lingering in his right eye. "You go on the town last night?"

"More like the other way around."

Johnny gave that a chuckle. "You never were one for sitting home and rolling socks, were you?"

Decker shrugged. "I like nightlife. You meet a lower class of people."

"Not me." Johnny stretched his big frame in a beam of mellow sunshine slanting through a window. "I need daylight. I got to have the sun, or I fade."

They were interrupted by a questioning voice.

"Hey, mister. Wanna feel me up for five bucks?"

"Sounds like a bargain," Decker said, turning to embrace a smiling freckle-faced woman. "How are you, Miriam?"

Miriam Wize—Miriam the Mouth, as she was called—had pleasant good looks complicated only by a mass of carrot-colored hair which fell to her shoulders. At forty-two years of age her full figure was a little on the dumpy side, but she carried herself well, and could draw a lot of second glances when she wanted to. On the street, fumbling in her handbag for an Instamatic, she could pass for just another tourist from the Midwest. Nobody would have pegged her for a Grade 12 agent who could score a 290 with a carbine.

"How they hanging, Deck?"

"Fine, Miriam."

"Fine?" Miriam's penciled eyebrows climbed a little. "You always used to say low and to the left."

"That's when I knew you better," Decker said, kissing her cheek.

"Careful with that agent," a new voice said. "You never know where she's been."

"Bumpy. Good to see you."

The man who shook Decker's hand had been born Donald Landing, but with a last name like that there'd been no way for him to hold on to his first one. Bumpy ran Intelligence for the office; made contacts, correlated information, got a line on the names and numbers of the important players, and kept a small computer humming.

"You two married yet?" Decker asked. Bumpy and Miriam had had a good-natured spat running for the last four years.

"Him?" Miriam sniffed. "Hell, he wouldn't know what to do. He'd put it under my arm."

"Listen," Bumpy said. "With what I've got it'd still give you a thrill."

"I know what you've got. I heard about it in the ladies' room at the Excelsior. It's no bigger than a Marlboro."

"That's a lie," Bumpy said emphatically. "I've never been in the ladies' room at the Excelsior."

"Hugh Decker?"

Another man had appeared at the open door: big, bulky, and approaching his fifties in a reluctant, rumpled manner. This was Ralph Dobrinski, the CA, the Country Attaché, the man who ran the Hong Kong office. Johnny Risotto introduced them, and Dobrinski invited Decker in for a chat.

Following the CA into his office, Decker nodded at a pretty secretary who was catching up on some filing. The desk beside her was empty, the desktop clean and polished.

Nobody had to tell Decker that this had been Angela Waters' desk. A typewriter sat on one side of it, hooded by a green nylon cover. In the context it reminded Decker of a blanket stretched over a bed in which somebody had recently died.

"You settled in okay?" Dobrinski asked, patting a chair and taking one himself. They spent some time talking about little things: formalities, and getting-to-know-you stuff. The CA appeared to Decker to be a reflection of his office: practical and unfussy. There was no flash to the man, but no guile either; just an easy, unforced pleasantness.

They talked about Eddie Fong, discussed that situation for a while, then moved on to the real reason for Decker's visit. They spent twenty minutes on that, going over the sensitive local ground rules which would have to be observed, what was known about the killing, and how best to investigate it without appearing to.

"We've got a break on the contact side. Do you know Doug Portloe?" Dobrinski asked.

"Lucky Doug? Sure. Narcotics guy. He's an old pal."

"He's in Homicide now. He's OC on the case."

"I didn't know that. That's got to help."

Dobrinski bobbed his head in agreement, and was silent for a moment. Then he scratched at a section of his thinning hair, and introduced another subject, this one with reluctance.

"When you were posted here before, I understand that you, um . . ."—Dobrinski frowned, as if the head scratching was hurting— "made a bit of a boo-boo."

"It wasn't a bit of one. It was triple-A-rated."

Dobrinski seemed pleased by the answer. It wasn't a bragging reply, merely an honest one. He liked that: straightforwardness. He had no time for guys who'd try to bullshit their way past you.

"I see," Dobrinski said, and struggled a little with what was coming next, wanting to put it as diplomatically as he could.

Decker saw his discomfort, and helped him out. Dobrinski seemed to be a nice guy; it would certainly be a change to have a boss he could get on with.

"I know what you're gonna say, and you don't have to because I'll say it for you. I'm not I Street's first choice to run an investigation in this town. Not their second or third either. But I happen to fit the bill because Eddie Fong's my responsibility, and he turned up here. You've read my OPF, so you know what I Street thinks of me. I've read my file too." Decker said mildly. "It says that I suffer, from time to time, an irrational and uncontrollable personality loss. I'm sorry to have to say that it's right. But I promise you this," Decker said, coming forward in his chair. "While I'm in this town, and attached to this office, I'll do my best to just keep nodding and smiling, whatever happens. But if it doesn't work out that way, and ordure hits the fan, I'll try to make sure the blades aren't pointing in your direction. Okay?"

Again Ralph Dobrinski was impressed; this was a guy who knew the score, and wasn't trying to fool himself. To solve a problem, a person first had to admit he had one. So this guy Decker had a chance.

"Fair enough," Dobrinski said. "We know where we stand."

At that point the pretty young secretary popped her head in the door to tell her boss that the people he'd been expecting had arrived.

Dobrinski introduced them to Decker, two men from the U.S. consulate across the street: the Legal Attaché—which was what an overseas FBI man was called, the Bureau having no charter to operate outside of the United States—and the RSO, the Regional Security Officer, a standard position at every U.S. consulate of any size.

They were both new to Decker, and he wasn't interested in them enough to get their names, although he found out later that the rest of the office called them Bob Boring and Sam Superfluous.

Dobrinski had the three resident agents brought in. Then everybody found chairs, and traded small talk while they waited for coffee. Decker, joining in the chat, felt good and relaxed to be where he was, although he was conscious of the disparity between the two groups. Ralph Dobrinski, Johnny Risotto, Bumpy Landing, Miriam Wize, looked anything but what they really were. Dobrinski could have been a factory floor manager who'd reluctantly put on a jacket.

Johnny, with his round face and lasagne stomach, and the socks which showed an inch of white skin above his ankles, could have been a novelty salesman from New Jersey. Bumpy—balding, thin, and slight, his mouth breaking down a wad of gum, his quick, sharp eyes missing nothing—might have been the guy who sells you a hot tip at the racetrack. Miriam the Mouth could have doubled for any attractive suburban housewife with a station wagon full of supermarket sacks, and something going with the local tennis pro.

Conversely, the two men from the consulate looked exactly like what they were. The RSO man, the security man, was probably ex-Secret Service, Decker decided: tall, with not an ounce more flesh than he needed, he had that austere, dedicated look of somebody who's been trained to throw himself in the path of an assassin's bullet.

The FBI man was a typical three-piece-suit-and-tie Bureau agent: neat, together, no seams showing, no loose threads; a wall-plaquer, as a friend of Decker's described the type: a good office man with a crisp telephone manner, and awards and framed citations on display. About the only thing the DEA and the FBI had in common was that their respective names were shortened to three initials. Outside of that, they were two vastly different organizations which didn't quite approve of each other's mode of operation.

The Bureau men tended to be button-down types, correct and formal, with not a whole lot of personality. Traditionally most FBI men had been either lawyers or accountants, and approached their law-enforcement duties with a propriety inherited from their previous professions.

DEA agents, on the other hand, were recruited from an astounding variety of backgrounds, and tended to be far more relaxed and unstuffy. They spent a lot of time getting their hands dirty on the street, mixing with pushers and dealers and money men. An FBI agent put in a lot of street time too, but when things got hot for a Bureau man—when the local villains tumbled to him, and threatened him—he could request a transfer, and get it. But when the same thing happened to a DEA agent, that agent was expected to stick around and tough it out.

When the coffee arrived, Ralph Dobrinski gave everybody time for a couple of gulps, then switched on a desk recorder and said, "Okay, let's formalize it. This is the first official meeting of the inquiry into the murder of Angela Waters, former employee of this office, DEA, Hong Kong. The code name for this operation will be

Tea Leaf. Tea Leaf," Dobrinski repeated, his eyes traveling around the assembled group. "All communications with I Street concerning this investigation will carry that heading, and are to be sent via the consulate by secret cable."

Both consulate men nodded portentously at this, and scribbled something in their open notebooks.

The four DEA agents watched them, and drank their coffee.

"Special Agent Decker." Dobrinski continued, "assigned this office on TDY, will act as GS, and will direct and coordinate all agent activity, reporting to me, Ralph Dobrinski, Country Attaché, regarding same." With mild relief at finishing a boring chore, he clicked off the recorder and said, "Thus endeth the first part. Now for the stuff we don't want on tape. How we handle Arsenal Street."

At the mention of the local police headquarters, the Bureau man edged forward uncomfortably in his chair, and the security man frowned in worried concentration.

The four DEA agents drank some more of their coffee.

"They're on top of it," Dobrinski said, "and when they come up with something, they've promised us a complete report immediately it's been approved for release. They've assigned a full task force to the case, so there's no question about them not going at it full-bore. On the other hand, they know we're not gonna just sit in the bleachers on this one. They know we're gonna intrude on their patch, and that's something that they won't tolerate."

"Fuck 'em." Miriam said. "If we want our own answers, we have to ask our own questions."

The two men from the consulate looked quickly at Miriam, then just as quickly looked away.

Dobrinski, used to Miriam's breezy vocabulary, and undisturbed by it, explained something to her. "It's a case of appearances. We can stand outside the cookie jar and look all we want. We can lick our lips, roll our eyes, and rub our tummies. But what we can't do is get caught reaching into the jar."

"Exactly," the security man said. He tapped his notebook with the end of his pen in steady cadence with his words. "If they caught you actively investigating, there'd be a lot of red faces at the consulate."

In his starched, dry manner the Bureau man backed up this opinion. "We can't afford to upset Arsenal Street. It's imperative that our working arrangement remains a viable one."

"Absolutely," Bumpy and Miriam said together, both of them nodding gravely.

Dobrinski flashed them a look, then said to the consulate men, "Liaison shouldn't be a problem. Agent Decker already has a good relationship with Doug Portloe, who's handling the case. Portloe's a good man, and a sympathetic one. He'll bend rules up to a point."

"Bend but not break," the Bureau man cautioned Decker, turning toward him. "It's important you make that distinction."

Decker pointed a finger at him, and nodded sagely, as if the man had made a major and well-considered observation.

"Okay," Dobrinski said, sitting up a little straighter. "We're off and running. Agent Decker, seeing you're GS on this, maybe there's something you'd like to say before we wrap it up."

Decker put down his coffee cup, got to his feet, and addressed the room. "There were only three rules in my day: go at 'em fast, go at 'em hard, go at 'em low. If they get up, knock 'em down again. You've got to play guts football."

He sat down.

The room was very quiet. Johnny, Bumpy, and Miriam, their lips compressed, were being very careful not to catch each other's eyes. The Bureau man looked at the security man; the security man, whose job brought him into daily contact with what he privately described as "weirdos, DEA agents, and other eccentrics," shrugged wearily.

The Bureau man pursed his mouth and addressed Dobrinski. "I have a few points I'd like to make."

"By all means," Dobrinski said.

The FBI man took several pages of closely typed notes from his briefcase, and fiddled with a pair of reading glasses.

Decker interrupted him. "Excuse me, but Agent Dobrinski mentioned Doug Portloe at Arsenal Street."

The Bureau man scowled. "So?"

"Well, I think I should talk to him as soon as possible. Like now."

"So go ahead," the other man said, irritated.

"Thing is," Decker said, getting up again, "if I'm Group Supervisor, no meeting regarding Angela Waters' homicide should be convened without me being present. Similarly, no meeting concerning the homicide should continue without me being present. And I have to go see Doug Portloe."

"He has a point," Johnny Risotto said, pushing his bulk up out of his chair.

Bumpy and Miriam immediately stood too.

The security officer, who had politely been given the shaft many times previously, and was used to it now, also got up.

The FBI agent, who had the Bureau's honor to consider, checked with Ralph Dobrinski in a silent request for a ruling.

Dobrinski raised his hands in a feeble gesture, giving a good impression of a powerless man.

The FBI rep glowered at Decker, tossed his notebook into his briefcase, and shut it with a bitchy click.

Decker nodded to him, nodded to the security man, and walked out of the room.

Ralph Dobrinski watched his new Group Supervisor leave, the meeting breaking up in his wake.

Hugh C. Decker.

He'd admired the guy when he'd first met him.

Now he was beginning to like him too.

The blood from the woman's nostrils had spread as it flowed, and had congealed on each side of her nose in the shape of a stage villain's mustache.

She lay on rumpled sheets, in a position of collapse, the facial expression totally bland, like a flat and undecorated carnival mask. On the best day she ever saw, her face would still have been ordinary and unremarkable, yet death had taken it a stage further toward dull blankness.

"Her boyfriend was sleeping right next to her," Lucky Doug Portloe said, taking the ten-by-eight glossy from Decker and putting it back into a folder. "He claims he didn't hear the shot. Woke up at his regular hour and found her like that. Sleeping right next to her, and that's what he says. Said she'd been depressed. He claims she must've got out of bed, got his gun, loaded it, got back into bed, and shot herself. If somebody told you a story like that, what would you say?"

They were sitting in Portloe's office on the sixth floor of May House, the main building of the Royal Hong Kong Police Headquarters on Arsenal Street, the street which forms the western border of Wanchai.

Decker and Portloe had already spent ten minutes catching up on each other's careers since Decker had last been in Hong Kong, and the policeman was now showing him something he'd just finished working on.

"What kind of gun?" Decker asked.

"Standard issue. Four-inch Special. He's a beat PC. Been with us three years, and never even been late for roll call."

"Powder burns?"

"Powder burns? There were pieces of her brain lodged inside the gun barrel."

"Probably suicide," Decker said.

Portloe blinked at him, then said in his soft Cornish accent, "You mean you would've believed his story? Lying right next to her, and he didn't even wake up? A thirty-eight going off within a few feet of him?"

"It's possible."

"Why?"

"Because if she rammed the muzzle against her skull tight enough for her brain to explode out into it, then her skull could have acted as a silencer."

Portloe opened his mouth, then snapped it closed again. "Bloody DEA know-it-all."

Decker raised his hands in an exaggerated no-problem gesture. He could joke with Doug Portloe, they went back quite a way, back to the time when Decker had first been posted to the colony, and Lucky Doug Portloe had just been Doug Portloe, a subinspector assigned to Narcotics.

They were about the same age, but the Englishman was thirty pounds heavier than Decker and, at six-feet-two, three inches taller. Portloe captained the police rugby team, and played for Hong Kong at the annual International Sevens Festival. In regular games he played at the back of the scrum, at Number 8, his job being basically to knock over the man with the ball, a chore he performed with swift and graceful ferocity.

Anybody meeting him for the first time had no trouble believing he was a policeman, built the way he was; but somebody who didn't know him, talking to him on the phone, hearing the musical rise and dip of his speech, might have got a picture of a plump, rosy-cheeked farmer picking apples in the sunshine of a southern English orchard. He'd earned his nickname in a sensational way.

Early in his career as a narcotics cop his cover had been blown, and a car full of Wo Hop To members had jumped him in broad daylight in the middle of Fat Kwong Street. They'd wrestled him

into the gutter, where one of their number had put a .45 automatic
to Portloe's head and pulled the trigger.

The gun hadn't fired.

The gangster had recocked it, put it to Portloe's head again, and
pulled the trigger a second time.

And again the gun had failed to go off.

The lodge man had cursed, and fussed with the pistol while the
leader, impatiently revving the car, urged a faster execution.

The automatic had been shoved into Portloe's ear for the third
time. And for the third time the loaded gun had refused to function.

The lodge leader had shouted something, the gang had jumped
into the car, and the car had screeched away, leaving the Cornishman lying in the gutter, stunned at having survived three attempts
on his life inside of ten seconds.

Lucky Doug Portloe.

The policeman leaned to his left, dropped the photograph into a
file cabinet, and slid the drawer closed. He had, of course, guessed
the real reason for Decker's presence in Hong Kong, and sensed
that Decker was about to broach the subject.

He was right.

"Doug?"

"Yeah?"

"Tell me about Angela Waters."

"Investigations are proceeding," Portloe began, "and—"

"And an arrest is imminent," Decker finished for him. "A dog
and two Martians are helping the police with their inquiries. Tell
me about Angela Waters."

The Cornishman moved his thick neck to check beyond the large
glass window which made up half the interior wall.

"If Waxy drops in, and we're talking about Angela Waters, he'll
kick my arse."

"But you're not talking about Angela Waters. You're talking
about your arse."

Portloe glared at his pal, and said with a slow burn in his voice,
"With all those handguns in America, how come nobody's shot you
yet?"

"They've tried, but I'm faster than a speeding bullet. Tell me
about Angela Waters."

Portloe checked the corridor again, then pulled at a drawer in his
desk, and had trouble opening it. The furniture in the office was

spartan and drab; budget quality. Most of the offices in May House were similarly furnished, yet the building was modern and quite impressive, having a tall white stone exterior. Police Headquarters had once been described as looking like a Hilton on the outside, and an aging YMCA on the inside.

Doug Portloe muscled the drawer into submission, and removed a blue folder with a white label gummed to its cover. It read, "Crime No. CCB 2478. Waters, Angela."

"I suppose you want the whole kit and caboodle?"

"Yes, please. From the top."

Portloe, with another cautious glance at the interior window, began to read.

"Angela Jane Waters. Unmarried female, age twenty-eight. American national, Hong Kong ID number 356692J. On March 28, at approximately eight-thirty A.M., Miss Waters' body was discovered by Rosetta García, Filipino national, employed by the deceased as part-time maid, at the deceased's residence, flat Six B, Cloud Regency Apartments, MacDonald Road.

"Mrs. García, immediately dialed nine-nine-nine and reported the find. Call was routed to Regional Command and Control Center, Central District. Ambulance team and emergency unit dispatched, Staff Sergeant Wong, and Station Sergeant Lo Fu responding.

"Upon investigation, Sergeant Wong confirmed existence of dead body, and went next door to telephone Command Center, whereupon CID group was dispatched."

"Why didn't he just radio in?" Decker asked.

"Because the media boys have gotten really bad. They monitor the police frequencies now. Couple of months back one of the bastards beat us to a homicide scene and moved the body out onto the terrace because his flash gun wasn't working."

"It's the same in the States. Screw the evidence, buddy, we gotta make the six-o'clock news."

Portloe grunted, found his place in the report, and continued reading. "Duty Superintendent Henshaw arrived on scene, and apprised ADC Crime of situation. Duty Super then designated order of examination for investigative teams. Forensics examined body, Pathology then did same. ID Bureau then photographed and dusted."

"They get a break?"

"No fingerprints besides those of the deceased and the maid.

Exhibit team collected and bagged all relevant items. General Examination by Organized and Serious Crimes Bureau, Chief Inspector Douglas Portloe, Case Officer in Charge."

The Case Officer looked up and said without much hope, "You sure you want all this?"

"Every syllable," Decker said with his best and most pleasant smile.

"Murder Report, Pol. form one-sixty. Preliminary initial examination revealed naked body of the deceased lying in bathtub. Congealed blood on nose and mouth indicated possible cracked skull. Upper trunk and genital area had been subjected to massive wounds. Meat knife, bloodstains on blade and handle, found on bathroom floor next to tub.

"Pathologist's subsequent postmortem report states that victim was killed between midnight and four A.M. by a blow to the top of the skull administered by a heavy, nonmetal object. Traces of the victim's scalp skin and hair were found on the seat edge of a chair in the living room, indicating chair as probable murder weapon. Other wounds suffered by victim, as previously mentioned, both breasts severed, vagina cut away. These parts found on a dinner plate on glass-topped coffee table in living room."

"Christ," Decker murmured. "I didn't know about that. A dinner plate?"

Doug Portloe went right on reading, welcoming the chance to sift through the facts once more and maybe spot something, some small detail, he might previously have overlooked.

"Blood sample and oral, anal, and vaginal swabs taken from victim, plus scalp and pubic-hair sample, and fingernail clippings. Organs sent to Toxicology and examined for presence of drugs, alcohol, foreign matter. Presence of alcohol only."

Portloe turned a page quickly, hurried on.

"Semen was found in victim's body, and on sheets in main bedroom, indicating that victim engaged in sexual activity on the night of the murder, possibly with the murderer. Forensic report states that condition of semen taken from the woman's body indicates that intercourse could have taken place after death."

Decker used his hand as a stop sign. "Back up a minute. You're thinking he screwed her after he killed her?"

"Looks very much like it."

"You can tell that from the semen?"

"Sure. If the woman was alive during intercourse, her body fluids would've degraded the semen. But there was very little degradation, according to the report, which could mean her body fluids weren't functioning properly or, more likely, weren't functioning at all. And there's something else too."

Decker waited to hear.

"They found stains left by a blue fluid on the sheets. Some in her body too. The lab says it's kitchen detergent. Okay, we're dealing with a madman here. He might have sprayed it on her because he felt she was unclean. Cutting her up like that, cutting off the parts he did, it's a reasonable assumption. Except there were no traces of detergent found on the breasts, only on and in the vaginal section. So he might have used the detergent as a lubricant, which would further suggest that the woman was dead."

Decker nodded at the reasoning, agreeing with it. He wasn't shocked by what he was hearing; he'd been with the DEA for eleven years, and in that time he'd been exposed to the darker side of life, to a lot of traffickers and their warped and brutal philosophies; Mafia middlemen, desperate amateurs, blasé free-lance pros who didn't care who got hurt, or how badly, just as long as they got their end of the deal. Decker had found that when it came to people doing things to other people, sane or crazy, there were no rules of propriety, no line beyond which lay the unacceptable.

"There were no drinking glasses anywhere," Portloe continued, "no cigarette butts found, and he didn't kiss her, lick her, or bite her."

"So you don't know whether or not the guy's a secreter."

"It doesn't matter. We were able to blood-type him from his semen. On the ABO system he's an O type, which doesn't tell us if he's Chinese or a Westerner, if you remember the breakdown."

Decker rubbed at a corner of his mouth. "I don't think I ever knew the breakdown."

"In Britain," Portloe told him, 'O's make up forty-six percent of the population. In Hong Kong, forty percent of the population. There's not much in it."

"It would've helped if he was a B type, huh?"

"Sure. In Hong Kong twenty-five percent are B's. In Britain, eight and a half percent. And if he was an AB, the chances of him being Chinese would've been twice that of him being British. But he's type O. Incidentally, so was Angela Waters."

The glass of the interior window blurred as somebody went by in the corridor. Portloe's chair squealed, his linebacker's body torturing its swivel when he turned.

"We better wrap this up. My Cornish sixth sense tells me that Waxy's skulking around."

"You're a superstitious Celt. Finish the report."

"How can I? You keep asking me questions."

"Okay, I'll shut up."

"Promise?"

"I promise," Decker said. "No more questions till you're finished."

Portloe fixed him with a look loaded with doubt, but resumed reading. "The PGM count was one plus, two plus."

"What the hell's a PGM count?" Decker asked.

Lucky Doug Portloe looked off at a far corner of his office and let out a lot of breath from his forty-three-inch chest. "PGM," he said very deliberately, "stands for phosphoglucomutase enzyme. A person inherits one of ten common types from each of his parents. It shows up in a man's semen and in a woman's vaginal secretions. In this case, a one-plus, two-plus reading means that either the man who had sex with Angela Waters is a two-plus, and she is the one-plus, or he is the one-plus, and she is the two-plus. It's very hard to pinpoint who's what."

The reply brought slanting lines to Decker's forehead. He would have made a lousy detective, he knew; he would never have had the patience to grind though all the zeros and decimal points as Doug Portloe was doing. For Decker lab work came after the arrest: serious types in white jackets analyzing the contents of the glassine bags he found on the street guys he busted. And he wasn't much interested in the purity or the weight or the suspected country of origin. Dope was dope, and it was all life-destroying shit whatever the latest fancy word for it was.

"Then how does a PGM reading help you?" he asked Portloe.

"It doesn't, really. Except if we'd got a reading of, say, one-plus, two-minus, we could have hoped the two-minus was the guy. Because you only get a two-minus count from one person in a hundred."

"Okay," Decker said. "What else you have, doctor? What did you do then?"

"Checked the woman's PGM count by hair-root analysis. She's probably the one-plus."

"Probably . . . ?"

"If she was Chinese we could tell for sure," Portloe explained. "Chinese hair roots are a lot bigger than the Western variety, so a reading's easier to get. Anyway, we ran a third kind of test on the semen, looking for a GLO reading, and if you open your mouth I'll kill you."

Decker pointed to himself in surprised innocence, and Portloe went on uninterrupted.

"A GLO reading is what you get when you test a glyoxalase enzyme. He's a GLO two, which doesn't give us anything because just about every guy in the world's a GLO two. One of these days, if I make it to old age, I'll get a GLO one. Only one guy in fifty falls into that category."

"All right. So now you've checked all those numbers and initials, and the bottom line is still a maybe. Maybe he's Chinese, or maybe he's a Westerner."

"True. But in this case, I'm pretty sure he's a Westerner. The prints would indicate that."

"What prints? You said there weren't any prints."

"I said no fingerprints. But there were gloves prints. On the knife handle, on the chair, on the detergent bottle, on the corpse. Forensics reckons the gloves were fine-mesh string gloves. You know the ones, sports-car drivers like 'em. And I don't know about you, but I've yet to see a Chinese wearing any kind of gloves in hot weather. It's purely a British thing. Goes with a TR Six, or an MG."

Decker asked if anybody had spotted a sports car at the apartment house.

Portloe told him they weren't having that kind of luck. "The watchman said he didn't see anybody pull up, but he was probably asleep. Neighbors saw nothing, heard less. It was pretty late, anyway."

"Do you know where she'd been?"

"Mad Dogs. We know she left there around eleven-forty-five. The place was jammed. The usual boy-girl make-out scene. A bartender and one of the waitresses knew Angela Waters. The waitress served her a drink around eleven-fifteen. She was sitting with a man. Tall, light brown hair, British-looking, sleeveless shirt and tie, no jacket, is the best she can do. She didn't see Angela Waters leave with him, but it seems a good bet."

"So we're looking for a tall, light-haired Brit?"

"Or a Swede, or a Dutchman, an American, or any other light-haired Western male who dresses like everybody else around here."

"And who drives a sports car," Decker concluded.

"Or a van, or a petrol lorry. Or he may not drive at all. They may have taken a taxi to her apartment house, although we checked with the cab companies and turned up nothing. Anyway, Portloe said, "the murderer doesn't have to be the guy she probably knew whoever killed her. Firearms and Toolmarks say the front door wasn't tampered with, and no sign of a forced entry. Forensics got a zero on contact evidence—no blood or fibers in the fingernail clippings, nothing on her clothes—so we have to assume there was no struggle. There was certainly no evidence of one in the flat. The woman's body showed a fresh bruise in the midsection, as if she'd been jabbed with something. We found a kitchen broom next to the sofa, and some meshglove prints on it."

"He gave her a shot with the broom," Decker said. "Stunned her, then killed her with the chair."

"Had to be that way. Then he dragged her into the bedroom, there were marks on the carpet, undressed her there, that's where her clothes were, and screwed her. Then he dragged her into the bathroom, dumped her in the tub, and took a knife to her. The knife was one of a set mounted in a rack in the kitchen. He put the parts he cut off her into a towel, carried them into the kitchen, evidenced by a blood-and-water trail, put the parts on a plate he got from a cupboard, left the towel there, took the plate into the living room, and put it on the coffee table. And that's as far as we've been able to reconstruct it."

Decker had taken a rubber band from the top of Portloe's cluttered desk and was pensively stretching it around his fingers. He pulled at it, testing the tension, concentrating on what he'd just heard. "He mutilates her, and puts the parts on a dinner plate. Why a dinner plate? And why put the plate on a coffee table? Did he leave it there for somebody to find? Somebody he had in mind? A roommate, maybe? Did Angela Waters have a roommate?"

"Yes, she did. But you're looking for a logical explanation, and I doubt very much that there is one. With madness there seldom is. I mean," Portloe said, kicking back in his chair, "there's an obvious sexual oral association between a dinner plate and the particular parts of the woman's body that were cut off and left on it. There's no doubt in my mind that we're dealing with a good old-fashioned sex maniac."

Decker doubled the rubber band around his fingers, eased it back, flirting with the tension. "You sure of that? I've heard of revenge killings similar to this. A jilted boyfriend out of his gourd on booze and uppers . . ."

"True," Doug Portloe admitted. "Plenty of blokes have sliced up their unfaithful girlfriends. Even cut off the offending parts. But to put them on a plate and leave them on a coffee table like a bowl of fruit, that's not revenge, that's madness."

Decker ran it through the processes for a minute, saw that his pal was right. The horror which had taken place in Angela Waters' apartment had been generated by insanity. Had to be.

He asked the detective what he'd been able to find out about the dead woman from the people who'd known her. Portloe told him much the same thing Johnny Risotto had reported when he'd driven Decker in from the airport.

"We've gone through her letters, her diary, her phone book. Talked to her friends and colleagues, including, of course, everybody up at St. John's House. The consensus is that Angela Waters was a popular, good-looking girl. Very outgoing. Perhaps," Portloe added with a sober twist to his mouth, "a little too outgoing. She had a reputation for being a bit free and easy with her favors, which is probably what got her into trouble. Although she had to be incredibly unlucky. There hasn't been a sex crime like this in Hong Kong since the broomstick murders."

When Decker reacted to that with a quick lift of his head, Portloe killed any connective thought.

"I know. A broomstick was used on Angela Waters. But the man who killed the other woman is doing life in Stanley. First thing I did was to check to see if he was still behind bars, and he is. So it's either a bloke who's new in town or whose madness has taken a while to surface."

Decker stretched the rubber band wrapped around his fingers. It lengthened, thinned, and snapped. He wondered if the same thing could happen to a person. Could he be stretched by stress, extruded to a breaking point, and then snap, bang! just like that?

Or maybe a person could spend years keeping something at bay in the back of his mind, something with jaws and vicious little teeth that gnawed away, year after year, trying to break loose, take over, until one day it burst through.

He flicked the rubber band toward a wastepaper basket, and got his thinking back on track.

"What about a boyfriend?" he asked Doug Portloe. "Did Angela Waters have anybody steady?"

"Nope. If she had, he would've been the first person we'd have talked to. Her roommate gave us several names of recent acquaintances, but there's nothing cooking there."

"Where was the roommate when it happened?"

"Thailand. On vacation." Portloe moved his wide shoulders as if they were constrained by a seat belt. He closed the folder. "So that's as far as we've got. And as far as we're going to get unless we get lucky. Our best hope, based on available evidence, and a stunning lack of leads, is that the guy will volunteer something himself. Something like that happened on the last—" Portloe quickly dropped the folder and got up from his chair. "Good morning, sir."

Decker, rounding slowly, saw that the Cornishman's sixth sense had been right. Assistant Commissioner James Crane stood in the doorway, his usual severe glare touched by a hint of surprise.

Surprise and annoyance.

Decker tried for a smile. "Good morning, Commissioner. Nice to see you again." He rose as he said it; when Waxy Crane walked into an office in May House, he expected people to get to their feet. Decker made sure to stand straight and tall; Waxy Crane was the last person in Hong Kong he wanted to antagonize. He'd already done that once, and suffered the consequences.

"Good God! *Decker!* What in blue blazes are *you* doing in Hong Kong?" Decker starched the smile into place and spoke through it.

"I've been assigned to temporary duty here, sir."

"Temporary. Well, I'm damned glad to hear *that*. They assigned you *here*?"

"Yes, sir." Decker wanted to laugh; he was remembering how Bumpy and Miriam, when they'd go drinking together at the Bull and Bear, would imitate Waxy Crane's speech pattern, using Up-Periscope English and hitting every third word.

"Well," the man sniffed. "All I can say is Washington must be fielding a pretty *poor* side these days if they're sending a rabbit like *you* in to bat."

Assistant Commissioner Crane also liked to pepper his dialogue with cricket analogies. He'd been nicknamed Waxy after a character, an irascible schoolteacher, in an English boys' magazine which had once been famous. Crane reminded everybody of the headmaster of a strict and venerable boys' school. Like many Englishmen of his age—late fifties—and social class—mid, with pretensions of upper—Crane had spent his early years at boarding school, and his thinking and attitude had been shaped by the experience forever.

As far as he was concerned, May House was aptly named; he saw himself, literally, as housemaster and principal. His officers were his "staff," and everybody else, certainly all those below gazetted rank, he regarded as unruly students who had to be kept firmly in line. He was a snob and a tyrant, but he'd earned the top spot by being a very good cop, and he retained his position by making sure his teams got hard-and-fast results.

If he had a fault, apart from his abrasive personality, it was that he always pressed for a good, clean solution to every case; everything resolved with no flapping edges, no loose ends. The trouble was, there were often times in policework when a case defied straightforward answers. When that happened, Waxy Crane had it squashed into shape anyway, and wrapped and bound so that it appeared to be as neat a package as any of the other cases. Decker assumed that the word Crane had used, "rabbit," was a cricketing term for a no-talent player.

"I wouldn't know about that, sir," he said.

"You *wouldn't*, eh?" Waxy Crane, with his red wattled face, his perfectly parted white hair, and his freshly pressed gray suit worn like a uniform, stood with his hands clasped behind his back, his eyes raking Decker with disapproval. He liked to rock slightly on his heels and, having good height, and being ramrod straight, the action achieved considerable menace. "What are you doing talking to Portloe here? It *wouldn't*, by any chance, have anything to do with a *homicide*, would it? That woman from your office?"

"No, sir. I was asking Chief Inspector Portloe about a man he might have run into during his time in Narcotics."

"And just *what*, may I ask, is this gentleman's name?" Along with the cane, heavy sarcasm was a popular weapon in the Great English Boarding Schools.

"Eddie Fong."

Waxy Crane switched his acid gaze, poured it full strength, onto his staff member. "Is this true, Portloe?"

"Yes, it is, sir. Eddie Fong." Portloe had never heard of the man. "A known trafficker, sir. I was telling Agent Decker what I could remember about his habits and associates."

"Crane's steely ray switched again, his mouth thinning in censorious compression. "A *drug* trafficker. *That's* why you're here in Hong Kong, Decker?"

"That's right, sir."

The assistant commissioner snorted his way into a deeper scowl.

He appeared even more dyspeptic than Decker remembered, and he had a good idea why: Waxy Crane would be out of a job when Peking took over. He'd have to either leave Hong Kong soon, and start looking elsewhere, or accept early retirement. Either option, as 1997 got closer, would not have improved an already choleric disposition.

"Cock! Hot cock! A load of old *cobblers*! You're lying, Decker. I'd rather have a thief than a liar. Specially if the liar was as lousy at it as *you* are."

Decker considered the accusation. He wasn't lying about Eddie Fong, and he could have insisted he wasn't. But he didn't want to do that: get pulled into an argument, get mad, walk out on Waxy with a line like, "Goodbye, Mr. Chips," and get banned from Arsenal Street. He needed Arsenal Street, needed Doug Portloe. So he just nodded tolerantly.

"Whatever you say, sir."

The head of May House peered at Decker as if his vision had clouded, actually leaning forward to shorten his focus.

"What's wrong, Decker? They knock you for six back there in Washington?" His voice had lost some of its iron, and he no longer emphasized his words. "The Hugh Decker I had the displeasure of knowing wouldn't have taken a remark like that. He would have told me exactly what he thought of me, and gotten himself kicked out of the building. What's happened to you, man?"

"Nothing, sir. I'm just trying to lead a more Zen-like life these days."

Waxy Crane took a moment to to digest that.

"Have I read you *wrong*, Decker? Are you trying to be *funny*?' "

"No, sir. Zen-like. That's the God's honest truth."

"Well, I'll give you *another* truth, Decker. Narcotics is on the tenth and eleventh floors. This is the *sixth* floor. And if I catch you up here again, hobnobbing with Homicide, I'll have you escorted to the airport and put on the first plane *out*. I don't care if it's going to Timbuktu, you'll be *on* it. Do you get my drift?"

"Perfectly, sir."

"Right, then. On your *bike.*' "

As Decker, nodding to Doug Portloe, began to leave, Waxy Crane, miffed at not getting a rise out of the American, fired one last shot. This time he chewed the words into bullets and spat them out.

"Decker, do you know why you're such a rotten agent?"

With a considerable amount of effort Decker managed to absorb that, and keep his smile working.

"There are several theories making the rounds, sir."

"Because you've got no finesse, Decker. No technique. You're nothing but a slogger, Decker. You just grab the bat down at the very end, close your eyes, and lash out."

Decker, soaking it up like a sponge, and extremely pleased he was able to do it, said, "Well, sir, I have to admit that holding the bat down at the very end doesn't bother me."

Waxy Crane bristled, his wattled neck throbbing with a deeper color. "And why not, I'd like to know?"

"Because," Decker explained, pushing his luck a little, but feeling confident, "as a famous American ballplayer once said"—he walked to the door and delivered the last part of his answer as he went by the assistant commissioner—"that's where the Cadillacs are."

5

"Eddie Fong," Decker said, just back from Arsenal Street, and sitting in Bumpy Landing's office with his three co-agents, "is like a pebble in my shoe. I've been walking on it for days now, and I'm beginning to limp."

"Then pop him," Johnny Risotto advised from a chair by the window. "He's only in Mong Kok. Four stops on the MTR."

Decker had taken them through his meeting with Lucky Doug Portloe, and told them he'd decided to hold off on the investigation until Portloe had something to go on. It would only be a rubber stamp anyway; the local police, with their vast network of beat constables, auxiliaries, and plainclothes people, plus an army of street informants, were far better equipped for a homicide inquiry than four American DEA agents. Meanwhile, there was always Eddie Fong, and the ten thousand dollars. Decker looked over at Bumpy. The little man was seated behind his Wang computer, his left hand prancing on the keyboard.

"Who's running this at Arsenal Street?"

"Dave Ramsey. New since your time, Deck. I talked with him this morning. He says that Eddie Fong met a guy last night in a restaurant in Hung Hom. They were still talking a couple of hours after the last noodle went down. Ramsey figures they were definitely cutting a deal."

"Eddie's pal Chinese?"

"Yes, sir. Ramsey had him followed and hauled in."

"What was the charge?"

Bumpy lifted his shoulders. "I don't know. Consorting with a known bore. Failing to stop after farting, who cares? This is Hong Kong, remember? You don't need much of a reason. They just wanted to get a look at his ID. He claimed he'd lost it, but he had a driver's license. His name is Wu Chih Tsung. The cops checked that in their sinners' file and got zilch. No wonder. I mean, look at this," Bumpy invited, thrusting his thin frame forward and holding up a computer printout. "Wu Chih Tsung is Wade-Giles Romanization. In the Yale it's Wu Jr Dzung. It's Wu Zhi Zong in Pin Yin, Ng Tsz Tsung in Hakka-Rey, Eng Chi Chung in the cops' own variation, Ong Chi Joong in Cantonese, Goh Chee Tsung in Chiu Chow, while in Mandarin—"

"Fantastic, Bump," Decker said, cutting him off. Bumpy had taught French and German before joining the DEA, loved languages, and would often explain more than anybody wanted to know.

"As you can see, Deck," Miriam said, sitting on a corner of Bumpy's desk, "Old Bumpy still loves to play with his Wang."

Deflated by the interruption, Bumpy picked up the phone, asked if anybody wanted coffee.

"And something to munch on," Johnny Risotto said.

"Hilary," Bumpy said into the phone, "you got something out there for Agent Rizzo? Doughnuts, Lo Pan buns, old typewriter ribbons? He'll eat anything. And coffee for him and me and Agent Decker. Two regular, one black, no sugar."

"Hey," Miriam protested, "how about me?"

"And one regular mouthwash," Bumpy said into the phone, and hung up.

"You were up to the part," Johnny said politely, "where the name Wu Chih Tsung had the best minds in the Royal Hong Kong Police Force baffled."

"The Romanization beat 'em, sure," Bumpy said, warming up again. "And the CTC code too." He turned toward Decker. "You see, a Chinese can Romanize his name any way he wants to, and it's completely legal. But he can't change the way it's spelled in Chinese, can't change the Chinese characters. And every Chinese character has a CTC, a Chinese Telegraphic Code, equivalent." He patted the cover of a fat book lying on top of the computer. It bore the insignia of Special Branch, a division of the police which was the British equivalent of the political section of the FBI.

"Bumpy," Miriam said, sounding tired, "Deck spent four years in this town. He knows all about the CTC."

"Maybe he forgot," Bumpy said defensively. "He's been gone a year and a half."

Decker, swinging up his wrist, glanced at his watch.

"Bumpy, I'm gonna give you exactly one hour to get to the point."

"I'm coming to it. Look at this." Bumpy waved another printout sheet, pointed to an underlined part. Under the name Wu Chih Tsung three Chinese characters were written, and under each character was a four-digit number. "Wu Chih Tsung, in the CTC code, comes out as seven-zero slash six-four, and eight other numerals each more thrilling than the last. Okay, Arsenal Street ran that through and got nada again, so they figured Wu Chih wasn't a sinner because he wasn't on file. But what I tried was a nickname, Ah Wu Chih Tsung, which is like putting an L and a Y on somebody's name in English, like Bobby or Billy."

"Or dreary and lengthy," Miriam said.

"So when I punched that in, the twelve numerals of the original name, plus four new numerals for the addition on the front, bingo! I hit paydirt. Look at this. Ah Wu Chih Tsung. Known member of the Wo On Lok."

As if he'd magically changed the printout sheet into a goldfish bowl, Bumpy now had everybody's attention.

"Holy shit." Miriam said.

"Lemme see that." Johnny Risotto was out of his chair; Bumpy handed him a Xerox copy of the printout.

"Eddie's going in pretty deep," Decker said. "I thought maybe he'd buy a couple of pounds for somebody to walk through customs in LA."

"No way," Johnny said. "The Wo On Lok buys big enough to hold Fourth of July sales. And if Eddie's talking to them, then he's got to be buying real weight."

Decker was thinking about Little Gladys Goodlay and her cheery explanation of how she'd lost her arm. Six members of the Wo On Lok, she'd said; the same lodge Eddie Fong was talking to. Decker looked over at Miriam. Each of the resident agents had an area in which they specialized: Bumpy was the info man, the facts-and-figures king; Johnny kept abreast of the current drifts and trends of the triad lodges; and Miriam had a good understanding of their mode of operation.

"I hear they're still as mean as ever, the Wo On Lok."

"Meaner," Miriam answered. "They could play for the Chicago Bears. They're chopper freaks. Slash artists. Fucking ruthless, too. They've been using a cute little trick to get dope ashore from the junks. They take a baby away from its mother, gut the child, fill the body with a heroin bag, and sew it up. They shoot up the woman to keep her quiet, and she walks ashore like any other junk wife carrying what looks like a sleeping baby on her back."

Decker winced: the brutality of the triad lodges in Hong Kong exceeded even the worst excesses of the Chinese gangs in New York. There, it was violence American style: the Shadows, the Tigers, the Dragons, the Frogmen had gone native and used .357's on their victims. They killed shopkeepers, restaurant owners, delinquent borrowers and, of course, each other; still, just standard stuff. "Charming outfit Eddie's running with." He checked with Johnny. "What else do we know about them these days?"

"Around the pool tables they call 'em the Hei Shuh. Maybe thirty thousand members, all of 'em very active in Yau Ma Tei, Sham Shui Po, and Castle Peak. They're into the usual things— extortion, sharking, et cetera. Deadly enemies of the Lo Shing. Every six months or so they have it out in back of the market in Western. You clean up after that, you need mops and aprons."

Decker leaned across, took the copy of the printout from Johnny, scanned it, then carefully creased it into the beginnings of a paper dart.

"Big in dope, huh?" he asked, getting the folds just right, but thinking about something else.

"Big going on tremendous," Bumpy replied. "About a year back, some of the Stateside lodges came over here and burned yellow paper with them. Miriam covered it."

"New York, Vancouver, San Francisco," Miriam said, "sent their Four Thirty Eight guys, and they sat down with the Wo On Lok's Four Eighty Nine, the fucking lodge leader himself. That much we know for sure. The rest we can guess."

Decker bent two small corners of paper; some people didn't approve of wings on the tail part of a dart, but Decker had always thought they improved the flight pattern.

"Three Fu Shan Chus from the States in the same room as a local Shan Chu," he said. "That's got to be good for five hundred keys."

"Maybe more," Bumpy suggested. "The stuff's not coming through Hong Kong anymore. The smoking crap, yeah, but not the arm magic. They've started up in Laos again in a big way, ponypacking it into Thailand, processing all the way to pure south of Bangkok, and shipping it out in the false ends of containers."

"Containers," Johnny Risotto said, sounding disgusted. "Remember when it went into the States in hollowed-out golf clubs, or starched into a consignment of shirts?"

"That was before the Chinese found out they could talk to the Italians," Miriam offered. "Those days the triads just had the Chinatowns, but now that the Maf and them are asshole buddies, they got the rest of America too."

Decker, almost finished with his model-making, said, "In New York the Chinese have bought most of Little Italy. About seventy percent of the real estate between Canal and Houston. Except the restaurants, of course. The Italians insisted on keeping the beaneries."

"Yeah." Johnny nodded. "The Mob always did like to eat."

Everybody watched Decker fashion the paper airplane, waiting for him to make a decision.

Eddie Fong.

To pop or not to pop.

The decision was delayed when the door opened and the pretty young secretary brought in coffee and doughnuts.

"Hilary, light of my life." Bumpy jumped up to help her with the tray. "This is Hilary," Bumpy said to Decker. "A very efficient secretary. I've been trying to get into her files for three months now."

The young woman grinned, looked over at Miriam, and said, "Honestly, what are we gonna do about him?"

Miriam had a suggestion. "Get him pants that button up the back."

Hilary left the tray, went back to her typewriter.

Everybody drank coffee, the mood gone pensive.

Johnny Risotto scoffed a second doughnut, dabbed at his mouth, and put the question to Decker.

"So how about it, GS? Eddie's maybe a hell of a lot bigger than you thought. You want to give him more time to get deeper into his deal, or do you want to pop him now?"

The dart looked finished, ready to try its wings. Decker held it up, sighted on a beer stein full of yellow pencils, launched it. It sped evenly through the air, sleek and quick, then, for no apparent reason, fluttered nervously and side-slipped to the floor.

Decker got up out of his chair and, to nobody's surprise, said, "Let's pop him now."

* * *

The streets of Mong Kok, a section on the west side of Kowloon, about a mile and a half north of the famous ferry terminal, have been compared with the crush outside of the main gates of a football stadium a few minutes after the finish of a close game. The sidewalks were solid with people, waves of bodies spilling into the road, beating back traffic, choking it to a standstill. No place in the world—not Tokyo's Shinjuku, nor Shanghai's Bund, nor Calcutta's Temple Road—beat Mong Kok for the largest number of people taking up the least space. It was the undisputed king of congestion, the most densely populated piece of real estate on the globe.

Like a sea parting for an ocean liner, the crowds broke for Johnny Risotto's bulk, flowed around it, joined up again in seamless procession. Following in Johnny's wake, Decker ran interference for Bumpy and Miriam, and the four of them made it finally to Tung Choi Street, to a part given over entirely to the sale of pocket bleepers. There were no radios, no watches, no jewelry, just row upon row of bleepers displayed in the shiny glass counters of an unbroken line of shops.

Above the shops, adding to the extraordinary density of the neighborhood, the usual indiscriminate riot of signs blocked off the airspace, forming an artificial ceiling overhead which stole a good deal of the daylight. Behind the signs, supporting a phalanx of rusting stanchions, a block of tenements stumbled down the street. Their metal window frames, peeling red and yellow paint, were hinged wide on the heat and noise, standing out like tattered flags in a stiff breeze; their balconies, caged in and crammed with a jungle of green things growing, were shadowed by ripped canvas awnings, rope lines looping down them like halyards from a wrecked square-rigger.

From top to bottom, like a brilliantly mounted exhibition, the tenements were fronted by acres of multicolored washing. Pegged out on straining wooden poles, their watery residue dripped down like the last stages of a tropical cloudburst.

Outside the grimy entrance of one of these buildings a young Chinese was handing out leaflets to anybody who'd take one.

Johnny Risotto, still ahead of the group, reacted in discomfort as a leaflet was thrust into his hand.

"Hey, I can't read this, it's in Chinese. I can't read Chinese."

"It say very good sale on bleeper. Make you special price inside."

The young Chinese pointed to a shop, took his voice down. "He came out for breakfast, went back up. Hasn't been down since."

"When he does, I want to know about it," Johnny murmured. He made his way back through the crush to where the others were waiting, reported on what the man he'd hired had told him.

They moved slowly from window to window, talking prices, intent upon the miracle of miniaturized electronics.

Nobody gave them a second glance, even though they deserved one: freckle-faced Miriam in a dark skirt and a green blouse which set off her tumbling red hair; short and slight Bumpy, in a knit shirt and suntans, looking like a Vegas gambler; tall, rangy Decker, in jeans and his favorite slim-cut Hawaiian shirt; and the blimp figure of Johnny Risotto in an unbuttoned sports jacket and generously cut golf slacks—just another polyglot bunch of American tourists who'd met in the hotel coffee shop and decided to go look for bargains together.

At the entrance to one of the shops a petite twenty-year-old girl, a page-boy haircut framing the perfect skin of her smiling face, said in a singsong Hong Kong accent, "See anything you like?"

Bumpy's quick eyes roamed her pert body. "Yeah," he said, expanding the word into two syllables.

"We're just browsing," Miriam told her, steering Bumpy away.

Bumpy looked back, slid his tongue out of his mouth, and fluttered it lasciviously. "I'd go down on that," he said.

"You'd go down on a crack in the sidewalk," Miriam responded.

An hour dragged by.

Then half of another.

Then a sweatshirted youth with winning ways popped up in front of them. He pulled a thick piece of tissue from his pocket, something shiny poking from the top.

"Rolex? You want Oyster Rolex?" The glint of his teeth matched that of his offering as his eyes arrowed toward the other side of the street.

Over there, barely visible through the crushing throng of bodies, the youth with the leaflets was walking backward, hurrying to keep up with a man while badgering him about low, low prices.

The potential customer, irritably uninterested, wore a narrow-striped Sea Dragon T-shirt, the kind the street peddlers sold out of cardboard boxes, baggy gabardine pants, and black lace-up shoes. His hair had been cut in mixing-bowl style, short, with a lot of skin showing in a straight line two inches above his ears.

Decker watched him trying to ignore the leaflet man. He'd made a good attempt at mimicking a certain type of local male, but there was no doubt about it: that was Eddie Fong on the other side of the street.

The group split up; Bumpy and Miriam hurrying ahead, Johnny Risotto crossing the street to get behind Eddie Fong, who was moving north. Decker tailed him from the opposite sidewalk as their quarry led them down a block strident with honking cars and impatient buses, then turned left into the jammed expanse of Prince Edward Road. Half a block farther on, Eddie Fong entered a doorway. Above the doorway, a huge vertical sign announced the Dah Gee Family Entertainment Center.

They gave it a minute, then everybody assembled outside, everybody except Decker. From inside, from the street-level floor, the click and crash of mah-jongg tiles being sorted sounded like heavy machinery. The place had bowling alleys in the basement, then the mah-jongg room, a billiard parlor on the floor above that, and, on the top floor, the inevitable restaurant.

When Decker arrived he looked a little different. He'd acquired two items from a stall: a pair of cheap sunglasses and a blue cap that said "Gola Shoes" above the brim.

The group moved through the doorway and mounted the stairs. If Eddie Fong was meeting some lodge members, he'd probably be meeting them in the billiard hall. Most of the triads in Hong Kong fancied themselves as hotshot snooker players.

The room they entered was long and low-ceilinged, neat and clean, with a freshly vacuumed smell to it. It was dramatically dark in the corners, but brilliantly lit in the center by rows of strip lights hammering down onto flat fields of bright green baize. Only one of the tables was in use; three Chinese youths standing around it, plus Eddie Fong, all of them squeaking blue chalk on to the tips of cues. Apart from a man at a cash register near the door, there was nobody else in the place.

The four players looked incuriously at the Americans walking in, dismissing them as a boring intrusion. Tourists wandered in from time to time; Hong Kong's billiard parlors are open to all. "Oh, my Gawd," Miriam said loudly. "Bernie, will you look at the size of the tables."

"This is snooker, Martha, not pool," Bumpy said. "It's almost the same game, only you try to pot the black ball."

"I'm gonna hustle the socks off you guys," Johnny claimed as they pulled cues from a wall rack.

Decker, saying nothing, spent some time choosing his stick, checking over the youths at the other table. They were wearing their daytime clothes: nondescript jeans and sneakers, and message T-shirts. At night, he knew, they'd look a lot different; they'd come zooming up Leighton Road, in the back of a BMW, and swagger into the clubs they protected dressed like George Raft in striped blue suits, wing-tip brogues, and loud ties, and, getting their movie metaphors mixed, with heads of hair like James Dean.

Johnny racked the balls, and they began to play, keeping up a stream of stupid-tourist comments.

Enjoying the situation, and wanting to delay the delicious moment of surprise, Decker watched Eddie Fong move to a jukebox and feed it. He returned to the table and began to line up a shot, squinting along the cushion at the position of a red ball. Eddie sawed his cue over his bridged hand a few times, then slowly drew the cue back. The jukebox came up with his first choice: lush strings behind Harry Nillson's plaintive voice singing "As Time Goes By."

Decker, unnoticed, moved silently. He reached out and gently grasped the end of Eddie's cue just as Eddie was about to make his shot.

The stick's forward motion was halted as if it had hit a rock.

Eddie Fong looked around.

As the tune boomed from the jukebox, Decker said to him, "I thought I told you never to play that song."

Eddie Fong's face stayed closed in frowning bemusement for half a second, then opened rapidly as Decker removed his sunglasses and his Gola cap.

Eddie Fong said one word, yelling it out—*"Ging chat!"* which meant "Cops!"—and hurled himself backward, out of the way of the action.

The youth on his right, who was closest to Decker, spun his hand into the back pocket of his jeans, sprang the blade of a knife, and had it raised shoulder-high for a throat slash when the thick end of Miriam's snooker cue whipped down and broke the thumb of his other hand.

He screamed, dropped the knife to clutch at the pain, and Decker forgot about him.

The kid at the other end of the table had been slower to react, and Johnny Risotto caught his wrist before it came out of his back pocket. He thrust his other hand under the youth's crotch and, in one grunting motion, lifted the Chinese, took a single step forward, and tossed him through the air. The youth back-flopped onto the snooker table, scattering balls, rolled, and disappeared over the other side.

The fourth member of the party had run for it, had already made the door, and was gone.

Decker, with a pleasant expression on his face, moved closer to Eddie Fong, who had remained backed up against the table.

"You owe me ten thousand dollars, champ. I'll take it now."

"No spee Inlish! No spee Inlish!" Eddie Fong cried.

Bumpy confronted him. "Meng?" He asked. Name?

Eddie Fong's voice warbled. "Lee Yuen Chee."

Bumpy, with surprising ease for a little guy, spun the Chinese, fished out his passport, and quickly flicked through it. He passed it to Miriam.

"What do you think?"

Miriam held it under the table lights, flipped the pages from back to front.

"A piece of crap. Where was it made?" she asked Eddie Fong. "Battle Creek, Michigan? Collect five of these, you get a set of tumblers?"

The passport was a genuine one which had been stolen, then altered in the usual way. The first three original pages had been unstitched and discarded. Three blank pages from the center had been removed and their page numbers changed. Fake information had been printed on them, and Eddie Fong's photograph had been mounted and embossed under a clear plastic strip on page number two. The three altered pages had been sewn into the front of the passport, while the three fake pages, bereft of even a watermark, had been sewn into the center to give the document the right weight and feel. It was a quick, clumsy product, but good enough to get by the average immigration official at a busy airport.

The passport's owner was trying to shrug and shake his head at the same time. "No unnerstan! No spee Inlish!"

"Eddie." Decker said patiently, turning him around to face him. "This is your life, Eddie. It's me, Hugh C. Decker, remember? Your old buddy from Chinatown, New York?"

"No spee Inlish."

"Sure you do. It's easy. Say after me, Mott Street. Doyers Street. Nom Wah Tea Parlor."

Eddie Fong looked bewildered and miserable.

His friend with a broken thumb groaned and tucked his throbbing hand under his arm. His partner was still on the floor, on the other side of the table, breathing slowly through his mouth.

"Shall we get Eddie outta here?" Johnny Risotto asked. "The punk who beat it has probably gone for some fighters."

They marched their prisoner in front of them, down the stairs, and out the door; kept him going for three blocks into Shanghai Street, an intense, pulsating thoroughfare which, at night, was visited mainly for its cheap massage parlors and two-bed tiger-girl brothels. By day it was just a good place to eat, a fact which Johnny Risotto was well-acquainted with. Leaning close to Decker's ear, he asked him where they were taking their captive.

"To lunch."

"Why? Not that I'm not all for it."

"I want to see just how Chinese he is," Decker said as they arrived outside the restaurant he'd been making for.

A hostess welcomed them. Decker took her aside and told her about their Chinese pal, whom Johnny was affectionately holding by the elbow, and how he wasn't feeling too well. Decker slipped her money, and arranged for a private room, and a very special dish to fix up his friend.

They were led across a huge area which sounded more like a frantic stock exchange than an eatery; young girls, wide leather straps around their necks supporting steaming metal trays, shouted out the names of the trays' aromatic contents, while tables full of hungry diners chorused, "Goa lei! Goa lei!" Over here! Over here! and competed with each other for favorite dishes.

The private room was located in a far corner, red-and-gold screens partitioning off the clamorous patrons, a round table set for eight in the center.

Decker ordered beer for everybody, and they sat down, Eddie Fong taking a chair as if it were mined. He looked wary and, at the same time, stubborn. It was clear that he'd figured out what was happening: he was about to get the nice-guy treatment, the Let's-have-lunch-and-talk-it-over routine. The set of his jaw indicated that they were wasting their time; he'd been on the street far too long to fall for kid stuff like that.

Speaking Cantonese, Bumpy said politely, "You born and bred in Hong Kong?"

"Hai," Eddie Fong answered.

Bumpy had a pen in his hand, and was scribbling on a piece of notepaper. He slid the paper across. "In that case, you shouldn't have any trouble pronouncing this."

What he'd written on the paper, in Chinese characters, translated as, "I have 188 white ducks." It was a phrase only a native Cantonese speaker could rip off quickly and get the tones right.

Eddie Fong saw the trap, and easily avoided it, "Mm sick dook," he said. I can't read.

It was a smart answer, there were hundreds of thousands of Hong Kong residents who couldn't read. They signed their names with a chop mark, a seal, which was the way Eddie Fong's faked passport had been signed. Decker reached over, patted Eddie's wrist, and said in English, "It doesn't matter if he can't read. Just as long as he can eat."

Johnny, remembering what the restaurant was famous for, knew what Decker had in mind now. His fat cheeks swelled when he grinned. He said conversationally, "I hope you're hungry, Eddie. And thirsty."

"No spee Inlish," Eddie insisted. "No unnerstand."

"Lemme have him," Miriam growled. She tossed her red hair, her emerald eyes flashing. "I'll cut off his cock, sew it to his fucking nose."

Eddie Fong looked shocked.

"I think he understood that," Bumpy said.

The door opened on a busboy balancing a tray of beer and a teapot full of yellow wine. Behind him came a smiling waiter carrying a sagging rice sack which he held in front of him, one hand keeping the top closed.

There was something lumpy in the sack.

And it was moving.

The waiter, clued in by the hostess, spoke to Eddie, the honored guest. It came out as something close to, "Got the hot winds, huh? This'll do the trick."

The busboy banged down a large bowl in front of Eddie, and half-filled it with a wine which, to many Westerners, tasted like shoe polish. But Eddie wasn't bothered by the wine; he was staring at that wriggling sack, a look of great foreboding beginning to replace his stubborn expression.

The waiter plunged his hand into the sack.

And pulled out a six-foot rat snake.

The busboy passed over a kitchen knife.

The snake, sensing its fate, looped and slithered, but the waiter wapped its head against the table and, with an easy, practiced movement, slit the serpent's belly.

He reached in and explored the innards for a moment, found what he was looking for, and used the knife again, just a pinprick this time. Then he bent the dead snake over the table and expertly squirted a jet of dark green bile into Eddie Fong's wine bowl.

Everybody else poured beer and raised their glasses.

"Kan pei!" they said, the traditional Chinese toast. Eddie Fong didn't want to hear that; it meant, literally, "Empty cup."

"Eddie, you're not drinking," Decker said in English. Then, switching languages, "No male born and bred in Hong Kong would ever refuse a warm, healing bowl of seh dam."

"Revives the pulse and refreshes the bladder," Miriam added.

"It's also a powerful aphrodisiac," Bumpy contributed. "Not that I ever needed one."

Eddie Fong, his mouth gone slack, was appalled by the stinking concoction bubbling warmly in front of him: there was a hell of a difference between being New York Chinese and Hong Kong Chinese. He knew he was trapped this time; but trapped didn't mean beaten! He fought the trembles as his hand reached for the bowl. He got it halfway to his mouth, but the foul odor almost made him gag, and he hesitated.

Johnny Risotto, sitting next to him, slipped a friendly arm around his shoulder, gently fixed a thumb and forefinger at the pressure points each side of Eddie's slim neck.

"Go ahead, Eddie. It'll make your teeth grow black and curly."

Eddie Fong hung tough. He licked his lips. Took a breath. Steadied his hands, and raised the bowl again.

He took a quick mouthful.

And, with a stupendous effort, swallowed.

He sat there for a moment, in the red-and-gold private room, thinking about what he'd just done; riding it out, justifying it. Then his eyes went wide, he clamped a hand over his mouth, kicked back his chair, and rushed for the door.

Johnny went with him.

They returned in a few minutes, Eddie Fong looking awful.

"You okay?" Decker asked. "We were all worried about you."

"No unnerstan," Eddie said weakly.

Decker motioned to the waiter. "Another snake. And keep 'em coming."

Eddie Fong folded.

He waved a hand as if cleaning a dirty window, and said in English, "Okay. All right. Just get this outta here."

Decker spoke to the puzzled waiter, who spoke to the puzzled busboy, who cleared the table. They both left the room, the waiter taking the rice sack, now limp and lifeless.

Decker didn't waste any time. No smiles now, no jokes; he wanted fast answers.

"Where's the money?"

"I got it in my room."

"Where in your room?"

"Hidden under the bed."

"The whole ten grand?"

"Yeah."

"What did you do with the Kel? The wire we put on you?"

"Sold it," Eddie Fong said, sounding flat, disgusted with himself.

"For how much?"

"Five hundred."

"Say again . . ."

A grand."

Decker hammered away at him. Johnny, Bumpy, Miriam, had faces of stones.

"Tell me about the deal."

"What deal?"

"*The* deal. With the lodge."

What lodge?"

"With the fucking Wo On Lok. Come *on*!"

Eddie Fong started. He hadn't been prepared for Decker to have that kind of information.

"When's it going down?"

"Soon."

"How much?"

"Lots."

Decker could see the guy growing cautious again, tightening up, his eyes dropping to the tablecloth.

"I want in, Eddie. I want to go up the chain."

Eddie Fong was shaking his close-shaven head, moving it like an old man with a nervous complaint.

"Forget it. I get cute with these guys, they'll leave me in sections."

"Get used to the idea, sport. You're taking me in. You owe me for the miss in New York."

"No. In New York I could've given you that guy, and still come out the other side. But not this bunch. I mean, those kids you chased in the pool hall back there, they're just Chung Wa, younger brothers. Pals of a buddy of mine. Rinky-dinks into cabdrivers and waiters. But this other group, the one I'm talking to, Jesus, they even hear I go narked over, even though I ain't talking deal, they'd bone my legs for me, buy me a goddamn goat cart."

"Listen," Decker began.

"Uh-huh. No, sir. You can do any damn thing you want. I'll sit here and drink snake soup till next New Year's Eve, but I ain't taking you into this one. Period. Finito. The end."

Decker stared into a face gone stiff. He flicked his eyes to the group, silently enlisting their opinion. It was unanimous; everybody recognized a man who had well and truly dug in his heels. There was only one way to handle it; slow, but tried and true.

"Aw, shit. I'll go," Miriam said, and pushed back from the table.

Bumpy handed her Eddie's passport on her way out of the room.

"What's up?" Eddie asked, worried because they were doing something he couldn't figure. "Where's she going?"

He didn't get an answer.

Johnny picked up a menu and turned the pages with slow contentment. "We got an hour and a half. Let's order."

"An hour and a half for what?" Eddie wanted to know, shifting position, uneasy alarm raising lumps in his chair.

Nobody told him.

The waiter answered their call. Johnny ordered crabmeat and mustard greens, stewed peanuts in chili, garlic pork, sesame porridge, and a double order of chow fun, Johnny's favorite dish.

They drank more beer with the food when it came, only the three of them eating, Eddie Fong understandably abstaining.

They talked while they ate, chatting together, forgetting about Eddie Fong, not allowing his morose presence to intrude on what had now become their lunch break.

"Hey, I got a new Hong Kong story," Bumpy claimed.

"There are no new Hong Kong stories," Johnny said, heaping his bowl with fried rice. His chopsticks reached across the table for a plump piece of crab and, in passing, speared some sliced pork.

"You want to hear this story, or not?" Bumpy asked, and launched into it. In contrast to Johnny, he ate like a bird. "This guy's over here from Italy, right? Meets this Chinese chick in the Mandarin bar. The girl is doing a little light hooking, okay? Well, he doesn't speak Chinese, she don't speak Italian, so they limp along in English, which is tough for both of them, but what are they gonna do? Anyway, she tells him she's from Soochow, a city of canals and bridges. Now, there's a coincidence, because he's from Venice, also canals and bridges. And she says, Venice all the same Soochow? Much water? He says, Much, much water. I have boat. I have gondolier. And she says, I have gondolier too. But don't worry, have good doctor."

Decker had heard it, of course, but he still laughed. He'd missed this, sitting around a restaurant table, shooting the breeze with Johnny and Bumpy; Johnny with his bright mind hiding behind a slow, considered manner; Bumpy's quick alertness and easy way with a line. He'd missed Miriam too, her colorful dialogue and uninhibited approach to her job. They were a hell of a lot different from the agents he'd worked with in New York. He'd liked those guys well enough, and they'd liked him, but they'd been uneasy working alongside Hugh Decker. They'd known his reputation, and hadn't wanted to get tarnished by proximity. As for his bosses, they hadn't been crazy about getting stuck with damaged goods, and had just been waiting for him to screw up again. They'd been counting on it, in fact, and had probably congratulated themselves on their prescience when it had happened.

But here in Hong Kong the atmosphere was different. It always was when you got away from home base. Here he was working with people who'd stay with him if things got controversial.

Decker felt at ease in this teeming, clamoring city; happier and far less constrained. It was easy enough to explain in the short term: things were shaping up for a change: he'd found Eddie Fong, and would get back the ten thousand dollars, if Eddie hadn't been lying. And he'd lucked into a score which was potentially very big, once he could persuade Eddie to take him in. It would be very nice to return to New York and toss their damn money down in front of them; extremely satisfying to report to Old Blood and Guns in Washington with a big Hong Kong collar to his credit. As for the Angela Waters thing, that would take care of itself. The Hong Kong police force had had some rough years in the past, but it was a highly efficient organization now. Doug Portloe would find the madman, probably sooner than later, and then it would be merely a case of putting Portloe's report into DEAese, coding it, and getting it on the wire to I Street.

Decker's thoughts drifted back to his own situation. The only cloud hanging over his return to the colony was Kate and her out-of-the-blue marriage. That still jangled, dug at him, the knowledge worming around in his vitals.

He'd taken a good shot, more of a blow than he'd realized. It hit his vanity.

Male pride, maybe.

Whatever it was, something had been scooped out of him, and the hollow filled with a nagging ache.

Decker shunted the thought aside, looked over at Eddie Fong, and got back to business. The guy was stewing in apprehension, wondering what the bit with the passport was all about.

It was another thirty minutes before he found out.

Miriam arrived back. "You bastards owe me a lunch," she said, tossing Eddie Fong's passport to Decker.

Its owner's worried eyes followed its flight.

"What she do with it?" Eddie asked.

"Took it back to the consulate, and got you one of these." Decker held up the document, opened to a brand-new U.S. visa.

"They gave him a B One, B Two," Miriam said, sitting down and pouring herself some tea. "Good for six months."

"He'll be there a tad longer than that," Bumpy said.

"What do you figure he'll get?"

"Well, if he was looking at a tenner before, and this time goes up for stealing money from a federal agent, plus misappropriation of government property, plus consorting with known traffickers for the purpose of illegally importing a controlled substance into the United States . . . all in all, I'd say he'll have his mail redirected for at least fifteen years."

Eddie Fong, shocked, bit teeth which needed brushing into his thin bottom lip. He closed his eyes, exhaled hopelessly.

"Okay, you win. I'll play ball."

"Eddie," Decker said, "You're about as hard to read as the front page of the *Daily News*. You say yes, we drop you back at your flat, and you beat it on us. Disappear into Ching Man Village, or the Shun Tin Estate. That's what's up there in the frontal lobes, isn't it?"

"No. Nothing like that. Honest."

"It can't be done, Eddie," Johnny said. "You picked a good town for a Chinese to fade into, but they made you at the airport. So now you're in the worst town for a Chinese to fade into.

Eddie Fong's head swiveled as Miriam spoke; pressure on him now from all directions.

"This isn't New York, Eddie, where if the cops want a new Chinese face they have to send to San Francisco. They got over thirty thousand Chinese policemen in this town, and it only takes one phone call to get five hundred of them on the street in jeans and T-shirts."

"It's a tiny little town, Eddie," Bumpy told him. "You can't jump into a Chevy and drive all night and lose yourself. There's just no place to go where there won't be somebody waiting for you."

Eddie Fong was hearing the truth, and his face showed it. There was a battle going on inside his head.

"I can't do it," he burst out. "They'll take off every limb I ever owned."

"You've never been inside, have you, Eddie?" It was Decker's turn again. "I know lots of guys who've been there. They say it's a lot like freeside, same old rackets going on. Like, for example, you get a guy in there used to run a string of hookers, he doesn't see any reason to stop doing what he knows best just because there are bars on the windows. So he gets a string together, and rents them out."

Johnny Risotto clarified it, in case Eddie didn't get the point. "A string of guys, Eddie. Rents them to the inmates for a carton of Winstons or a bag of coke."

"And a nice Chinese boy like you," Miriam said, "is gonna get snapped up by a prison pimp, because he knows the cons will pay to take your pants down to see if your asshole runs sideways."

Sweat had broken out on Eddie Fong's forehead. He gulped tea down a dry throat. He was badly shaken, but still holding together.

"Let me tell you what you have ahead of you, Eddie," Decker said to him quietly. "We take you to the airport, put you on the three-o'clock to Seattle. You get a drink, a headset, a meal, a movie, all of it served up with a smile. The hours drag by, the Pacific's a monster. You doze a little, get up, walk around, rat through the airline magazine for the third time. You think you're never gonna land, but finally you do. You shuffle through the plane, which has now become a slum, newspapers and plastic glasses everywhere. Tired people bang you with bags and drop coats on your head, but at last you reach the door. And who's waiting for you at the end of the walkway? Two hard guys. One of them will stop you, and he'll say in a voice that's all bass, no treble, Is your name Eddie Fong? And you can tell him it's really Donald Duck, and that he's got the wrong duck, but it won't do you any good."

Decker paused for a moment, giving his little speech time to sink in.

"How old are you, Eddie?"

The reply was little more than a squeak. "Thirty-five."

"Thirty-five. Well, that man, the hard guy, will flash his tin, put his hand on your arm, and tell you what to do. And from that moment on, you'll have hard guys telling you what to do every hour of every day until you're fifty. Think about it, Eddie."

The Chinese was breathing through his mouth, moisture hanging on the bony ridge above his fast-blinking eyes. He started some words which came out frazzled at the edges.

"If I take you in, take you up the chain, you guarantee to get me out?'

Decker didn't lie to him; he never had, never would lie to anybody who was risking serious retribution.

"I guarantee to try. I can't guarantee success. The only one-hundred-percent guarantee I can give you, about your future, is if we take you out to the airport."

Eddie Fong drank more tea quickly, gazed into his empty cup as if he could see his future at the bottom of it. But the choice was clear enough: possible maiming or definite incarceration.

One a maybe, the other a certainty.

He had to go for the maybe.

"Okay," he said, shaking his head in bleak despondence. "I'll take you in."

And this time Decker believed him.

6

A hard-edged, jangling sound, naggingly insistent, pulled him out of the hot lock of Kate's thighs, cruelly jerked him away from her quick, rhythmic thrusts, the slam and buck of her pelvis hinging up to meet him.

With his eyelids unopened Decker rolled across his hardness and cut off the telephone's shrill interruption.

"Yeah?"

"Deck? You awake?" Doug Portloe's voice.

"Hard to tell."

"A man named Brian Fairweather killed Angela Waters. God told him to do it. You want to meet me in the Hilton coffee shop in thirty minutes? Better make it forty-five."

The line went dead.

Decker, putting the phone down as if it were crystal, watched it all the way to its cradle. He climbed out of bed, his virility chastened by the sudden news. He went down the hall to the bathroom, stood under a hot shower thinking about the big differences you got in homicide cases; some got locked away in filing cabinets with the letters SP stamped on the folders: Still Pending. Pulled out once a year for review, they got locked away again, the stamp unchanged. Other cases unraveled like the sleeve of an old sweater; a quick pull in the right direction was all it took. And this one was like that because Lucky Doug Portloe wasn't the kind of cop who'd make a claim unless he could support in nine ways to Sunday.

Back in his room, the brain cobwebs washed down the shower drain, the early-morning phone call appeared in his mind like movie credits:

Victim: Angela Waters.

Killer: Brian Goodweather? Fairweather? Fairweather.

Director: God.

It was about what he'd expected. Madmen often believed they'd been given a divine mandate. Doing the work of God was the ultimate impeccable excuse. Entire wars had been justified for that reason; why not the odd killing or two?

Out on the street Decker exchanged the clang and clamor of the auto shops for the marginally lower uproar of the morning rush hour on Hennessy Road.

He added his weight to a packed tram, rode the gaudy, trembling machine into the white canyons of Central, and got off opposite the old Bank of China with its impassive stone lions. He walked through the landscaped garden of Chater Square, past beds of canna lilies and crimson flame trees and flowering bamboo. He'd always liked this little square, with its terrapin pond, and fat golden carp glistening in the sunshine. He felt good—things were looking up, professionally, anyway: Eddie's bed, was locked up at St. John's House, and Angela Waters' murderer was on ice. All that in less than forty-eight hours. Not bad.

Coming out onto Des Voeux, Decker spotted a gap in the traffic, ran for daylight, headed up the slope to the cobblestoned port cochere of the Hilton.

It was a good spot Doug Portloe had chosen to meet; there was little chance of Waxy Crane finding them together here. The assistant commissioner, disliking Americans as he did, shunned any place they congregated. He often referred to the Hilton as the Officers' Mess. This was because, back in the years when the U.S. Seventh Fleet had regularly visited the colony, and the sailors had been entertained in the Wanchai chicken houses on Lockhardt Road, the officers had been taken care of on the twenty-second floor of the Hilton—by young ladies who knit socks outside their permanently rented rooms, and who would invite the brass inside to help them wind their wool.

Decker found Portloe at a corner table of the street-level coffee shop, wreaking havoc on a plate of bacon and eggs. Decker got coffee from a circling waitress, and watched the policeman's iron jaw crunching the last of his marmaladed toast.

Portloe, a lapsed nonsmoker, moved his muscular rugby-player's body, lit a Carlton, took two quick puffs, and ground the cigarette into an ashtray as if he were burying an opposing player. When he started speaking, the content of his message didn't jell with his soft Cornish accent.

"About an hour after Waxy saw you off the premises yesterday, we got a call from the owner of a camera shop near the market, one of those places with a full service. Something came through the bath that looked a little different from the usual mum, kids, and sand castle at Deep Water Bay. Can you guess what it was?"

"Angela Waters' body on the bed?"

"No. Just certain parts of her body. On the dinner plate."

Decker stopped his coffee cup halfway to his mouth. "Jesus! They were just props, the plate and the coffee table . . ."

"Right."

"And he took the shots in for regular processing? Nobody in his right mind would—" Decker, hearing the inanity of what he'd just said, cut himself off.

"Exactly."

"It's still hard to believe."

"Look, there are crazy people, and there are people who do crazy things. And there are crazy people who do crazy things. Anyway, it was a hell of a break for us. We went down to the shop and hung around. It could've been a week, a month, or forever, but it wasn't. The bloke walked in around three with his claim slip in his hand."

"Is he a talker?"

Doug Portloe's nose had been broken at the top of the bridge, and when he nodded it looked like a hatchet coming down.

"Told us everything, and it was pretty much the way we thought. He picked her up at Mad Dogs, took her home, stopped off at his place on the way to get his camera equipment. He told her he was going to record their first date. When they got inside her flat he killed her with the chair. Then he screwed her on the bed. He put it on tape."

"You find that too? The cassette?"

Portloe looked down at the ashtray, at the crushed cigarette, as if he regretted ending its life so soon.

"Yep. A slightly out-of-focus replay of a man having intercourse with a dead woman. He dragged her into the bathroom, sliced her up, took the still shots, left the apartment house, dropped off the roll of film, then went back to his place and watched himself in action."

Decker drank the rest of his coffee, looked around for the waitress. He could use a little more stimulant; he was thinking of how he was going to have to give these macabre details to everybody at St. John's House, the people who'd worked with Angela Waters, known her pretty well, liked her a lot.

"The guy's name is Fairweather?"

"Brian Haydin Fairweather. English, thirty-seven, been here three years. It turns out that, five years back, he was arrested in Sarawak on suspicion of murder. A sex crime, naturally. The case was bungled, and thrown out. Fairweather was probably terribly disappointed by the verdict."

Decker nodded, agreeing with that, then asked Portloe about Fairweather's confessed motive, about God telling him to do it. "I take it he's a religious nut . . ."

Portloe went around his mouth with a paper napkin, crumpled it in his thick fingers. Saturday-afternoon rugby got all that violence out of his system for the week; the rest of the time he was just a big, quiet man.

"Yeah, but he's not up on a soapbox with a Bible. He's pretty calm about it. Said she was a scarlet woman. Sees himself as the good right hand of a vengeful God. Thankfully, he's only had one previous outing, the Sarawak thing. If there were any more, he would've told us. He's proud of what he's done."

"Proud of screwing a dead woman? Taking a knife to her?"

"One of our shrinks had a quick session with him. He says he's a screaming sexual repressive. No problem chatting up women, but all kinds of problems getting their clothes off. The servant-of-God bit would appear to be a convenient excuse, but Fairweather certainly seems to believe it."

"Where've you got him?"

"Hei Ling Chau. They're running some tests before we make our case. Look, I have to fly. You haven't heard any of this. Or at least keep it inside St. John's House. If it gets back to I Street before it's officially released, Waxy Crane will have me washed over a waterfall without a barrel."

"All I know is what I hear at the hairdressers'," Decker said. Then, as the detective moved back his chair, he tacked on some genuine gratitude. "I appreciate it, Doug. Let's grab a bean together next week. Roam the town, see if we can't find some good Somerset cider."

"Sure, if we can't find any good Cornish cider," Portloe answered, already striding away.

Decker remained at the table, only half aware of the life going on around him: tourists from California and the prairie states comparing wristwatches, some severely and identically suited Japanese businessmen going over some figures, a group of Canadian banker types in silent thrall to the *Wall Street Journal,* a table of rich and bored Filipino women wearing diamonds and short fur coats and sucking on long brown cigarettes like vampire bats at blood: the usual Hong Kong four-star-hotel mix.

A man named Brian Fairweather killed Angela Waters. God told him to do it.

Lucky Doug Portloe had a cop's concise way of putting things. Brian Fairweather, an English madman; normal enough on the outside to do anything any normal person does: feed himself, dress himself, drive a car, hold down a job of some kind. But, at the same time, crazy enough to mutilate a person on God's behalf, warped enough to photograph his handiwork, and dumb enough to have the shots processed commercially. Or maybe this was his way of making sure was caught; the maniac's traditional remedy for his own recognized illness. And was that recognition the thing which had drawn him, a crazy person, to a pub called Mad Dogs?

Decker didn't know.

All he knew was he had to do now what he'd been charged to do: check out Brian Fairweather for himself. "We're DEA," Paul Johnson had said, his mouth like the slot in a steel mailbox. "We don't take nobody's word for nothing."

Pretty lousy English for a guy who'd started out as an editorial assistant in one of Boston's most prestigious publishing houses.

Decker left the coffee shop and walked around the curve of the hotel onto Garden Road, climbed the short rise to St. John's House. Hilary, the young secretary, was the only person in the office. Decker asked her to check the files for any past correspondence with the psychiatric prison on Hei Ling Chau, then, while she searched, he typed up a quick FIS report of his meeting with Doug Portloe and left it on Ralph Dobrinski's desk. The letters FIS stood for Fuck I Street. Nobody knew just which particular agent in which distant DEA office had invented the term, but it had stuck. It meant, simply, that a report was for internal eyes only, and was not to be coded back to Washington.

It took Hilary ten minutes of searching before she found something Decker could use: a letter concerning a dope pusher who'd been treated at Hei Ling Chau. It was signed by a Malcolm B. Crealy, Assistant Governor, H. K. Prisons. A quick phone call was all it took to verify the fact that Malcolm B. Crealy still held that post.

Decker pocketed the letter, went downstairs to the street, got into a taxi at the Peak tram station, and was driven down the hill into the morning crush of Queen's Road. He quit the cab when the traffic silted up, and walked the rest of the way to the futongs, the narrow little alleys in Western that specialize in a variety of commodities and services. The shops in these alleys, lined up in solid, unremitting competition, offered everything from rattan furniture to rope, linoleum, cleaning solvents, and bright-feathered singing birds in bamboo cages. The alley Decker arrived at, Tit Hong Lane, was entirely devoted to printing. It was bordered on each side by stalls made of rough wood roofed over with corrugated iron, and no bigger than the average big-city newspaper stand. Inside the stall Decker chose, whose sign claimed a printing facility in both Chinese and English, a man sat working an offset press which was no larger than a portable typewriter. The machine clacking and chattered as its printing plate, the size of a small teacup, rose perhaps two inches, then snapped down again, effecting a loud and sudden reunion with its flat steel bed. The man inside the stall, a lugubrious Chinese with sticklike arms, wore a Ford-logo cap, bottle-lensed glasses, and a floppy white undershirt which a thousand random ink smudges had turned into a Jackson Pollock painting. He was feeding the diminutive machine with business cards, thrusting a blank onto the tiny bed, whipping away his hand as the plate slapped down, darting his hand in to remove the printed card, and repeating the process, with an exact and insouciant timing, at an astonishingly fast rate. When he saw, out of the corner of his eye, Decker standing there, he shut off the machine.

"A job for nimble fingers," Decker said in Chinese.

"Sometimes nimble, sometimes tardy," the printer answered, fanning out his right hand. Three fingernails had been crushed into shriveled scales, and the tips were like spatulas.

"It's the nimble kind I need today, master." Decker held out the letter he'd taken from the office files. "A rush job."

The printer adjusted his heavy glasses, examined the letterhead, and nodded when Decker asked him if he could exactly duplicate it.

"A hundred dollars for five hundred," the printer proposed.

"I don't need five hundred."

"How many, then?"

Decker fessed up with a smile, "Just one."

The bottle lenses flashed with understanding.

"Two would work out cheaper," the printer said, which, under the circumstances, was a very Chinese thing to say.

"Okay, two. How much?"

"Fifty dollars each," the printer answered, which was also a very Chinese thing to say.

"Done!" said Decker.

The little ferry, as flat and even on its keel as the bubble in a carpenter's level, turned sluggish green bow water into slow-dancing white foam.

The harbor on which it worked this miracle reflected the congestion of the city it served: sampans, lighters, billowing Hovercraft, lazy dredgers, flag-bedecked tourist junks, swift police boats, naval launches, sailboats, hydrofoils skimming the waves like sleek float planes, tankers, freighters from all around the world, everything claimed its own patch.

Decker, sitting upstairs in the hot sunshine, the sky like a bright blue hood over his head, watched the action and marveled at the close tolerances of the traffic. There just wasn't room for the traditional maritime-safety gaps between vessels, and so everybody missed everybody else by alarming margins, slicing through fresh-laid wakes, nipping in front of pluming bows. It had often occurred to Decker that Victoria Harbor might just be the first stretch of water to suffer from gridlock.

The ferry shrank from confrontation with a Kwangtung liner, then bullied a Chris Craft gin palace out of its path, and, with its confidence restored, rounded the low sprawl of Kennedy Town. The steel-and-glass monsters of Central began a slow recession behind the foothills of the Peak, and a salt breeze, blowing in from the China Sea, flattened the morning heat, and took the tops off the waves curling in through the narrow chute of Sulphur Channel. From there on it was a warm and pleasant half-hour trip to the little island of Hei Ling Chau, which, topographically, isn't much different from the other 237 islands which make up the Crown Colony of Hong Kong: amorphous-shaped, hilly, semideserted, and covered with a scraggy stubble of trees, none of which has any decent height or spread. A thin line of beach, broken by clumps of lumpy gray rock, rims the island like the residue on a mug of boiled milk. Hei Ling Chau isn't featured on any picture postcards.

Decker got into the island's only taxi, an aged Toyota with

treadless tires, rode in its broken rear seat up the hill toward a yellow brick building at its crest. The building's architect, perhaps dreaming of adventures in the Foreign Legion, had designed a Moroccan fancy, a crenellated fort with massive doors and with watchtowers at all four corners. Instead of pitiless sand dunes, miraging off into sun-warped distance, the structure was surrounded by a ragged lawn of Bermuda grass and a high Cyclone fence. Several Hakka women, the only sign of life, were bent over a bed of geraniums, the black cloth fringes circling their straw hats swaying desultorily as they moved hoes around in the soggy heat. On top of the building, the red of the geraniums was picked up by the flag of Hong Kong hanging limp and spiritless from a high white pole. The prison, a sorry, morose-looking place, wore its exile like a black armband.

Decker took a quick look at the letter he'd typed in an office-supply store before he'd boarded the ferry. Under a perfect copy of the prison's letterhead, the missive gave permission for Charles J. Milligan, Attorney-at-Law, to visit with prisoner B. Fairweather at prisoner's own request. It appeared to have been signed by the jail's assistant governor.

The letter had a business card clipped to it, a card that Decker had had in his wallet for a long time. ID's of all description were part and parcel of a DEA agent's artillery, although there were some agents who were a little cavalier about their identities. One man Decker had known in Philadelphia had invented a law firm named Hiley, Insulten, and Slandress, and claimed he's used it twice without trouble.

Decker had no problem with the gate man, and no problem with the second piece of security, a staff sergeant and two guards behind a long counter immediately inside the building's main entrance. This anteroom had shiny parquet flooring and surprisingly fine-quality wainscoting gracing plain white plaster walls. High up on the rear wall a large Victorian clock kept track of time with a loud exactitude. The air, which smelled of furniture polish and floor wax, was being slowly stirred by the languid blades of ceiling fans, the only interior memory of the prison's exotic facade.

"Charles Milligan to see prisoner Fairweather at prisoner's request," Decker said, holding out the letter of authorization.

The metal chevrons on the sergeant's arm caught the light as he reached for the sheet of paper and the attached card.

"Fairweather," he said, turning pages in a book the size of a hotel register. "Pretty quick. Only process him yesterday."

Decker gave the man, Chinese, like the guards, a half-shrug. "Ever known a new con didn't start screaming for a lawyer?"

"That be the day," the sergeant said, and nodded an okay to one of his men.

The visitors' room was a junior version of the anteroom, with high ogee-arched windows admitting shafts of light which arrowed down like probing searchlight beams. The rest of the room was chillingly bleak, the walls dead white with not even a notice to relieve their blank stare.

Two scrubbed wooden tables, chairs in back of them, faced each other, separated by a gray expanse of heavy wire mesh strung wall to wall and from ceiling to floor. The tang of polish was present here too, but layered over the thin, institutional smell, closer to a mood than a scent, of failure, punishment, atonement.

When Brian Fairweather was brought in, there were no surprises: a 37-year-old Englishman a glamorous woman had found attractive enough to go home with, he looked very much the way Decker had imagined he might: slim, and on the tall side, a good head of hair, good facial features without any dramatics—a slender, handsome pleasantness. He would have made an excellent impression in a good blue suit, but at the moment his attire added nothing to his presence. He looked bedraggled in a pinkstriped long-sleeved shirt —no tie, it had been taken away from him; prison-issue slippers— his shoes had had laces in them; and a pair of debelted pants which were now supported by a breakaway nylon cord. A prisoner in Hong Kong had certain rights, but suicide wasn't one of them.

The uniformed guard stepped away to give them privacy and they had the room to themselves. Prisoner and visitor took chairs, drew them up to the tables, and regarded each other through the wire mesh.

"I didn't expect a visitor so soon," Fairweather said. He had an achingly correct Oxbridge accent built into a well-modulated voice, the kind which had no doubt made some telling points in student-union debates.

"Did they tell you who I was?" Decker asked.

"No. Just that I had a visitor."

"Well, that's exactly what I am, Mr. Fairweather. I've come here to talk to you. Ask a few questions."

"You're American? You sound American." Fairweather paused,

then emitted a soft "Ah," as something occurred to him. "Of course. The woman was American. I expect you're from the consulate. One of the diplomatic staff."

Decker neither confirmed nor denied it; he wasn't going to lie to a crazy person if he didn't have to. He went back to his original statement, speaking politely; wanting the man to feel easy with him, open up.

"If you wouldn't mind, I'd appreciate it if you'd tell me what happened. For my records."

"Yes. Well, I've already given the police a full account, but," Fairweather added reasonably, "I can quite see how the American consulate would have to make inquiries too." He could have been talking about a window he'd broken at an American club. "Where would you like me to start?"

"When did you first meet Angela Waters?"

"At Mad Dogs. On the night."

"The night you killed her . . ."

Fairweather's head bobbed. "Yes."

Decker was stopped by the matter-of-fact confession; no dropping of the eyes, no tortured, guilt-twisted mouth, just a plain and simple answer to what evidently appeared to be a plain and simple question: Yes, the night he killed Angela Waters.

"How did you meet her?"

"Went over and introduced myself. Chatted her up. It's not hard to do with a woman of that sort."

A moment ago Decker had felt something for this guy, a sympathy for his situation—reduced to a clumsy shuffle by ill-fitting slippers, his pants held up by an undignified piece of rope, his pallid lost look which even the briefest incarceration stamps on a person —but now sharp little nails of anger pinched at him. If Johnny and Bumpy and Miriam had been fans of Angela Waters', there was no way in the world she would have been anything but a terrific kid.

And this man had murdered her. Savaged her.

"Just what sort of woman would that be, Mr. Fairweather?"

"An extremely immoral one. One of easy virtue. She was a scarlet woman."

"Who told you that?"

"God."

Again the man answered in that peculiar conversational manner, as if direct information from the Supreme Being were to be had by picking up a ringing phone.

After a moment Decker said, "I see," the edge off his words. Feel what you want toward him—sympathy, pity, revulsion, disgust—anything but anger. Hard to justify getting angry with a person whose mind was out of control. "So you introduced yourself. And then?"

"We talked about this and that. The usual preliminaries. Then I suggested we go to her place. She agreed, of course, so off we went."

"You went straight there?"

"No, we went to my place first. To get my camera equipment." Fairweather stopped and dry-coughed. It was merely a mannerism, Decker saw; he wasn't at all embarrassed by his confession. What was there to be embarrassed about? "Then we drove to her flat. Apartment, as she called it."

"Yes . . ."

Decker waited.

"Then I killed her."

"How?"

"Cracked her skull with a chair. Didn't the police tell you?"

"Then what did you do?"

For a brief instant, madness spun behind Brian Fairweather's eyes. They were pale, bleached eyes, like pennies dropped into a fountain long ago.

"Then I took her into the bedroom and purified her."

"I see. And then?"

With no change in his reasonable, considered tone, Fairweather said, "I carried her into the bathroom and rid her of the parts that had been the means by which she had sinned." He paused as if expecting a comment here, but Decker just watched him, Listened to him, a man politely repeating the same anecdote for the umpteenth time. "I put them on a plate I got from the kitchen, and photographed them with my Nikon. I isolated the evil and recorded it," Fairweather explained in his perfect-pitch BBC voice. "In order to master evil, one must record its presence so it may act as a constant reminder. Don't you agree?"

"Was that the only time you used a camera?"

"No. Actually, I used a video camera as well."

"When?"

"During the act of purification."

"To record evil?"

"To record its purification," Fairweather corrected.

"Then what did you do?"

Bland face, neutral tone. Keep him going.

"Left the flat, drove into Central, and dropped off the film. Although I must admit"—for the first time, Fairweather's good looks darkened, his mouth slimming into a prim line—"I certainly didn't expect them to reveal the contents of a customer's snapshots. After all, photographs are personal items, like letters, or a diary. That sort of thing leaves a bad taste in the mouth, don't you agree?"

Decker stared through the heavy wire mesh at this privileged-background, upper-class Englishman who was peeved by what he considered an inexcusable lapse of manners.

Perhaps reading some kind of censure into Decker's silence, Fairweather said, "I suppose you think I'm off my rocker. That's certainly what the police think. They've been giving me some rather insulting tests. But I'm not, you know. I freely admit I contravened the law, but only man's law, civil law. Quite frankly, I can't see myself being convicted in any Christian court when all I did was obey God's directive. And that, of course, is our overriding duty during our brief time here on earth. Don't you agree? To do God's bidding as He directs us?"

Decker sat on the hard wooden chair and listened to the man asking him whether or not he thought it was a duty to murder a person. At least this guy was insane, Decker thought. There were plenty of people in the world who were killing other people in the name of duty, and they were all regarded as mentally stable.

He got back onto the line of questioning; it would all go into his report to I Street: firsthand stuff, nothing echoed from the Hong Kong police transcripts. They would have done just as well, but nothing but the horse's mouth would be good enough for Old Blood and Guns Johnson.

"You said God told you that Angela Waters was, as you put it, a scarlet woman."

"As He put it. His words, not mine."

"Right. As He put it. When did God tell you this?"

"At my flat about two weeks ago. He appeared to me there."

"Oh?"

"Yes. I woke up in the middle of the night, and there He was. Standing by my bedside. He told me about this woman whose evil offended Him, and that He'd chosen me as His servant of vengeance. He told me where I might find her the following week. And that He'd be there to point her out to me."

Decker sucked it into his memory, waited for more.

Fairweather cocked his head, his brow corrugating slightly. He looked at Decker as if he were disappointed about something.

"You know, it's a funny thing," he said.

"What is?"

"Just that I've told the police, and two or three other people here, all that I've told you. And yet not one of them has asked me what God looks like."

It was obvious to Decker that the guy wanted very much to tell him, just like somebody busting to talk about a celebrity he'd rubbed shoulders with. God, the ultimate celebrity. What did God look like, anyway? The old joke flashed into his mind, about the man who'd died and been revived, and claimed he'd gone to heaven for a few minutes. When asked what God looked like he'd replied. "Nothing special. Like any ordinary middle-aged black woman."

To keep the answers flowing, not wanting to jar anything, turn the man off, Decker asked Fairweather the question the world had been pondering for several thousand years.

"Nothing like the Old Testament God," Fairweather said, taking pleasure in imparting a surprising piece of news. "Nothing like the Renaissance painters depicted either. Or Blake. Or any of the mystics. It was quite a surprise, really." Fairweather ran a hand though his hair, and looked inside himself. "He took the guise of a modern man. He looked like any of the regulars at Mad Dogs. English, with a mustache, blue blazer, and cricket-club tie."

God is an Englishman, was Decker's first thought. It made some kind of weird sense: God was supposed to have made man in His own image, so here was somebody returning the favor: making God in his own image. The only surprising thing to hear from a religious nut was that God would hang out in an ersatz British pub in Hong Kong. But then, he, or rather, He, had to be there in order for Fairweather to justify his story; a story he clearly believed to be the absolute truth.

"What did God say to you?"

"He pointed out the scarlet woman, as He told me He would, and the rest you know."

"Yes, the rest I know," Decker said, and watched the crazy man looking back at him, his story told, silent, and somehow contented-looking; a person who'd been given a difficult assignment, and had accomplished it successfully.

Decker caught the guard's eye and rose from the table.

"Thank you for talking with me."

"Not at all," Fairweather said, allowing himself to be led away.

The guard took big steps across the polished floor. His prisoner, handicapped by the too-large slippers on his narrow feet, had to shuffle quickly to keep up with him.

Wanting to stretch his legs after the confines of the jail and the half-hour ferry ride back to Central, Decker passed up a cab and walked east on Connaught Road.

Brian Fairweather filled his mind: the spectacle, the phenomenon of polite, orderly madness. There was an educated brain behind the man's well-bred good looks, but it was as if rain had soaked through his skull and shriveled and twisted the gray matter out of shape.

A block away from St. John's House, waiting to cross Lower Albert Road, it occurred to Decker that Mad Dogs was only a hundred yards along to his right. It would be an easy matter to drop in, chat to somebody who might have seen Fairweather talking to Angela Waters. It wouldn't advance anything, since Doug Portloe had a full and proud confession plus some stunningly conclusive photographic evidence, but it was the kind of backup detail I Street would be happy to see on a report. Anything to keep I Street happy.

Decker walked around the curve of the road under the high stone ramparts of the governor's residence, toward a lone sign sticking out over the sidewalk. It was rectangular and made of wood, and had been hand-painted in the style of a British pub sign. The illustration was a visual pun on the old Noël Coward song "Mad Dogs and Englishmen," and featured a bulldog standing in front of a Union Jack. The bulldog looked arthritic, and a little puzzled, as if it were trying to remember where it had buried a bone. The draped flag in the background had too many folds in it, and looked rather more like a patriotic shower curtain. As an attempt at a British pub sign, it was a good example of a Chinese pub sign.

The place lacked authenticity on the inside too; it resembled a New Yorker's idea of a British watering hole: bentwood chairs drawn up to restaurant tables, unupholstered banquettes along one wall, and sawdust on the plain board floor. But authentic or not, Mad Dogs was a popular place because the atmosphere was good and friendly, the prices were fair, the beer was imported, and the management believed in good food and plenty of it.

Being as close to the office as it was, Decker had been a regular for lunch, and had often popped in in the evenings, but he didn't recognize the young girl who brought him a bottle of Bass and poured it with too much of a head. She was just off the boat, this one, an ex-secretary maybe, trying her hand at something new. Decker asked her if there was anybody around who'd been on nights last week, and a few minutes later a waitress working the other side of the room came over. Tall, angular, and Scots, she was new since Decker's time, skin as white as the inside of an apple, shiny brown hair falling almost to the waist of her floor-length pinafore dress.

Decker told her he was with a section of the U.S. consulate, and suggested that she probably knew some of the staff, people who dropped by now and then. The girl confirmed that; she had a distinctive Edinburgh accent thick enough to spread.

"Did you happen to know a woman who worked at St. John's House? Angela Waters?"

The girl's face folded, and her spindly body got close to a shudder. "Och!" she said, using the Scottish guttural. "That was terrible. Everybody here was shocked. Did they catch the fiend who did it yet?"

"They'll get him. Did you happen to know Angela?"

"Aye, I did. And more than a wee bit. That's what makes it doubly awful. She used to come in for a spot o' lunch a couple of times a week with a group. I think they all worked together. Two men and a woman. Real characters."

"I think I know them," Decker said, beginning to smile. "The big guy has a double order of the daily special, no matter what it is."

"That's him."

"The other guy always has something light, and when you bring it, he propositions you."

The waitress nodded a shy confession, and showed long teeth as part of a giggle.

"And the woman has red hair and a way with words."

The girl's eyes went to the ceiling. "We have to be careful not to seat her near the parrot."

Decker laughed; the Scots girl did too, the living a far more welcome subject than the dead.

The waitress excused herself, hurried away to pick up some orders, delivered them to a clutch of young women in English travel-agent uniforms. The lunchtime rush had come and gone, and theirs was the only other table occupied. A couple of coatless shipping clerks were settling their tabs at the cash register and, at the bar, a beefy, florid-faced man was ordering a second Irish coffee, the first one still working.

Decker reduced the foamy head of his pale ale and watched the Scots girl skirting tables, coming back toward him. Decker asked her her name.

"Jeanne."

"Okay, Jeanne. One more question about Angela Waters, if that's okay."

"Of course."

"Did you see her leave here the night she was killed? With a man?"

"Aye." The girl nodded her head fervently, then changed the action to a negative shake. "I've been racking my brains ever since the Old Bill talked to me. The police," she translated. "But I'm still a mile away from a decent description. I noticed him, but I dinna pay him a lot of mind, if you see what I mean." She shifted her tray on her bony hip, tossed her long brown hair, and said with a touch of chagrin, "I'm a ninny, and I know it. I should be able to describe him, because I served him when he was talking to his friend."

Even though his mind jumped to no instant conclusions, even though it stayed quiet and didn't pop off in any wild direction, Decker still experienced a reaction to the girl's last phrase; a tingling in his innards like a vibrating cord, and a quick, sharp charge which only then bumped his thinking onto an obvious track.

He went into his beer glass again for a long, slow pull, picked up a paper napkin, took his time blotting the corner of his mouth. He stretched his next question as if listening for its echo. "This friend . . ." He put down the napkin, smoothed its roughed-up crispness. "A man or a woman?"

"A man."

Voice steady, no special interest showing, Decker asked the waitress what this man had looked like.

The waitress clenched her eyes to see if it would help squeeze something from the back of her memory.

"Well, he was nothing a lass might want to take home for a bookend, I can tell you that."

"You mean he was ugly?"

"Not ugly. Just ordinary."

"When you say ordinary . . . one of the usual crowd?"

"I don't remember him in here before. But he was dressed like the usual crowd. And they're all Brits. Mostly from south of the border."

"English . . ."

"Aye." The girl's beaky nose wrinkled in mock disgust. "One of the drawbacks of the job."

"He was dressed like the usual crowd," Decker said, giving the girl back her own words. "Which is what?" He knew, but he wanted to hear it from her.

"The standard gear. The Hong Kong uniform. A blazer and a tie."

"Was it, by any chance, a cricket-club tie?"

The waitress pursed her thin lips. "Now you're asking me. Cricket, rugby, golf, I canna tell the difference. But a club tie, yes. They all wear them around here."

Decker had been sweeping the girl's answers into a corner of his mind, telling himself he'd leave them there until he was ready to gather them up and examine them one by one. Meanwhile, there were still one or two questions to go.

"How about his face, Jeanne? Do you recall any particular features?"

The waitress kissed the back of her front teeth with the tip of her tongue, irritated at losing the access number to her memory.

"Describe him," Decker urged. "Try."

"Forty, forty-five. Um, ordinary-looking." The Scots girl stopped; grimaced at the paucity of her descriptive powers. Then she lurched ahead, riding on the back of a sudden remembrance. "Although I do recall . . . but you wouldn't want to know that."

"Maybe I'd be fascinated."

"Well"—the girl leaned closer, like a coffee-klatch gossip with a juicy tidbit to impart—"he had dandruff something terrible."

"Really? Any other details?"

The girl went back inside her head, came out empty. "No. I'm sorry."

Decker examined the brown liquid in his glass and wondered, with most of his thinking blanked off, why fine ale was still brewed only in the British Isles when, once upon a time, ale had been what the whole world had drunk.

"You sure he didn't," he asked, "have a mustache?"

Surprise expanded the girl's expression, and she tapped Decker's shoulder like a schoolmarm singling out a bright student. "That's right. How did you know that?"

Decker shrugged; not so much in answer to the query as in reaction to what was in his mind: some people saw God as a wrathful, flowing-maned presence in a long white robe, gigantic of figure, fearful of countenance, eyes blazing with retribution. Another school pictured the Divinity as a searing bolt of pure white light, unwatchable, unknowable; and no more approachable than the incandescent heart of an exploding star.

Well, both groups were wrong.

Everybody in the world was wrong.

Except Brian Fairweather.

Because, in actual fact, God was an Englishman.

With a mustache, and a blazer, and a cricket-club tie.

And, so it was said—and who would have guessed?—a bad case of dandruff.

II

MURDOCH
AND
SLEMP

7

At precisely seven A.M., when the security light which monitored the front gates launched into its inflamed tap dance, Murdoch, knowing it would be Valerie arriving, shed his tailored pajama top, swung his body out of bed, reached for his crutches, and naked, propelled himself into his workout room. Rain, hail, or shine, Valerie came every Monday and Thursday morning at the same time to give Murdoch his erotic massage, whether or not Murdoch felt he needed sexual release.

Arthur Murdoch was a man married to routine. He believed that, given enough information and preparation, the unforeseen could be circumvented, and life bent into an obedient straight line without curve or corner to shelter unwelcome surprise. Murdoch worshiped control, and routine was his god. Routine told you exactly where you were every day, and when you knew that, you got a good idea of what was to be expected.

What an edge that gave you! When you were able to read the signals and, more important, had the power to have them moved, then the runaway locomotive that hauled fate around could be derailed or switched to a harmless siding before it had a chance to come crashing into your life.

That dark, mindless engine had already run down Arthur Murdoch once; he wasn't about to give it a second shot.

Bracing himself with crutches, he covered the distance to a bench press and stretched out on it awkwardly. He hissed in a breath and pushed a barbell weighing 220 pounds out of its cradle and into the air. He did it four times, settled the weight, hinged himself up to a sitting position, and grimly viewed his lifeless legs.

Wan Li.

Hardly a day went by when the name didn't pop into Murdoch's head and squat there like a foul and poisonous toad, keeping company with a stinging, fresh-as-paint hatred for the man, a man who'd been dead for fifteen years. Wan Li had died because Murdoch had hired three men to drown him. They'd done it in a deserted reach of the Jubilee reservoir over a period of five hours. Arthur Murdoch wanted Wan Li to understand what was happening to him, and who had orchestrated his prolonged demise.

Murdoch maneuvered himself toward a sit-up board just two "strides" away on his aluminum helpers. Wan Li had made him a present of these shiny poles for life. The man would never have got the chance if Murdoch had looked into the distance, seen what was coming down the tracks. He hadn't trusted Wan Li—Murdoch never trusted anybody—but he hadn't suspected him either, and he should have; should have played heads-up ball.

Instead Wan Li's man had shot him in the spine with a .25 auto, the kind of shitty little gun a car salesman might give his wife for her bedside drawer because he worked nights.

Wan Li had screwed up. I want Arthur Murdoch dead and buried, he'd told somebody. Instead, he'd got him alive and crippled.

Big mistake.

Murdoch reached down, hooked a leather strap over his dead ankles, and effortlessly ripped off twenty fast sit-ups, no problem at all for the washboard ridges corrugating his midsection.

His chest, his shoulders, his arms all popped and bulged with over-development. Thick muscles guyed his neck, running up like iron pipes into a head of gray hair as closely shaven as a boot-camp sailor's. The muscular display seemed to overrun his scalp and reach down to his face: he was fifty-seven years old, yet there was not a hint of sag in the cheeks, not the slightest droop beneath the chin; hardness only, tough eyes as hard as slate; strength in the nose, strength in the wide, slightly bulbous brow: a tight, unforgiving face with the tense, gritted fortitude of the marathon runner, the clutch player.

Arthur Murdoch finished the exercise, regained his hated crutches, and propped himself up on his senseless feet.

Perpendicular, the discrepancy in his body was strikingly evident; he had the legs of a man thirty years his senior, thin and withered, atrophied into limp stalks. The would-be assassin's bullet, with its nerve-shattering impact, had turned them into flaccid, dangling pendants, like the boneless tentacles of a jellyfish.

The rubber-tipped crutches made a squeaky, thumping noise as their owner strenuously jabbed at the floor on his way to the Swedish arm bars mounted on a wall. Valerie would be a few minutes yet; she always had coffee with the kitchen amah before she came upstairs to perform her hand magic. She and the amah were both into astrology, both convinced that the apparent conjunction of an earthly planet with a group of stars thousands of light-years away somehow affected the tides of life on a remote outpost of the Milky Way.

Murdoch had grown up surrounded by astrologers, fortune-tellers, soothsayers. It was all a bunch of crap, the practitioners either deluded fools or avaricious charlatans. Some of them were just plain crazy. Like the one he'd taken a date to, at the Wong Tin temple years ago when he'd been a whole person—instead of half-man, half-vegetable—when the walk through the crowded, narrow fortune-tellers' alley had presented no embarrassing challenge. The man had been old, with deep lines dividing his face into a dozen sections, a wispy white beard trailing from his chin like the roots of a ginseng plant, and eyes so buried they looked like marbles that had slipped down behind his sockets.

He'd looked into his date's hand—Murdoch remembered the girl, a wide-assed, big-titted humping machine from some dumbbunny town in Florida—and given her the usual pap about love and marriage, a long life, many grandchildren. But when the old man had taken Murdoch's hand and peered into his palm, there'd been no such cheery prognosis. Instead he'd shaken his ancient head and muttered something about death.

Murdoch hadn't been able to believe it; these guys earned their money by giving you good news, waffling on about how successful you were going to be, telling you what you wanted to hear. When he'd demanded to know more, the old man had reluctantly examined Murdoch's palm again, then had said, incredibly, "Bee. Death by stinging bee."

Senile old fool. It was going to take more than a goddamn insect to remove Arthur Murdoch from his ball of mud. If a pro hit man hadn't been able to do it, what chance did a lousy little bumblebee have?

Nevertheless, the old man's prophecy had played on Arthur Murdoch's mind. He'd never been able to shake it off; such a strong forecast had left an indelible impression that had etched deeper as he'd got older. Murdoch had seen his doctor, and had himself checked out for susceptibility to anaphylactic shock, the massive rush of histamine that a bee sting can induce. The result had been negative, but Murdoch had played it safe; he'd had the lantana bushes and the white flowering hedges pulled up out of his garden, and the lawn mown and raked daily to get rid of any clover. And whenever he went outdoors, in anything like a bucolic setting, he carried with him a specially made refillable insect bomb containing an extremely strong DDT. The bomb was attached to his crutches, chromed to match them; most people never even noticed it.

But in spite of the fact that Murdoch had gone to all this trouble because of a prognostication; he strongly maintained that all fortune-tellers, palm readers, graphologists, K'an Hsiang men, Pa Kua diviners, et cetera, were bullshit artists. Inside information, expert contacts, empirical insight—these were the things that brought future knowledge And an ability to react immediately and decisively on that was the recipe for success.

And there were few people who could give Arthur Murdoch lessons in success: one of the most powerful men in Hong Kong, worth at least two hundred million U.S., he could influence the vagaries of the Hang Seng index with a five-minute meeting; make or break a new enterprise with a couple of phone calls. He was a financial colossus with enormous clout, and was no less successful on the social level. He'd bought and bullied his way into the black-tie, diamond-studded monthly doings of All The Best People: chairman of this fashionable charity, sponsor of that worthy cause, a biggie in the Jockey Club, a benefactor of the Hong Kong Philharmonic. For an American, in this most British of colonies, it was a rare thing to be up there with the nobs.

Finished on the arm bars, Murdoch, blowing lightly, his skin sheened by a faint glow of moisture, thumped across the room and gazed out at the panoramic view.

It was like being in an aircraft up here: nothing beyond the glass except the tree-covered slope, diving down like a steep-breaking wave until it met the blue sparkle of Deep Water Bay far below. Golden pieces of the morning sun jigged across the water, gilding the yachts at rest in the lee of Middle Island, which, with its soft swell and rise and staggered double peak, floated in the bay like a cool green luxury liner.

Murdoch's aspect was of the south side of Hong Kong island; the soaring reaches of Central lay over the other edge of the Peak. Most of Murdoch's foreign business associates, invited to the American's house for the first time, expected to be rewarded with the famous view, the one that laid out the skyscraping spectacular of the downtown section, the magnificent two-thousand-acre harbor, and the brilliant shore of the Tsim-Sha-Tsui over in Kowloon. They were disappointed to find that Arthur Murdoch's house was on the unfashionable side of the Peak, the side that faced the Beaufort Islands, and the Po Toi group, and the glossy, flat emptiness of the South China Sea.

Murdoch had chosen to build his home on this side for a very simple reason: had he built on the north slope of the mountain, then on clear high days when the mist had burnt off, and the blue air shone squeaky clean, the mountains beyond Kowloon, beyond the New Territories, would have been clearly visible.

The mountains of China.

The southern boundary of a country containing one billion Communists.

No.

Arthur Murdoch would never, not even if the land were free, ever build a house facing north. Not with a view of an obscenity like Red China. And so, situated where it was, tucked into a leafy corner of Mount Cameron Drive, with its nearest neighbor, the Dutch consulate, a good three hundred feet away, not many people, unless they had either an invitation or a helicopter, got to see Arthur Murdoch's house. And a lot of people wanted to, because it had had considerable exposure in the up-market, consumer-oriented, house and architectural magazines.

It was basically a huge box anchored to a stressed-concrete base, cantilevered out over the slope, and held together by a skeleton of red-painted I-beams and tubular supports. Everything else was half-inch-thick plate glass, twin-paned and tinted green: the load-bearing walls, exterior and interior, as well as the entire roof.

All glass.

Over the roof, and down the front and end walls, water ran in a constant and dreamy cascade. Pumped up from an underground tank, and recycled, the water's gentle flow cooled the house and turned its hard reflective edges into soft, shimmering ripples.

If the outside was a visual knockout, the inside was merely stunning. An English cabinetmaker had been flown over to handle the floors. They were made of yellow furniture-grade yuan wood, each board cut in six-foot lengths and fitted, using the tongue-and-groove method. Covering a large part of the floor were Whampoa rugs, vast stretches of virgin wool woven in Shanghai in the twenties. Red and purple storks pranced on them, hunting mice in sunburnt cornfields; flocks of songbirds soared through a jungle's green mansions. In the pink-flowering trees kites chased white doves while hungry red tigers watched from below. Long, elegant chesterfields sat on these luscious rugs, the gray hides of ostriches buttoned to them.

There were no paintings, but ornaments instead: an orange glazed horse from an eighth-century tomb. A stoneware chicken-head ewer from the Te Ching kilns. A five-clawed dragon made during the reign of Hsuante. A pair of glazed white cups from the Nara period. A seventeenth-century Masunobu folding screen. Gorgeous.

Arthur Murdoch's house: liquidly transparent, and full of beautiful things.

And yet a number of jealous and envious people referred to it, a house of water and glass, as the Fish Tank. Others, with good and true reasons to hate Arthur Murdoch, saw the tank's inhabitant as a crippled fish swimming crookedly through sunken treasure.

Squinting for focus, Murdoch stared through the glass wall, challenging the azure distance, and caught the sun flash off the white-haloed chimney stacks shooting up from the new power station, a toy-size structure from this height.

There was an example of success, of power, of pressure applied to the right necks at the right time. Murdoch Construction had built that utility, although, initially, resistance to the scheme had been vociferous and well-organized.

Arthur Murdoch had squashed it piece by piece, bullied it through the various planning and permission boards; swayed, threatened, cajoled, bought. Buying people was always easiest; it was expected. It was the way things got done in Asia, something they didn't understand so well back in the States. Squeeze, it was called.

An apt word: the application of pressure by means of financial inducement. Often a very large inducement. But it was always worth it. And on those rare occasions when those in position wanted more squeeze than they were entitled to, and smirkingly dug in their heels believing that their price would be met, well, then you were forced to squeeze back.

Murdoch watched a gray curl of errant smoke climb thinly into the air from stack number three. A subinspector had insisted, in spite of the money-stuffed suitcase left for him in his flat, that the foundations of that building should be sunk a little deeper. There was nothing wrong with the foundations, they were plenty deep enough, but the subinspector's pockets seemed to be bottomless. The man was now permanently supervising those foundations, buried in the cement with one of the Major's homemade bullets lodged in the back of his head. A greedy Chinese who knew nothing about construction except how to make it pay.

No big loss to the world.

The faint sound of chimes broke into Arthur Murdoch's thoughts: Valerie out in the hallway.

He pivoted on his crutches, crossed to the rear wall, and pressed a button which released the hallway door. It was a piece of security he'd only recently installed; now nobody could wander around the upper floor without his knowing it, poking into things, prying. No more mistakes like that.

With some difficulty Murdoch backed his haunches onto the sit-up bench as Valerie walked into the room.

Nobody was certain whether Valerie was Japanese or Korean, and Valerie herself wouldn't say. Her age was a mystery too; she looked thirty but others claimed she was closer to fifty. Valerie remained silent on that score as well. But there was one thing about Valerie on which everybody agreed: she had the knack.

The masseuse had a diminutive figure, and a face that was classically Oriental topped by hair the color of charcoal jerked back into a pony-tail. The ivory clasp behind her head held her hair with such severity it appeared to contribute to the tightness of the wrinkle-free skin stretched over her tiny nose and rising cheekbones. She wore no makeup save for a thin dark line penciled through nonexistent eyebrows, and a hint of color on a mouth that enclosed brilliantly white teeth capped like a movie star's. Her figure was like a boy's: no bosom, no hips; she was ageless, sexless, and perfect as a brand-new doll.

She said good morning to Murdoch, a greeting which went unacknowledged, and put down a finely crafted rosewood attaché case, Valerie's box of tricks. When she opened it, two baize-lined trays hinged up. Set into the trays were a dozen squat inch-high bottles, and as many thin glass vials containing an almond-oil base and a mélange of other liquids. Nobody ever got the recipes out of Valerie, but she did admit to using lemon grass, orange oil, origanum oil, melissa, niauli, yland, and elemi oil.

She took the towels that were always ready for her, spread them over a chair, then turned up the sleeves of her dress. It was a white cotton dress buttoning down the front and stopping at knee level where white stockings took over, her feet encased in flat-heeled white shoes. It was almost a nurse's uniform, and was certainly as unsexy; Valerie always dressed like this, unflatteringly, to emphasize the fact that she did not deal in sex. While it was true she induced an orgasm in her clients, it was not done for their pleasure. The orgasm was a manifestation of the tensions and pressures and worries which besieged the vast majority of the people she ministered to, and it was her theory that the body's physical release allowed a corresponding mental one. People like Arthur Murdoch, a workaholic, a man of immense responsibilities with a huge payroll to meet, needed help in order to relax and forget for a restorative few minutes the insistent, urgent demands of a business empire.

Valerie actually had more women clients than men, the women being surprisingly immodest in the presence of the masseuse, and quite content to stretch out naked without any covering sheet. While the age of her male clients tended to be over forty, her women clients were from a much wider age group, anything from slim twenty-four-year-old models, who swore by her services, to plump, dumpy matrons who couldn't have got through the week without one of her visits. But young or not so young, male or female, her technique remained the same.

Murdoch lay facedown on the bench. Valerie selected one of her little bottles, thinking carefully about it, choosing one which she thought would be "right" for Murdoch on this particular morning. The underlying scent of the oil she chose was something which often defeated Valerie's clients, but Murdoch identified it: gardenia. It put him in mind of a warm night in Fiji the time he'd gone down there to make a deal with a group of Indians. A girl who'd given him a memorable mouth job had worn a gardenia in her hair. He remembered the white petals ending up all over his pubes, as if his dick had died and somebody had sent a floral tribute. Well, maybe his gams were dead, but the old schlong was alive and kicking.

Valerie spilled some oil into the palm of her hand and worked it into Murdoch's thick neck with her short, supple fingers. She talked as she worked; she found it helped exorcise the twin demons of strain and worry which blocked the way to a carefree interlude.

"Oh, yes. A lot of tension there. I can feel it. We'll have to get rid of that. That will just not do."

She had a warm, comforting voice, as pleasantly viscous as the oils she used: a rich voice, a voice of confidence, her Oriental accent imparting a rolling fluidity to her English.

"So much tension," she scolded lightly. "I can feel it here. And here. And here."

She put gentle pressure on his shoulders and arms; kneading, pressing, coaxing.

"We'll have to get that down," she said, as if the tension in Murdoch's muscular upper body were a lump in a tube of toothpaste that could be squeezed and manipulated in whatever direction she chose.

She worked the stress down toward his flat, hard waist, then started on his withered legs, comforting, correcting, moving the tension upward now. She talked on in that same syrupy tone, letting Murdoch know that she could feel the hard knots of pent-up anxiety which had sunk through him, and that she was triumphing over them, bending them to her will, easing them toward an exit.

With long, sinuous, gliding movements her hands stroked his calves, his inert thighs, the tight muscles of his buttocks. She had half the tension, she told him, right where she wanted it, centered around his waist now, all the anxieties gathered together, ready to be banished.

Now she could work on the remaining part, the front of his body. Murdoch turned over.

Valerie reached for another kind of oil, a touch of frangipani in this one. She pumped down the rigidity from, his nail-keg chest, from his solid flanks and shoulders, then squeezed it upward from his stringy shins and knees.

Long before her fingers got anywhere near his crotch, Murdoch was erect. Most of Valerie's male customers said that even the best lay they'd ever had had never given them the kind of hard-on Valerie was capable of producing; and that was without her even so much as looking at their cocks. In the ten to fifteen minutes that Valerie's massage took, she never touched the genitals except once at the very last moment. Her technique was reputed to be the same as the ancient Japanese Habu Jibu, which, literally translated, means Half Touch, a technique which was supposed to have taken a talented court concubine two years to learn.

"I can feel the tension gathering," Valerie crooned, her hands feeling to Murdoch as if they were inside his flesh. "You will release that tension, get rid of all that worry and tiredness."

"Yes," said Murdoch, eyes closed. A response was usual at this stage; whatever small initial resistance a client showed—and no client was ever completely relaxed from the word go—had usually been replaced by complete confidence by this time. By this time the client was usually wanting to give him or herself: men began to arch their backs, women to spread their legs.

But Valerie's fingers would ignore the invitation, and continue to push and smooth the tension down toward the loins and up toward the same area. "It's all there," she'd murmur in that mesmerizing tone. "I can feel it now. It's gathering. Getting ready to leave."

If it was a woman under her hands, she'd lower her voice and, at precisely the right moment—Valerie always knew exactly when—she'd start those subtle fingers at the inside of the woman's knees, and run them upward saying, "Here it comes. It's *here!*"

And then, and only then, would she touch her finger just once into the woman's dampness. And her grateful client would sob or cry out and hip-jerk into an eye-opening orgasm that lasted and lasted and lasted.

With men she was equally skillful. She had the ability to turn her fingers from electric sensors to lumps of cold stone if a man was ready before his tension had all been organized.

Murdoch, now, was very near, and she damped him down, stalled him, but kept him close.

"Almost there. So much worry. So much weariness. It's coming together now. I can feel all that terrible tension. It's all there now, ready to fly from your body and leave it in peace."

She moved her hands up the inside of his legs as if she were closing two zip fasteners, made scissors of her oiled fingers, caught them around his penis, and jerked them firmly upward.

"It's *here!*"

He didn't grunt or cry out; Murdoch shouted, the release was that strong.

She took him in a towel, no longer coaxing but praising now, reassuring him. She attended to him, then covered him with a fresh towel, a mother tucking a young one into bed.

Murdoch, his body numbed, his brain sucked dry, gazed up at the water shimmering over the glass roof, a gently babbling brook, a lazy stream turning the sun into soft diamonds.

Valerie gathered up her fragrant oils, nestled them in their green-baize bed, eased the catch closed on her attaché case, and crept from the room on her quiet, considerate, flat-heeled shoes.

Arthur Murdoch had another appointment that morning, one he made only now and then, and kept with considerable reluctance. His big brown Mercedes nosed through the high front gates and dropped down a road as green and tree-heavy as a jungle track. A quarter-mile below the great glass house, the chauffeur stopped at the edge of a small playground park on Wanchai Gap Road and helped his boss out of the rear seat.

Once he was on his feet, Murdoch impatiently brushed his driver aside, as he always did anybody who offered him a hand, and set off across the lush grass, heading for an empty bench. It was no more than sixty feet away, the sun was warm but not yet hot, and he was on time for his appointment, but Murdoch still crossed the empty space as if some invisible barrier had been placed in his path which would have to be breached by speed and power. It was the way Murdoch got around, scuttling on his metal supports as if fearing they might splinter any second and pitch him forward in a helpless and undignified heap. Loathing his crutches, Murdoch unconsciously tried to leave them behind, outdistance them, free himself from their constant and unwanted companionship. He'd tried other means of assistance: he'd had a man who lived in Crete, an Englishman, a genius in robotics, design and build a pair of walking metal legs which could be clamped to his real legs out of sight under his trousers. They'd been powered by a battery designed to be carried in a briefcase by his side. The metal legs were a marvel of ingenuity, but they jerked him along with the stiff, risible movements of a mechanical man, and he'd thrown them away.

He'd tried a number of other things to help him walk, but had finally had to settle for the crutches again.

Long John Silver. Tiny Tim. Arthur Murdoch hated the company he was in. He reached the park bench, looked and listened carefully for any sign of a bee, lowered himself, and sat there in the shade of a liana-choked pepper tree, the sun, struggling through the thick foliage, dappling his close-cropped hair.

He pushed at his sleeve, checked the ten-year-old Heuer ticking on his wrist—a perfect watch, unimprovable; unbuttoned his dark summer-weight jacket—a wool-and-cashmere mix, expertly tailored to elongate his fireplug figure; and wondered where the hell Slemp was.

Murdoch hadn't seen him since he'd given the Englishman his instructions; he liked to put space between himself and controversial happenings. And even though Slemp had proved adept at keeping a low profile after performing the quick and silent chores Murdoch paid him to do, his employer was still cautious enough to meet with the man sometime after the event, and always in out-of-the-way spots like this little park.

Nobody came here weekdays except the Filipino amahs to push their charges back and forth on the swings. The tiny space was protected by heavy stands of trees, cut off from everything: a perfect place to talk without fear of eavesdroppers, bugged cars, bugged phones. There was nothing more threatening here than the cries of children, the tinkling bell of the soda-pop wagon, and the intermittent whir of cicadas singing love songs to the sun.

Five minutes stretched into ten.

Murdoch jabbed at a bull ant negotiating a fallen twig, the hard rubber tip of a crutch messing it into a curling red blot, a spot of vibrant color against the green of the grass.

Another five minutes dragged, and Murdoch swore. Then at last Slemp appeared, coming down the path toward him.

Major Reggie Slemp.

Distaste whittled at a corner of Murdoch's mouth as he watched the man approach; not exactly a commanding figure: slack-faced, flabby-chinned, round-shouldered, and with a paunch that would start to balloon before very long. Not your typical British officer's military bearing, Murdoch thought. But then, as he well knew, "Major" Reggie Slemp had really been Sergeant Reggie Slemp. And he hadn't served in Borneo in the Blue and Grays during the Communist Insurrection, and been invalided out with a land-mine shrapnel wound as he claimed; he'd been a range instructor at Aldershot, England, and had been kicked out of the Army for bad-checking just about every little shop in town.

But no matter how spurious his claim to a distinguished service career, he did have one talent which was undeniable: Reggie Slemp was an armorer, small-arms artificer, and gunsmith of outstanding ability.

And an efficient killer.

Arthur Murdoch, every now and then, had need of such expertise. Personally, he couldn't stand the man. He was an embarrassment. He'd got him a job in one of his companies, and when the guy had blown that, he'd got him another. And then a third. The Major was a cheap little crook and rotten at it.

"Sorry I'm late," Slemp said, flopping down next to Murdoch. "But what can you expect with a Chinese mechanic trying to sort out a Jap car?"

It was exactly the kind of remark Murdoch had come to expect. Slemp was the type of middle-class Englishman who automatically puts down the indigenous population of whichever country he happens to be living in. It wasn't consciously racial; it stemmed from the idea that an Englishman abroad had to be a superior person if for no other reason than his country of birth.

Murdoch had news for Slemp: the Chinese were excellent mechanics, and he was a goddamn, know-nothing slob. Just look at the guy! Baggy, gray flannel trousers with a crease like a rolling pin, tattersall-check shirt bunching around his pudding waist, crepe-soled suede, brothel-creeping fruit boots which hadn't been brushed since new. And that corny cricket-club necktie with the pelican emblems, a stain on it like one of those dopey birds had laid a broken egg. And why the hell didn't he shave off that stupid mustache? It hung there under his vein-popped nose like a child's dirty hairbrush. The guy was a crapbag; the Brylcreem he used had to be a couple of days old, and was now matting his hair in thick brown strands each side of his center part. His scalp, buried beneath all that gunk, had a permanent flaking problem which was usually displayed on the lapels and shoulders of the navy-blue blazer he always wore, the one that was, no doubt, lying crumpled up on the passenger seat of his rusty, dogged-out little Honda. Murdoch resisted the impulse to tell him to for crissakes clean up his act, and instead launched straight into the reason for the bucolic meeting.

"I saw the newspapers. The woman was mutilated."

"Yes. He must have gone ape. Frankly, when I read about it," Slemp said, squinting into the bounce of sunlight skimming off the grass, "I wasn't surprised. He seemed pretty normal. But it's often the normal ones who are the most unstable."

"Where did you meet him that night?"

"Mad Dogs. Appropriate, what?"

"How did you arrange it?"

"I phoned the woman at her flat. Gave her a false name and told her I was a friend of a friend of hers in America. Told her I had a surprise for her. She wanted to know which friend. I told her it was all part of the surprise. I asked her if we could meet somewhere congenial in the near future, and she suggested Mad Dogs, which was fine with me."

Murdoch turned his head when Slemp raised his hand to flick sweat from his forehead. A wetness under his arm had darkened his shirt, and the odor that arose, unrepressed by any cosmetic application, was high and sour.

"I arranged to meet Fairweather there, and pointed the woman out when she came in. Don't worry," Slemp hurried on, knowing what was in his boss's mind, "I took a good look around first. There was nobody there who knows me."

"How about the staff?"

"All new people. Besides, I haven't been in there for two years. Not since they refused to take my chit." Miffed at the memory, Slemp snorted through his nose, the hairs peeking from his nostrils stiffening in umbrage. "I wrote out a check on the spot, and never went back, I can tell you. Anyway, it went off like clockwork. The woman got tired of waiting for a friend who never turned up, and responded to Fairweather's advances. And he did the rest."

"He sure as hell did," Murdoch muttered.

"Granted, what he did wasn't nice," Slemp offered in an assuaging, tolerant tone, "but it certainly does lend weight to the idea of a sex crime. There's certainly that to be said for it."

The cicadas quit their chant as their god ducked behind a cloud. The only sounds now were the shrieks of children's games and the squeak of the oil-starved swings. The bell-ringing soda-pop wagon had left for thirstier pastures.

"I'd feel better if you hadn't gone in," Murdoch said, frowning over it. "If they catch him, somebody might remember you together."

"Won't matter. There's no way I could possibly be tied in. It's ten to one they won't catch the bugger anyway. The loonies are usually far too smart. Nature compensating, I suppose." Slemp licked a finger, rubbed at an oil smudge on the back of his wrist. The area was discolored, not only by the oil mark but also by skin which a subtropical climate had freckled into dime-size spots. Murdoch had always found it hard to believe that hands as ugly as those could be expert with an automatic, although it was only in the preparation and smithing of a weapon, the technical aspects, that Slemp was so killed; he freely admitted to being a poor shot when it came to actually firing a gun. But then, a hit man's work with a pistol was all close-in stuff, so prowess at long range was not a necessity.

"And even if they could identify me," Slemp added, "it would still come down to Fairweather's testimony, if they were able to catch him. And they're hardly going to take the word of a madman against that of a member of the Malthusians Cricket Club. And, don't forget, I never even met the woman, so there's no tie-in there either."

Murdoch grunted, whether in agreement with his statement or not, Slemp couldn't tell. The killing had been planned and carried out so there could be no possibility of repercussions, and his boss knew it. But everybody likes to be reassured, even a tough-as-nails bastard like his employer. Tough in certain areas, that is; it was common knowledge that Arthur Murdoch had some kind of phobia about insects. He had that silver tube of bug spray clipped to the inside of one of his crutches. Everybody knew it, and laughed about it behind his back; an elephant scared of mice.

Slemp watched Murdoch reach into his jacket. He passed over an envelope fat with money. Slemp's spotted hand appeared to accept it with reluctance, almost distaste, as if being remunerated in this manner was too much like a coal miner lining up for his pay packet on a Friday afternoon.

"I'll call you if I need you," Murdoch said, grabbing his crutches and hauling himself upright.

He set off across the park, the aluminum poles stomping into the cushioning grass in their forceful, metronomic swing. Slemp had to hurry to catch up, walk at a trot to stay with him.

"I say . . . that old banger of mine . . . you couldn't possibly give me a lift into Central, could you? Nobody'll spot us together. I'll slip out quickly."

Without looking at him, without even a break in his driving rhythm, Murdoch said, "Don't be a fool," and kept going as Slemp tailed away like a dog grown tired of chasing something. With a mean curve to his mouth, he watched his boss moving on four legs, scurrying over the grass like a ruined beetle, bearing down on his air-conditioned Mercedes as if he meant to ram it.

Slemp was getting pretty bloody sick of Arthur Murdoch.

Sod the bastard!

He might own half of Hong Kong, but he didn't own Reggie Slemp, the damn cripple. One of these days Mr. Arthur Bloody Murdoch might just get his well-deserved comeuppance: a .22 slug fired behind the ear. You wouldn't feel quite so superior with a ninety-grain RSW bounding around inside your cerebellum, would you, Mr. Big Deal Taipan?

Slemp might have spat at the departing car if what he regarded as his superior English breeding hadn't mitigated against such coarseness. Instead he slashed at a thin fallen branch with a scuffed suede shoe, and set out for what he knew would be a bloody long hunt for a damn bloody taxi.

As the Mercedes hummed down the precipitous dip of the Peak Road, Murdoch sat back against the marshmallow comfort of the deep red leather seat and brooded about Reggie Slemp.

Going into the pub, talking to Fairweather, that had been bone stupid. All he had to do was point out the woman as she went in, then let the guy go in after her and pick her up. If Slemp was going to start getting sloppy, making mistakes, his contract was going to have to be canceled some dark, rainy night.

Trouble was, he'd be tough to replace. It would mean important talent, trusting somebody he didn't know, couldn't control. Get rid of Slemp before he did real damage? Or gamble that, next time out, he'd be tighter and cleaner, the way he used to be?

Murdoch decided it needed some thought; but not right now. Right now the car was approaching Baker Road, a junction which figured largely in Murdoch's trip downtown every morning. This section of the ride produced wild swings in his emotions; part of it made his blood boil, then, a few moments later, this clenched, seething feeling gave way to a suffusing glow of satisfaction.

The anger was occasioned by the green monstrosity the Mercedes was now passing: the embassy of the so-called People's Republic of China, the Reds' official residence in Hong Kong. It was, for all intents and purposes, deserted: no cars out front, nobody moving around, the front door looking as if it had been boarded up from the inside. The abandoned look was further enhanced by the building's tennis court, its asphalt surface heat-buckled and potholed, the basketball hoop mounted on a pole at the north end off-center and sagging like an overused gallows. And yet life was going on behind those ugly green stucco walls. They were in there, all right, the Reds—Murdoch knew that for sure—planning, gloating, waiting.

That's all they had to do: wait.

The liver-shitted British government had seen to that, handing the colony over to Peking like a roast-beef sandwich on a platter. Mercifully, it took the Mercedes only a few seconds to zip by the embassy, and Murdoch could then concentrate on a sight that never failed to lift his heart: the vista which opened up as the car lowered its hood for the final plunge down the slope into Central.

This was the famous view which Arthur Murdoch's extraordinary house turned its back on: the ship-filled harbor sweeping west in a broad and glittering S shape, the forested hills lapping the heights like a green river in flood, the three-mile ribbon of harbor front choked with rocketing steel and glass and granite, the structures reaching for a sky as flat and perfect as a paint sample.

One of those buildings was the headquarters of Arthur Murdoch's business empire: shipping, construction, real estate, textiles, import/export. Its owner had had a small revolving reflector mounted on top of a water tank forty-seven stories above street level, positioned so it would bounce the morning sun in a special way. People thought it was, literally, just another flashy touch in a city whose architecture majored in such showboat antics; Murdoch found it amazing that, in a town full of military people of one kind or another, nobody had yet recognized the pattern of flashes: one short, one long. A break. Then three long flashes.

The letters A M in Morse code.

This small added touch served no purpose other than to send a self-congratulating message of accomplishment to the building's proprietor each morning. Accomplishment was what life was all about. Accomplish nothing, and you were nothing. A man was measured by his success, rated according to the amount of money he had at his disposal, the height of the hill he sat on top of, the size of the whip he was able to crack, the wattage of power he could generate. Having received and been buoyed by the glitzy communication, Murdoch reached for a radiophone, called his personal assistant, checked on his schedule for the day. Along with the usual dross was a meeting with some people from the Mercantile Board bitching about what they insisted on calling glaring discrepancies in freighter manifest, then an interview with somebody from a business magazine who'd already been canceled on three previous occasions and would have to be seen this time. Then a time-wasting confab with the British American Cultural Group, of which Murdoch was chairman, regarding an upcoming visit of the Chicago Symphony. Then lunch with the people who'd bankrolled his development on the Queensland Gold Coast, followed by a full afternoon working on a bunch of stuff which had been hanging fire for too long.

Murdoch tossed the phone aside and pushed back in the red leather seat that wasn't feeling quite so comfortable anymore.

A thin brew of unease began to percolate in his mind.

The British American meeting bothered him. The Assistant U.S. Consul would probably be there, and talk would inevitably drift around to the awful thing that had happened to one of the staff over in St.John's House. It wasn't something that was going to be clucked over and forgotten in a few days. The phones would have been buzzing between the consulate and Arsenal Street, polite pressure applied. That fucking Rudyard Kipling idiot, Waxy Crane, would be running around May House beating a gong. The guy was a joke, but he was also a damn good cop.

Murdoch stared sullenly out of the window as the big car whipped by the straining uphill traffic. Taking care of a greedy local building inspector was one thing; with something like six million Chinese squeezed into the colony, the disappearance of just one of their number was not going to cause a tidal wave of response. But the brutal killing of an American resident—and a U.S. government employee to boot—that was different.

Still, he'd known all that; factored it in. And gone ahead and made the decision.

He'd done the right thing; no question about it.

The woman had been flattered by the invitation to the house, charmed by its waterfall exterior, entranced by its million-dollar decor. She'd wandered around it, naked and pretty, poking into corners like a cat, looking at things, listening to things. Well, the same thing that had done for the cat had done for Angela Waters.

Too bad. She'd possessed an understanding, an intrinsic thing that certain women have about men. She'd known that crutches might mean a guy couldn't walk, but they sure as hell didn't mean he couldn't perform.

So she'd come home with Arthur Murdoch, Hong Kong's most eligible bachelor, biggest Western wheel, and richest goddamn fuck a working girl would ever have in her entire life, something to tell her grandchildren about.

And she'd been great in bed, a real knack for the sack. A damn shame, having to zip a talent like that; but how long would it have been before she began to understand that the handsome gift he'd given her was a reward for her silence?

She'd been smart, that girl; bright. She would have realized, sooner or later, that anything worth a gift of a thousand bucks could be worth a gift of fifty thousand. And even if they'd been able to come to an arrangement—her own numbered account in Singapore or wherever—the danger would still have been the same: she might have started to wonder about what it was she was being paid to forget. And if she'd pursued it—had him followed, checked up on certain out-of-the-ordinary visitors to the house, like the general from Taiwan, for example, and put it up against what she'd heard on the tape—it was possible she could have got close to what was in the pipeline. And then no amount of money in the world could have bought her off.

No.

He'd done the right thing.

He'd just ride it out, that's all. And hope that Slemp's lack of judgment would pass unnoticed.

Murdoch started the morning with three secretaries and the overnight telexes, made a dozen phone calls, then stomped into the boardroom for the biweekly kick-ass session with his department heads. He emerged from that in a grumpy mood which was not improved by having to sit still for the thrice-postponed magazine interview. He hated giving interviews; he knew from past experience exactly the questions which would be asked, as well as the ones they were dying to ask, like had his handicap given him a fear of rejection when approaching women? And did owning a pair of legs like overcooked noodles make it difficult to go to the bathroom?

The interview started out, as they usually did, with the standard request for a personal biography, and the reporter received the standard rundown: born in Shanghai in 1932, parents American evangelists who were killed in the riots in '37. Adopted by an American banker, raised in the International Settlement, then sent, aged ten, to the U.S. for schooling. Arrived back in Hong Kong in 1950 and, through a loan from a kind friend, got started in the textile trade. Eventually sold that business, and took his profits into shipping for a while, got lucky speculating in commodities, then jumped into the real-estate market, which was just beginning to boom. Bought a construction firm with which to develop his land purchases and, from that point on the House of Murdoch had risen along with the financial rocket of the most dazzlingly successful city in Asia.

The biography sailed close enough to the truth to be credible. However, most of more interesting details had been omitted.

The friend who'd got Murdoch started in the textile business was the man who'd adopted him. He was Chinese, not American, and while it was true he was a banker, he was also the leader of one of Shanghai's most powerful triad lodges.

With the money he'd been loaned, Murdoch imported short-staple cotton from Pakistan, opened a factory—an illegal hut on a hillside behind North Point—and filled it with some cheap weaving machines, cheap because they'd been damaged in a suspicious fire. He'd then employed women and children to run the machines; women who, possessing no ID cards, were willing to work for an ounce of tea and three bowls of rice a day, and a pallet bench to sleep on.

The shipping endeavor sounded grand, but it was hardly that. Murdoch had bought a two-million-mile freighter that had come up to Hong Kong for breaking. He'd got it for scrap plus ten percent, borrowing the purchase price from a local bank at a favorable rate by offering a piece of the mortgage back to the bank for its memorial fund. After a marine surveyor had accepted ten times his usual fee to double the measured width of the hull plates in his report, and thus qualify the vessel for reregistry, and a greatly inflated hull insurance, Murdoch had put the ship to work hauling lumber from the Celebes to New Caledonia. It had foundered, with the loss of three seamen, on its second trip, but by that time it had returned a nice profit from its first voyage, and earned a handsome settlement from the insurance company.

As for Arthur Murdoch's next success, commodity speculation, it could be more accurately labeled commodity manipulation. The fix had gone in.

Impressed by the ability of Hong Kong printers to churn out wonderful fakes—IDs, passports, share certificates, bearer bonds, currency—Murdoch had got an idea and had taken it to a Chiu Chow businessman he knew, a biggie in import/export. This man had liked the scheme enough to go in fifty-fifty. He'd used his connections to secure an order from a major coffee estate in Kenya for a particular brand of pesticide. Murdoch had then bought several plain brown sacks similar to the kind the famous-name chemical company used, had paid an artist to copy the brand name and logo design, found an engraver to make the plate, and a printer to run off the sacks. He'd then had the sacks filled with a plain white powder dyed to match the color of the pesticide, and with a few chemicals added to give it that distinctive smell.

When the estate's early coffee crop had failed, the scare that had swept through the market had been sufficient to send prices rocketing, and Murdoch and his partner had both made fortunes. That had been around 1957, when the riots had erupted in Hong Kong, business had panicked, and property prices had crashed. Murdoch, cash-rich from his commodity scam, had picked up twenty apartment houses for the absurd price of ten thousand U.S. dollars apiece, a $200,000 investment which had later become worth forty million.

All this was Arthur Murdoch's real story, the one that didn't get into print. The one that did include the traffic incident of the failed competitor with an imagined grudge who, filled with madness and envy, had shot Arthur Murdoch, then thrown himself into the Jubilee reservoir.

The interviewer from the magazine, a nervous, emaciated New Zealand woman who couldn't seem to leave her ridiculously short ducktailed hairdo alone, recorded the official version of the orphan-to-tycoon story, then unsettled by the formidable personality of the man on the other side of the immense mahogany desk, asked him a more topical question, one which was being asked all over the East.

"Mr.Murdoch, when Hong Kong reverts back to China in 1997, do you think the one-country, two-systems idea, as proposed by Beijing, will work?"

Murdoch looked at her, looked away as if he charged for staring at people and she wouldn't be able to afford the rates.

"You kidding? It'll be one country, one system. What else? You think a Commie Marxist society is gonna allow Capitalism to continue here? Under Capitalism the people of Hong Kong take home money every week. Enough for them to buy food, clothing, and pay the rent on an apartment. And most of them have enough left over to take in a movie now and then, go to the track maybe, eat out, a little pork and fish with the rice, a glass of Cognac with the tea, enjoy themselves. You think Peking is gonna allow six million people to live like that, and the other one billion to live like pigs? Nothing in their lives except working land that isn't theirs all day, going to bed at ten P.M. after a swell evening watching propaganda plays on the box? The day the Reds move in here," Murdoch said, back to glaring at the New Zealand woman, with her little thin pen and her little thin body, "Hong Kong and everybody in it will be dragged down to the level of the peasants in every other city in China. And you can't get much lower than that."

The interviewer, having some nervous trouble with the tape recorder, had switched to some rusty shorthand.

"There is a theory," she began, shooting a timid glance at this man whom she'd decided to describe as a "tough-buzzard tycoon with a wrestler's chest and an air of impatience verging on irritability," "that instead of Beijing influencing Hong Kong, it will work the other way around. Do you—"

"Hogwash! Utter bull! That's what ought to happen, but it's not what's gonna happen. The Reds have got thirty-eight years of Communism to defend. If Peking allows the Hong Kong free-enterprise system to start influencing the rest of China, they'll be admitting that those forty years have been a disaster."

Flustered by the vehemence of the American, his jut-jawed abrasiveness, the woman pushed at her hair and said lamely, "You think it has been that? A failure?"

"Think?" Murdoch was just this side of incredulous. "Lady, I don't think, I *know*. And so does anybody else willing to take an honest, unblinkered look at the record." Murdoch slashed out his hand as he said this, ending the gesture by rapping his desk with his fist. "Take their vaunted agricultural policy. The output per capita in Red China today is exactly the same as it was under the Hans, two thousand years ago. That's progress? Take employment. A third of the entire work force sitting on their backsides, unemployable, unfirable, unproductive. The other two-thirds spends thirty or forty years breaking their sandals in the fields or churning out widgets in a factory, and what have they got to look forward to at the end of all that? Maybe a fifty-part-share ownership in a used bicycle. Some system, huh?" Murdoch glowered at the woman as if she were responsible for the whole thing. "Freedom. That's what it's all about. Individualism. Private enterprise. They're the basis of Western society, and they're the three things the Reds are committed to stamping into the ground. My God, the Red Guards destroyed all the private toilets in Peking because they said they were examples of bourgeois individualism. You take a crap in Peking now, you got to crouch down in a stinking latrine with thirty or forty people right there next to you. You call that civilized?"

With her eyes down on her notebook, the woman quickly switched away from politics, back to the safer, politer subject of business. "Mr. Murdoch, your companies are always in the forefront of things in the Pacific area. What's your next important project? Anything that you can reveal at this time?"

For the briefest part of a moment, Murdoch was tempted to tell her, tell her all about Doh Mei-Doh Day, and watch the stupid broad begin to grin at his joke, the grin looping to a round O as she realized he was serious.

"I'm working on something," Murdoch said quietly.

"Big?"

"The biggest thing I've ever done in Hong Kong," Murdoch answered. He could have said that it was the biggest thing anybody had ever done in Hong Kong. "It's gonna be breaking pretty soon. I can't talk about it just yet."

Or ever, he might have added.

The woman flipped her notebook closed and bullied her hair again as she rose.

"Thank you for your time, Mr. Murdoch."

Murdoch raised a thumb to his mouth, worried a tiny piece of ragged nail his manicurist had missed. He was thinking.

Doh Mei-Doh Day.

"You're entirely welcome," he said, a long way away.

8

"Motive," Ralph Dobrinski said, tenting his fingers and bringing his lumpy body forward in his chair. "There's no motive. Who'd want to kill Angie?"

"I don't know," Decker said. "But I do know that any secretary working in a DEA office has access to a lot of sensitive information. She could have been trying to peddle it. I say *could*. It's always a possibility, granted?"

"Sure, we'll grant you that." It was Bumpy speaking, talking in a subdued voice, unhappy with Decker's suggestion. "And if it had been anybody else, I'd say it was a possibility. But you didn't know this girl, Deck. There's no way she could've been into anything. Not Angie." Bumpy looked to Miriam for confirmation, and got it.

"Out of the question," she said. "I mean, if somebody from, say, the Soviet Trade Mission approached her, asked her to slip them a memo now and then, the names and numbers of the latest players to help them fight the East European dope biz, she would've told them to fuck off." When Miriam shook her head her carrot-colored hair splayed out like a flag in a breeze. "Angie wasn't interested in money. I knew her. She didn't give a rat's about it. A girl who looked like that could've married a million dollars anytime she wanted to."

Decker looked around the office at each of the four seated agents; they looked back at him, silently telling him he was wrong. Decker's eyes stayed on Johnny Risotto, whose large body hid his chair, crossed hands resting on his stomach like a man grasping a beach ball.

"Johnny? What do you think?"

The big man made a face as if his belt were too tight, which it was.

"Well, for one thing, Deck, I'm still trying to get my mind around what you've just told us. A nut case takes shots of his handiwork, then gets them processed at a shop in Central? I'm still reeling from that one. Then this guy . . . what's his name?"

"Fairweather."

"Fairweather. Okay, he tells you God told him to do it. And a waitress at Mad Dogs says she saw somebody that night talking to Fairweather, somebody wearing a blazer and a club necktie. Now, this fits Fairweather's description of God. And God created man in His own image. Fairweather's English, right? Probably likes to wear a blazer and club tie himself."

"Johnny, that's exactly what I thought. But Fairweather doesn't have a mustache. And he says God did. And the waitress says the guy Fairweather was talking to had a mustache. So it's not an exact image."

"Maybe Fairweather had one and shaved it off," Bumpy proposed, but without a lot of conviction.

Decker dipped his head, watched dust motes waltz around in the sunlight angling in through the big windows. He gave it a moment while the room waited for him, then looked up and spoke directly to Ralph Dobrinski.

"I think Angela Waters was murdered. Killed by a crazy man, yes, but not by chance. By design. I can't back it up with anything hard and fast, it's just a bone feeling. I'd like your permission to run it down."

Everybody knew what the answer was going to be because Decker's request was only a formal one, polite but unnecessary. By going to the prison and talking to a murder suspect, he'd put Dobrinski in what was potentially an acutely embarrassing situation; and yet, as long as the visit remained unreported, Decker had done the right thing in going out and digging for facts.

Dobrinski said, "You're GS on the case, Hugh. It's your ballgame."

"Sure, but I'll need help. and that'll cut into *your* ballgame."

"You want these three, huh?"

"Yes, please. Forty-eight hours. That's all."

Dobrinski hesitated, drummed his fingers on a fat folder on his desk; the folder was marked DCA: Drug Control Asia. He tapped the folder like a judge gaveling a decision.

"Okay, forty-eight hours. But not a minute more."

Decker checked with the three agents.

"Okay with you guys?"

Johnny Risotto answered for all.

"Sure. Hell, you may be right. And if you're right, you'll be a hero."

"And if you're wrong—" Miriam began.

Decker cut through her. "If I'm wrong, I'm a schmuck. Bumpy, I want to look at everything we know about Angela. Her history in the States, her time here, her friends, relationships, the usual thing. As for you, Miriam, you get the legwork for calling me a schmuck."

When Miriam bridled, her green eyes flashed.

"That's not fair. You called yourself a schmuck."

"What were you going to call me?"

"A scumbag."

"The kid's sheer class," Bumpy said to the ceiling.

Miriam asked Decker what he wanted her to do.

"Buy neckties. I want a sample of all the club ties in Hong Kong."

"You know what you're asking me? You know how many sports clubs, associations, they have in this town? They all have special neckties. I'm gonna have to back up a truck."

"It's an awful lot of ties, Deck," Bumpy said in his high, piping voice. "Hell, I met a guy the other day, he's in business security, and he was wearing a tie belonging to a field-hockey team called, and I kid you not, the Hong Kong Defaulters and Absconders. I mean, even they've got a tie. I'd better give Miriam a hand."

"I'd better help out too, Deck," Johnny Risotto said. "It's gonna be tough enough just getting hold of the established clubs' neckties, the big clubs."

"It's gonna be a regular hernia," Miriam said. "You're supposed to have a letter signed by the secretary of the greens committee, General Sir George Smallpiece, DSO, VD."

Frowning, uncomfortable with the words he had in his mouth, Ralph Dobrinski came back into the conversation.

"I hate to say this, but the best and quickest way of getting all those neckties is to get Arsenal Street to help. But I don't see how we can approach them."

"What if I snuck in through the back door?" Decker asked.

Hope elevated Dobrinski's craggy eyebrows.

"You mean Lucky Doug Portloe?"

"I could try him. I could call him now."

But Decker didn't have to do that because, a minute later, Doug Portloe beat him to the telephone.

"Deck? I want to talk to you." The lilt had gone from the Cornishman's voice; the sun was off the hills, and dark valleys showed through. "This morning an American lawyer visited Brian Fairweather out on Hei Ling Chau. He signed the visitors' book Charles Milligan. There is no American lawyer registered in Hong Kong by that name. And Immigration has no record of any Charles Milligan just passing through. So this unexplained prison visit, coming as it did right on the heels of our breakfast meeting, leads me to wonder if Charles Milligan, described as slim-built, five-ten or eleven, star-shaped scar under left eye, could be somebody we both know who looks like that."

Faced with a delicate situation, vis-à-vis the Hong Kong police, Decker adopted the standard all-court DEA defense: admit nothing, deny everything, and equivocate about the rest.

"I don't know a thing about it, Inspector. I wasn't anywhere near Hei Ling Chau this morning."

"You certain of that?"

"You kidding? It's twelve miles out to sea. You think I wouldn't remember it if I'd just come off a thirty-minute ferry ride twelve miles out to sea?"

"I forgot to tell you. This is not an official call."

"It isn't?" Decker paused; that changed everything. "Hold it a minute. Hei Ling Chau . . . by golly, now that you mention it, I believe I did swing on by this morning."

"Deck, you've got one foot on that plane to Timbuktu. And at the rate you're going, I might be sitting next to you. Questioning an accused homicide suspect in custody without police permission? Which you know would have been categorically refused anyway. You're going to have to cool it, fella. Understand?"

"Sure. Absolutely."

"I mean it, Deck."

"I get the message. You don't have to worry."

Portloe's voice softened, and some of the music returned to it. "Okay, then. Just as long as we understand each other."

"Doug, can I ask you a teensy weensy little favor?"

"What it is?"

"Can I go see Fairweather again?"

On the other end of the line black silence formed like a faraway thundercloud. Then Portloe said, "I swear I may end up on a homicide charge myself."

Decker told him then about the question-and-answer session with Fairweather, and about going to see the waitress at Mad Dogs; told Portloe everything.

"Doug, I think the guy was pointed at Angela Waters. He was the bullet, but somebody else pulled the trigger. However, nobody here at the shop buys it. And I'm sure you don't either."

After a long moment waiting for confirmation of this, Portloe surprised him.

"No. I think you could be right."

"You do? Why?"

"Because there are only two kinds of homicides, dumb ones that are too sloppy to succeed, and smart ones that are too clever to succeed. Getting a madman to knock off somebody for you isn't new, but it's still smart."

"Been done before, huh?"

"When it comes to people killing other people, everything's been done before. But look, Hugh, I can't take it any further. Not without getting Waxy's permission, and if I asked, he wouldn't give it. Right now he's got himself irrefutable evidence, and a self-confessed killer behind bars. I don't think he's going to want to disturb that."

"Sure. I can see how he'd be happy with what he's got. Trouble is, what he's got is the killer but not the murderer. I have to see Fairweather, Doug. I want to take him a whole bunch of club neckties and see if he can tell me which one God was wearing."

"Forget it. You can't see him again. That's asking for trouble."

A ball of silence choked the line for a second time, and for the second time the detective handed Decker a surprise.

"Send Miriam. Fairweather has a sister somewhere. She can be his sister. I'll fix the paperwork."

"Doug," Decker said, "for the life of me I can't see why everybody says you're a no-talent churl."

On the other end of the phone Portloe gave that a smile, then canceled it as he got back to a serious point.

"It'll be absolutely the last time any of you can see the bloke. No phone calls, no fan letters, no contact. You got it?"

"Check."

"And one other thing," Portloe concluded. "I never made this phone call."

"That's probably why I never got it. Listen, before you go . . . who would you say knew Angela Waters best?"

"Her roommate, Faye Keeble. And I didn't hear that question."

"I didn't ask it," Decker said.

They both hung up.

The apartment house in which Angela Waters had been killed was one of the tall white modern ones that stalk up in bunches on MacDonald Road in the Mid Levels, a high-rent area that makes up one section of the Peak foothills.

MacDonald Road is the first stop the Peak tram makes, a slow two-minute climb from the terminus at St. John's House; yet the incline is so precipitous that the view from even the first floors of the apartment houses is a real-estate salesman's dream.

Angela Waters had lived on the sixth-floor front, so Decker was sure that her view of the ship-clotted harbor, and the glowing brilliance of nighttime Kowloon, would have been built into the hefty rent such an address would command. But if you were on a U.S. salary in Hong Kong, it was affordable.

The lobby of the Cloud Regency Apartments looked like a set designer's idea of a billionaire's living room: antique carpets on grainy oak floors, tapestries hung on the slub cotton walls, a central chandelier like a glass Niagara, swallow-you-whole sofas and chairs. But once out of the mirrored elevator, on the sixth floor, the carpet no longer threatened to steal your shoes, and the walls were merely painted a serviceable tan.

A uniformed constable was stationed outside apartment 6B. Decker caught him in the middle of a slow tai chi movement; when you guarded an empty apartment for eight hours a day you had to make your own fun.

A sheet of paper was Scotch-taped to the door. Between the formal black letterhead of the Royal Hong Kong Police, and Chief Inspector D. Portloe's big-handed signature, was a typed message stating that the apartment had been sealed by order.

The abashed constable told Decker that the person he was asking about was staying in another apartment within the building. Decker rode the elevator six more floors, pressed the doorbell of 12B, and waited.

And went on waiting.

A second pressing brought a response, but only after a long half-minute.

"Who is it?"

A woman's voice asking.

"My name is Decker. I'd like to see Faye Keeble, please."

A bolt slid back; the door opened on a safety chain, and Decker got a glimpse of a vertical strip of face: a gray eye, a piece of nose, half a mouth. But there was enough on show to form an anxious expression.

"I'm attached to the U.S. consulate here. DEA." Decker took out his plastic and held it up, long enough for the gray eye to take a long look at it, long enough to read the smaller print, which the gray eye seemed to want to do.

The door closed, metal rasped through metal, then the door swung wide.

"I'm Faye Keeble," the woman said. "Please come in."

Decker walked into air many degrees cooler than the air in the corridor. The door closed, the woman turned into the light coming in through the big picture windows, and Decker got a good look at her other eye, the rest of her nose, the complete mouth. Seen as a whole, the face was well worth looking at. A little bit more of this and that and Decker would have called it striking.

"I'm sorry," she said, "acting like a little old lady."

A voice on the deep side, the words solid and rounded.

"Not at all. You did the right thing."

"Would you excuse me for a moment? Please sit down."

She was wearing a cotton dressing gown, wet patches at her shoulders from her damp hair; he'd caught her in the shower.

Watching her cross the apartment, a tallish, generously hipped woman, her buttocks swaying beneath the gown, snapping the folds from side to side, Decker felt a quick surge in his groin, a lurching sting of desire. He was surprised by the reaction. Sex had been a long way from his mind a moment ago, standing outside in the corridor, wondering if the woman he'd come to interview was going to be able to guess at a reason why her friend had been murdered. Now, watching her walk away in that hippy glide, he was imagining her legs, long and slender and naked beneath the gown, the cheeks of her rounded ass, the smooth hollows, the dark split dividing her thighs.

When Faye Keeble returned to the room her hair had obeyed a few fast commands of a brush, and she'd thrown on a green paisley-print shift and slid her feet into red rubber thongs. She hadn't bothered with a bra, Decker noticed; there was a full and exciting jut to the shift, a smooth, nippled roundness inadvertently shown off by a tightly drawn belt at the waist.

"Please sit down," she said again. "You're here about Angie, of course."

"That's right."

She took a seat opposite Decker, sat straight-backed against a sofa's deep cushions, and waited for him to begin talking with what seemed to be a fine, controlled presence.

Taking a longer look at her, Decker confirmed his estimation of Faye Keeble's good looks: striking, beyond question. But she would not have won any beauty contests; third place maybe, if the competition wasn't too steep. Her face was an amalgam of the good and the not-so-good: a jaw a little too round to match her slim tallness, the nose a straight bone rather than a button, with a high bridge to it and a mild suggestion of a hook. The lips, which should have been heavy and a little pouty to go with the full breasts, were instead lean and stretched a bit too wide, imparting a clamped look to her mouth, as if there were secrets held prisoner inside.

Her hair forestalled an overtly feminine look, being too short and strict. The brush she'd hastily used had arranged it in parallel wavy lines, like that of a woman just out of a swimming pool. But worn as it was, in a damp wave curling back over her head, it also put her plus features on show: skin so whitely perfect it looked edible. And eyes a misty gray color, like smoke from a fresh wood fire, the eyebrows set in faint curves, whispered lines suggesting slight surprise. A face, Decker decided, that you'd see different things in from different angles, different planes; a face he would not have minded checking out from a closer position.

She was very much the kind of woman Decker had always found attractive. Kate had been an exception: the only woman he'd ever been really involved with who could have been described as lovely. He'd never felt the tug of women who could fit into the popular conception of beauty; where most men saw glamour, he all too often saw vacancy, an absence of something. He'd found that many glamorous-looking women had discovered early on in the social whirl of their lives that good looks were all they were going to need and, accordingly, had majored in no other areas.

This woman, now, Faye Keeble, had all the signs of turning out to be a diamond mine: imperfect on the surface, but with the distinct possibility of hidden riches to be tapped.

"I understand you've been out of town, Miss Keeble."

"I've been on vacation in Thailand. I wanted to get away from the phones and the office, so I put myself out of touch, didn't tell anybody where I was going. I didn't find out about"—she hesitated for a moment, still coming to grips with it, Decker saw—"about Angela till I was stopped at the airport when I arrived back."

"And this place?" Decker indicated the apartment they were sitting in: a spacious, double-roomed living area full of good pieces of Chinese Chippendale, framed watercolors against French wallpaper, a long terrace beyond sliding glass doors giving onto a stunning northerly view. Whoever owned the place was not short of a bean.

Faye Keeble told him the apartment belonged to some friends who were away in England, and that they'd let her have it for a while. "Although I heard from the police this morning," she added. "They say I can move back into my apartment soon. But I'm in no hurry to."

"So they told you they caught the guy?"

She nodded, dropped her eyes to her hands, saw that they were tightly clasped, and untangled them. She let out breath, brought her face up, and looked at Decker for an interval before saying, "I don't recall Angie ever mentioning your name."

"I didn't know her. I've only been here four days."

"I see."

Faye Keeble went on looking at him, and Decker was very much aware of it. It was a curious, unreadable expression on her face; pink tongue licking her pale lips, her smooth neck moving as she swallowed. He wondered if she were afraid of him, nervous, after what had happened to her roommate, of being alone with a man in an apartment. And they were alone, he was certain of that; there were no sounds of anybody else moving around, no radio or TV playing anywhere. Her fear, if that's what it was, made her look extremely vulnerable sitting there, smoothing out the shift over her knees, the outline of her legs pressing against the thin green fabric, accentuating the long rounded shape of her thighs.

Vulnerable and sexy; and once more Decker felt the stabbing twinge in his loins, and was embarrassed all over again for wanting a woman he'd come to question about a dead friend. But she looked so appealing, so in need of comfort and reassurance, that Decker wanted to get up, walk over, take her by the hand, and lead her into the bedroom and take that shift off her very slowly so that her body was revealed very slowly, free those heavy breasts, watch the nipples pop and rise, get the shift down over that wide bow of her hips, down over the swoop and dip of her tummy, get his fingers damp going in beneath the dark thatch.

He cut off the thought and looked away, followed the silver interlocking lines in a cloisonné vase standing on the coffee table. Then he looked back.

The thought returned, sizzling hot and emphatic.

He wanted to fuck this woman, cover her with his body, get on top of her and protect her, hold her and tell her, while he split her, that it was okay, that it was all over, and that nobody was going to harm her while he was around.

Christ!

He wrenched the idea out of his mind again, but it was still in his body, showing up as a swelling.

For the second time he swung his gaze away from Faye Keeble, tried the spectacular vista beyond the sliding doors, then tried to think of the name of those faraway clouds hanging over the quarry scar in Sha Tin. Altostratus? Nimbostratus?

"I'd like to ask you a couple of questions, Miss Keeble, if that's okay." Decker brought his head around, concentrating on the sobering reason for his visit. "It's for the official DEA report."

"Go ahead."

"When did you first meet Angela?"

"In college. We were both at Sarah Lawrence together, graduated at the same time. Angie went back to Chicago, and I got a job in New York, but we kept in touch."

"What kind of work were you doing then?"

The question had no direct bearing, but Decker asked it because he wanted to know something about this woman; she was pulling at him like a full moon does a sea.

"The same kind of work I'm doing now," Faye Keeble answered. "I'm a securities analyst. Angie went to work for the DEA in Chicago, and was transferred here. Not long after, my firm sent me over here too, so we teamed up. Got an apartment together."

"When was that?"

"About a year back."

"Do you mind if I ask you about her personal life?" Decker said, looking into Faye Keeble's gray eyes, which were still regarding him in a manner he couldn't pin down. It wasn't fear, he saw that now; uncertainty, discomfort perhaps, but with something else folded into the mix as well, something elusive and fleeting.

Again he wondered if she could be holding on to a piece of information she wanted to keep hidden. Was that what it was? She had some kind of hole card, and was just a lousy poker player?

"Which side of her personal life?"

"The men she went out with."

"Angie went out with a lot of men. There was nobody steady."

"Did you ever double-date? You and your boyfriend?" Decker heard himself vocalize the words, had trouble believing he'd said them. What a question! But he wanted to *know* about this woman. Was there some guy in town who owned that body? Who was allowed to undress her, spread her legs, have them clench around him, feet locking behind his calves while she panted little yips of pleasure into his ear, or maybe high moaning grunts that got louder and louder and closer together until they ran into one long exhalation of release?

Decker coughed behind his fist, squirmed in his armchair.

"My boyfriend?" Faye Keeble asked. Twin lines like arrows zinged in and wounded the lovely clear skin of her high forehead. "We seem to be talking about *my* personal life, Mr. Decker."

"I'm sorry. That was just a clumsy way of asking you if you ever got to meet any of Angela's boyfriends."

"I met some," Faye Keeble said. Then, with a slight buckle in her voice, "But I never met the man the police say killed her."

"They showed you his photograph?"

"They were here about an hour ago. They said he's English. His name is Fairweather. I never heard Angela mention that name."

"Did Angela mention, let's say recently, another man who was English?"

"What's his name?"

"I don't know."

Faye Keeble moved back against the sofa cushions, but there was no relaxation in her posture; she was still tense, clenched within herself, and with the tip of her tongue going to her lips again, her mouth seemed to be drying up.

She said: "Angela probably knew a dozen men or more who were English. The social circle in Hong Kong brings you into contact with a lot of expats, as they call themselves."

Decker nodded at that, took his time before speaking again; her next answer could mean paydirt.

"The guy I have in mind has a mustache and wears a blazer and a club necktie."

"That sounds like half the Englishmen I've ever met. The older ones, anyway."

"Yeah," Decker said. He'd known it wasn't going to be that easy, and hadn't really expected a positive reply. There was just too much latitude. A blazered, mustachioed Englishman in Hong Kong? It was like asking somebody in Los Angeles if he knew somebody who drove a foreign car and owned a flashy wristwatch. "Do you have anything of Angela's I could look at? An appointment diary, something like that?"

"I could let you have what I gave the police. They brought it back today. A photo album and a scrapbook."

"That'd be great."

For no apparent reason, Faye Keeble took a fast breath, like a lap swimmer making a turn, then got up abruptly and left the room. Decker welcomed the break; it gave him a chance to get up out of his chair without revealing the embarrassing bulge which was still present in the crotch of his slacks. He pushed open the sliding doors, went out into the warmth of the terrace, and willed his blood to stop pounding. He focused his mind on the gilded buildings in Central, staked out like clumps of candlesticks five hundred feet below. The whole collection was spectacular, but there were still several standouts: the gold rocket of the Far East Finance Center—the Hakka's Tooth, as the locals called it; the soaring, circular spiral of the Hopewell Center; the Connaught Center with its zillion portholed windows turning it into an elegant cheese grater; the ribbed and rounded floors of Exchange Square rising like four stacks of bone-white saucers the sun had fused together. But the winner and grand champion was the new Hong Kong Bank Building. No building in the world had ever cost more to construct, but they'd got their money's worth: with its stressed tubular steel supports mounted on the outside of the structure, instead of on the inside, it looked like a cross between a skyscraper and a suspension bridge. Unique. Like the city stretched at its feet.

Behind him Decker heard Faye Keeble coming back into the room, coming onto the terrace carrying a glass of water. He checked his nether regions, and was relieved; there was nothing like a little modern architectural appreciation to cool the blood and stem the passions.

"I'll be able to wave to Charles and Di," Faye Keeble said. She nodded down to the left at the white wedding cake of Government House set in its own little park, the encompassing trees like thick bunches of parsley viewed from the heights of the terrace. "That's where they'll be staying, of course."

"Well, there goes the neighborhood," Decker said.

Faye Keeble smiled, seemed relieved to do so, relieved to have something else to discuss besides a hideous killing. She sipped at her water, then had a stab at playing hostess.

"Would you like some ice water? Or coffee, maybe?"

"No thanks. I'd better be leaving," Decker swiveled toward her, squinting slightly as hard daylight hit him direct. A thin track of moisture glistened on her brow; not heavy, clinging moisture, like sweat, but the kind an ice cube might leave behind.

Decker knew she'd rubbed one on her face.

Because she was hot? In an apartment where the air conditioning was just this side of chilly? Or because she was bothered?

Bothered.

This lady was definitely troubled by something.

A DEA agent comes to ask a few routine questions about a dead woman, and her ex-roommate gets flustered. Why?

An Englishman with a mustache, a blazer, and a club necktie. Did Faye Keeble know exactly who he was talking about?

What the hell was going on?

"You mentioned a photo album, Miss Keeble. And a scrapbook. Could I take them with me now?"

When she nodded, that look was back on her face, staring at him again, her eyes flicking briefly to the starburst scar on his cheekbone, her mouth going thirstily into her drink, ice cubes colliding with her white even teeth.

Standing on that sun-soaked terrace, Hong Kong a softly roaring dazzle far below, Decker got the feel of precyclone weather, the way he remembered the day standing still when he was a kid in southern Nebraska, the air like it was up on tiptoe, balancing something; static electricity humming and crackling, riding point for the gathered forces massing close by.

He was getting emanations from this woman; something skittery and nervous was dancing between them. Fragile, apprehensive.

"Miss Keeble, is there anything you'd like to tell me about Angela Waters?"

She caught the accusative note, spotted the blatant hook in the probe. But Decker didn't get the reaction he'd thought he might: a guarded retraction, a shrinking behind thin defenses. Instead Faye Keeble looked genuinely puzzled.

"What do you mean?"

"Something you didn't tell the police, perhaps."

"Like what, for instance?"

"I don't know. Something you maybe thought was none of their business."

Moving now, both of them, walking back into the living area with its framed watercolors and fine furniture and overzealous air conditioning; its plain white walls, and Faye Keeble standing out like a beacon against them, the green cotton shift clinging to her like something starved for affection; the curling wave of her hair, overmatched against Hong Kong's infamous humidity, losing some of its sweep, taking an inch away from her tallness.

"No. I told them everything. She was a lovely person. I'm going to miss her terribly. What happened to her was . . . I still . . ." Faye Keeble's swelling face stifled the words, and her control hovered on the edge.

Decker spoke quickly. "Are you a judo student, Miss Keeble?"

Any topic would do, and there was a white cotton judo outfit lying folded on a chair.

The woman's breath shuddered as she settled herself. "Yes."

"I did kendo in New York. Never got around to judo."

"I never got around to kendo," Faye Keeble said, grasping at the subject change. "I've watched it at the dojo. I'd like to try it one day."

"Which one do you go to?"

They were walking toward the door now, Faye Keeble handing him something in a bulky plastic bag.

"It's in Western. Cleverly Street. You'll let me have these back?"

"Absolutely. Thanks for talking with me, Miss Keeble."

She acknowledged that with a flutter of her hand and said, "Call me if there's anything I can help you with."

In his mind Decker said: There is something you can do for me: you can hike up that clingy shift you're wearing, slip out of your panties, stand with your legs open, and let me see just how far I can stuff my tongue up you.

Weirdly, it seemed as if she'd read his raunchy thought. Her eyes expanded the merest fraction, and she was back to looking at him in that strange, unreadable way again.

Decker mumbled another thank-you, made the door, and got out of the apartment before he made a fool of himself.

He stood in the tan corridor, on the other side of the closed door, wondering at the strength of his reaction to Faye Keeble. Why? Did she just happen to be the kind of woman that rang his gong? Or was he just feeling super horny, alone with a sexy chick just out of the shower, and his libido at oven-ready temperature?

Waiting for the elevator to arrive, Decker went over the interview, and the two entirely different reactions it had generated. He'd been close to grabbing and stripping her, and she'd seemed to be holding her breath as if dreading some loaded question she was afraid he was going to ask. So frazzled and edgy, Faye Keeble; almost as if—

Dear God in heaven!

Decker slowly turned, stared back up the corridor.

He'd never been that great at reading women's signals, signs, body language, whatever you wanted to call it. Was that what had been happening in Faye Keeble's borrowed apartment: a mutual turn-on? Was what he'd mistaken for nervous evasion actually sexual tension?

Decker took a step toward her door, then halted.

He played back the scene, viewing it from a different angle, still not certain of this new interpretation.

But what if he was correct?

His scrotum tightened, his throat tightened, his blood raced.

He walked back down the corridor. Stood outside apartment 12B looking at the metal numerals screwed into the dark-stained wood, the curling second letter of the alphabet. Maybe 12M would be more appropriate: M for mistake.

Was he about to make a big one?

He rang the bell.

The door opened.

Not on the chain this time.

"Could I see you for a moment?" Decker heard the desiccation in his throat.

Wordlessly Faye Keeble stepped back, the same uncertain expression on her face, eyes blinking, nostrils stiffening for breath.

Decker closed the door behind him, put the package she'd given him on a side table, put it there carefully and deliberately.

"I came back," he began, "because . . ."

He stopped talking, unsure of how to take it further without botching it.

Faye Keeble helped him out.

With perfectly flat intonation she said, "I know why you came back."

He waited for her to add something like, "And you're wasting your time," but she said nothing more; just stood very still, unfathomable. Waiting.

So there it was, Decker. Either go for it or get out.

He stepped closer, put his arms lightly on her shoulders where she could brush them aside if she had a mind to.

Faye Keeble did nothing, just watched him with those large gray eyes, a soft liquid depth to them.

Decker kissed the corner of her mouth, a tentative move, unsure and experimental.

There was no resistance, but neither was there acceptance. She kept her hands at her sides, stiff and tight like her body; he could feel the tension zinging through her like a plucked guitar string.

Decker kissed her again, just as lightly as before, and again there was nothing there. And yet it wasn't the response of a woman rebuffing an unwelcome advance, turning herself into a block of wood, because her mouth was slightly parted, enough to give him access to the soft, silky inside of her bottom lip.

But it was still just a kiss; passive allowance at best.

Decker gave her the chance to give him an emphatic no. He slipped the tip of his tongue just inside the edge of her teeth, and got ready for a sharp stab of rejection.

It wasn't forthcoming.

Faye Keeble's mouth opened like a flower in the sun. She made a sound like a sigh, and tried to snake her tongue around his, her body sloping in against his hardness as her arms slid around him, her pelvis rising in a slow-motion hip thrust.

They didn't even make the bedroom.

They pulled and jerked at each other's clothes; popped buttons, stretched elastic as if the garments were on fire and had to be got rid of before they burned flesh.

They clashed together like two breathless people getting air from each other's mouths.

They wrenched apart, went at necks and faces.

He spun her around, backed her up against him, his cock rigid beneath the perfect globes of her bottom, not yet entering her but grasping her to him, hands cupping her breasts, fingers nippling her, teeth worrying the slim muscle along the smooth white ridge of her shoulder.

She twisted back, spun into him, going for his mouth, stretching up on her toes when his fingertips squished into her dark ripe fruit. They wanted the impossible: everything at once; hands and mouths all over one another.

Decker dropped to his knees, exactly as he'd imagined himself doing not three minutes back. She half-crouched to accommodate him, grasped the back of his head as he fastened his mouth on her yoni, tongue deep-probing, rocking violently the man in the boat.

He pulled at her hips and, like clumsy wrestlers, they tumbled to the broadloom in a combined collapse, instantly melded together, and pumped and bucked and thrashed against each other for a few furious moments, their voices melding too, crying out, gasping as they shared a stupendous shuddering climax.

They flopped like limp, boneless things, separated, flaked out on the thick broadloom, and sucked air in response to the thump and charge of their pulses.

For five minutes they lay there, a soft, acrylic prickle at their backs, gazing up at the decorative molding on the ceiling. And thinking.

Then Faye Keeble rose, took Decker's hand, led him into a lacy, blue-painted bedroom, and stripped the bed of its counterpane, baring the slightly mussed sheets she'd slept between last night. They did everything they'd done out in the living room, but at a far slower pace. They savored each other, making up for their initial hectic clash with careful, pronounced movements and little considerations; silent questions asked and answered, pleasuring in their bodies' swap and exchange.

Still later, the light shifting in the bedroom, the sun angling louvered shadows against the blue wall, they lay side by side again, basted in their sweat, sweetly marinating in their fluids, the room funkily perfumed by their spent bodies.

There were few sounds to break their thoughts: some high cries of children dashing down the exterior corridor faded quickly, leaving a faint residue of traffic noise wafted up the slope form Central by a hot harbor breeze.

It was Faye who eventually snapped their silence.

"I want to explain why this happened so I can listen to myself and understand."

Decker rolled over onto his tummy, one side of him mitered into her, his face close to the shampoo scent of her neck.

"Go ahead," he said, wondering why he'd thought Faye Keeble

wasn't lovely. He traced a finger around the swift curve of her jaw and over the sensuous lips he'd thought thin and repressed. From a fine high cheekbone he brushed away a tiny droplet, the product of a glistening line of moisture rimming her hairline. Thick and richly textured, her hair was a glossy chestnut color, qualities that, for some reason, he'd always associated only with tresses that were long and flowing.

"I want you to understand too," Faye said. "Because I don't want you to be fooled."

Decker watched her eyes switch from the ceiling to his face. He knew those orbs pretty well now. A thin slash of faded blue liner at the corners seemed to tug at the big round irises, pulling them into an apparent elongation. The lashes were long and spaced, their upward curl emphasizing the mildly surprised look her eyes awarded her face. She'd kept those eyes on him all through the lovemaking in this bedroom; prettier than gray, they were getting on toward blue—quiet, deep receptors opened wide for a message; trying to glean something, trying to read him.

"I'm not going to tell you," she went on, "that this is the first time I've ever done anything like this, because it would sound trite. Even though it would be true."

When she drew breath and swallowed, the tip of her tongue licked briefly at her upper lip, and Decker had to resist the impulse to trap it with his mouth and taste it again like a luscious pink bonbon. He thought about his candy comparison: the lover as sweet-toothed cannibal.

"I just needed somebody," Faye said simply. "Pretty badly, as I'm sure I demonstrated. I'm sorry to be so frank."

"Don't be. You haven't wounded me. I didn't think what happened happened because I drive women crazy with my hot Latin glances."

She drew away from him a few inches, just enough to put a little sober distance between them.

"You're thinking it was because of Angela, aren't you? That I was scared and needed . . ." She broke off to consider the direction the sentence should take . . . "Whatever a person needs when they're brushed by a horrible death. Well, that certainly has to be part of it. But not the main part."

Perched above her now, not that far away from her kiss-bruised mouth, Decker waited for her to continue; then, realizing what she was about to say, beat her to it.

"Somebody walked out on you."

Faye Keeble, slowed by Decker's unexpected prescience, said, after a moment, "How did you know? Was mine a cliché reaction?"

"I knew because I managed to lose someone too." Decker followed the confession with a shrug of his uppermost shoulder. "I still would've tried to jump your bones, a sexy woman just out of the shower, the two of us alone in an apartment on a warm and lazy day, but it wouldn't have been anywhere near as intense."

Faye moved her head in a tiny affirmation. His words seemed to make her feel better about the situation, as if, having been used herself, she didn't feel so guilty about using him.

"I met him here," she said. "Knew him for about eight months. We worked in the same office. Then he was transferred to Tokyo, and when I told him how much I liked Tokyo, he said he'd send me a card."

"And off he went, huh?"

"And off he went. So off I went. Flew down to Bangkok to wander the temples and buy a splint for my busted heart."

"Is it knitting together okay?"

"Slowly. But it's going to be a bit stiff for a while." Faye let him have half of a quick smile, embarrassed by her part of the conversation, but needing to get it out. "I'm twenty-eight years old, and I was crazy about him like I was eighteen years old. It's nice to fall in love, but it's bloody awful if you get in too deep and get stuck with it."

"Sounds like you've been burned before."

"Not this badly. This time it was third-degree, with bandages up to my neck."

Decker noted the second use of a medical analogy—splint, bandages—paraphernalia of the hurt and damaged.

"And you?" Faye asked, moving back closer to him, closing the gap she'd opened up. "You were left behind too?"

"No. I was the one who did the leaving. Also a transfer. I was working here in Hong Kong, and I got shifted back to New York."

"And you didn't ask her to go with you?"

"It was high on my list of things to do, but I left in kind of a hurry."

"Too fast to make a phone call, huh?"

"Ouch," Decker said. "Yeah, you're right. I could've done something about it, and I didn't. At first, when I started missing her, I was seriously thinking about making that phone call. But New

York's full of attractions, lots of legs walking around that town, and it took the edge off the memories. Then when I found out I was coming back here for a while, I suddenly remembered how crazy I was about her."

"But she was no longer available."

"You must have a script," Decker said. "Yep, I let geography dictate my feelings. Always the easiest way of handling things." He looked away from her steady gaze, forced by it to examine his actions. "I behaved like a bastard, right?"

"It depends. Did you have an understanding with her?"

"Nothing I could get sued over. I mean, there was nothing ever said, but lots that was probably assumed."

"Then you didn't behave like a bastard. You merely behaved like an idiot."

Decker grunted, gave her a tight little grin. "I'm pretty talented at that role."

Faye raised a finger to the indentation beneath Decker's eye, traced the ridged folds of its star shape.

"Wounds," she said. "Some people have them on show, some don't."

Decker kissed her cheek, gentled her hair with his fingertips. The gesture changed her eyes, and she regarded him in a way she hadn't displayed before: a question there, although of what kind exactly, Decker couldn't have said. He'd never met a woman so difficult to fathom, and he wondered if that were part of the reason why Faye Keeble's appeal was sneaking up on him with increasing intensity.

She lifted her arms, crossed them behind his head, brought him down to her.

The way they made love this time was different yet again. They took turns moving on each other, slow, measured performances full of awareness, empathy. But the excitement was still there, in some ways higher and headier than it had been during their first urgent coupling, a deep and sense-numbing pleasure that enveloped them in a warm skein of contentment.

Separated, on their backs, side by side once more, they watched the new slant of the louvered shadow on the blue wall. It had made quite a bit of progress, and was now burnishing the silvered frame surrounding a wash drawing of a Chinese orchid.

"What's his name?" Decker asked.

"Ray."

A pause for the shadow to shift marginally, or appear to.

"What's her name?"

"Kate."

Another pause. The shadow snuck toward the purple flower as if it meant to trim its spotted abundance.

Decker said, "I think that was us that time."

Faye turned her head toward him, moved in closer.

"That's a nice thought."

They began to talk, words coming easily, flowing from them now. They talked about themselves—their jobs, interests—began to know each other.

"Were you sad or glad to leave Hong Kong? I mean apart from having to leave Kate behind."

"Sad. I love this town. Also, I didn't leave it the way I would've liked. I was booted out. That was part of the reason why I left Kate here."

"Why? Why were you kicked out?"

"Screwed up on the job."

"I'm surprised," Faye said. "I would have said you're very good at your job."

"Sure. I do a good job. It's just that every now and then, well"— Decker smacked his lips together, shook his head, some sadness and regret in the movement—"I blow it."

She asked him what had happened here in Hong Kong, and Decker wondered for a moment if the question was some kind of test she'd set him; would he politely evade it because it was none of her business? Or answer it and so pay her the compliment of including her in a very personal part of his history? Quite a few people in New York had eventually got around to asking him why he'd been thrown out, but he'd never told anybody the real reason. However, he found that he wanted to tell Faye Keeble; to do so would be a kind of sharing of himself, and he hadn't done much of that with a woman for a long, long time.

In fact, not since Kate.

There'd been a lot of women in New York, several of whom he'd seen for more than just a few weeks. There'd even been a couple of relationships which could have been described as firm. But none of which could have been called close.

"I made two mistakes," Decker said, "The first was thinking that I was a smarter narc than this chief inspector at Arsenal Street. Police headquarters. I hear he's retired now. Anyway, I had this informant, a Straw Sandal in the Chuen Kwan Lok."

"A what?"

"A messenger in one of the big triad lodges. The Chuen Kwan Lok runs the brothels in Yau Ma Tei, and the fishing junks in the shelter. At that time the dope was coming in on Thai trawlers and being dropped off near the outer islands for the local junks to pick up. This guy's info was one-hundred-percent reliable because he wanted to emigrate to the States, and wanted me to write a sugar letter for him."

"You'll have to explain that one too," Faye said, reaching down for a sheet to cover them. The air conditioning was making itself felt as their bodies cooled, the moisture on their skin beginning to chill them.

"A sugar letter? A letter of recommendation he could flash at the consulate. They don't do anybody any good, and I explained that, but the Chinese think the State Department operates on squeeze and influence like their government departments, and you can't tell 'em different."

"So he was willing to talk . . ."

"Talk?" Decker whistled a curving note. "Lady, that guy babbled. He wanted to score points, and he could, because he was right in there, part of the chain. He knew which junk in the shelter was going out to make the catch, where the pickup point was, and when it was supposed to happen. So I passed all this on to this chief inspector, because the DEA can't make an arrest outside of the United States. We can only sit on the bench and coach."

"I know. Angie told me that."

Decker noticed that she was able to say the name as she'd said any other; no hesitation, no tremor. Because she was feeling safe? Even though she was just six floors above an apartment where her friend and roommate had been bloodbathed? If that were true, if she felt secure now, that would be a very nice thing: great for her, and a hell of a compliment.

"My triad guy fed me info on two separate occasions," Decker told her. "He waited till he knew it was surefire stuff. And I passed on that information both times. To Arsenal Street. And both times this narcotics cop, the chief inspector, went out and intercepted a junk. He tossed those two boats up, down, and sideways and couldn't even come up with a pack of aspirin. Clean clear through. And yet the stuff was on board. Exactly where, my guy couldn't tell me. But there was no question about it. He knew for definite sure it was somewhere on those boats."

Faye levered herself up and assumed the position Decker had been in a little while back: propped up on one elbow and looking down at him. With her shoulders raised, her breasts hung a full and irresistible invitation, and Decker kissed the goose bumps ringing the large pink areolae, not so much a sexual thing, more a gesture of closeness, intimacy.

Faye dropped her head, brushed her lips against the bridge of his nose, moved back, waiting for him to tell his story.

"He came to me a third time, my guy, the Straw Sandal. He told me he had something that really was worth a sugar letter. Maybe two. There were twenty keys coming in. To Stanley. Told me when, told me which junk. Same thing all over again. So I met with the narcotics cop and politely told him to search the goddamn junk properly this time. The captain had clearly found a new wrinkle, some new way of either wrapping the base or hiding it in the traditional five-pound bags. We had a little discussion at the top of our voices. He called me an interfering Yankee bastard, I called him an incompetent Limey son of a bitch. Then we both felt better. So he went out to intercept the junk, even though he was positive this trip would be as big a waste of time as the other two had been."

Decker paused; he wasn't looking at Faye but at the opaque glass bulb cover fixed to the ceiling. And he wasn't seeing that; he was seeing a dark beach and a crumbling jetty, and a hot, moonless night a year and a half back.

"But I was ready this time. I went over to Stanley and hired a sampan with a couple of Caterpillar D four-hundreds powering it. And I also hired six horn-fisted fishermen and passed out tire irons. We followed the police launch right out past Wong Ma Kok, and watched the cops intercept the junk coming into the bay. It was coming from Waglan Island, the little one with the lighthouse, a drop-off point for the Thai trawlers. Toss the stuff over the side in waterproof bags, the junks would haul it up, sail it in.

"Anyway, the narcotics team was on that junk for two hours, tossing it pretty good. I mean, the guy tried. Then they started back toward Stanley. I had the sampan brought over in front of the launch. The guy nearly blew a fuse demanding to know what the hell I was doing out there. No right, gross interference, et cetera, et cetera, blah, blah, blah. Part of the reason he was so mad was that he'd come up empty again. So I waited till the launch had burbled off, then went out and boarded the junk."

"What did the junk crew think about that?"

"It didn't matter what they thought. I had these hard-case fishermen with tire irons backing me up. I told the captain I was going to toss his boat. He knew who I was, or what I was. I speak passable Cantonese, but I can't get rid of the American accent, so he had me pegged for DEA. I wasn't the cops, I certainly wasn't a rival lodge, so who else could I have been?"

"I went on a junk once," Faye said. "It looked like a wrecker's yard. How do you search something like that?"

"It ain't easy. I put a man over the side first, see if they were trailing anything. He went under the keel too. Nothing. So then we started inboard. A nightmare. We lifted, unrolled, untwisted, prized, poked, broke open. I sent a man up the masts, into the sails, even took up the bilge boards, which was an aromatic experience I don't recommend. Nada. Zilch."

"Were you beginning to think that maybe it wasn't there?"

Decker moved his head in a slow negative. "No way. My guy was a Four Three Two boy, a Cho Hai. He helped set up the collections, so he *knew*. And he wanted that letter from me. So I kept on looking, rechecked everything, top to bottom, stem to stern. And all the time that junk captain just watched me work, grinning at me, enjoying himself.

"We were playing button, button, and he knew where it was and the gweilo couldn't find it. He even decided to have dinner while he watched. You know how the Chinese are, if they're not doing anything, they'll start cooking. That's what he did, got a wok going over a butane stove, and just stood there eating pieces of fish and leering at me, watching the Big Nose strike out. And, oh boy, did I want to find that stuff! I wanted to see that captain choke on his foo yung when I found it. I wanted to take the stuff back to Stanley, throw it at the narcotics cop, and say, What do you think that is, sporto, baking powder?"

Decker swallowed, rubbed a finger quickly at a spot on his eyebrow. When he spoke again, slower and more deliberately, the color had drained from his voice. He sounded flat, punctured.

"About an hour later I realized I wasn't going to find it. I knew I'd be going back to Stanley with nothing to show, and I could've lived with that, I guess. But knowing beyond a doubt that the dope was there somewhere, and that that leering, grinning junk captain was gonna beat me, well . . . I just did my nut. Flew off the handle."

Very still now, Faye waited for him to conclude.

"I ordered everybody off the junk and into the sampan. The captain, the crew, everybody. I grabbed an ax and ran down below-decks, down to where we'd pulled up the bilge boards. It was wet and slimy and reeked of fish and garbage and God knows what, and I went at the wooden hull with the ax. Chopped a hole in the fucking thing. Came out of there covered in seawater and slime, hopped into the sampan, and watched that junk settle and disappear. Thirty fathoms to the bottom of Tai Tam Bay."

Decker let out some breath. Faye felt his shoulders rise in the ghost of a shrug, a hapless movement.

"Two days later I was escorted to the airport and put on a plane for Los Angeles. So that's what daddy did in the war. Pretty dumb, huh?"

Faye allowed some time to pass before she spoke; she sensed that telling the story had cost Decker something, and she was pretty sure, by the way it had affected him—living it, not just relating it—that he hadn't done it all that often.

"Were you ever vindicated? About the drugs?"

"What, the new wrinkle? Oh, sure. It was a beauty. Remember I told you the captain was eating while we went through the junk? Cooking with butane? A fat steel bottle, two feet high, fifteen inches across. You've seen 'em, usually painted blue, and beat-up, paint peeling off them. Turned out that most of that bottle didn't contain gas. It'd been cut near the top and fitted back on again so neatly you'd never spot it in a zillion years. Two canisters in one. Enough gas in the top part to run a burner for an hour or two. The dope was in the lower part. Ten keys. The other ten keys was in another butane bottle. They got a lot of weight in that way, not that the discovery did me any good. I was long gone by that time."

Decker suddenly felt strangled by the sheet that was covering them. He tossed it aside, swung his legs over, sat on the edge of the bed. Faye sat up with him, but not touching him, recognizing the discomfort the recounting had brought on.

"Look," she said, trying to lighten it. "You were right and you were wrong. The drugs were there, and that makes you right. But you blew your top. Maybe you shouldn't have, but it can happen to anybody."

"Thanks, but you have to blow pretty big to do what I did. And besides, it wasn't just a one-time thing. I did something similar in New York. It wasn't quite as spectacular as scuttling an entire Chinese junk, but it was enough to make an idiot of myself again."

"When did this happen?"

"A little over a week ago."

"But you said—" Faye cut herself off, shook her head in a forget-it gesture.

Decker got off the bed, moved his shoulders, swung his arms, feeling freer now.

"Hey, I got an idea. Let's take a fast shower, go have a few drinks, eat a little Chinee, come back here and take a slow shower."

"That's just about what I was going to suggest," Faye said.

They did, more or less, what Decker had proposed: spent a long time over drinks talking about themselves, talking about Angela Waters, took a long time over dinner, returned to the apartment, and got back into bed.

It was midnight by the time Decker made it back to his hotel, but his head was too full of Faye Keeble to get to sleep right away. He was still having trouble believing it had happened the way it had; astonished, too, at its swift development. They'd met around three in the afternoon, two people with an itch to scratch, and had ended up eight hours later half in love with each other. He wondered if Faye was thinking the same as he was, mistrusting the circumstances. If they'd met in a normal way, neither of them coming off a bad romantic trip, would a relationship still have blossomed?

And did it matter worth a damn anyway how two people came together?

Decker finally dozed off into a thin layer of sleep, the street outside quiet for the night, the thump of the faulty air conditioner a low mumbling lullaby.

Had he been sleeping deeply, he probably wouldn't have heard the sound that woke him.

It had been like a key fitting into a lock; somebody out in the corridor—probably some late-arriving drunk trying to get into the wrong room.

He listened for other sounds.

There weren't any.

Whoever had been outside the door had gone away.

Decker closed his eyes again, tried to conjure up his sleep mantra, a visual one: a little white rowboat that would rock him gently, drift him into a still lagoon.

He had it drawn up alongside him, about to board it, when a certain, sure knowledge jerked him wide-awake.

He was lying facing the wall, wearing just pajama bottoms, his back naked, the covers down at the end of the bed.

Under his arms pores popped moisture, and the skin between his shoulder blades tweaked and prickled, picking up the radar bounce given off by somebody's stealth.

The saliva under his tongue vanished and sawdust seemed to fill his throat.

He knew he was no longer alone in the room.

Dark in the room, but not pitch black, his naked back a broad and easy target. Yet Decker stayed quite still, trying to breathe as if sleep had hold of him.

Lying on a bed in the Orient, with his back to the room.

From fifteen feet out a Japanese with a knife would have begun his rush. The Chinese liked to creep up all the way, make sure with the first thrust. And whoever was in the room with him would certainly be Chinese: one of Eddie Fong's associates.

Decker listened for the squeak of the floorboard, the one that was loose underneath the ratty carpet, and thought about a weapon: a glass ashtray, a water jug, something.

The bedside table held a lamp with a burnt brown shade which might have done had it not been tethered by a very short lead. There was nothing else within easy reach except the Sayings of Buddha, left there to compete with the Gideons' offering.

But there was always something you could use. Decker had been taught that a weapon didn't have to be hard or sharp, and there was something right under his head that was neither; and not a bad thing against a man with a knife. And there would be a knife, because Hong Kong was Blade City.

Brain cool, body hot. Sweat dropped into a hollow of his rib cage, took a wet ride down his flank.

A noise then, just on the edge of sound.

Not the floorboard pinching against a joist, but wood against wood all the same: the wardrobe door being eased open.

The taste of salt fell onto his lip, the sheet dampening beneath him. The smell of sweat would tell a good man that his hit was awake and waiting, so Decker knew he had to make his move now.

His right hand had crept very, very slowly toward the old-fashioned switch on the cord of the lamp. He needed light; in the dark the advantage has to be with the man who can chop and cut. His left hand was also in motion, taking a good grip on the pillow that cradled his head. He risked doing nothing for a half-second more, coiling himself, holding his breath, then did two things at the same time: hit the lamp switch and, in a fast, explosive movement, threw himself the other way, toward the room.

He spun across the bed, landed on the floor on his feet, his momentum surging him forward.

The intruder, shocked by the light, whirled around from the open wardrobe in time to take a stinging, blinding blow: Decker backhanding him, wapping him with the pillow full in the face.

It stopped the man cold, long enough for Decker to get in a heel shot at the man's knee. It hit too high, but was still enough to tumble him. The man fell, rolled against the wall, and came up again headfirst, like a sprinter getting out of the blocks. Decker swung the wardrobe door into a shaven skull.

The man collapsed, falling forward this time, and Decker dived on him. He pinned his arms, searched quickly for a sleeve or leg scabbard, checked back pockets.

Not even a flick knife. And there'd been nothing in his hand when he'd gone down.

Decker got up off him, stood over him, one hand protecting his groin. The man, who looked to be no more than twenty, was blinking and stretching his jaw as if his ears were popping.

"Ney gue mut yea meng?" What's your name? Decker asked, chopping harsh Cantonese at him.

"Yun. Yun Kai Lo."

"Who're you with? Speak!"

"Nobody. I never joined." The youth had a Swatow accent, his tones produced from the front of his mouth. They came out a little groggily; the wardrobe door wasn't light, and the bottom half was now split.

"Yeah? How many meals you had?"

"What?"

"Three and a half, right? You're black society." Decker was referring to a lodge initiation ceremony where the Incense Master pricked the new member's thumb. The initiate then ate fruit, which counted as one meal, drank water, which counted as two meals, red date wine, three meals, and sucked his bleeding finger, which was half a meal.

The youth wobbled his wounded head, partly to clear it, partly to further deny the accusation.

"I'm not black society. I'm against black society."

"Listen, you cow's egg. I saw you the other night in the Sai Gai billiard hall. You're San Hop Sin. Where are your cards? Show me your cards."

Decker had never seen him before. He was accusing him of belonging to a triad gang, an indictable offense in Hong Kong, to get him scared and malleable. He knew the kid wasn't connected; no eagles flew on his arms, no tigers reared in red tattoo. And he babbled instead of lapsing into a bored, superior silence.

"No cards. I never got into it."

"Pig shit! The night clerk's a Sze Kau in the Heavenly Queen. He let you in here, didn't he?"

"No. I bought a key," the youth sputtered, scared, caught out, authority threatening him. "From the floor maid. I swear it." He fumbled in his pocket, brought out a poorly cut blank, held it toward Decker like an offering for an angry god. Decker accepted it with a relief he didn't let show; the kid was a hotel thief looking for cash, traveler's checks. He could have been an amateur from Eddie Fong's crowd, an expendable soldier sent to check out the castle defenses. Decker didn't want that; he was hoping that Eddie would stay straight this time, and take him in for real.

"I don't know," Decker said, a tall Westerner with long, lean muscles standing over a Chinese youth. "Maybe you're a Hung Kwan." It was a ridiculous suggestion; a Hung Kwan was a Red Pole, a lodge enforcer, and they were usually forty-year-old tough-buddy thugs with knife scars and faces flattened by bamboo canes.

"No." The youth stroked a hand over his sore head and dropped his eyes. "I'm a thief."

"If you are, you're a rotten one. Get up."

The boy made it to his feet, then took a woozy second to reply when Decker asked him where he lived.

"The Ming Wah Estate."

Decker knew it: east near Shau Ki Wan, about three thousand families living in concrete sky rockets; father, mother, big brothers, little sisters working with their hands all day, then coming home and taking the elevator to the thirty-third floor. But not to a penthouse; to a shoebox apartment shared with a cousin, an uncle, and a couple of elderly grandparents. This was Hong Kong. Everybody ate as long as everybody worked. This was the "too" city—too many people in too little space, too much competition for too few jobs. And if you were too sick or too old or too tired or too infirm to go out and compete, that was too fucking bad.

"What did you say your name was?"

"Yun Kai Lo."

"What do you do in the daytime?"

"I'm a street sweeper in the Ma Shan village."

"And the pay's miserable, right?"

"Yes."

"And your family relies on you to bring home money, don't they?"

Flushed with shame, the youth spoke to the floor. "That's why I steal."

"Yun, if I'd had a knife in my hand a minute ago, instead of a pillow, the most you would've brought home tonight would have been your dying body. Correct?"

The boy's shaven head, a duck's egg rising on it, nodded mournfully.

"Okay," Decker said. "So maybe a sweeper's pay is miserable, but it's more than a dead man makes. Now, get out of here. Go on home. And stay away from the floor maid."

The youth walked unsteadily across the room, paused for a second, and said politely, "M'goi nai," then let himself out, quietly closing the door he'd opened with such high expectations.

Decker double-locked it after him, got back into bed, and lay there waiting for his pulses to slow. There was no doubt about it, it certainly did get the adrenaline pumping when you thought a steel blade was heading for your gut. It occurred to him, without too much effort, that if that kid had been black society, a 426 boy, say, with a beef knife in his fist, then Special Agent Hugh C. Decker, GS 14, DEA, TDY Hong Kong, would be lying in a mess of blood and slashed foam rubber.

He had to have a weapon. Eddie Fong could go either way: play ball or say fuck it and send a fighter after him.

Okay, a weapon. Something a little more efficacious than a lumpy hotel pillow. He'd heard of an agent in Kyoto, sometime back, who, similarly banned from carrying a gun, had bought himself a perfectly legal antique sword. Another had carried a weighted sap, and worn safety shoes with steel caps in the toes.

A sap was no good; a man with a knife had the reach on you. Swing at him and, if he was any good, he could slash an arm artery, then while you thought about that, move in and hash your kidneys for you. And a sword was too final. Had he had one tonight, Decker realized, he would have slaughtered a twenty-year-old street sweeper, which would have been another small blot on his record. Not to mention the blot on the street sweeper's record.

A weapon.

Legal, effective, and something he could carry without raising too many eyebrows.

It took Decker several hours before he got an idea. And that idea segued naturally into another.

His mind was back in the apartment with Faye, when he'd been lying close to her telling her how he'd scuttled the junk, and how he'd screwed up again later in New York, blown his top again. She'd started a question saying, "But you said—" and had stifled it. He knew now what she'd been on the brink of saying. She hadn't completed it because it could have sounded accusatory, a little too personal for that early stage of the relationship.

"But you said you'd studied kendo in New York," was what she had planned to say.

She studied judo, so she knew what they taught you in the Oriental martial arts: that the head governs the hands. Which was why they called them disciplines. She'd been surprised that, having studied kendo, he hadn't learned discipline.

Well, he could have answered that, if she hadn't been too polite to finish her observation. The kendo he'd studied had been sport kendo, ninety percent action, ten percent intellectual application. Also, the school was a cheap one, around the corner from where he lived in Chelsea. The master, a Korean, had gone American and was just out for the bucks. It was a lousy school, come to think of it, and it certainly hadn't given him what it should have. But then, maybe he hadn't gone looking for that side of it anyway.

Okay. Tomorrow was another day.

Correction. Tomorrow was already here: a gray streak of light was bending past a corner of the window curtain where it dropped from a broken ring. Decker closed his eyes, whistled up the little white rowboat, got in. And this time made it all the way out on the still, placid waters of the sleepy lagoon.

9

A gentleman's umbrella.

That was the object that Decker went looking for bright and
early that morning. He found one in a shop in the Prince's Building, a men's outfitters trying hard to reproduce the restrained opu-
lence of Bond Street and Savile Row.

The umbrella was plain black, very large, and with a traditional
curved handle. It would have been perfect for a bankers' golf tour-
nament on a wet day.

Decker took a cab through Sheung Wan into Kennedy Town, the
western edge of Hong Kong Island. It was old here, an unchanged
prewar district, the waterfront, called the Praya, thick with lighters
just in from working cargo ships out in the roads. They were part
barge, part house, these lighters, with green-painted superstructures
and red-painted living quarters, the upper decks looking like apartment balconies with their jumble of potted plants and washing
spread for the sun. Deck cranes moaned and squealed swinging sack
after sack onto rusty blue trucks, or straight onto the bent backs of
laborers for the short, staggering trip across the Praya to dark and
cavernous godowns.

Decker watched all this noisy industry as his taxi took him down
the aptly named Belcher's Street, and round into Cathick Street,
the spicy jute aroma of the godowns swamped now by the heavy
blood smell of the abattoir and the fresh-meat wholesale market,
their floor gutters running red.

Facing the market was one of the ugliest apartment houses in the
city: only five stories high, and running back for half a block, it
appeared to be constructed entirely of filthy glass panes and paint-
chipped metal window frames. In miniature it might have resem-

bled a glass cigarette box that had been buried in a garbage dump for two years. There were a number of grubby shops at street level: a ship chandler's selling used merchandise, mainly coils of stained rope and dented brass, the inevitable duck and noodle stands, whose cooked products also looked stained and dented, something called the Kai Dang Welfare Association, and the place Decker had come to visit: a metalworking business. It was no bigger than a one-car garage, the interior stacked to the roof with a fantastic mélange of bronze and tin and aluminum jumbled together like the aftermath of an explosion. The workshop was the sidewalk.

Two men in shorts and undershirts banged heavy hammers on galvanized iron, shaping what looked to be a commercial air duct. They drank from pop bottles as they worked, warding off the heat of a compatriot's flaring acetylene torch, and that of the already humid morning. They seemed glad to stop their cacophonous din and talk to Decker. He explained to the boss man what he wanted.

The man took the umbrella, opened it, examined it, and nodded a can-do. He accepted some money, told Decker when to return, took a swig of Fanta, and resumed his hot and deafening trade.

Decker cabbed it back to Western to a herbal shop he knew on the Bonham Strand. They had a pay phone inside their aromatic door, and a phone book in good condition. He called the office. Hilary, the young secretary, had a message for him from Johnny Risotto: be there at noon. He said he would, then hung up and checked the phone book. He got the name and address of the martial-arts school Faye had told him about, the one on Cleverly Street. It wasn't far. Decker walked it.

The dojo was upstairs on the second level of an old stone building. It wasn't very impressive—most dojos weren't—an empty space the size of a basketball court, broken by four thick pillars supporting a stamped tin ceiling, a sanded and lacquered wooden floor, rough brick walls painted a pale cream, and some makiwara at one end of the hall, punching boards for Tang Hand, as the Chinese called Karate. In the center of the floor a group of middle-aged men and women posed in balletic slow motion: midmorning devotees of tai chi chuan, "soft fist" Chinese boxing. Decker had taken lessons during his time in Hong Kong, not that it had done him much good; he'd mastered the physical aspects, but the mental state, the structured thinking, had eluded him, overwhelmed by his own particular devil.

Decker watched the class rock with smooth grace onto their back feet, front feet raised on poised heels, extended fingers moving like languid underwater creatures to positions of attack and defense. The various moves, their names and meanings, came easily to his memory: weight to the left leg, pivot on right heel, grasp the bird's tail.

Circle hands past waist level, palms facing down, form a right loose foot, and the white stork spreads its wings.

Strike, parry, punch.

Part the horse's mane. Fair lady works at shuttle. Ride the wild tiger. Lower the left arm, circle the right hand, step forward and repulse the monkey. Lovely stuff.

Decker watched the class break up, head for the changing rooms. He thought he had the floor to himself until he saw a man step from behind a pillar pushing a soft dry mop over the boards. Decker moved onto the floor, bowed to the dojo, as etiquette demanded, and walked toward the man.

He wore a navy-blue quilted keikogi jacket that looked hand-made, and black, wide-pleated hakama trousers, bare feet showing beneath them. Even if the jacket hadn't been navy blue, the teachers' color, Decker would have recognized him as a yudansha, a man of dan rank, by the way he held the mop handle—fingers and thumb perfectly laced around it, hands wide apart—and by the way he worked it over the floor: with short, considered movements, strong and economical. He looked Japanese, and was perhaps nearing sixty, with a lined forehead and a web of twisted skin closing one eye. He stood straight-backed, a slight-bodied man who seemed underweight, thin hair graying at the wings and caught behind in a short pigtail.

"Can I help you?" he asked, stopping his chore. His English had very little accent.

"I wanted to ask about instruction. In kendo."

"Are you a beginner?"

"A novice. I had fifteen, sixteen months' instruction in New York."

The master appeared to need time to process this information, his dark eyes taking in Decker's breadth of shoulder, then straying to the asterisk incision on his cheekbone. Decker noticed the ridged knuckles, the sinewy wrists, and wondered about the man's ruined eye, wondered who'd been good enough to do that to a yudansha.

For a long moment they stood in silence, two scarred men on a deserted dojo floor, the recognition of power and strength a mutual one. The master told Decker he'd need to assess his ability in the discipline in order to assign him to a class. He called an assistant, who escorted Decker to the changing room and found some gear for him. Decker came back onto the floor wearing the uniform of a novice: white jacket criss-crossed with heavy black stitching—a design like a star map—and flowing black pants hanging wide and loose like a woman's formal skirt. He wore body armor made from thick wadded leather, a lacquered bamboo tare—an apron designed to protect stomach and hips—and heavy gauntlets on his hands.

The master, waiting for him in the middle of the floor, was wearing similar equipment, with the addition of a face mask resting on flaring shoulder pads. The mask was protected by a horizontal steel grid and was divided down the center by a single vertical steel bar. It looked like the eye of a giant insect, all-seeing, unwavering. Decker didn't have a mask; he didn't need one: a dan-rank teacher didn't make any mistakes with a student.

The master held two shinai, long bamboo swords capped at the ends with protective rubber tips. Decker accepted one, stepped back, bowed, and assumed the middle position, ready for basic practice. The master peered at him through the grille.

"Did you not sit mokuzu in New York?"

"Pardon?"

"Mokuzu. Before and after training, it is important to rest and compose the mind."

"We never did that," Decker said, adding, in the resulting silence, "It wasn't a very good school."

Behind the mask the master's face was without expression, his voice polite but flat.

"Which style were you taught?"

"Kendo-kata. We learned the standard ten sword forms, and the names of the cuts and thrusts."

"Very well. I would like you to demonstrate them, please." The master bowed and stepped back, and like Decker, assumed the middle position: body upright, one foot advanced, sword held straight out from the waist, almost like a man carrying a flag in a parade. He took a breath, breathing from the bottom of his diaphragm, exhaled, and said, harshly, sharply, *"Shomen!"*

Decker responded with what somebody who'd never seen kendo before would have thought was phenomenal speed. His bamboo sword flashed above his head, his elbows already bringing it slashing down again as he lunged forward shouting the attacking kiai. *"Ya!"*

The blow would have landed on top of the master's mask with a fearful crack had the master's sword not deflected it with an easy grace.

"Hidari-men!" the Japanese cried. It was the second exercise, an oblique cut at the left temple.

Decker went straight into it, swooping around, getting his wrists and forearms into a fierce slice that warped the air.

It was parried with ease.

"Migi-men!"

A shot at the right temple this time, which, once again, didn't come close to finding its mark.

There were five more cuts and thrusts, all performed with increasing strength and speed; the clash of swords, the shouts of the attacking *"Ya!"* and the defensive *"Ho!"*

Eight chances Decker got, and he couldn't even get near the Japanese. When they went straight into it again, running through the series a second time, Decker bore down, put all his skill, all his strength into the cuts, trying at least to get close, but the elderly master brushed away the blows like a man bothered by a lazy blowfly. When the master turned aside a kote cut, which had always been Decker's best move, warding it off almost as an afterthought, Decker felt the demon start up inside him, locking up his body, stretching his jaw, gritting his teeth.

He began to hit harder, yell louder, tried to power his way through the master's defense. Finally, after a hard, stabbing tsuki thrust had been deflected with the barest of movements, and the master cried *"Migido!"* calling for a cut to the right side of the breastplate, Decker, gripped by the sharp, digging claws of a hot anger, swore and lunged, came back with the tsuki thrust again, a surprise move aimed at the beard of the face mask.

The Japanese, even though expecting a different blow, cracked Decker's sword aside, slashed with his own, and pulled the blow at the last instant so that it landed with a feather touch against Decker's padded collarbone.

A real sword, with a fine edge to it, would have split him to the waist.

The master, with a quick movement, stepped back and removed his mask. Decker, his bamboo shinai raised high over his head, froze the cut, killed it in midair.

Sweat on his face, breathing hard, he sucked air, slowly lowered the sword, the anger fading like a breeze-blown mist, leaving him silently cursing it; embarrassed.

When he saw the sword lower to Decker's side, the master, whose respiration seemed entirely normal, bowed to his student. Decker bowed in turn, wristed sweat off his flushed forehead, slowed the bellows inside his lungs.

The master, his lined face composed, bone-dry, began to speak. "You have good speed. Your technique is poor, but you move well, and you are strong."

Decker, still catching his breath, brushed at an eyebrow, listened.

"However, you lack discipline."

"Yes," Decker said. "I know."

"It is the basis of all the martial arts. There must be a balance of body, brain, and intellect. Fear, doubt, surprise, and confusion are the four positions of kendo. These do not afflict you. But there is a fifth poison worse than the others. Lack of self-control."

Decker slowly nodded his head. "That's why I'm here. That's the instruction I came for."

The master grunted, an enigmatic sound that could have meant anything. He said, after an introspective moment, "It may take more time than you care to put in."

"I can come every morning for as long as I'm in Hong Kong."

"How long will that be?"

"A week. Maybe two."

"A week," the master said, as if his understanding of English had suddenly deserted him. "To learn self-discipline takes some people a lifetime."

"Master," Decker said, leveling with him, leveling with himself, "without it, I may not have a lifetime."

The Japanese took the helmet liner off his head, a white cotton towel, and wiped it slowly over the hilt of his bamboo sword. He remained silent for perhaps thirty seconds, concentrating on the chore, then began to speak in his quiet, even tone.

"In Japan, in the Sengoku-Jidai, the Age of War, one of the greatest swordsmen was a man named Tsukahara Bokuden, a minor baron from Niigata, a soldier poet. He fought nineteen duels with the live blade, and killed nineteen men. In battle he was said to have killed two hundred. There is a record of a match that Bokuden fought against a famous swordsman from Kurashiki named Rinsai." The master folded the towel into his tare apron, and stood there, five-feet-seven, perhaps 115 pounds, radiating calm, his damaged eye giving him the look of a benign pirate.

"Rinsai," he said to Decker, "won his matches by enraging his opponents past the point of clear thinking, and thought to do the same against Bokuden. He killed Bokuden's wife, and broke the news to Bokuden before the match, and was surprised when his opponent failed to rush at him. Instead, Bokuden spoke to him in rhyme. 'Rinsai,' he said. 'Tactics do not depend on the sudden charge or the cowardly blow. What matters is a mind kept cool as winter's snow. You have slain my wife. Pray to Buddha, Rinsai, you are about to lose your life.'"

The narrator stopped speaking, lapsed into a pensive silence. Decker knew he was supposed to guess the rest, but he was caught up in the story.

"What happened?"

"Rinsai was confused by this placid reaction. He fought badly and died quickly."

The master bowed to Decker again, stiffly from the waist, then turned and walked away.

Decker watched the slight figure crossing the floor like an actor, his lines delivered to a hushed audience, departing the stage. Decker went the other way, to the changing rooms. He took a shower, thinking about the story he'd just been told, got dressed, found the assistant, paid him some money, and went out onto the floor again. Down at the far end, like a shadow in his dark, flowing outfit, the master was pushing his dust mop over the polished boards as if he'd spent years perfecting the correct technique.

Like a pond disturbed by a stone, the waxed wood seemed to ripple as the mop passed over it.

Then flatten.

Then gleam with an untroubled stillness.

They used Ralph Dobrinski's office. He was out, and his space was the largest, so they met in there: Decker, Johnny, and Miriam.

Bumpy joined them while they were ordering up lunch.

"Sorry I'm late." He was walking painfully. "My date last night . . . teeth like a barracuda."

"Wounded in action, huh?" Decker said.

"Goddamn right." Bumpy eased himself into a chair. "I had to stop off for a three-inch Ace bandage."

"Three inches," Miriam said. "You'll have some left over."

"A three-inch-*wide* Ace bandage."

From the telephone Johnny Risotto said, "You want some lunch, Bump? I've ordered four pizzas."

"What are the rest of us having?" Bumpy asked.

Decker was busting to know how they'd got on yesterday with the neckties, but he didn't hurry them. He knew them. All three liked to ease their way into the business of the day. But once in, they'd work around the clock if they had to, with no real complaints. He waited till the food had arrived and everybody was munching before he got around to the neckties, asking Johnny if they'd had any success. "You bet," Johnny said, halfway through his pizza and already eyeing Bumpy's. "Doug Portloe came through with a Farnsbarns letter, and then it was all over but the legwork."

The type of letter Johnny referred to was one typed on official police stationery and signed by Chief Inspector Farnsbarns, a mythical member of the force. A letter like that opened a lot of doors, and if anything did go wrong, nobody got the blame except the non-existent inspector.

"We ran around town and bought about a hundredweight of ties, then Miriam sailed them over to Hei Ling Chau. Miriam?"

"No problem with the prison," Miriam said, finishing a swig of Diet Pepsi. "Lucky Doug Portloe had the fix in, and I went into the visitors' book as Fairweather's sister." Miriam looked at the slice of pizza in her hand, put it back on its cardboard tray, not so hungry anymore. "Jesus, that guy, Fairweather. I'll tell you, I honestly didn't know how I was gonna feel talking to the man who did that to Angie, but you know something? I felt more sad than mad. The poor bastard's out to lunch before breakfast."

"I know what you mean," Decker said. "His mind's gone. He's just a talking head."

"However"—Miriam snapped back into her investigative role—"he was definite about God's necktie. I showed him the lot. He picked this one." She dug into her pocketbook, pulled out a folded tie, let it unfurl as she held it up. Red pelicans flew in a frozen formation across a navy-blue sky. "He said he remembered the birds. Said he likes pelicans. Likes to watch them glide over the harbor, pounce on a fish. That's why he's sure about the tie. Over to you, Bumpy."

Wincing a little, Bumpy got to his feet and took off his sporty hessian-fabric jacket. Everybody was dressed a little more formally today: Johnny wore a gray suit, and Miriam had on a dark skirt and blouse that slimmed her generous figure. Decker disliked suits and wore, every chance he got, chinos and a flowered Hawaiian shirt, with a pair of faithful track shoes. Right now he wore penny loafers and a jacket over a polo shirt as a nod toward the rarely enforced DEA dress code. On the street, undercover, anything went; in the office, no shorts or sandals, please.

"Big Red called me from the prison," Bumpy explained, clicking open the attache case he'd brought with him, "and described the tie. I checked it against my list. It's the official necktie of the Malthusians Cricket Club, over there in Victoria Park. I went there, found the club secretary, spun him a tale about trying to locate one of their members, English, in his mid-forties, has a mustache. He gave me eight names from memory, plus I was able to buy these." Bumpy dumped magazines onto Ralph Dobrinski's desk. Everybody gathered around. "The current copy of the club's annual magazine," Bumpy announced, "plus four backdates. I've been through them and found shots of the eight members he gave me, plus several more jokers all in their forties, or thereabouts, and all with brushes." Bumpy picked up a magazine and opened it to a marked page. Ringed in red crayon was a halftone cut of two men posing in cricket flannels. One of the men had hair curling like lettuce leaves from beneath a small cloth cap, prominent teeth, and a mustache. Both men seemed on the verge of exploding with laughter.

Decker took the magazine from him, leafed through it. It was a parochial affair printed on inexpensive paper, no more professional than a high-school yearbook. Most of the photographs were of men holding drinks, faces flushed, eyes blinking against the power of a flashbulb. They wore either tuxedos or blazers with club ties at their throats, or knotted ascots. The rest of the shots were underexposed daytime photographs of men swiping at cricket balls or looking determined behind a tennis net. The copy was the standard mix of cliche jokes and snappy headlines, with a liberal use of members' nicknames, childish nomenclatures like Buzzer and Banger and Binky. The jacket featured a poor line drawing of a pelican flying through an elaborate scroll. The scroll had a Latin inscription which Bumpy translated as: Be ye ashamed to come in last. "Or, as we used to say at school, last in lousy."

"All right," Decker said. "How many shots did you mark?"

"It works out at a total of eleven different guys who could be our man. Some of them appear in two or three or all five of the magazines."

"What we need to do," Johnny Risotto said, "is schlepp the mags over to Fairweather and ask him to ID God. But I don't know how we can do that."

"We don't do it," Decker told him. "The deal was Portloe gets Miriam in, and that is it. No mail, no contact, nothing till after the trial. If we try to bluff our way in, we'll lose Lucky Doug for all time."

"The waitress at Mad Dogs," Johnny said. "Let's give her a look at the magazines, see if any of the faces ring a bell."

"Sure, we'll do that," Decker said. "But before we do, I got something here." They watched him open the plastic bag he'd brought to the office; after he'd left the dojo he'd gone back to the hotel for it. "I got this stuff from Angela's roommate. A woman named Faye Keeble."

"I've spoken to her on the phone once or twice," Miriam volunteered. "A nice lady."

"I thought so too."

Decker said it quite naturally, as if it had just crossed his mind. But Faye Keeble hadn't been very far from his thoughts since he'd woken that morning. The thought of her now zinged through him, touched him like electric sparks. The memory of being with her yesterday afternoon, yesterday evening, last night, was like a live wire he'd grabbed hold of and couldn't let go. All that time with her, hours and hours, and yet there was a shadowy quality to it, like a vivid dream you know didn't happen. He took out the scrapbook, the photo album, placed them next to the magazines.

"I haven't looked at these yet, and I'm glad I waited. We'll all be coming at them fresh, first time for everybody. Yell out if you see any familiar faces."

Decker opened the cover of the snapshot album, and Angela Waters smiled out at him. He saw once again how attractive she'd been, how sexy: lots of shiny brown hair worn high on her head, humor in her eyes, a figure just this side of voluptuous, a mouth made for pouting prettily. There were some shots of her in the States with what had to be her family, standing outside of what looked like a Midwestern church, as well as some snaps of her nicely filling out a swimsuit on an unmistakable Waikiki beach. Most of the shots had recognizable Hong Kong backgrounds, the smoky red-and-gold interior of the god-filled Tin Hau temple in Aberdeen;

Angela near the mouth of an ancient cannon built into the gray brick walls of Kam Tin; Angela against a green mountain of vegetables in the Southorn Market.

Many of the photographs recorded her at social functions. She'd had a pretty busy calendar, Decker saw: barbecues, dances, parties, formal balls. Other shots showed her as the star of some overly ambitious amateur theatricals: Eliza Doolittle, Nellie Forbush, Annie Oakley.

The scrapbook contained numerous items culled from the *South China Post*, some of them reviews of the musicals she'd appeared in. There were also three pages from the *Hong Kong Tatler* a local version of the snooty British publication. It was famous in the colony; the masthead read, "The Business, Cultural, Social, and Sporting Life of Hong Kong," which, as everybody said, only left the triad lodges uncovered. It was a glitzy publication full of ads for expensive restaurants and smart boutiques, and once-in-a-lifetime watches.

The first of the pages, from the current edition of the magazine, showed a black-and-white layout of a dozen photographs, groups of people, mainly couples or threesomes, with fluted wineglasses held at waist level. "Moore Expression" was the catchy headline, a cocktail reception, hosted by a big-name bank, for the opening of an exhibition of works by a famous sculptor.

Angela Waters had been captured unawares in one of the shots, deep in conversation with a short, thick-set man balancing on shiny crutches. The copy under the photograph read, "Miss Angela Waters discusses a fine point with Mr. Arthur Murdoch."

"Arthur Murdoch," Decker said with a twist to his mouth, "still has an eye for the ladies, I see."

"Hong Kong's richest free-lance penis," Miriam said. "Angie went out with him a couple of times. Said he was strong and interesting."

"I heard he was married once," Bumpy said. "Got a divorce. He got custody of the kids, the wife got the Philippines and New Guinea."

Everybody laughed.

Decker turned to another page from an earlier issue.

Angela Waters, flanked by two attractive men wearing name tags on their tuxedo lapels, appeared to be laughing at Bumpy's joke too. In another shot she sat at a table in a supper club, a glass-bead curtain behind her, an enraptured gentleman by her side regarding her like a faithful cocker spaniel.

There were several more photographs of Angela, all in cocktail surroundings, and in each one she was attended by a different man. Only one of them had a mustache, and he was Chinese.

"Nothing," Johnny Risotto said. "Let's try that waitress."

"Which one?" Bumpy asked. "What's her name?"

Decker told him. "Jeanne. The Scots girl."

Bumpy, with a lascivious glint in his eyes, began to gather up the magazines. "I'll go."

Miriam shook her head at him. "She's the tall one. You won't even come up to her shoulder."

"With what I have in mind," Bumpy replied, carrying the magazines toward the door, "that's plenty far enough."

He was back inside of thirty minutes, a cool excitement working on his sharp features.

He dumped the magazines on the desk, opened the top one to a marked page, pointed to one of the red-ringed photographs.

"Here's your guy, folks."

In the shot a well-dressed Chinese woman presented a trophy to two delighted men in white tennis shirts. The headline read, "Club Pips HMS *Tamar* in Tennis Tourney." There was an accompanying blurb bragging about the club's victory over the team from the local Royal Navy base. The copy beneath the halftone cut said, "Mrs. Caroline Chuen presents the winners' trophy to team captain Allan McDougal, watched by vice-captain Major Reggie Slemp."

"Major Reggie Slemp," Bumpy said, stabbing the shot with his finger. "The waitress, Jeanne, took a long look at this shot, thought it could be him, wasn't quite sure. But I found him in two of the other magazines as well." Bumpy flipped them open, both relevant pages marked by paper clips. "Here he is here. And here. As you can see, he also plays golf. A bit of a jock. When Jeanne saw these two shots she had no doubt. Major Reggie Slemp is the guy she saw with Fairweather that night."

Nobody said anything; nobody had a chance because Bumpy hadn't finished.

"And it gets better. I called a buddy at Arsenal Street, called him from Mad Dogs, asked him for a readout on this guy Slemp." Bumpy dived a hand into his jacket, pulled out a notebook, flipped it open. "British passport, came in from New Zealand, 1982. Got a job as a shipping clerk with Tai Kok lines. Fired from there, left under a cloud. Theft, apparently. No charges brought. Incidentally, you know who owns Tai Kok?"

Johnny Risotto knew. "Arthur Murdoch."

"Right," Bumpy said. "Okay, it only took Slemp two days to get relocated. This time with Natural Fortress Insurance. Do you know who owns Natural Fortress?"

Miriam fielded that one. "Arthur Murdoch," she said, and everybody looked at everybody else.

"Right." Bumpy slowed his delivery, a man getting to the punch line of a story. "He didn't last long. Fired again. But once again he relocated within a few days. He's now working as a sales rep with Saint Mathews, the sports-store chain. Saint Mathews is owned by the TRK Group. Guess who owns the TRK Group?"

"Is there a central hiring system for Murdoch's businesses?" Decker asked.

Bumpy was shaking his shiny bald head. "No, sir. It's obvious somebody went to bat for Slemp, and it could be any one of twenty or thirty Murdoch executives. Now, I'm not making any wild charges here, I'm only talking about what we know. We know Fairweather killed Angie. We know that Major Reggie Slemp is the guy Fairweather was with that night, the guy who played God. And we know that Arthur Murdoch was involved socially, romantically, whatever you want to call it, with Angie."

Johnny Risotto looked over at Decker. So did Miriam. Bumpy shut up, and nobody said anything.

Decker left the office, went into Johnny's, punched buttons on his phone.

Faye Keeble answered on the second ring.

"Hi," Decker said. "How are you?"

"Fine."

Just that one word, her voice low and warm, made memories of their time together leap into sharp focus for Decker, the electric wire back in his body sparking again.

"I've missed you," Decker said.

"I've missed you."

A pause, listening to one another's presence on the line; plugged into each other, remembering.

"Can I see you tonight?"

"Come for dinner. I'll cook something."

"Better make it supper. I may be late."

"Okay. What would you like?"

"Something we can bolt quickly."

"That can give you indigestion."

"There are other pains that are worse," Decker said. "Specially for boys."

"Get here as soon as you can," Faye said.

"Listen, before you go. There's a guy around town. Owns half of it. Arthur Murdoch. Did Angela ever mention his name?"

"She went out with him a couple of times."

"When was this?"

"About a week before I went on vacation. Why?"

"How about a man named Slemp? Major Reggie Slemp. She ever mention his name?"

"There *was* somebody named Reginald for a while. English. But his name was Burnley or Bromley."

"What did Angela think of Murdoch?"

"I think she was flattered he was interested, in spite of his reputation."

"They went out twice, huh?"

"That's all. It was only brief. The second time didn't go too well."

"Oh?"

"He was angry at her over something."

Decker gave it a beat. "Angry about what?"

"Something trivial. I've forgotten exactly. Is it important?"

"Tell you what," Decker said. "Have a think about it. See if you can remember what it was. Will you do that?"

"Sure. But as I say, it was no big deal. Some kind of misunderstanding."

Decker told her he'd see her later, hung up, and returned to Ralph Dobrinski's office. Miriam was playing homemaker, gathering up empty pizza trays and pop cans. Johnny and Bumpy were studying the red-ringed pictures in the magazines.

"I'm gonna need Reggie Slemp's address," Decker said.

Bumpy put the magazine aside. "Easy Peasy. Need anything else?"

"Nope. I already know where Arthur Murdoch lives."

"What are you gonna do?" Johnny asked.

Decker gave a casual shrug and said, "I read somewhere that the rich are different from you and me. I thought I'd maybe go and check that out."

* * *

The security lock on the high iron gates made an angry buzzing noise, as if annoyed at being disturbed.

Decker, behind the wheel of the office Toyota, drove through as the gates hinged open, and parked on a drive whose red herringboned brick had been laid as evenly as a ballroom floor.

A waiting servant told Decker that Mr. Murdoch was on the tennis court, and directed him to the side of the gleaming house. Decker was impressed; he'd never before been to any of the great houses of Hong Kong. There were maybe a dozen that were famous in the colony, most of which belonged to big business wheels like Arthur Murdoch. During his time in the city Decker had known of Arthur Murdoch just as he'd known of all the other movers and shakers, but had never come into contact with any of them, although he could have socially. These people, had they lived in Palm Beach or Palm Springs, New York or LA, would have moved in a circle few outsiders would ever have glimpsed, but in Hong Kong, with its relatively tiny social circle, the high and the mighty mixed with the hoi polloi, which was why it was possible for a good-looking secretary like Angela Waters to meet somebody from the upper stratosphere. Like Arthur Murdoch.

Decker went where he'd been directed, the house beginning to work its spell on him. The water that cooled the acres of glass bubbled and dripped down the wall he was walking past, forming an opaque curtain which shimmered and billowed as if ruffled by a breeze. The sun, losing height in the western sky, struck small bright rainbows the entire length of the wall, hovering in the fine spray curling up from the pink-tiled gutters set into the footpath. The rainbows dazzled momentarily, then vanished, to reappear somewhere else. Arthur Murdoch's humble abode. Not bad.

Decker heard the thwack of a tennis ball as he reached the end of the great house, and saw the court nestled one hundred feet away in its trimmed-green-grass surround: high green wire fence, backed, low down, by green cloth wind dampeners. To break up the monochromatic effect, a ring of topiaries, sprayed white, had been placed around the fence; from the air the court would have looked like a square green peg in a round white hole.

The court itself had made news too. Arthur Murdoch had been a player of some repute before he'd lost the use of his legs. He'd brought a team of experts up from Sydney to lay the court for him, an *en tout cas* surface resting on three layers of crushed rock. It was as flat and immaculate as a pool table, and could drain off a tropical downpour inside of ten minutes.

Decker followed a path bordered by clipped bamboo and dwarf banyans that led to a landscaped Japanese garden devoid of any flowering trees or floral plants. The garden ended in a lawn opening onto a vista that stopped Decker for a moment: quick, slanting, green slopes dropping away like an immense land spill, and miles of still-bright sky coloring the mini-ocean of the South China Sea. Way off in the squinting distance a super tanker, it's 300,000 tons reduced to ant size, crept along the edge of the horizon, mired to it as if it had sailed into a pool of glue.

The view figured, Decker thought; if you build a house of glass, you may as well put it where you can see something from it.

Lawn sponged under Decker's shoes as he crossed to a gate in the high wire fence. He slid it open and walked onto the perfect tan surface of the tennis court.

The far end was littered with yellow tennis balls being rounded up by a Chinese teenager in a smart blue track suit. At the other end another boy, similarly dressed, was bouncing a ball to Arthur Murdoch, who was perched three feet off the ground on a high metal chair, the numerous legs of which fanned out to form a solid, unrockable base. The seat he sat on was like a tractor seat made of molded plastic, and without a back support. The chair, which looked like a giant steel spider, was clearly a custom job, the seat riding on a complicated arrangement of gimbals and ratchets.

Murdoch, a plain white racket in his hand, caught the ball the boy bounced to him, tossed it into the air, and, swiveling his upper body on the seat, brought the racket lashing down from above his head and walloped the ball. It was all done with arm and shoulder and wrist, Decker saw; the man's legs, encased in light seersucker pants, boat sneakers on his feet, were folded away underneath a rung of the chair, as useless as the racket cover next to them. Decker stayed where he was for a minute; there was a rhythm on the court he was reluctant to break: the boy at the far end would pounce on a ball like a shortstop, scoop it up, and chuck it to his pal, who'd field it and feed it to Murdoch. Murdoch would catch it, set himself, and go into his windup. The seat would swivel, then snap back hard as the man unleashed the power in his heavy shoulders, slashing the racket through the air with a big slicing follow-through. The balls flew with savage pace off the strings, flashed over the net, gouged out dust a few inches inside the service line, then wapped into the green-cloth backing of the wire fence.

Watching him serve, Decker got a small insight into the guy. The very fact that he was out on a tennis court at all said something about the way he regarded his handicap. And the way he hit the ball, getting every ounce into the shot, whipping his arm over, ferociously pounding the ball as if it were something dangerous to be gotten rid of—that said something about him too.

Decker had seen the type before: the hard-driving captain of industry, the company president who, after a hard day at the office running his empire, comes home and works off the pressure, burns it off like surplus fuel, does something physical because booze won't wind him down anymore. A twelve-hour workday, but a body and brain stoked for fifteen.

The ball boy, errant for once, bounced a ball Murdoch couldn't handle and, swinging to try to grab it, Murdoch spotted Decker standing there.

"Mr. Decker? Come on over."

Decker walked along the edge of the court. He'd called Murdoch's office from St. John's House, spoken to a secretary, and told her the truth: that he was DEA and wanted a word with Mr. Murdoch. The secretary had got back to him with the message that her boss was busy all afternoon, but would see him if he cared to come to his house, say, around six P.M?

"Good evening," Decker said.

"You play tennis, Mr. Decker?"

"No, I don't."

"You should, you've got the build. A lot of the pros are built like you."

Murdoch swung away to accept another ball, and blasted it harder than ever. He hit two more serves like that, pumped-up muscular shots full of clenched energy. He reminded Decker of a fighter in a gym grunting body blows into the heavy bag, making believe the bag was his next KO victim.

What was it supposed to be, a warning? Was this the bicep-flexing, chest-thumping routine to soften up a prospective opponent? Why should Murdoch regard him as that? Or did Arthur Murdoch look upon everybody as an opponent?"

Questions Decker pondered.

He also wondered about the giant insect bomb that was in easy reach of Murdoch's chair. Then he remembered that Arthur Murdoch was said to have a thing about bees. Apparently so.

Murdoch lashed one more serve, then broke off to get his first good look at his visitor. Decker felt the hard gaze land on him, a look that drilled like a test well being sunk. Arthur Murdoch's pale blue eyes in a well-barbered face; not an inch of flesh on that face or the throat that was surplus, nothing but muscle pushing at his jaw, sinewed development expanding the black T-shirt he wore on his compact, welterweight body. Iron-gray hair, iron-gray stare.

"Timing," he said. "In tennis or business, timing's the secret. What's your sport, Mr. Decker?"

"I don't have one."

"But you used to, right?" Again the eyes appraised him. "In college, maybe?"

"I'm afraid not," Decker said, lying to get a little early advantage.

"An intellectual, huh?" There was no dig in the question, it was delivered with a brief smile. Decker saw that he was being treated to the charming, flattering side of Arthur Murdoch. The disarming side. It was a tried-and-true tactic: come on strong, forceful, then relax, slip in a few compliments, get the other guy to think you weren't so tough after all; get him to ease his defenses. Well, Decker's job had given him considerable experience in doing exactly the same thing.

"Even though I don't play tennis, I've watched a lot. And that's a very professional serve you have there, Mr. Murdoch."

"Yeah, back when I was healthy, it was my best shot. They say I could've turned pro, you know, a serve like that, even though I was only five-eight standing on a Kleenex. And you know a curious thing? People think the famous big servers were all big men. That's a myth. Rod Laver had a great serve, and he's the same height as me. And Segura and Rosewell are both shorter."

But they didn't have big serves. And neither did Laver, Decker could have said. Funny; Arthur Murdoch didn't appear to even notice that he lived his life on crutches, but he was sensitive about being short.

"Equipment's another myth." Murdoch held out his racket like a duelist's second offering a weapon. "Look at this. Hardly fancy. A Wilson right off the peg. I learned a lesson about gear once, down in Australia, in buffalo country. I had an under-and-over the Purdy people tailored for me in London. Gave me a choice of barrel weight, barrel length, ventilated or raised rib, beaver-tail fore end or English splinter. I could choose chamber length, action pressure, straight, semi, or full pistol grip. They measured my arms to get the right stock length, and because my right eye, my shooting eye, was slightly stronger than the left one, they corrected the cast of the barrels, curved them a few hundredths of an inch off true. Two and a half years in the making, that piece."

"Incredible," Decker said, suspecting he was supposed to be impressed, even intimidated, by all this macho Hemingway gun talk.

"But you know what? I screwed up." Murdoch did his best to look chagrined, but the emotion was beyond him. "A bull buffalo coming right at me, and I missed him twice with this fantastic gun. If my guide hadn't dropped the animal it would've taken me out. So I learned a lesson, Mr. Decker. It's never the tools, it's the way they're used." To illustrate the truth behind this little lecture, Murdoch cracked a serve which almost tore a hole in the backstop at the end of the court.

Decker could have laughed; Murdoch with his cracker-barrel philosophy trying to make out he was really just folks, as humble as anybody who could afford to pay thirty grand for a bespoke London hunting rifle. The guy was an actor. Men like Arthur Murdoch never learned a lesson, never learned anything. They were always right; and if they were wrong it was everybody else who was out of step.

"So, Mr. Decker. You're temporarily attached to the consulate, and you're here about Angela Waters, correct?"

"That's right, sir. One of our people gets killed, we have to open and close a file on it. It's only backup to the local police inquiry, but it's Justice Department policy."

"I already talked to the police. They came to see me. They knew I saw Angela about three or four days before she was killed. This is a small town, Mr. Decker. A guy like me takes a girl for some chow mein, and all Hong Kong knows it."

Decker nodded at the obvious truth of that, and waited.

"I can only tell you what I told them. I didn't know her very well."

"I see."

Murdoch reached down for a towel folded on a rung of his custom-made chair. He ran it around his short, powerful neck, then examined the towel as if perspiration seriously interested him.

"It was a terrible thing what happened to that girl. The newspapers said she was mutilated. I was sick when I read about it. I mean, you live in this town, you get used to picking up the Post and reading about a triad slashing. You get so you expect it, you're dead to it. But when it happens to a Westerner, an American, and a woman at that, it really shakes you up. Specially when you knew the person."

"Then you think this could be triad-related?"

Murdoch had the towel working behind his ears now; then he began to snap it between his hands. His handicap seemed to have turned him into two people: nothing from the waist down, a bundle of moves and restless energy from the waist up.

He said: "When somebody gets cut in this town, sliced up like that, you can bet it's a lodge killing. After all, she was DEA. And you guys are always getting threats from the gangs for crabbing their act, right? Maybe this time they went through with it."

"Could be," Decker said, and waited for more. Murdoch was a talker, and you always let the talkers ramble; you never knew what they might tell you in a fit of logorrhea.

"I met her at a cocktail party, asked her out. She was a damn fine-looking woman. Bags of personality too. Our second date we had dinner here. She wanted to see the Crystal Palace. That's what the locals call the house, the Crystal Palace."

Murdoch tossed the towel away and began to bounce a ball on the wooden throat of his racket, watching its quick, nervous rise and fall while he waited for a question he knew was coming.

"And that was the last time you saw her alive?"

"Alive or dead. It was a closed-coffin funeral. I just hope they get the bastard who did it."

"So do I," Decker said, perhaps coloring the words a little too much.

Murdoch's raised chair put him on a level with Decker, and for a fleeting moment their eyes locked and jarred.

The moment vanished as the tennis ball caught an edge of the white racket. Murdoch's head turning to watch it hop away.

"I wish I could be of more help, Mr. Decker."

It was the end of the interview, except for the final little coda, and Decker was pretty sure how that would play. In fact, he would have been willing to bet a week's salary that he could predict how it would end: Murdoch would make some comment about him taking up tennis, something complimentary, the object being to send a visitor away with the impression that Arthur Murdoch was a pretty good fellow after all, and surprisingly approachable, considering his exalted position in the community.

"Thank you for your time, Mr. Murdoch. Good of you to see me on such short notice."

"No problem."

Decker shook his hand, turned.

"Incidentally, Mr. Decker . . ."

Decker turned back.

"Think about taking some tennis lessons. With shoulders like yours you'd have a hell of a backhand."

"I'll give it some thought," Decker replied, starting off again and wondering why it was that the best bets were always made with yourself.

The answer: Yes.

The question: Was Arthur Murdoch involved in Angela Waters' murder?

Decker, negotiating the roller-coaster bends that looped down the slope toward Central, had no hard-and-fast facts to back up his decision; could not have explained why he was sure it was correct; was not entirely certain how he'd arrived at it. It was just a street thing, something learned from a lot of years talking to people and looking behind their words.

Either Arthur Murdoch was lying, or he wasn't. He had to trust instinct, and his instinct told him that Murdoch was covering up.

He knew something he didn't want to admit to. And maybe he knew *somebody* he didn't want to admit to.

Like a man named Slemp who a maniac thought was God.

"Decker stopped the car, checked the address Bumpy had given him, Slemp's address, and started driving again.

10

Decker left the car in Central, rode the subway to Kowloon Tong, and switched to the KCR, the fast, modern railway that runs up through the New Territories and connects with the train to Canton. He got off at Fo Tan, five stops before the border, asked directions, and began walking toward the road where Reggie Slemp lived. The street soon branched off, narrowing into a rural country lane lit by a few haphazardly placed mercury lights, blue against the darkening sky, beetles zooming under their tin surrounds. He walked on broken bitumen, tractor-lumped and sticky, past market gardens and fields of wispy corn and rolling hills topped by the spare and ghostly outline of wind-bent trees.

Slemp's house was set off by itself, a one-story stucco bungalow with a wooden veranda. A fruitless banana tree, its limp fronds split and sagging, guarded the board gate of a dilapidated picket fence which had no sides, only a front.

Decker climbed the rickety stairs and rapped on a colored glass pane set into the door. A door god, which appeared to have been in place for many years, scowled suspiciously at him.

Decker waited, looked around. Behind him came the low roar of the KCR tracks, and the buzz of traffic on the four-lane highway that ran north and south. Beyond the highway the calm liquid spill of Tolo harbor led all the way to the remote outpost of Ping Chau, the little island's lights faint like a weak pulse. Footsteps scuffed behind the colored glass.

The door opened, and Decker got his first look at Major Reggie Slemp, recognizing him easily from the photographs in the club magazines. His first thought was that Brian Fairweather must have been extraordinarily crazy to believe that this person could be God:

yucky Brylcreemed hair, a nose that booze was beginning to lump, a mustache shaped like a fat Band-Aid, jowly cheeks, and a double chin. He wore an Ashford checked shirt, sleeves rolled up the forearms, baggy pants, and brown carpet slippers. He looked to Decker like a man who'd once been obese, had lost the weight on a crash diet, but retained the flab.

"Major Slemp?"

"Yes?"

"Can I come in?"

The major peered at his visitor, looking annoyed. He'd been chewing something when he'd come to the door, had opened the door in the act of swallowing, and there was a red sauce mark on his mouth.

"Who are you?"

"The name doesn't matter."

"It bloody well matters to me, old boy. I like to know who I let into my house."

Decker looked away, along the veranda to where a rattan table and chair stood, an unwashed glass and an empty beer bottle by the side of the chair. "Why don't we say"—he looked back at Slemp—"that Murdoch sent me."

He hadn't been sure of what kind of approach to take with the guy, or how to find out for certain whether or not Slemp was involved with Arthur Murdoch. But the direct approach always took some beating; his training had taught him that: extemporize, ad-lib, play straight man to the criminal comics, or comedian to the bad-guy straight men. Or just come right out with it and watch the effect.

"Who?" Slemp asked. But the beat was there, a fraction too much hesitation. And his frown of noncomprehension was too heavy for a simple question.

"Can I come in?"

Slemp blustered. "I don't know what this is all about, but I suppose you'd better."

Scowling, he stepped aside as Decker walked past him. One glance at the room and Decker recognized a bachelor's quarters. A cleaning amah came once a week probably, but because there was no Mrs. Slemp to keep on her hammer, the amah faked it, left the dust where it was, and got home early. A cheap landlord had furnished the place with what looked like surplus stuff from other properties. Nothing matched: a broad armchair had had its past sins covered by terry cloth; a second chair was made of scraggy cane; and a third was an old Naugahyde Barcalounger, low on one side like a car with a flat tire.

The plaster walls were bare except for a print of the Taj Mahal, and the light in the room came from large tasseled lampshades stuck on high wooden poles: they looked like a very thin man doing his party trick.

In one corner a battered portable record player was spinning a record to a close: a late-fifties Sinatra pressing of an old show tune. Slemp crossed to it and killed the sound as if embarrassed by his choice of music.

"I was just having a bite before going out to the club," Slemp said, moving toward the kitchen. Decker followed him, and was glad that the revelation had not been followed by an invitation to dine: waxy green linoleum covered the floor, holed in places like the sole of a badly worn shoe. The walls had been painted with a lead-based paint and had sweated in lumpy parallel streaks. In the sink, which was an old-fashioned china tub, dishes were sunk in the scummy water of a plastic baby bath. Lying on a moist dishcloth, on a table, were a stick of Anchor butter, an open can of Heinz spaghetti, and a gaping package of sliced white bread.

"Now, what's all this about? Who's this chap Murdoch?" Slemp picked up a sandwich and bit into it, evening up the red sauce smear on his mouth. He was trying to act cranky at being disturbed at his repast, Decker figured, but his eyes were not those of a man eating a sad little sandwich; they leveled at Decker like a zoo keeper watching a python while he cleaned its cage.

"Our mutual employer," Decker said.

Slemp chewed, swallowed, examined the sandwich, choosing a good spot to go into it again, "I work for a sports-store chain. A man named Robinson is my boss."

Slemp had been reading while he ate; next to a pewter mug of beer was an open magazine. It was upside down from Decker's angle but he was able to recognize, on the front cover, a photograph of a tarted-up big-caliber revolver. The logo was familiar too: *Guns & Ammo*.

He picked up the magazine, checked the gun on the jacket. "I meant your nighttime job. Your now-and-then job." It was an S&W model 27 with an engraved bone handle. A useful piece if you were after a bull moose.

Alarm made Reggie Slemp chomp at the sandwich. He gulped it like a savage getting rid of a threat by vigorously eating his enemy.

"I don't have a nighttime job."

"That's not what Murdoch says." Decker lifted the magazine, waved it a little. "He says you're a good man with a gun."

Slemp wasn't very fast on his feet; he reached for the mug of beer, gulped some to give himself time to get an answer together.

"I used to be damned good with a gun. I was a range officer in the British Army. In Borneo. Perhaps this man Murdoch knew me in Borneo."

"Boy, you're cagey. I just come from talking to him. Up there in that glass palace of his, except I didn't get inside it," Decker said, easing into the role he'd created for himself: imported talent, an American mechanic. No trigger-happy street bopper talking like dis and dat, but the other kind, the ordinary Joe just doing a job, hiring out his expertise like a doctor or a lawyer. "We had our little meeting on the tennis court. I listened, he talked, in between belting balls over the net. Gutsy little guy, the crutches and all. Anyway, that's why I'm here in Hong Kong," Decker said, letting the statement dangle.

Slemp couldn't resist it.

"Why? Why are you here?"

Decker, interested again in the magazine, turned a page.

"Because I'm a good man with a gun too."

Slemp stopped drinking, stopped eating; stared in suspicion, confusion, at his visitor, this Yank in a bright floral shirt. "What do you mean?"

"I mean, you and me, we're both in the same union. Murdoch imported me for a job he wants done. Some biggie he wants to put down. Told me he didn't want his regular guy doing this one. When I heard that, that he already had a man he used regular, I asked him who. Like, what was his name. He said I didn't need to know that. I told him if he wanted me for the hit, I did need to know that, because I like to know who I'm aceing out of a job, so I can protect my ass. He saw the point of that, Murdoch, and he give me your name. So that's why I'm here. In this house talking to you."

Decker turned another page. Slemp had gone rigid. Decker knew why: the guy thought he'd come to kill him.

"The way I figure it," Decker explained, "I don't want what happened to a buddy of mine to happen to me. He was in the biz, and he got this job, only there was a regular guy too, and the boss wanted my friend. So when the regular scout heard about it, he tracked down my buddy and switched off his lights. Didn't want the competition, so he got rid of it," Decker said, engrossed in a lurid four-color spread for Nissan trucks. "Now, I wouldn't want that to happen to me, so I'm here to have a little chat with you so we don't have to get into anything. I let you know what's going down and square it with you. Did I do the right thing? Because I don't know if you're the jealous type or not."

Blood came back into Slemp's jowly face, and his chest rose and subsided in a flood of relief.

His imagined escape chinked holes in his armor.

"I don't understand it. What reason did he give?"

"For what?"

"For bringing you in."

"Who?"

"Murdoch," Slemp said irritably.

So there it was.

It had just been a guess on Decker's part, Slemp being a gunman, but it had made sense: he was a man who did dirty work, and his choice of contemplative dinnertime reading matter was a gun magazine. Ergo, it was a safe bet that he shot people for a living.

"Who knows?" Decker asked. "Maybe the hit is somebody you'd have trouble getting close to for some reason. Murdoch didn't tell me."

Slemp, looking like a man on the verge of being canned, asked if Murdoch had said anything about a retainer.

"You mean signing me on permanent? No, sir. I wouldn't go for that anyway. I'm happy in LA. I wouldn't want to live here. Too many people and not enough acres."

The Englishman pressed his upper teeth into his lower lip, teeth that were stained red now, but would be a natural brown/gray color. Decker could imagine the guy's toothbrush: splayed in all directions and unchanged for a year. His comb would have murky pieces of old hair dressing clinging to it, interspersed with little white flecks of scalp skin.

"It's just a one-time job," Decker said. "You're not out on the car tracks, nothing like that. But I wanted to clear it with you. Make sure we don't have a beef. Okay?"

"I'm not going to act against you," Slemp said, mollified a little by his role of feared gunman. "My argument is with Murdoch."

"I'd play dumb I was you. That way you know something he doesn't. And it's always nice knowing something the boss don't."

"You're right there," Slemp said. He tossed the half-eaten sandwich into the dishwater in the baby bath, wiped his mouth on his wrist, removing most of the sauce.

"You brace him with it." Decker said. "a guy like that, a guy with his own goddamn building downtown, he won't like it one little bit. He'll feel his authority's being questioned. He could get mad and fire your ass."

"Yes, there's that to it. He's a touchy bugger all right. I don't think he likes me much anyway."

"Okay, then. Subject closed." Decker rapped the magazine with his hand. "I'll bet you didn't buy this at the corner newsstand. The gun laws in this town are wacko. The NRA would have a heart attack they came here."

"Yes," Slemp said, still thinking about Murdoch's slight.

Decker turned a page. "Hey, look at this. A Steyr Hahn, 1911. I used to own one of them. A sweet little piece, but a real bastard to get ammo for." He held up the magazine so that Slemp could view it. "I thought the thirty-eight Colt Super case looked like a possibility, but the rim diameter's too wide, and the wall was too thick. Goddamn thing wouldn't chamber."

Slemp cast a professional eye over the photograph of the ancient straight-up-and-down pistol. "You could have used thirty-eight Special brass. You would've had to shorten it, of course, and machined the rim away, and cut an extractor groove. But it would've worked."

"Yeah? I never thought of that. I finally traded it for an Astra A Eighty."

Decker was prepared to run through a whole range of guns until he struck a responding chord, but he got lucky with his first choice. A look of pleasant interest softened Slemp's expression. "I used to own an A Eighty. A four-incher."

"How about that?" Decker said, pleased. "A couple of A Eighty fans. I don't know what you did, but I switched the original grips for a pair of Mustangs, aced the Partridge front sight, and pegged on an MMC."

"I changed the sights too. I preferred the Millets, myself. Blade rear, ramp front. But I didn't peg them, I silver-soldered them, melted the edges just a touch, and lamp-blacked them. I also reduced the pull to eight pounds double action."

"Hey," Decker said, moving his head in admiration. "You really know guns."

Slemp brightened another notch; he very seldom got a chance to talk small arms in a place like Hong Kong. In a city which abhorred guns, it was a lonely hobby.

"I say, would you like a glass of beer?"

"Sure. You bet."

Slemp pulled a bottle from a small refrigerator, snapped the cap, poured amber liquid into a glass-bottomed tankard, unwashed like his own.

They both drank, Slemp measuring Decker, sizing him up, thinking. With the image of a smile tugging at a corner of his mouth he said, "How are you at keeping secrets?"

"Pretty good. If I wasn't I wouldn't be standing here drinking your beer."

Slemp put down his tankard. "Come on. I'll show you something."

Decker followed him out of the kitchen, through a rear door, and down some broken stone steps into the darkness of an overgrown back garden. Slemp took a bunch of keys from his pocket, inserted one into the keyhole of a basement door—a steel door, Decker noted—turned a triple throw lock, and pushed the door open. With no light on, there was nothing to be seen, but the smell was there: the faint aroma of blued steel, oil, and a lingering scent of nitrocellulose.

They went in, Slemp closing and locking the door before hitting a switch. Strip lights popped and flickered, then held, washing the area with a blue-white brilliance. The basement ran the length and breadth of the house, with windows front and back sealed and covered by boards and acoustic tile. The ceiling had been soundproofed too. On a long workbench against a wall, laid out in careful symmetry, was a variety of hand-loading equipment, all of it topquality: a powder measure, a repriming tool, an eighty-shell loading block, a bullet mold with a sprue-cutter attachment, a case trimmer, a bullet resizer with a full set of swaging dies, plus assorted reamers, brushes, mallets, pliers, tweezers, oils, lubricants, and gels.

Decker was struck by the difference between this room and the one upstairs. Here everything was spotless, sparkling clean, the cement floor swept, the paneled walls glossed by varnish.

"Come and meet my children," Slemp said, pointing across the room.

Next to a lathe and a drill press was an old blackwood sideboard shiny with polish. A new top had been made for it, fretted shapes had been cut into the top, and snug in pockets of dark green velvet lay Slemp's gun collection.

Slemp took the guns out in turn, handling them like a man fondling a kitten, passing each one to Decker, then replacing it. His voice was full of pride and affection.

"A Chemelot-Delvigne twelve mil rimfire."

"French, huh?" said Decker, although he knew it was Belgian.

"A Dan Wesson Model Fifteen Two."

"Is that a twelve-inch bull barrel? Wow!"

"A Sig-Sauer three-eighty. I accurized it by inserting cone bushings here and here. Reduced the barrel play considerably."

"Sweet."

"A four-fifty-four Casull. That'll fire two-forty grains at two thousand feet per second."

"Hell of a weapon."

"Can you identify this one?"

"Looks like a Colt of some kind."

"It's a Texas Patterson thirty-six."

"I've never seen one before. A classic."

"How about this one?" Slemp asked.

"A British Webley. But what did you do to the barrel?"

"Reamed it out and shortened it. Fires a silenced round."

"That could help in certain situations," Decker allowed. He gestured around him. "With all this stuff, I guess you can make pretty much what you want."

"Within reason. Here's my pride and joy." He handed Decker a large automatic pistol, elegant and sporty-looking, the molded walnut grips raked back at an acute angle. The long slim barrel had been blued, and hundreds of tiny holes had been drilled into it.

"You been playing with this one too. Looks like a water sprinkler. What the hell is it?" Decker asked, although he knew what he had in his hands: the tiny holes were bleed-off holes. Slemp had moved up from a gun that fired a single silenced round; this one would fire eleven rounds with just a slight phtt!

Slemp smirked, enjoying the little lesson he was giving; he'd yet to meet a Yank who knew beans about guns.

"A Ruger Mark Two target pistol. I turned down the barrel, machined on a sleeve, and drilled all those holes! Took me quite a while, I can tell you."

"Hey," Decker said. "This here's a silenced gun, right?"

"Exactly. No bulky silencer to carry around, screw on, replace when the baffles get clogged. I can put a couple of hundred rounds through this piece, and it'll still fire as quiet as a mouse."

"You're some kind of genius, you know that?" Decker said, turning the pistol in his hand. The hard bright lights flared on it, an evil-looking thing, slick and slim and deadly as hell. "You're gonna have a hard time throwing this baby in the harbor."

"What do you mean?"

"After you do a job."

Slemp released a superior little grin as he took the gun and returned it to the sideboard. "Ah, but you see, I don't have to throw it away. When you drill a barrel, you distort the rifling inside. So if the police dig a bullet out of somebody, they'd have the devil's own time getting a slug and barrel match. The only problem," Slemp said, the pedantic instructor with a student willing to learn, "is that you give up a bit of accuracy. Still, I didn't make it to win target competitions."

Decker chortled. "Goddamn right. What do you load in it, anyway?"

Slemp motioned him over to a workbench, reached up, and took down a pipe-tobacco can. Inside, bullets were clumped together like tiny rockets on a launchpad, their points tipped bright red. Slemp extracted one, placed it in Decker's palm.

"That's a seventy-five-grain hollow-point slug on four-point-six grains of slow-burning Bullseye. It's sitting in a twenty-two long-rifle cartridge."

"Hollow point? But you filled it in."

"With phosphorus," Slemp said.

Decker put a slow grin on his face. "A tracer? That's what you fire?"

"That's what I fire."

"I don't get it. Why a tracer in a hit gun?"

Slemp took back the long slim bullet, reclosed it in its tobacco can. "So they know they've been shot," he said.

"Thoughtful sonofabitch, ain't you," Decker said, his laugh turning an insult into a compliment.

Slemp chuckled with him, two pros sharing a naughty joke about the tricks of the trade.

The tour completed, they left the basement, still chatting about ammunition, muzzle velocities, down-range energies, continuing the gun talk upstairs in the grubby living room, Slemp telling Decker how he'd bought the guns in Manila and Taiwan and smuggled them in one by one. Slemp's date at his club, if he did have one, seemed to have been forgotten. He was enjoying himself. They drank more beer.

An hour later Decker said he'd better be going.

"It was good talking to you. I'd say let's get together again, but Murdoch wants the job done pretty soon, then I'm outta here."

The mention of the man's name brought a tart look of discomfort to Slemp's face.

"Damned insulting," he said.

"Don't let it throw you. Like I say, it can't be any reflection on you. You know more about guns than Billy the Kid."

Slemp muttered something; the beer had made him morose.

Decker, with his hand on the knob of the front door, said, "Take my advice. Play dumb. Don't let him know that you know. Turn *him* into the sucker."

Slemp nodded glumly. "You're quite right. Only thing to do."

"So long now."

"Good-bye."

Slemp watched Decker go down the stairs into the overgrown path, knowing he should offer him a ride to the station, but he was in a rotten mood now. The cheek of Murdoch, bringing in somebody else! Why? He'd killed four men for him, and they'd all been perfect jobs. And getting rid of the Waters woman had gone according to plan, hadn't it? If there was anything he couldn't stand, it was ungratefulness.

Slemp went back inside and got himself another bottle of beer. And brooded.

"Hi, there," Decker said when Faye Keeble answered the bell.

"Hello." She stepped back to let him in, closed the door. A delicious smell of roasting chicken came from the kitchen.

Decker kissed her, a short, gentle kiss, a careful bridge between the passions of the previous day and this new meeting.

"Sorry I wasn't here an hour ago."

"You weren't expected. You said supper."

"I didn't mean because of the food."

Faye smiled at that. They watched each other, standing there just inside the door, both wanting to be reassured that what had happened between them hadn't been a fluke.

"There's something I want to ask you." Decker put his mouth against the throb of her throat.

"The answer's yes."

"That gives me a lot of latitude."

"Take it," Faye said.

He stepped back to get another look at her: short brown hair worn in a wave again, deep clear skin, the gray eyes he remembered —a smoky haze in them—the gorgeous mouth waiting for him like pink fruit.

"You like the outfit?" she asked. She was wearing jeans and a white oxford shirt.

"I'd like it better hanging over a bedroom chair."

"I'd still be wearing panties." She brushed her lips against his chin. "Silk ones," she said into his neck.

"They'd have to be aluminum to stop what I'm getting right now."

"Arabian Nights stuff, huh?"

"What?"

She opened her mouth a fraction, allowing his tongue to flutter under hers for a moment, disengaged, and murmured, "I've read that the ladies of the harem were sometimes serviced through their silk pajamas."

"Any pictures in these books?"

"I think we should discuss this inside."

They took a while to reach the bedroom, entwined together, reluctant to let go. They left a trail of clothes on the broadloom, sank down onto the bed, locked into each other, hammered together briefly like driven pistons, released together, lay together.

When they began again it was a gentle struggle to get closer, deeper; hands moving, fingers gripping, breathing each other's air. They traveled for an hour through warm seas, cool space; swam, flew, glided on each other's bodies.

Submerged beneath him, she was a taut ship drifting him on a calm and easy tide; reversed, she was a full spread above him, sweeping him away, taking him with her.

"What happened between us last night," Faye said at last, "is something I've been thinking about all day. I wasn't sure what it was made of, the feeling. I thought maybe soap bubbles. I just couldn't tell."

"And what do you think now?"

He felt her shoulder raise against his chest in a tiny shrug. "I'm still not sure. But it's obviously something tougher than soap bubbles. You have any idea?"

"I don't know either. Maybe just very tough soap bubbles."

"Maybe," she said. But she was smiling when she kissed him.

They ate supper out on the terrace, the softness of the warm night settling quietly around them.

Below them the forest fire of Central burnt itself out on the harbor, which glittered as if a high wind had layered it with sparks. Beyond the water, over in Kowloon, the white conflagration broke out again.

Decker and Faye ate slowly, watching each other, cool and relaxed. Decker was barefoot, his floral shirt worn lazily outside of his tan chinos. Faye had on a toweling bathrobe, her shower-damp hair streaked back very much as it had been when Decker had first met her thirty-two hours ago, although it seemed to him a lot longer than that. He felt he knew her mind and body like he would have somebody he'd been living with for months.

"Faye Keeble?"

She raised her palm. "Present."

"You're not just a pretty face. You're a lovely face. Did you know that?"

"No, I didn't. But if you say I am, maybe there's something to it."

"Let's go out tomorrow night. So far, all I've seen you wearing is jeans and a man's shirt, or that terry robe, or nothing."

"Which do you prefer?"

"Let's stay in tomorrow night," Decker said.

"No, let's go out. Then stay in."

"Deal."

They ate the food, sipped chewy red South Australian wine, watched the incandescent city laid out below, easy with each other, happy. They drank coffee from Africa, brandy from Spain. Then Decker, with an inward sigh, started talking about something he knew would make them a little less happy.

"I asked you about Arthur Murdoch today. Something happened between him and Angela, you said. Did you remember exactly what?"

Faye put down her coffee cup and stared at the unimprovable symmetry of cup and saucer: two perfect circles of white bone china.

"My roommate is killed, and because of it you come to Hong Kong, and we get together. It's a weird world, isn't it?"

"And getting weirder. What do you remember?"

"Not much more than I told you."

"She didn't discuss him with you?"

"Not in depth, no. We didn't natter like that. We talked about our jobs, Hong Kong, the States. But our private lives remained private."

"I don't get it. This wasn't a flute teacher taking her out." Decker pointed off the terrace. "It was a guy who owns one of those entire buildings down there. Didn't she at least mention going up to that glass palace of his?"

"She said it was like coming in on an aircraft. A feeling of floating." Faye, who hadn't touched her dessert, picked up a fork and took a healthy mouthful.

Decker watched her eat. He had a feeling she wasn't going at the cake because she was hungry.

"Hey, Faye."

"Yes?"

"I've only known you for a little while."

"Less than that."

"Right." Decker smiled at this bright girl. "So how come I think I know you well enough to wonder if there's something you're not telling me?"

She moved her fork for another stab at the cake, then quit the deception and let the utensil clatter to the plate.

"Probably because you're a quick learner."

Decker waited. Faye gave it to him.

"Angie had a funny philosophy. She was quite happy to accept gifts from men who took her out, men she hadn't known for more than a few days. I never said anything, but she knew how I felt about it."

"Did Murdoch give her something?"

"A watch. A very expensive one."

"After the first date?"

"After the second. He took her up to his house, and something happened up there that upset her."

"What exactly?"

"She told me she was left by herself, and she wandered around the house, found her way into his office. There was a microrecorder on his desk with some business papers. Angie played back the tape.

Or some of it," Faye said, then hurried on in reply to Decker's surprised look. "She was like that. Angie liked to kid around. She said she was going to tease Murdoch about his business secrets. Murdoch came in and yelled at her to drop it. He was furious. But he calmed down quickly and apologized. Told her his business affairs affected a lot of people and that he was naturally sensitive about such things. Next day he sent her the watch."

"To atone for his outburst?"

"Sure."

Decker picked up his brandy. It had been served in big snifters, but he didn't twirl the liquid; it was a cliche he liked to stay away from. He took a sip, then asked Faye the big question he had all ready to go.

"What was on the tape?"

"It certainly wasn't anything to get excited about. Murdoch dictating some kind of memo about . . ." Faye stopped, furrowed her brow. "It was a Chinese name . . ."

"Think."

"Why is all this so important?"

"Anything concerning Angela is important. What was on the memo?"

Faye looked up as if the answer was on the terrace roof. She concentrated for a moment, then grasped at a swirling memory. 'Doh something . . . doh mei-doh. He was talking about something or somebody named doh mei-doh. Angie said she only heard half a sentence. Something about Taiwan being happy about CND."

"That's exactly what she heard?" Decker asked, trying not to put too much weight into the question.

Faye nodded. "A reference to doh mei-doh, and being on schedule, and that Taiwan would be happy about CND. It didn't make any sense to her, and it doesn't to me."

Decker looked away from her, looked down at the Central, and fanned the information in his mind like a poker hand.

On Schedule.

Taiwan.

CND.

Doh-mei-doh.

"It makes no sense to me either," Decker said. "Taiwan is Taiwan. And the only CND I ever heard of is the Campaign for Nuclear Disarmament, the British peace movement. As for doh mei-doh, I'd have to research it. It doesn't sound Cantonese. Some other dialect, maybe." He thought for a moment. "You didn't tell the police any of this?"

"They didn't ask me any of this. And again I have to wonder why it fascinates you."

Decker flirted with telling her the truth, decided against it, then, looking at her concerned loveliness, Faye Keeble, Angela Waters' best friend, on the other side of the table, he reversed himself. Maybe she had a right to know. And maybe he wanted to tell her in order to share something he wouldn't be sharing with anybody else outside of the trade. He wanted to get closer to this woman, and confiding in her would be a big step in that direction.

"I think Angela was murdered because of what she heard on that tape," Decker said, putting his hands flat on the tabletop and facing her square-on. "I think Arthur Murdoch had her killed. And to get him for it," Decker said into Faye's shocked silence. "I'm gonna have to find out who or what doh mei-doh is, what CND really stands for, why Taiwan would be happy, and what exactly it is that's on schedule."

11

At eight A.M. Decker had already been awake for two hours worrying the same questions that had kept him from getting much sleep. He needed some input, some feedback from Bumpy and Miriam and Johnny Risotto, but it was too early to go to the office, so he decided to go to the dojo instead. It wouldn't be a bad way to start the day; rid his mind of Murdoch and the meaning of the tape for a while, and concentrate on simple things like eye and arm coordination; get up some sweat.

The master's assistant kitted him out as he'd done the previous day, then Decker went out onto the floor.

The master, waiting for him out there in his dark, flowing uniform, bowed to Decker and gave him some instructions.

"You will sit mokuzu, please. Compose your mind. Dwell on strong and placid things. The sun steady on the ocean and the riptide surging below. The hawk gliding in the summer sky a moment before its thundering dive. Strength from within."

Once again Decker was impressed by the man's double persona; he exuded a sense of immense and implacable calm, and yet beneath the navy-blue tunic, hard, lean muscles were ready to trigger instantly: the sword and the chrysanthemum, the classic Japanese samurai mix.

Decker walked off a ways, sat cross-legged, straight-backed, the bamboo shinai across his knees in a position that was supposed to turn the sword into a forgotten twig of wood.

He tried to focus on serene strengths, but there was no way an image of calm oceans and soaring hawks would form. He saw, instead, power of another kind, overt and show-off: Arthur Murdoch's corded arms tossing up a tennis ball and lashing it over a net. And a third kind of power, this one buried in flabby unkemptness: Major Reggie Slemp in his beautifully ordered gun room holding that deadly silenced target pistol.

Doh mei-doh.

On schedule.

Whatever it was, it had been worth the risk of killing a DEA employee to keep it quiet.

Why?

Because Angela Waters was simply a woman out on a date who got unlucky and found the wrong thing? Or was it *because* she was DEA, and Murdoch had been afraid that what she'd heard, or might have heard, would sooner or later mean something to her?

Arthur Murdoch, Hong Kong taipan: insurance, construction, shipping, textiles.

Heroin?

Decker became aware of the master waiting for him. He rose and went to the center of the floor. They bowed, then looked at each other for a moment, a moment that wasn't supposed to be there. Two men, the Japanese with his scant figure, his thinning pigtailed hair, the creased web of skin obscuring his left eye. And Decker, so much taller and broader, and twenty years his junior, his jaw getting tight as he recognized some kind of challenge in his instructor.

As the man placed his steel face mask on his head, Decker thought he caught the briefest impression of a superior smile.

Both gripped the bamboo swords, hands apart on the rough leather mounts. Both assumed the middle position.

"Shomen!" the master shouted.

Decker yelled *"Ei"* and they were into it.

Eight steps forward, eight steps back; attack, defense, their long bamboos cracking together, echoing around the quiet of the dojo. A rare thing happened. A small group of tai chi exponents left off their ballet, riveted by the intense surge of action in the middle of the floor: the superb, deft skill of the yudansha against the fierce outpouring of concentrated strength, the sheer aggression of the tall Westerner.

It lasted for six furious minutes, the master calling the disciplines, Decker hurling himself into them, trying for a touch, a score, and not even coming close.

"Enough!" the master cried.

Decker could have held his blow, a migi-do cut to the right side of the breastplate, but he let it go, his sword slicing through the air.

"Ya!"

The master's shidachi counter cut the sword with a terrible whack, killed its powering descent dead.

They stood for a moment like two men holding swords for a wedding couple to pass underneath, then slowly relaxed.

The Japanese removed his mask, took two long breaths, a faint glow of moisture at his temple. Decker was panting, the heaving in his chest taking his shoulders up and down, sweat smarting his eyes, soaking his ribs.

The master began to speak, surprising Decker by telling him something he'd heard before: the story of the duel between two famous swordsmen.

"In Japan, in the Sengoku-Jidai, the Age of War, one of the greatest swordsmen was a man named Tsukahara Bokuden, a minor baron from Niigata, a soldier poet. He learned his art at the Kashima Shinto shrine. He fought nineteen duels with the live blade, and killed nineteen men."

The master told the story with the same precise detail, and with little variation.

". . . Tactics do not depend on the sudden charge or the cowardly blow. What matters is a mind kept cool as winter's snow. You have slain my wife. Pray to Buddha, Rinsai, you are about to lose your life."

"What happened?" Decker asked, because he knew he was supposed to.

"Rinsai was confused by this placid reaction. He fought badly and died quickly."

The master bowed to Decker, signifying the end of the lesson for the day, asked him to sit mokuzu, and left to take another class. He was joined by his assistant, a young Japanese with a shaven head. "Yoshio," the master said, "what is your assessment of that student?"

The assistant looked over to where Decker was sitting, his face glistening, his breathing still not back to normal.

"His reigi is deplorable," the young man replied, referring to the etiquette of kendo. "His technique is poor, his timing rushed, his defense sloppy. He fights with his arms and shoulder, and not his head."

"But . . . ?"

Yoshio frowned, said grudgingly, "But he has commendable

power. Enormous drive. On offense he strikes each blow as if it were his last."

"And what of his chances were he to fight with the live sword?" the master asked, putting his assistant to the test.

"He would die at the second thrust. But if only his right arm were cut off, I think he would switch hands and attack with his left."

"A man like that," the master said, watching Decker slowly recovering, "what would you say his job is? A salesman? A business executive?"

The young assistant, ramrod straight, stared down the hall, shook his shaven head. "No. That one is a warrior of some kind."

The master smiled.

"Yoshio, you are learning."

With Ralph Dobrinski giving him the nod, Decker said, "I'm going to talk for some time. Anybody who wants to go to the bathroom better go now."

He told them about his visit to Murdoch's house, what was said, what he thought was left unsaid. He told them about his trip up to Fo Tan, and how he'd bluffed Slemp, how he'd won the man over, and what was in Slemp's basement. Last he related the information Faye had given him, about Murdoch's squabble with Angela Waters, and what she'd heard on the microrecorder.

He spoke for fifteen minutes uninterrupted, then said, "Okay. the bottom line. I don't like Arthur Murdoch. I suspect he has people killed who are in his way. In my opinion he's cold, vicious, and driven by some kind of evil engine. I admit that's emotion on my part, so let's talk about facts. It's a fact that Brian Fairweather killed Angie. And I believe that Fairweather is telling the truth when he says that God told him to kill her. It's a fact that Reggie Slemp fits his description of God. And it's a fact that Slemp has been identified by the waitress at Mad Dogs as somebody Fairweather spoke to that night. It's a fact that Slemp is a killer, certainly based on the evidence I saw. And it's also a fact, by virtue of his own oblique confession, that he works for Murdoch as his hatchet man.

"It's a fact that Murdoch has extensive interests in Southeast Asia, including Sarawak. It's perfectly possible that he found out about Fairweather being arrested down there on a sex charge. It's perfectly possible that he knew Fairweather was a religious nut, and came up with the idea of using him to kill Angie so it would look like the work of a madman.

"Slemp, Murdoch's enforcer, did his part, and Fairweather sure as hell did his. There's no question in my mind that Murdoch did it through Slemp, who did it through Fairweather. And I think it all happened because of what Angela heard on a tape at Murdoch's house. That's it, lady and gentlemen. I rest my case."

Everybody had things to say, questions to ask, but they deferred to Ralph Dobrinski.

"Did this guy Slemp admit to talking to Fairweather?"

"I didn't want to get that close to the bone. If I was who I claimed to be, I didn't figure there was any reason Murdoch would've told me about any of that."

"So the line below the bottom line," Dobrinski said from behind his desk, his bright eyes out of whack with his stolid face and thick body, "is that we have one crime, three killers, and no legal rope to loop 'em together."

"Not yet, no."

Johnny Risotto spoke next, made the request both Bumpy and Miriam were about to make.

"Run it by us again, huh? What Faye Keeble thought Angie heard on that tape."

"Something or somebody called doh mei-doh. A reference to being on schedule, and that Taiwan would be happy about CND."

Bumpy had perched his thin frame on a bookcase in a corner. He hopped down and left the room without a word.

Miriam said, "CND is the Campaign for Nuclear Disarmament. But I can't see Taiwan being happy about anything like that. So it's a good bet CND stands for something else."

"There's a CND in town here," Dobrinski said. "It's an ad agency. But I don't know where that gets us."

"Maybe Murdoch owns the place," Miriam offered.

Dobrinski said no. "I know the guy who owns it. Hal Daley."

Nobody said anything for a while, they were waiting for Bumpy's return, suspecting that he'd gone to do some checking.

He arrived back a few minutes later with a fat, odd-shaped book under his arm. He said, "There are two CND's listed in the phone book. One's an ad agency—"

"We've covered that," Miriam said.

"—the other's a freight outfit. CND Freight Forwarding Limited."

"How about this?" Johnny Risotto asked, spread out in his chair. "Let's say there's an outside chance that Angie's murder was drug-related. Taiwan's huge in dope. Maybe the people in Taiwan are happy about CND Freight being on schedule with a delivery."

"Sure, that'd play," Bumpy said, putting down the book. "The United Bamboo handles most of the dope out of Taipei. But not through CND Freight. I ran them through the computer, and they're clean."

"Maybe they just started a new line of business," Johnny suggested.

Miriam's red hair bobbed in agreement, but Bumpy looked doubtful. "It's possible, although the info's pretty well up-to-date. Unless they're brand-new in the biz, we'd have them on file."

"All this," Decker said, "is presupposing that Murdoch's running dope. Can we check on that?"

"I already got a discreet call in to a buddy at Arsenal Street," Bumpy answered. "He's getting back to me." He opened the book he'd brought in, a Chinese dictionary with two pages marked by paper clips. "As to doh mei-doh, the nearest I can get is something in Hakka Rey. Burnt ground." Bumpy shrugged his thin shoulders, slapped the book closed. "That's only a literal translation. Best I can do."

"It's a long shot anyway," Decker said, sitting on a corner of Dobrinski's desk. "Faye doesn't speak much Chinese. And I don't think Angela did, did she?"

"Kitchen Cantonese, that's all," Miriam said.

"So," Decker continued, "Faye's only repeating what she thinks Angela thinks she heard. It may be correct. It may be something a lot different."

The phone rang then; Dobrinski picked it up, listened for a moment, waved to Bumpy. Bumpy took the handpiece, grunted into it twice, thanked somebody, hung up.

"Narcotics has nothing on Arthur Murdoch. No overt involvement, no suspected involvement."

"Then he's either in the biz and running it through an intermediary, or doh mei-doh is a code name for something entirely different," Dobrinski said. He didn't look happy.

Heavy silence swam through the office.

Decker took a stroll over to a window and watched the traffic pouring down the hill, down Garden Road. A couple of police Land Rovers peeled off in the direction of Government House, protected by its thick stand of trees. The scene looked like a river in flood shooting by a lazy green sandbank.

Still facing the window, Decker said, "Who do we know in Special Branch these days?"

"Forget it," Johnny told him. "They're as tight as ever."

"Tighter," Miriam said. "I know a guy in Special Branch. Had him up for a drink last week. When I asked him if he took an olive or an onion in his martini, he said: 'I'm sorry, I'm afraid I can't tell you that.' "

Everybody smiled at Miriam's little joke, knowing, at the same time, that it wasn't far from the truth. Special Branch, being involved in things like counterespionage and other sensitive areas, was notoriously close-mouthed.

"Too bad," Decker said. "If we had a contact, he could tell us a little something about Murdoch's background. Something that Special Branch would know and ordinary folks wouldn't. And that might give us a clue to what the hell's going on."

"Is he a U.S. citizen?" Dobrinski asked. "We could go to the Bureau."

"He's a Hong Kong citizen," Bumpy told him. "Besides, he's a famous anti-Communist, so the Bureau wouldn't be interested anyway."

"How about Jack Sanders?" Decker asked. "He still in the Branch? I seem to recall this office did him a favor once."

Johnny Risotto, peeling the wrapper from a candy bar, shook his head. "There's no way in, Deck. Those guys have to sign a piece of paper that puts them smack up against the Official Secrets Act. Even after they quit the force they can't set foot in a Communist country for three years. That's how tough it is. Sure, Jack Sanders owes us, but he won't dip into his files for us. If it ever came to light, they'd hand him a suit with arrows on it."

"I'll tell you what," Miriam said. "Why don't you give Slemp to Arsenal Street? Let 'em haul the fucker in for gun possession. They take it easy on him in return for what he knows about Murdoch."

"Hey, Red." Bumpy was tapping his temple. "You're not thinking, kid. If he's Murdoch's enforcer, he can't pull Murdoch into the mud without getting splashed himself. One whole gun charge will get him two years. A third of a murder rap will get him fifteen to twenty."

Miriam nodded at that. "You're right, Bump. You've got a keen, analytical mind. Intuitive, probing, and icily deductive, you sneaky little rat."

"Thanks, Miriam. I know I sometimes take a dig at you, cast aspersions on your womanhood, stuff like that, but I want you to know that, deep down, I think you're a genuine clumsy slut."

While Bumpy and Miriam smiled tightly at each other, and Dobrinski ignored them, and Johnny Risotto finished the candy bar, Decker got an idea. It wasn't anything stunning; just something to get them back to basics. Legwork in lieu of brainwork.

"Let's put a tag on him. Murdoch. A round-the-clock surveil. See who comes and goes at that house of his. If whatever it is that's on schedule is coming off soon, maybe it'll show up in the company he keeps. Okay, Ralph?"

"Why not? The four of you can do six-hour shifts. Do a little thinking while you're watching."

"We'd better roster it so that you and I are free tomorrow afternoon," Johnny said to Decker. "A call came in from Eddie Fong. He's got a meet set up."

"Eddie Fong. I'd almost forgotten about old Eddie." Decker checked with Dobrinski. "What are you gonna tell I Street in your report?"

Dobrinski knew that Decker wasn't referring to Eddie Fong. He dismissed I Street with a one-handed "safe" signal. "I'll tell 'em the truth. That we've got a strong lead, and we're hoping for a break."

A lead and a break.

Decker figured it. They had one; what they needed was the other.

The silver-and-red China Airlines 737 successfully negotiated the high-rise hazards of the western approach to the airport and completed its run-out a good half-mile short of the beckoning sun dazzle of Kowloon Bay. The plane had began its flight in the smoggy, traffic-polluted city of Taipei, the unlovely capital of the island of Taiwan, formerly called Formosa, the Beautiful One.

Among the 174 passengers was a man in the first-class section who'd come to Hong Kong to meet secretly with Arthur Murdoch.

Another man, this one a courier, squashed into a center seat in tourist class, had come to make a delivery. He was unaware that he was making it on behalf of the man sitting in splendid comfort in first class, just as he was unaware of the true nature of the goods that had been placed in his charge.

The flight was cleared through Customs and Immigration without problem. The courier, a young man good at his job, produced a commercial customs form which stated that he was bringing in a number of electronic items urgently required by Chung Wah Components Ltd. He opened the case he carried, a large black Samsonite with combination locks, the devices were routinely checked, the form was stamped, and the young man carried the case through the concourse to where a battered pickup truck was waiting. Release and acceptance forms were signed, the case changed hands, and the courier, with four hours to kill before his return flight, went downtown to lunch in his favorite Peking restaurant.

The man traveling in first class, whom the courier was unknowingly working for, was accompanied by a bodyguard, their relationship clearly that of servant and master. The servant was six-feet-seven, and had been a basketball star with the Taiwanese national team. Now he was a full-time security attendant attached to the man he called General, the man being a lieutenant general in the Taiwanese Air Force. In Taiwan the ex-ballplayer watched over the general's well-being, carrying an open sports bag in which lay an Italian Socimi, a fully automatic submachine gun which could be fired with one hand. But, on this trip, because of the colony's gun laws, he'd had to content himself with a concealed pistol made of plastic that fired Teflon bullets. He felt very undergunned after the Socimi, but at least he had no trouble passing through the airline's metal detector.

The general was five inches shorter than his bodyguard, which still made him a tall man. A pronounced tummy, and bulk in the buttocks and thighs, made him a big one as well. He was fifty-four, with a circular face that was beginning to crease above the cheekbones and beneath the chin. He had puffy and extremely elongated eye folds inherited from a Manchurian grandparent.

The general often came to Hong Kong, and always with the same forged passport. In Taipei he exited the country through a VIP area, and by spreading a little money around, his departures were not recorded. Not officially, anyway. The ICA, the Taiwan Internal Police, was aware that the general made little illicit trips now and then, but put it down to the attractions of the second wife they knew he had stashed in an expensive apartment in Repulse Bay. It was a normal enough double life enjoyed by any number of high-ranking Taiwanese officials and military men, most of whom had money out in the Hang Seng, and dividends going into a Hong

Kong bank account which they neglected to report. All standard stuff: the perquisites of rank and privilege. It was never thought necessary to put a tail on the general, so his connection with Arthur Murdoch remained unknown.

The general lingered at the airport long enough to observe the safe transfer of the Samsonite suitcase, then turned his attention to the rental car his tall bodyguard had just picked up.

Frown lines increased the cross-hatching on his face; he liked to ride in a Jaguar but, as his bodyguard explained, a Toyota Crown sedan was all they had left.

The general settled grumpily into the rear seat with its fussy nylon lace headrests, and handed his bodyguard the address Arthur Murdoch had sent him: a girls' school up in Fan Ling, the main city of the New Territories.

A girls' school . . . The general wondered, with a pleasant and familiar feeling stirring in his loins, just what Murdoch had prepared for him. The man was a generous and creative host, and had never failed to come up with something novel in the way of entertainment.

The general mused about it as the car took off: three Chinese and a Big Nose; the association was working smoothly now, but after Doh Mei-Doh Day? Who could tell? Murdoch would give them away if it suited his purpose; the general had never yet met a Big Nose you could trust. Too bad; the man really knew how to treat a guest.

The car circled the jammed decrepitude of Kowloon City, headed north toward the Lions Rock tunnel and the freedom of the expressway. The general lounged in the rear seat, still ruffled about having to accept a lesser car. He was used to fine automobiles; he'd been born into wealth. His father had been in command of a regiment under Chiang Kai-shek and, for bravery in battle, had been awarded the silk-stocking concession in Chungking: trading ammunition to the Japanese in Shanghai, who just happened to be the enemy at the time, in return for stockings, which he traded for battlefield morphine, which he then sold for gold.

His son, the general, had gone to military college in Canton after the Japanese defeat in 1945, then moved to Taiwan ahead of Mao and his armed peasants in 1949, got a commission in the army, then switched to the new air force Claire Chennault had formed for the Nationalists. He'd trained as a pilot on piston aircraft, then trained on jet fighters, then moved up to twin-engined attack fighters.

Stripes had sprung to his sleeve as if he'd had his own tailor, until, at last, when the correct and proper financial arrangements had been made, he'd succeeded to the Department of Arms Procurement as a technical adviser, which, in Taiwan, was like being allowed to rob any five banks of his choice.

Eventually, with seven figures stashed away in various offshore depositories, the general had been graciously allowed to buy his own command.

He'd met Arthur Murdoch when Murdoch had bid on the contract to build an office complex on the outskirts of Taipei. As the projected complex would overlook a road leading to the sea, it needed military permission for plans to move ahead, and when Murdoch had looked around for a reliable and connected middleman, somebody had mentioned the general's name. From then on the general and Arthur Murdoch had enjoyed a pleasant and profitable relationship.

And one that was supposed to continue that way.

It took twenty-five minutes for the Toyota to reach Fan Ling, a junior-size town of small parks and busy roads, and with a no-nonsense downtown section where the signs were made of economical plastic rather than the metal and glass excesses of Hong Kong.

The bodyguard recognized Murdoch's Mercedes parked outside a long low school building and swung in behind it.

The general got out, walked to the other car, bent to the rear window.

"Good morning, General," Murdoch said as the big man, looking more like a prosperous banker than an air-force officer, gave him a mock salute.

"Mr. Murdoch. How nice to see you again." When the general smiled, two curved lines like parentheses bracketed his high flat cheeks, and his eyes were stretched into slits. The general had the whitest teeth Murdoch had ever seen. They'd been capped in Los Angeles, so he'd been told, by a man who was a dental cosmetician to several Hollywood movie stars.

"Good flight?" Murdoch asked, shaking the general's large and fleshy hand.

"Excellent, thank you."

"No problem with the extra baggage?"

"I saw it transferred myself. So we are indeed on schedule, as your tape indicated," the general said. He was referring to the microtape Murdoch had sent him the previous week inviting him for dinner and apprising him of the status of the endeavor on which they were embarked, he and Murdoch, and two Hong Kong Chinese. Murdoch had found that the ordinary mail and a good drop-off address were by far the safest way of communicating. He'd sent copies of the tape to the two local men as well.

"You're right about the timing," the general went on, still displaying his Hollywood dental work. "I'm delighted about it."

"Fine," Murdoch said from his hunched position, looking up at the general's height. "We'll talk later at dinner."

"I'm looking forward to it." The general half-turned toward the school. "And whatever you've arranged for today."

"Basketball. I know how much you like the women's game," Murdoch said, giving his guest a little bit of shaft.

The general wasn't offended; he looked excited.

"You're expected. Everything's ready." Murdoch handed him a card. "Just give this to the man at the door."

The general bowed and said, "Doh-mei-doh," as if it were a traditional phrase of thanks, then turned and walked toward the school.

Murdoch watched him go, his mouth tight. The general had been having a little joke, the goddamn fool. Let him; he was living on borrowed time anyway. Soon after this thing was over, the general would meet a major in Taipei—Major Reggie Slemp—and the general and his gun-toting bodyguard would be found shot to death in a car with a half-kilo of heroin hidden under the dash; just one more military man who'd decided to dabble in drugs and been spanked by the big boys. Murdoch knew it would only be a matter of time before the general started hinting about having his payoff improved; the guy was extremely greedy, and not too bright; a dangerous combination. Murdoch ordered his chauffeur to take him back to Hong Kong, then reached for the phone beside him.

He pushed the off button.

He didn't want to be disturbed for the next thirty minutes; he had a lot of heavy thinking to do.

The gymnasium was large by Hong Kong standards, big enough to contain a three-quarter-size basketball court with space at the end for dressing rooms.

From inside came the stamp of feet, the cries of high-school girls. The general gulped.

A sad-faced Chinese in workclothes, a janitor or a caretaker, accepted the card the general handed him, a piece of red pasteboard with the characters for Good Luck printed on it in gold. Wordlessly he led the way toward the rear of the building, pushed open a fire door, went down a dark hall, unlocked an interior door, and gestured inside. It was some kind of storeroom: there were mops and pails, and the smell of floor polish and disinfectant.

The general broke into a mild sweat as he realized what Murdoch had thought up for him, and his throat took on an ashy dryness when he saw what was laid out in a corner: a box of tissues and a tray containing two large black-and-yellow papayas, peeled.

The janitor left the general to his pleasures. The general locked the door and, with his heart belting his ribs, moved farther into the dim little room and found, in the wooden wall, what he'd been certain he'd find: a peephole.

He pressed his eye to it. His breath lurched, and he began to tremble: several girls, fifteen or sixteen years old, no more, were stripping off their sweaty basketball uniforms and reaching for towels. More girls were coming in off the court behind them, not one of them over seventeen.

It took the general but half a minute to get out of his suit, tear off his shorts, shove his eye back to the peephole.

He groaned with pleasure and anticipation, forced himself away, moved quickly to the tray of papayas, and noticed something: a sliver of light coming from another tiny hole. He hurried to it, his penis stiff and throbbing in time to his racing heart.

He peered through the second hole.

A shower room!

Empty, but it wouldn't be for long.

He scrambled back to the other hole, almost wounded his eye ramming his face to the wall, peeped into the changing room. He could hardly stand it; that group of little lovelies were all naked now, heading for the showers.

The general fumbled for one of the papayas. It was so overripe it was oozy in his hands. Holding it like a football in front of him, he turned side-on to the wall, and once again glued his eyes to the peephole. There, right in front of him, not ten feet away, busy chatting with her friends, a sixteen-year-old with stand-up tits, curving and hanging but jutting too, areolae it would be hard to get your whole mouth around, nipples like pink thumbs.

Another girl next to her, but turned away—a bottom bowed like a violin, firm-cheeked, split high, marvelous!

The general sank his penis into the squishy ripeness of the papaya and began to gently fuck it, dry little whimpering sounds grunting from his open mouth, except he was really fucking that cute little sixteen-year-old just beyond the wall, a swivel-hipped little darling with a fine sheen of perspiration glossing her perfect honey-skinned body.

The girl turned.

The general felt as if he'd been struck in the balls.

The thatch on her! Wildly matted, a jumble of black bush.

God! Ahhh!

The general climaxed, his vision blurring, eyes gone wild, a strangled sound in his mouth like a man being choked.

The papaya, in large shredded pieces now, dropped away and splattered on the floor. He snatched at some tissues, dried himself, leaned against the wall, gave himself a a few minutes to recover, then moved to the other peephole.

Bliss!

A girl under a slow shower, this one older than the others, much more mature, but still not a wrinkle, not a crease in her luscious body, except the glorious one that counted.

She began to soap herself. The general, erect again, reached for the second papaya, sank his born-again member into its juicy richness.

The young girl, proud of her body, was soaping it slowly, humming an inane pop tune, and luxuriating under the warm water, swaying in time to the tune in her head. She lathered the soap in her hands—it bubbled up white and creamy—ran the soap over her thighs, up over her hips, around the dip of her navel, turned to face the tiled wall, and lathered the globes of her perfect rump.

Still humming, she turned back, her breasts jiggling as she moved her shoulders in her song. She looked down at them, drew lazy soap lines around her nipples, cupped both breasts, and rotated her soapy fingers in slow, sensuous revolutions, a young girl enjoying her new womanhood.

On the other side of the wall the general, gripped by a pounding sexual ecstasy, had tears in his eyes and a pain in his chest. He'd once confided to Murdoch that he'd searched for years for a partner who could raise him to the heights, but without success. He had the money to buy any woman in the world who was for sale, including those who didn't know they were. On one of his visits to his Hollywood dentist he'd paid the star of a hugely successful TV series fifty thousand dollars to go to bed with him for one hour, and even she, a woman with the body of a goddess, even she had not been as pleasurable as a melon you could buy in the market for thirty cents. Murdoch had remembered, and had thoughtfully supplied a visual stimulant as well.

The young girl raised her arms over her head like a diver entering a pool, and shook her body to a pop beat, shook and swiveled and swayed.

The general's response was quick and massive, and he sank to his knees while his chest heaved and his tubes pumped.

He got some tissues, wiped away the mess of fruit on his cock, knowing he'd have trouble urinating; the soft fruit would lodge in there for a while, but pleasure often brought its own price.

He dressed, unlocked the door, and left the gym, walked in the hot blare of the sunlight toward his bodyguard, waiting beside the car.

The bodyguard, taking the Toyota away in the direction of the expressway, twitched his nose and wondered if the fool in the rear seat had stepped on a ripe banana.

Repulse Bay, on the south side of Hong Kong island, had always reminded the general of the French Riviera, with its snaking littoral road swooping past the fine homes, the cool green mountains above, the glistening sea below, lapping the white bight of sand. Indeed, the apartment he rented for his number-two wife cost as much as a similar one would have in Nice or Cannes. But nothing was too good for a woman who'd been Miss Dragon Boat Festival of 1981, and had a talented crotch to go with the good looks.

The general showered as soon as he got inside, came out naked, and took the woman on the broadloom in front of the picture window overlooking the beach. It was good—she still had a fine figure even at age twenty-six—but all the way through, he kept thinking of that beautifully budded seventeen-year-old in the gym.

He fell asleep on the broadloom, and awoke refreshed two hours later. He ran a videocassette of himself making love to his number-one wife in Taipei, his number-two wife watching beside him, and pointed out to her the areas in which his Taipei wife's technique was superior. He put her through her paces to see if she'd learned anything, then went inside and slept till early evening.

His tall bodyguard, whose name was Lim, picked him up around eight P.M. and drove up the winding incline to Wong Nai Chung

Gap, then around the other side to Arthur Murdoch's house. Lim had driven the general there many times, and knew the way well. He also knew the great glass house well, and the layout of the grounds.

So he knew exactly where he was going to place the little device he had in his pocket.

It was one of the devices the young courier had brought in on the flight that morning. Lim had picked it up from a warehouse in Sai Ying Pun a few hours back while the general had been coaching his second wife.

When they reached Murdoch's house there were two cars parked on the red brick drive, evidence that the other guests had already arrived. The front door of the glass house opened on a soft yellow glow and swallowed the general into its rich luxury. Lim, as usual, found his way to the servants' quarters, where dinner was served to him and the other two chauffeurs, both of whom were merely drivers. The men they drove for had no need of protection; they were both so powerful, in a certain area, that anybody would have been crazy to try to harm them.

Lim joined in the car talk at the servants' table—boring stuff about engine sizes and zero-to-sixty times—then got away when the meal was finished, to smoke a cigarette outside.

Standing near the high black gates, he watched a car arrive, and three sensational-looking women get out of it, which meant that the business meeting was over, food was being served, and the after-dinner entertainment would be ready and waiting in the wings. Lim gave it another twenty minutes, then moved.

A yellow floodlight at the side of the house stretched his figure to impossible dimensions as he silently crossed the manicured lawn. He turned a corner, walked into the reflected white excitement created by garden spots positioned beneath rows of flowerless shrubs. His long shadow snuck ahead of him, bent across a flagstone path, the opaque gleam of the glass house barely reaching him now, the trickle and splash of water coming off the roof receding into the creak of the night: crickets, a lonely bird, the soft hum of music. The trimmed landscaping ended at some boxed bay trees, and beyond these, beyond a discreet wire fence set above the cliff face, the grassy bank took a sudden nosedive and fell away into a mountain wilderness, dark for a thousand feet until it hit the clustered lights of the southern beach towns far below.

Lim's stalky legs took him swiftly down some concrete steps to a passage that ran underneath the back of the house. Above him now were the massive red steel triangular beams supporting the great glass balcony which cantilevered out into the air.

It was dark where he was, the lawn lights unable to reach this space, but a three-quarter moon bent enough ambient light into the passageway for him to see by. He stepped lightly to a point about halfway along the path, where a plastic tube of electric wiring descended from a junction box. He didn't need the wiring for his purpose, but the box was a convenient place to attach the device. He took it from his pocket—it was no bigger than a miniature AM radio—peeled off its strip of sticky paper, revealing a layer of thick black Bostick.

He pressed it against the wall above the box, activated the timer, then went back along the passage, up the steps, around the lawn, back to the servants' quarters, where the talk was still of automobiles.

The general kept him waiting for another two hours.

Driving home, back down the slope to Repulse Bay, the general burped softly, then said in Cantonese, his tones slurred by fine wine and single-malt Scotch, "Where'd you put it?"

"Where you told me. Underneath the back of the house."

"Good," said the general, and smiled out at the warm night gliding by the window. He'd had an excellent evening; doh mei-doh, as Murdoch's chef had produced a superior minced pigeon in lettuce leaves and a delicious dish of garlicked eels, and the woman he'd had after the meal had been delicious too—an expert with the rosin bow; she'd delayed his climax for ten brain-searing minutes. The general dozed in contentment, and had to be shaken awake outside the apartment house.

Upstairs he tumbled into bed beside the hot nakedness of his number-two wife, but couldn't perform. He settled for holding on to those wondrous prizewinning breasts and foggily conjuring up the memory of the adolescent schoolgirls taking off their clothes in the changing room at Fan Ling.

What a host the American was.

What a shame he had to go.

Around about when the general's bodyguard had been placing the little device under Arthur Murdoch's glass veranda, Decker had been at the bottom of the slope on the other side of the Peak, in a restaurant in Central, sitting opposite Faye.

Riding down from the Mid Levels, they'd talked briefly about Angela Waters and her association with Murdoch. Decker had asked Faye about Reggie Slemp again, and whether she'd been able to think of any possible tie-up with Angela and the Taiwan/CND riddle. They'd got nowhere again, then agreed to drop the subject, come back to it later. They both felt a little guilty about this, but the plain fact was, the thing that had sprung up so quickly between them was becoming stronger and stronger, and talking about Angela's death was getting in its way. They wanted to talk about each other.

"Tell me something about yourself," Decker said. "Something you've never told anybody else."

"I cheated once on a seventh-grade history exam."

"I'm sorry, but I'm gonna have to report you."

Decker had one hand on a glass of beer, the other lying flat on the table. Faye reached out and twined her fingers around his.

"Now you. You tell me something personal."

"I'm a Junior Miss, size six."

When Faye's mouth expanded, her eyes widened marginally, imparting a look of slight surprise to her face. Decker had noticed this before; it made her smile that much more complimentary, as if the speaker had also told her something she didn't know.

"I already guessed that," Faye said. "Come on, personal. How did you get that scar under your eye?"

"What scar?" Decker touched a finger to the deep scouring on his cheek. "Hell, I'm gonna have to buy a new razor blade."

"Come on, tell me," Faye urged, laughing a little. She looked irresistible: a cream cotton dress with some neckline, minimal makeup, her hair blown dry and sitting high on her head, leaving a lot of fine, grainy-skinned neck on display; vampire bait, Decker thought. He answered her then; he found he wanted to tell her something personal, and he'd told very few other people about his scar. And he'd been asked a lot.

"A dealer took a shot at me."

Faye's lips moved back sharply on her teeth. "The bullet hit you there?"

"Not the bullet, a piece of the wall the bullet hit."

"A little higher and you would've lost your eye."

"Yeah, well, he was a thoughtful dealer. How did you get to be a securities analyst?"

"Clerked on Wall Street for a year, moved into sales, closed my eyes, stuck a pin in the Dow Jones list, and presented my findings to my boss as my considered recommendations for performance stocks for the quarter. When seven out of ten hit, they made me an analyst full-time."

"That's what you use? A pin and a blindfold?"

"Good heavens, no. I'm all scientific now. Plant research, management lunches, performance charts, competitor comparisons, et cetera. I only average five out of ten now, but at least I'm doing it in the approved manner." Faye swallowed some of her drink, still with her hand on Decker's. "How did you get to be DEA?"

"It's a long story. You want to talk, or shall we order?"

"Both. You can talk with your mouth full. I've seen you."

"You're bad, you know that?"

"Tell me," Faye said. "I told you. Did you go to college?"

"You have to, to be DEA. Have to graduate too. After that you're allowed to go back to being stupid."

"What did you do after college?"

"Journalism. Got a job on the *Inquirer* in Philly. Interviewed a couple of DEA guys for an article, and they impressed the hell out of me. I saw them off and on for a drink after that, and one day they told me their outfit was looking for a few good men, as they say." Decker tossed off the last third of his beer. "I wasn't about to win a Pulitzer, so I had my Olivetti bronzed and went to Basic Agent school."

"At Quantico? The Marine base in Virginia?"

"How did you know the school's there?"

"Angie told me."

"When I went through," Decker said, "it was in Glencoe, although I trained at headquarters in Washington." Decker chuckled at the memory. "It was a little cramped, but fun."

Faye crept a little closer, put some gentle pressure on his hand. "Tell me." She wanted to know everything she could about this man who'd exploded into her life; it was a bit like coming into a movie halfway through, a movie in which you quickly became involved, caught by; you wanted to know what had happened at the start, how it had begun.

"Well, for a start, Combatives were a little weird. The Administration bought this old bank on J Street and converted it. They put a gym on the first floor for hand-to-hand training, and that was okay. And the machine-gun, shotgun, carbine training was okay too, because we did that at Fort Blair. But they used the bank for the handgun instruction, put in a firing range on the second and third floors. I tell you, walking into that place with an S&W two-incher in your pocket, you felt like Willie Sutton out to make a big haul."

A hostess came, they ordered refills. The room was only half-full, a small place, some Chinese couples, some Western couples, no businessmen, no tourists. A sizzling smell of crisp duck predominated, accented by ginger and garlic. White damask mirrored the low-key lighting, and bottles of wine and beer crackled in beaded ice buckets. A nice spot for a quiet meal.

Faye raised her drink and a drop of frosted water dripped onto Decker's knuckle. She raised his hand, licked at the water drop, smiled into his eyes. "More," she said. "Keep going. What else did they teach you?"

"How to swim fifty yards dressed and in a semiconscious state."

"You're kidding."

"Nope. We used the pool at the old Sonesta Hotel on Thomas Circle. Unheated and freezing. I thought you just had to swim a length, show 'em you could do it wearing a suit. So I was waiting for the word to go, and I certainly got it. The instructor clipped me on the neck and shoved me in. And that was when I realized you were supposed to do it stunned."

"Pretty tough. Do the FBI trainees have to do that too?"

"Sure. But they get water wings."

"I'm loving this," Faye said. "I may join myself. What else?"

"Tradecraft. Clandestine ops. Clerical work, plus the legal side of the business. Surveillance techniques. A little electronics. Street ops, all kinds of things."

"Tell me about that one, street ops. That sounds like fun."

"The most fun in street ops," Decker said, wanting to put his arms around her and kiss her for five minutes, "was learning high-speed automobile control. Used to drive the local cops crazy, four of us doing seventy through a thirty-mile-an-hour zone in Fairfax, Virginia."

"You sound like a bunch of teenagers."

"That's basically what we were. There was one little number they always pulled on the rookies when you were learning street surveillance. They gave you a Polaroid shot of a guy you were told to spot on the street and tail without him noticing you. So, okay, we stood around on J Street for half an hour, and sure enough, the guy comes by. Big, tough-looking cookie. So we tagged him the way we'd been taught in class, and we thought we were doing okay. He walked us all over Washington for about three hours then, around about two P.M. he goes into this lunch counter, sits down, and orders. So we sat down and ordered too. Not only does this look natural, we were starving, okay?"

Faye was starting to grin, anticipating the punchline.

"So," Decker continued, after a pull at his second beer, "his food arrives, and he starts wolfing it down. Then our orders arrive. And what happens? The guy puts money down, gets up, and leaves."

"And what did you guys do?"

"Went after him, of course. We put down money too, but hell, we were famished, pounding the streets all morning in this guy's wake, so we grabbed our burgers and hot dogs and ran out after him. We went around the corner, and there he is, standing there facing us right in the middle of the sidewalk. And he yells at us, right there in the middle of Salem Street, 'You're not supposed to bring your fuckin' lunch with you.' "

When Faye laughed, she laughed with her whole body, tossing her head back; a good laugh, hearty and genuine. It was another thing Decker liked about her: she didn't hold back on anything; she was up front with her feelings, and the unexpressed invitation was there to either take 'em or leave 'em. A very together lady, Miss Keeble; and in that clingy cream dress, and with her white even teeth showing in her laugh, and her eyes on him like warm electric things, a very sexy one.

"How long did it last?" she asked. "The training."

"Three months. Then we all graduated as Special Agents Grade Seven."

"Then what? Straight onto the street?"

Decker winced. "Good God, no. If you don't know what you're doing on the boulevards the bad guys'll hammer your head in. No, I spent two years as a gofer. I remember my very first assignment on my very first day. My boss asked me how I'd done on the high-speed evasive-driving course. My heart jumped. I thought I was gonna be wheelman on some big Mafia bust. So when I told him I'd done pretty well, he said, fine, take the car and get it washed."

"What a waste of talent," Faye said, teasing him."

"Oh, I did more than just wash cars. I drove burnt ones around the country, cars that had been made by the other side as DEA vehicles. A year of that and they finally let me go undercover, let me loose on a simple knockoff. I'd sit in the front seat and hold the flash roll. I went on a couple of those, did okay, didn't let my ID fall onto the sidewalk, backed up the guys once or twice, and then I had my bar exam."

"I'm going to need subtitles."

"A bar exam," Decker explained, setting his glass exactly in the center of a table coaster, "is when a group of Grade Fourteens you've been working with get together in a bar and unofficially decide whether or not you're DEA material. If not, the word filters back to you, and nobody bursts into tears if you go in and quit."

"So you passed . . ."

"Scraped through, yeah. Made Grade Nine, started working with a senior partner, impressed him by not getting bitten by our sniffer dog, and was assigned to San Francisco as a Grade Eleven. Did okay, they sent me to language school to study Cantonese."

"The Berlitz crash course?"

"Even better. The U.S. Army language school in Monterey. I spent two years on Grant Avenue disguised as a bowl of wonton soup, then I was posted here when a vacancy came up. I blew it, as I told you, and was kicked back to New York. Blew it again there, and here I am back in NT."

"This is NT? I thought it was HK."

"Not in a DEA cable. We give every major city a code name, something that reflects a particular city's personality. Hong Kong is NT. Stands for Neon Tough."

"Neon Tough," Faye said, trying out the name. "I get the first part, the sign capital of the world, and all that. What about the second part?"

"Tough? Because of all the triad gangs. They're everywhere. And if you get in their way you can lose a limb. It's a shiny-bright, hard town we're having dinner in. Incidentally"—feigning bewilderment, Decker looked around him—"why did we come out for dinner? Do you realize it'll take us at least fifteen minutes to get from this table to your bedroom?"

"We didn't think it through," Faye said with a little sigh.

A hostess glided up to their table, an order pad in her hand. "Are you ready over here?"

"Oh, my, yes," Faye said, smiling at Decker, squeezing his hand.

Decker checked the menu, ordered scallops in black-bean sauce, fried lemon chicken, and fan chow rice.

To go.

* * *

"If you weren't in the money business," Decker said, moving his cheek over her throat, kissing its fragrant smoothness, "what would you be? If you had your druthers."

"An architect. Crisp, clean drawing board, a T square, a ruler, everything correct. All the lines either meeting at exact points or running dead parallel."

"Order. Is that the real Faye Keeble? Everything in its proper place? No surprises?"

"Probably not. But it's the opposite of what I do now, which is largely guesswork." She moved to pull the sheet over them so they could snuggle in the chill of the bedroom's artificial air. "How about you? If you weren't DEA, what would you be?"

"Oh, I don't know. A corrupt Southern sheriff. Something that pays good."

"No, you wouldn't. You don't care about money."

"How do you know that?"

"Because I know you."

"How could you? We only met a few days ago. I don't even know your middle name."

"Julie."

"Or your hometown."

"Youngstown, Ohio."

"Or if you have any brothers or sisters."

"One elder brother. Richard."

"And all you know about me is that I'm a DEA fuck-up who used to be a journalist. So how do you know I'm not kidding about the Southern-sheriff bit?"

"Because," Faye said, kissing his eyebrow, running her hands over his flat stomach, sliding them up to his tight-knit flanks, "I learned your mind while I was learning this body. I know the map of this body now, and I know the person it belongs to. I know what he would do, and what he wouldn't do, by the things he does to me."

Decker raised his head so that his eyes were on a line with hers in the darkened room; just the vague outline of her face visible, the soft curl of her hair, the warm, tart-sweet aroma of her juices.

"All the time we weren't talking," Faye said, "we were sending and receiving signals. Messages. So I know you, Hugh C. Decker. I know why you joined the DEA. And I know why you fucked up, too."

"You do? What else do you know?"

"That you couldn't be a cop, anyway. Even though you were joking."

"Why? I'm a narc, aren't I? That's a cop."

"A special kind, though. If you were a regular cop you'd have to enforce all the laws, some of which you wouldn't agree with. You'd have to arrest some guy because he doesn't have a home to go to. Or pull in some woman for peddling her hips."

"I wouldn't arrest her. I'd make a deal with her."

"Listen. I'm serious. Nobody becomes a policeman because he hates crime. That's for Batman and Robin. But drugs are something else, aren't they? They're very specific. A heroin pusher's dealing in weakness. He's the ultimate coward, the ultimate hypocrite, selling a good time to somebody, knowing the good time's going to result in a bad one. And that irks you, Hugh. It's not the moral consideration, the bad guys make you mad. You get angry because they're out there walking around dealing in the disgusting stuff, and it's damned difficult to do a hell of a lot about them."

Staring at her, but unable to see her face clearly, her words halted Decker, held him motionless.

"Like the captain of that junk," Faye said. "You couldn't find the stuff, and that made you mad because, like anybody in the drug business, that bastard didn't care who ended up a bag of bones in the corner as long as he got paid money."

Decker nodded in the darkness, said quietly, after a moment, "It's not just the bad guys. It's the so-called good guys too. The fun folk who snort a little coke at a party. They've got their fingerprints on the gun that kills a DEA agent in Mexico or Colombia. They help pull the trigger but they wouldn't believe it if you pointed that out to them. They get me mad too, the casual users who don't have anything better to do with a hundred bucks."

"They wouldn't be users if there weren't any sellers."

"They'll always be sellers." Decker flopped onto his back, tried to make out the pattern on the ceiling. "You know what their favorite cop-out is? If I don't sell the stuff, somebody else will. Jesus, that's a pathetic piece of reasoning. When Joe says that, he's admitting that he's willing to swim in the gutter with Jack, but they're too greedy and too bone stupid to see it that way. Faye, I've had guys tell me that if they get killed pushing dope, then it's just too bad, it's the chance you take. They'll brag to me that it's a game for high rollers. They think it's fair. They kill people for a bigger slice of the action, and if the same thing happens to them, tough shit. Guys like that make me very mad because there's no appealing to them. You can't threaten them with anything. A jail term? So what? They go on dealing inside for a few years, build up good contacts for later. You're right, Faye," Decker said to the ceiling, "they get me angry. The whole thing's so fucking cynical I sometimes wonder if I'm living on the wrong planet."

Faye found his hand, folded it into hers, pressed it to her side. She said, "The world's been going through a tough patch for a long time."

"The world? That's the word, all right. It's global now. It used to be the villains stayed home and did evil things on their own patch. Whatever they did in France or Sicily or New York stayed there. But now it's all interconnected. You've got people in Bangkok making decisions about what happens in San Diego. People in Montreal calling the shots in Tokyo. You've got the American Mafia running Australia, for cris-sakes. The bad guys are in black, and there are armies of them. Legions. The guys in white? You've got to be kidding. People have this idea that there's a DEA guy under every bush. Would you believe me if I told you that the DEA Race in Cairo, the Resident Agent in Charge, has a territory that covers twelve thousand square miles? One man."

Faye heard him take a long breath to diffuse the tension stiffening his body.

He said, quieter, his delivery slower, "The drug business generates something like a hundred billion dollars a year, yet there are countries that still officially refuse to believe that it touches them. You've got diplomats flying the stuff in in their unsearchable baggage. You've got cops, clergymen, congressmen, plus three reigning presidents, plus a member of a royal family, we know all this for sure, carrying junk across borders. The problem is, drugs have become part of the fabric, like nuclear reactors. Nobody wants 'em, everybody knows they're dangerous as hell, but there's so much money being made, you're not gonna be able to close 'em down."

Faye laid her head on his chest, felt the pace of his heart, the heat of his skin. She kissed him under the jaw, calmed him with her gentle presence. After a minute Decker's hand came down to stroke her hair, the anger seeping from him, drained by her nearness.

"Sorry about the soapbox."

Faye let some time slide by before she got back to the subject she was loath to introduce, but it was one that couldn't be ignored; they were both held by it, linked together because of it.

"I want to talk about Angela again. On the way downtown tonight you mentioned a man named Slemp. You asked me about him once before. Who is he?"

"He's Murdoch's pistolero. He kills people to order."

"Can't the police pick him up?"

"I'm pretty sure they don't even know about him, unless I tell them. We could get Slemp off the street on a possessions charge, but that would tip Murdoch, and I don't want to do that. He had Angela killed because something's on schedule. Because of Taiwan and CND and doh mei-doh, whatever the hell all that means. I want Murdoch running around operating on normal. It's the only way we have a chance of getting a line on what's up."

Faye pushed herself away, fumbled for the bedside lamp. The light threw a pale wash over Decker, the cool illumination shadowing the definition in his shoulders and above his collarbones. The bounce off the blue wallpaper tinged his flesh, marbled it in wavy streaks like water reflected from an aquarium. Lying on his back, the sheet flat across his waist, and with no movement to him, he looked, for an instant, like a corpse laid out.

Faye shivered, moved closer, leaned over him. The angled light caught the wound under his eye, gouging it deeper, spreading it like a pursed expression.

This was a man whose job had caused somebody to shoot at him.

With fear taking small bites at her, Faye knew the same thing could possibly happen again.

"Hugh. You're not allowed to carry a gun, are you?"

"Nope. But I've got a man making me one hell of an umbrella."

Thinking he was trying to keep it light, Faye didn't come back at that.

Instead she said, "When it's time, you'll let the police handle it, won't you?"

"Handle what?"

"This man Slemp."

"Goddamn right. He buys guns the way I buy eggs."

He wasn't lying—she could see that—he thought he was telling the truth, but he wasn't. It wasn't in his nature to back off, and that scared her.

"Well, there it is," she said, almost to herself.

"There what is?"

"The downside. I get involved with you, a lovely man, and there's nothing but positives, and you wonder when a big fat negative is going to appear. Well, it's here."

She saw understanding pop into his eyes, and wondered if she'd been right about him not knowing he was lying.

"If you're worried about my hide," Decker said, "don't be."

"I wouldn't worry if—" Faye froze the rest of the sentence, let some silence plug an awkward gap. "Sorry. I'm beginning to sound like a wife."

"You were about to say," Decker said, "that you wouldn't worry if I didn't have this habit of blowing my cool. Am I right?"

For an answer she came down to him, spooned herself into his side, moved her head in a small forget-it gesture.

"You're worrying about nothing," Decker told her, turning toward her, bringing her against him. "There's no way I'm gonna let a piece of crap like Reggie Slemp upset me."

III

DECKER
AND
SLEMP

12

It was in the parking lot two floors below the lobby of the Murdoch Building, and quiet too, the only sounds the tick of a car engine losing its heat, and the hum of the air registers in the low ceiling.

The smell was a compound of gasoline fumes and warm vinyl, and tires hot from the ovenlike streets above; a comforting place if you liked automobiles, which Slemp didn't. A lucky thing, he reflected, because there was no place to bloody well drive to in Hong Kong.

He'd stationed himself in a dark corner, the strip lighting creating large pools of shadow. He'd got there on time, while Murdoch was already ten minutes late. Naturally.

He heard the elevator doors open, and a steady, quick clump/scuff, clump/scuff, which had to be Murdoch's surging crippled progress. Pumped up by alcohol and indignation, Slemp put a scowl on his face and stepped out from behind a car to show himself.

He stepped back into darkness again as Murdoch joined him. Murdoch did not look pleased. The man was a stone, Slemp thought: stone-dead legs, stone-hard through the chest and shoulders, stony facial features with a mouth like a chip of granite.

"What the hell is it?" His tone said it better be good, meeting like this, taking a risk.

Slemp's nostrils strengthened and narrowed as he bit down, matching Murdoch's delivery.

"I'll tell you what it is. I've been insulted, that's what it is. And I'm damned if I'm going to stand for it."

Slemp hadn't been able to shake it, the embarrassment of Murdoch bringing in somebody else; the thought had been expanding in his gut like tainted meat. The American mechanic had been

right, of course, "Don't let Murdoch know you know. Make *him*
the sucker." But his professional pride had been sorely wounded,
and it had begun to eat away at him, affecting everything he did.
This morning, having a knock in the cricket club's nets, that old
gaffer Jocko Simpson had clean bowled him, and crowed about it.
"Bit off your stroke this morning, aren't you, old thing? One too
many behind the collar last night?" That had been the last straw.
How could he concentrate on the flight of the ball, or on anything,
when his professional abilities had been downgraded? He'd
marched into the clubroom and called Murdoch, demanded an
immediate meeting.

"Insulted you? Who's insulted you?" Murdoch asked, thinking
that it wouldn't be hard: eighty-nine degrees outside and the guy's
wearing an ascot and a heavy cable-knit cricket sweater, for cris-
sakes; plus his grungy hair was salted with dandruff, as usual, and he
smelt like a goat.

"You have, of course! Why do you think I'm here? I know about
the Yank you brought in. Don't think I don't."

"What Yank?"

"The one you brought in."

"You just said that," Murdoch growled, looking around him. The
man would have to go; risking a face-to-face meeting for some
goddamn trivial offense. "Why don't you tell me what the hell
you're talking about?"

"The American mechanic," Slemp hissed, stinging himself into
outrage. "He came to see me. Wanted to make sure I didn't come
after him in a fit of professional jealousy. Was damned decent about
it. I thought I was supposed to handle matters of that sort. If you
think I'm losing my touch, I'd like to know about it."

Arthur Murdoch, his stumpy figure propped up at the armpits,
but somehow appearing to stand six feet tall, hunched his eyebrows.
"A hit man? You talking about an American hit man I'm supposed
to have hired?"

"Not supposed to have hired. *Have* hired. He told me all about
it. What I want to know is, why?"

Slemp had known Murdoch for a number of years, witnessed him
in all his moods, but he couldn't recall ever seeing him quite as
rocked as he was now. He was motionless, lizard-still; a man zapped
by a lightning bolt. Slemp was almost surprised to hear him speak,
even though it was just two barely audible words.

"Describe him."

"Mid-thirties. An athlete's build. American face, open, pleasant, but a large blemish under one eye. Scar of some sort."

"He's DEA."

"What?" It was a reflex answer; Slemp had heard perfectly well. His mouth dropped half an inch, and his indignant body sagged. "What did you say?"

Murdoch's eyes, his voice, were like whirring drills. "His name's Decker. And you showed him your fucking guns, didn't you?"

"How do you . . . he told me that . . ." Bewildered, yet recognizing the truth ahead of understanding, Slemp's questions foundered on Murdoch's basalt gaze. "Are you sure?" he finished weakly. The enormity of his mistake climbed over him, flattened him, halted all connected thought.

"And you didn't think you did any harm going into Mad Dogs," Murdoch said from the middle of his throat.

Slemp's head moved from side to side as he spluttered something in his own defense.

Murdoch spoke through him, his voice low and hammering. "How the hell else did he get to you? Somebody identified you, you goddamned idiot! Christ only knows why he suspected me. Maybe I'm not as good a liar as I thought." Murdoch looked away from the Englishman, away into the dark recesses of the garage. Blue light skimmed off metal, winked off windshields. Tires slid on the cement floor as somebody took a car out of the exit at the far end; then silence rolled back in again. "The Waters woman probably talked to somebody. Her roommate maybe, somebody at the office, a friend. Told them I got mad at her when I caught her nosing around." Murdoch's eyes slammed back at Slemp. "But Decker wouldn't have had a thing if he hadn't got to you. He bluffed you, you damned fool. You've fucked up everything."

Slemp opened his mouth on nothing, his cricket sweater feeling awfully hot now. He fumbled at his throat, untied the ascot. Murdoch seemed to have shrunk; there was something clenched about him, like the way his hands were clenching around the supports of his crutches. He spoke in his thinking voice, the vitriol missing now; a man quietly verbalizing a problem which needed solving.

"You showed him your guns, right?"

"Well, yes. I was utterly convinced he was what he said he was. And, well, I don't get a chance to talk firearms with anybody in this city."

"Never? You never told anybody? At the club, maybe: Keep it under your hat but I have a gun collection?"

Slemp's head was moving like a metronome. "Good God, no. I've *used* some of those guns."

Murdoch knew it was the truth. A hit man wouldn't take a risk like that. Not unless he thought he was talking to somebody in the same line of business.

"The man tricked me. Lied to me." Outrage was beginning to creep into Slemp's demeanor. "A damned con man."

"If he's the only person who's seen your basement, then he's all we have to worry about. He's probably told his offsiders, but that's just hearsay as long as there's no actual witness. You're gonna have to put him down."

"Of course," Slemp said, in high dudgeon. "No question about that now. I mean, the man's seen everything."

Murdoch ran his stubby manicured fingers slowly over his cheek as if testing that morning's shave. He said, almost abstractedly, "He probably won't have blown the whistle yet. He's gonna wait awhile. So here's what you do. You get into your car and you drive home fast. And you take all those guns and you dump 'em."

For a second Slemp was too shocked to reply. Dump his guns? His *collection*? "What do you mean, dump them?"

"I mean get rid of 'em. What the hell do you think I mean? One word from Decker and the cops'll be out at your place busting in the basement door. They do that, they'll have you. And if they get you, they could come after me by asking the same questions Decker did. Get rid of the guns, all that junk you got down there, and we're both okay."

"The junk? You mean the reloading equipment? You want me to throw that away as well?"

"Everything, goddammit! Wake up, Major," Murdoch said, putting weight on Slemp's bogus title, "we've been found out."

Slemp nodded, sweating heavily now, reeling from three pieces of terrible news.

"Get that basement broom-clean. Swab it out. Then fill it with some kind of oily crap. Get hold of a scrap motorcycle. Take it to pieces. Get some oil and grease around the place so the cops can't find one little grain of powder. Nothing to connect you to guns."

Slemp looked ill, as if he were suffering cramp. Bits of old engine in his immaculate basement? Grease on those workbenches which he scrubbed regularly with sandsoap and dried with a chamois cloth?

"Get it all done immediately. As for Decker, I want him down as soon as possible. Tonight. I'll set him up. But it's got to look like he stuck his nose in some other kind of business. He's DEA, so we'll make it look drug-related."

Slemp ran a hand through his greasy hair, only half-thinking about what Murdoch was telling him, his mind still on the loss of his guns, the defilement of his basement.

"We'll fix it so it looks like a lodge killing. What do you think?" A blunt edge of derision showed in Murdoch's question. "You're the expert in this area. Think that'll work?"

"A triad killing? Yes."

"What'll you need?"

"Three men should be sufficient," Slemp said, beginning to like the idea; this man Decker had made him look like a fool. "Three men with beef knives."

"You got 'em," Murdoch said. "I'll get back to you." He spun around and thumped back toward the elevator, and his office. And his matchless Hong Kong connections.

Arthur Murdoch.
Reggie Slemp.
Hugh C. Decker.
Seven hours before the underground meeting of the first two, Decker had begun his day as he had the last two mornings: with a kendo class at the dojo. And for the third time running, the master, after putting him through a furious workout, had recited the story of Bokuden, the soldier poet, and his victory over Rinsai.

Once again the master had said no more and no less, but left Decker sitting mokuzu and wondering about the curious lessons, wondering if he was supposed to take the story with him as some kind of personal mantra. Whatever it was, if it was part of the course, so be it.

He went from the dojo to Stanley Street, to the Luk Yu, the last authentic teahouse in Hong Kong. It was part of old China, this place, a high square room with beautifully carved latticework around the walls, floor-length tablecloths, and elderly waiters in starched white jackets. At the red-doored entrance a glass box displayed several types of tea, a weighing scale, and a velvet antler signifying the beneficial qualities of the national drink.

This early in the morning there were only three customers besides Decker: Johnny Risotto, Bumpy, and Miriam.

They ordered Yam Yeung, the slightly bitter tea from the north, then Bumpy led off with his report of the previous day's surveillance. "I tagged Murdoch up to Fan Ling. He met a big, prosperous-looking Chinese who has a chauffeur who's gonna be rich if he hires out by the foot. The car was a rental. Rented to"—Bumpy slipped a piece of paper from his jacket—"Sing To Hin. And he lives in Taipei."

"So there's your Taiwan connection," Johnny said to Decker. Then added, "Probably."

"Probably's right," Bumpy said, "I called the office in Taipei, and they did some checking. There are several people by that name living in the city but they all stayed in Taipei yesterday, so the guy's faking it."

"Okay," Decker said, "we'll get back to him. What did Murdoch do with this guy?"

"Had a word with him, then drove off. The Taiwanese went into this school building they were parked outside of. I stayed with Murdoch, tailed him back to his office, where he stayed put all day."

Decker asked if they had anything on the school. Bumpy told him he'd been able to get a list of the teachers there, all the adults employed, and not one name had excited the computer.

"All right, who tailed Murdoch from his office?"

"That was my shift," Miriam said. "He went home to that fishbowl he lives in up on Mount Cameron Drive. It's all bush up there so I hung around in the trees opposite his front gate, just me and some gaily-colored snakes. Around about eight three cars arrived within ten minutes of each other. I got their tags and checked them out. One was the rental that Bumpy already got, the guy from Taiwan. The other cars belong to two local businessmen, S. J. Lam and Sai Ho Koo." Miriam put her notes down on the table and slid them across to Decker, who glanced at the names and checked with Bumpy.

Bumpy shook his head. "Nothing. They're clean. Both very wealthy, and apparently made their loot legally."

"How long did they meet for?"

"Three and a half hours," Miriam said. "Murdoch threw a screwdo for them. Around about nine-thirty three starlets arrived in a car driven by a guy who was probably their clap doctor. Everybody left a couple of hours later looking tired and exhausted. I tagged the rental to an apartment house in Repulse Bay and put the big Taiwanese to bed."

Johnny Risotto ate an almond cookie that had come with the tea, and pensively reached for Bumpy's.

"Murdoch, two locals, and a guy from Taiwan," he said. "Could be a regular business meeting with after-dinner girls to ease the way to a deal. We won't get anywhere without pointers."

Decker agreed with him. "We need to know about these guys. Who they are, what they are, and if they're part of doh mei-doh, whatever that is. The Taiwan connection leads me to think maybe yes."

Bumpy sighed, regarded the tea leaves in the bottom of his cup. They didn't augur anything promising. "We're back to Special Branch again. And they're not gonna tell us gringos anything."

"Does it have to be Special Branch?" Decker asked. "All we need is somebody who knows the players and the numbers of their shirts." Miriam's cup came away from her mouth as if her tea was too hot.

"Bertie Winters," she said. "What's wrong with Bertie Winters?"

Johnny sat a little straighter in the chair he was having a hard time fitting into. "Hey, now," he said slowly.

Bumpy was grinning; Miriam had solved it.

"Red," he said, "for a nervous virgin, you get some pretty good ideas."

"Will he talk to us? What happened to the guy?" Decker asked. He remembered Bertie Winters, an incurable gambler who'd gone to the Nineteen Brothers for a loan. The lodge had demanded a curious security: Winters' officially issued revolver. But the gun had then been used in a holdup; a payroll guard wounded with it. As the barrel was registered with Arsenal Street, the gun had been traced back to Winters, and he'd been sacked.

"He's living over in Macau, close to the casino. And sure he'll talk to us," Miriam said. "As long as it didn't threaten national security, he'd tell us a few things, long as he was sure we wouldn't blab."

"You guys want to get onto it?"

Bumpy and Miriam pushed their chairs back. "Check with you later," Bumpy said as they left.

Johnny Risotto drank more tea. "This could work out, Deck. We might just be getting a little bit closer."

"If Winters knows the guy from Taiwan, maybe a lot closer." He glanced at his watch. "What time are we meeting Eddie Fong and his merry men?"

"Five. We got lots of time."

"Good. I want to stop off at Kennedy Town on the way. I got to pick up an umbrella."

Johnny looked out through the window at the sunshine beating down on Stanley Street.

"Sure. No sense in getting wet," he said.

Once upon a time Kennedy Town, or West Point as it was once called, had been a fashionable area of fine restaurants and classy, licensed brothels. In those days a gentleman hired a sixteen-year-old maiden for a week, and returned her at the end of seven days, slightly shop-soiled, to be rented out again at a far lower price. There are still some brothels in Kennedy Town but they are tiny back rooms now staffed by schoolgirls who offer only a yu daan massage. Yu daan is a fish dumpling made for soup, and it is fashioned by using a swift up-and-down hand action. The schoolgirls, wishing to retain their virginity, and thus make a good marriage, finish their homework, then hop around to the room they've rented, and dispense this limited sexual thrill to whatever client comes calling. Fondling of the breasts is permitted, and perhaps a little chow sow jee, smelly finger, but nothing else.

Decker directed Johnny to the clamorous metalworker's shop on Cathick Street, and found the boss man hammering away at a piece of galvanized ducting on the sidewalk.

The umbrella was ready, hanging from a wrought-iron hook on an interior wall. Decker lifted it down; it had a very weighty feel to it, and a very satisfying one. He unfurled it, pushed it open, revealing a new shaft running from the curve of the handle to the rubber tip at the point: three feet of half-inch-thick steel. The man had done an excellent job, and Decker thanked him, closed and furled the umbrella tightly, and carried it out to the car, where Johnny Risotto took a long look at it.

"You always buy your raingear at a metalworker's?"

"They have the best prices," Decker told him.

Johnny took the car away, heading east toward Causeway Bay and the harbor tunnel.

"So," Decker said. "We're finally going to come face-to-face with the dreaded Wo On Lok."

"Just don't get cute with 'em. They're running the place these days. They've even got the formula-one concession."

"I like it. What is it?"

"Car races over in Wang Tau Hom. Two o'clock in the morning, they just clear the streets and hold a Monte Carlo rally. Hotted-up Z cars and stripped-down Colts. They run a book, naturally, and everybody bets. Nobody gets any sleep but somehow the cops never arrive."

"It's always nice to deal with the top," Decker said.

They picked up speed once they emerged on Kowloon-side and got on the four-lane road. Johnny took a second tunnel, this one buried beneath the airport. They came into daylight on a vast piece of landfill which jutted into Kowloon Bay like the airport runway it paralleled. After running ruler-straight for a quarter-mile, it notched in and the artificial bay thus formed, a typhoon shelter known as Kwun Tong, supported a large and vibrant floating population: junks and covered sampans, and chunky red and green lighters moored side by side.

Johnny drove to the western end of the shelter, to a stretch of fill as flat as a desert plain. To Decker it looked like a reflection of the giant housing development shooting up behind it. The place was a rabbit warren of boxy metal sea containers: orange and silver and yellow and red, row upon row of them, laid out in dusty avenues and sandy cross streets. Everything smelled of hot earth and baking steel, and jet fuel wafted in by a slow and steamy breeze.

They got out of the car in front of a peculiar-looking structure. It had been fashioned from two rusty containers, each of which had had one side removed. They'd been butted up against each other and soldered together to form a rectangular metal shack which had then been mounted on breeze blocks. The regular hinged doors had been removed, and a front wall had been fashioned from inch-thick plywood, and a new door mortised into it.

"You all set?" Johnny asked.

Decker picked up his converted umbrella.

They pushed through the plywood door into a makeshift office: two gouged wooden desks, several bright red filing cabinets, some cheap folding chairs, a couple of flashy electronic phones, paper rubbish scattered on the metal floor. On one of the desks documents and in/out trays had been pushed to one side to make way for a jumble of Styrofoam takeout cartons and a big serving dish set in the center.

Four men were seated around the desk, bowls in one hand, chopsticks in the other. They were busy spearing food, too occupied to talk or do anything else but go on eating as they looked over the new arrivals. Then Eddie Fong, who was one of the diners, said to them, in English, "Come on. Grab a bite."

Decker checked the group quickly, his eyes settling on the man sitting to Eddie's left. He could have been Eddie's older brother: severely scissored haircut, plain sleeveless white shirt and navy-blue pants, black lace-up shoes. He had a thin and sallow face, as if he'd just got out of bed after a long illness, a prominent, un-Chinese nose, and eyebrows so light they appeared to be missing. He wore no wrist jewelry, no rings, not even a watch. Decker figured him for a Pak Sze Sin, a 415 man, an adviser and planner whose responsibility was to organize the deals and liase between the lodge and the customer.

The two other men at the desk were men whose duties were obvious: a twenty-year-old runner, an odd-job initiate, who jumped up to get bowls and chopsticks for the guests, and a man fifteen years his senior with solid weight to him, nostrils as large and dark as his distrustful eyes, and frown marks that crawled across his prominent brow before arrowing down each side of his slowly chewing mouth. His jaw had been broken sometime in the past and was lumpy and out of line with the rest of his face. There was muscle through his shoulders, muscle in his stare too, which took in Decker's umbrella. The man was clearly a Hung Kwan, a Red Pole, a 426 enforcer responsible for meting out physical punishment to errant lodge members, and a lot worse to members of a rival lodge, or informers. Like Little Gladys Goodlay. It would have been men very much like this one, Decker knew, who'd held her down on the butcher block and hacked off her arm.

"This here's Mr. Bruno." Decker said. "From New York."

Johnny Risotto moved his head in a quick upward motion, as if he was jerking a string with his chin. "Eh," he grunted.

He found a chair and pulled it up to the desk. Decker did the same.

The runner put food in front of them. One box held noodles marinated in chicken stock, then crisp fried in oil and vinegar, the other featured Kwang Swao, hot spiced yams with pieces of plump duck. It was Chiu Chow cooking, Johnny's favorite kind.

"Ey," Johnny said, poking in the first box with a fork the youth had found for him. "They fried the fucking spaghetti."

"It's a specialty of Hong Kong, Mr. Bruno," Decker said, apologizing for the food. "It's the way they do it here."

"So what's so special about fucked-up pasta? I want that I go to my sister-in-law's. What else they got?"

"Try some of this, Mr. Bruno." Decker maneuvered another couple of containers in front of Johnny: cold steamed fish in a tau cheung bean sauce, and a classic Swatow dish: slices of pickled goose layered with a thick ruby-colored jelly.

Johnny prodded it as if expecting an explosive substance.

"What's this Jell-O shit?"

Decker, sounding embarrassed, said, "It's traditional, Mr. Bruno."

"I don't care what the fuck it is. What the fuck is it?"

"Dried goose blood."

Johnny tossed his fork into a plastic out tray. "I ain't hungry."

The parts they were playing, they'd played many times before. Johnny had set it up on the phone with Eddie Fong; Decker would be the American middleman who knew the local scene, while Johnny, just off the plane from JFK, was on a buying trip for one of the East Coast families.

The role was easy for Johnny, having grown up on New York's Grand Street. As a sixteen-year-old he'd been a runner for a Mob coffee bar. Later he'd waited tables to put himself through college. He claimed that was how he got so fat: snacking on all the orders he carried out from the kitchen.

He sat back from the desk, sucking noisily at a can of San Miguel, moodily watching his hosts eat stolidly and without pause until the food was all gone.

The 415 man, the planner, the senior man present, wiped his knobby knuckles on his thin mouth and turned his head toward Eddie Fong, signifying that he was ready to talk deal.

Eddie, who was using a piece of torn typing paper to clean his teeth, waved the paper at his boss and said, "This is Mr. Chu. It could be he's got something to sell."

"A wristwatch? A Parker pen? What?" Johnny rumbled.

"Mr. Bruno would like some details," Decker added superfluously.

"Twenwty-five keys of base," Eddie Fong announced.

Johnny drank off his beer, popped another can. "Purity?"

Eddie and the planner held a whispered conversation.

"Sixty. Mr. Chu says it'll go to ninety, ninety-five easy."

"Yeah?" Johnny didn't sound impressed. "He guarantees that, does he?"

The planner nodded, showing that he understood English.

"Where's it from?" Johnny asked, turning to look at a boxed air conditioner that was thumping icy air toward the back of his neck.

"It's quality merchandise," Eddie told him.

"Where's it now?"

"On a freighter. Coming in from Kaohsiung."

The name jarred through Decker; it was one of the big ports in Taiwan.

On schedule. Taiwan happy about CND.

Was CND a Taiwanese shipping line? Why the hell hadn't he grabbed a Lloyd's list and checked on that?

Like a paper flower in water, the idea that Arthur Murdoch was running drugs was blossoming in Decker's mind. A hell of a coincidence if this deal Eddie Fong was into was Murdoch's deal, but that was the kind of thing you always hoped for: some kind of luck, some kind of break.

"What happens when this boat gets here?" Johnny asked.

Eddie conferred with the planner once more.

"It's coming in the East Harbor anchorage. A special delivery offloaded over to the barge."

"What kinda special delivery?"

"The stuff's in a crate of fireworks," Eddie told him. "It's a smart move. Nobody's gonna want to hold up a crate of fireworks, seeing as how they're for the royal visit."

Johnny looked over at Decker, doubt lifting from his plump face.

"Hey, that ain't bad. Prince Charming and his old lady. I read about 'em. They're coming here tomorrow, right?"

Decker confirmed it.

"And they got fireworks for 'em in their honor. And the boy's gonna be in the fireworks," Johnny said, as if it were all his idea. "When does the boat get here?"

"Early tomorrow morning. Mr. Chu's ready to do the deal then if you want," Eddie Fong explained.

"Yeah? What do I use for cash? Think I got it back at the hotel in a sock? We get together on price, I call my people in Manila, a guy'll bring it in tomorrow, we'll deal tomorrow night." Mr. Bruno checked with his lieutenant. "What'd he mean, off-loaded over to the barge?"

"It's where they let the fireworks off from, Mr. Bruno. A barge anchored in the harbor, the western side. There won't be anybody around 'cept for the guys working the rockets. And the fireworks'll be a good cover, we do the deal at night. It's a smart idea, Mr. Bruno."

"They okay? The guys with the matches?"

Eddie answered him. "No problem. Most of them are members of the lodge. And anyway"—he nodded at the starched-faced enforcer, who was sitting like a block of wood watching Decker, suspicious of the umbrella—"there'll be lotsa muscle around."

Like a man swayed by a brilliant argument, Johnny began to ponderously nod his head. "Not bad. I like it."

The planner whispered into Eddie's ear, and Eddie delivered the news.

"The price is a hundred-thirty a key."

"Yeah? Well, now, I don't like it. In fact, I hate it."

They spent fifteen minutes arguing about price, then agreed on a figure which left everybody grumpy. Then Johnny really upset the other side. "Okay, here's how it is. Tomorrow night we're on the barge. I look at the stuff. It tests out at sixty, and it ain't gonna be a hernia taking it up thirty points, we got a go project. I hand over the dough. But I hand it to the boss. Nobody else."

"Mr. Chu is the boss," Eddie claimed.

"Horseshit. The guy's a deal maker. We're talking two and a half million American here. I don't hand over that kind of glue to nobody who ain't running the show."

Mr. Chu, the planner, spoke out loud for the first time, and in English. "Not possible."

Decker jumped into the conversation. He knew they'd never get a lodge leader present, but somebody close to him maybe, somebody who'd be a real prize if he was caught with his hands full.

"Mr. Bruno doesn't mean the big boss. Just somebody in charge. Like a Sheung Fa."

"The hell's that?" Johnny muttered.

"A Double Flower. A Four Three Eight, Mr. Bruno. Very high in the lodge. You deal with him, you're dealing with a guy in charge."

"Okay, then. One of them whatever you said. Or I don't deal."

They spent another fifteen minutes arguing about that until the planner, in the face of Johnny's scowling and loud intransigence, finally agreed. They went over some details, then Johnny went through a series of conciliatory hand motions and moved his chair back.

"We got a deal then. Nine tomorrow night."

"Mr. Chu would like some cash up front," Eddie Fong said.

"Sure. Long as I can have some boy up front."

"Mr. Chu, demonstrating his familiarity with the term, gave that a quick negative. "Not here yet."

When Johnny rested his hands on the desk, it shifted under his weight.

"Neither is my money," he said, turned, and lumbered toward the door.

Decker, picking up his umbrella, went with him, noticing, as he did so, that the enforcer was still puzzled by it, perhaps wondering how the American would use it in a fight—like a bayonet maybe, thrusting, stabbing it forward.

Out in the sudden heat and grit of the container yard, walking between the ordered rows toward the car, Johnny said, "How was the e-fu?"

"Best noodles I ever ate. And the nok mai gai was symphonic."

"Bastard," Johnny said, but he sounded pleased. The meeting had gone well. Decker was more than happy too; the delivery and the buy would take place in an ideal spot: there was no chance of anybody escaping in traffic or vanishing into the subway from a barge anchored in the harbor. If it all went down as planned, they could score a couple of pretty heavy collars.

They discussed it on the way back, along with another subject: the fact that they had a tag. Decker had spotted a green Datsun with a busted wing when they'd left Hong Kong-side, and it was still with them: two young Chinese in the front seat.

"Arsenal Street keeping tabs on me," Decker said. "I don't think Waxy Crane trusts me."

"Yeah, I spotted them way back," Johnny replied. "Terrible tail job. Any closer and they'd risk a charge of buggery."

Johnny called the office from the car, just to check in. When he replaced the phone he had a message for Decker.

"A guy named Harris called. Wants to meet you for a drink ten-thirty tonight. The Jade in the Edinburgh Tower."

"You sure it was Harris? I don't know any Harris."

"It could have been Harrison. Hilary said it was a bad line. He said he's a friend of a friend of yours in New York. He has a letter he was asked to deliver to you. Sounds romantic."

Decker grunted. There were a couple of people who might want to contact him, give a letter to somebody who was going to Hong Kong to beat the regular mails. At least the timing was okay; Faye had a business evening she couldn't get out of and wouldn't be back till after eleven. He'd see this guy Harris, then go on up to her apartment.

"You want to grab a bean tonight?" Johnny asked when they came up Hong Kong-side. "You can buy me the Chiu Chow you owe me."

"Sure. What happened, you get let off the chain?"

"June's taking her sister to the movies. She wants to see one of those snickerty-snack, angry sword epics. I told 'em I'm against screen violence, and got out of it."

"Okay. Let's do it."

"Pick you up at eight," Johnny said, letting Decker out at his hotel.

Decker didn't want to go up to his room right away; instead he walked around the corner to the Singapore, an old hotel that had been refurbished since Decker saw it last. The bar was still a pleasant place for a quiet drink if you got there early enough.

He went up to the bar, nodded at a Brit who had yet to be served. The Brit asked for a G and T, and when the barman grinned uncertainly, translated, "A gin and tonic. Lime if you have it."

Decker got himself a beer, took it to a booth, wondering why the English were so fond of diminutives and initials.

He concentrated on more important things, like how he was doing so far. It seemed like several weeks, yet it was just five days since he'd come back to Hong Kong to pinch Eddie Fong and find out some facts about Angela Waters' murder.

So how was he doing?

Not bad. Eddie Fong looked like working out nicely, as long as old Eddie didn't have second thoughts about the buy. They'd be a touch vulnerable out on the barge if he did a number on them: two DEA agents against several fighters and a couple of Red Poles. They'd get a quick burial at sea without a flag or a rifle volley. But Eddie Fong, and people like him, were something Decker had faced before, had experience with. He couldn't say the same thing about the Angela Waters thing. It was like one of those puzzles they sold on Lascar Row; open one box and there was an even smaller one inside.

He'd opened the one marked Arthur Murdoch. And the one marked Reggie Slemp. But what about the ones inside those? CND. Doh mei-doh. Burnt ground. On schedule.

And what about Murdoch, anyway? What the hell was he hatching? And, while he was on people, what about Faye Keeble, the thought of whom made him feel like a lottery winner?

What happened when his temporary duty here was over? What did he do about Faye?

The same as he did with Kate?

And there was somebody else he had to figure out what to do with—somebody he'd known for a long time: Hugh C. Decker.

One more explosion and he'd be looking for a job with some security firm somewhere: ex-DEA man hired to cut down on waterfront pilferage, or something.

Decker looked over at a group at the bar, the usual Hong Kong mix. If he walked up to them now, right this minute, and started to bad-mouth them, cuss them out, insult the memory of their parents, how many of them, Decker wondered, would eventually fly off the handle?

Two out of ten?

One out of ten?

None out of ten?

How did people do it? Was there a trick to holding it in, keeping control all the time?

How to get mad, and not forget how to behave.

Aye, that's the rub.

Decker sipped his beer, blanked his mind to see what would pop into it.

And discovered a funny thing.

The Brit at the bar, when he'd ordered a G and T; those initials were echoing inside his head. His subconscious, like a movie wonder dog, was trying to tell him something.

The Brit had pronounced it "G 'n T," not doing much with his upper lip.

And when you said G 'n T that way, or any way, it sounded a lot like GNT.

CND.

Maybe Faye had heard Angela Waters wrong. Or maybe Angela

had heard the tape wrong. Maybe what she'd heard had really been C *and* D.

Taiwan happy about C and D.

C for cocaine? C for crack? D for drugs?

That was really reaching.

Names, then. Back up and fill in the gaps. Taiwan—the guy from Taiwan with the tall chauffeur. He was maybe a biggie with the United Bamboo in Taipei. Was he happy about two guys named Chuen Fu and Den Pi; some kind of C/D combination?

The phrase "on schedule" had to mean the drop on the ship, the freighter that was coming in.

And doh mei-doh was the code name for the operation, a name that meant burnt ground. Why burnt ground?

Decker thought about it. Went by it once. Went by it twice.

The third time, he went into reverse and got a piece of it. Then the rest fell neatly into place.

So simple.

Like all puzzles when you can turn the page upside down and read the printed answer.

13

With a screwdriver in one hand and a wrench in the other, Reggie Slemp stood in the middle of the cement floor and gazed at his basement.

The naked benches looked wounded, bereft, like something shorn because of ill health, like skin clipped and cleaned around a wound. How many nights had he spent down here, a Scotch and water to one side, his Sinatra tapes playing, humming along with the fine old Cole Porter tunes, working on his hand-loads, working on his guns, refining, changing, correcting?

How was he going to replace all this equipment, lovingly collected; all top-drawer stuff?

Standing there, looking around him in misery, Slemp began to experience another kind of emotion.

Slemp began to feel very, very angry.

That bloody DEA *bastard*!

It was all his fault. If he hadn't seen all this, tricked his slimy way down here, there'd be no reason for touching any of it. He was directly and totally responsible for this . . . carnage.

Well, Mr. Decker would pay for it. Oh, yes. Not for him the quick stab in the heart. Let him live awhile. Gut thrusts, groin thrusts, he'd tell the three fighters Murdoch had promised him for tonight. Gut slashes. Nothing deep; something that would allow the bastard an hour to bleed to death in agony.

With his teeth gritted more in anger than exertion, Slemp hefted a big cardboard box, carried it out into the high grasses of the jungly backyard. At the end of the yard a small fire licked at the blackened remains of the wardrobe top, the one with the velvet-lined fretted pockets which had held his gun collection. Slemp carried the box around the side of the house and out of the front gate to where his battered Honda Civic was parked. Attached to the rear was a small wooden trailer he'd rented. He placed the box in it, went back for another box, this one also full, then covered everything with an old sheet.

He returned to the basement and mopped it out—floor, benches, all the surfaces—then locked up, reflecting bitterly that there was nothing to keep safe or hidden anymore; nothing to glory in. Carrying his guns in a suitcase, he went back to the car and drove toward the highway.

It took him just fifteen minutes to make Tai Po Market, a nondescript town with tall white cluster blocks climbing into the sky on its outskirts, and an old and new market section farther in. Slemp stayed on the southern side, drove into a scrappy field that was home to a junkyard: wrecked cars, ruined refrigerators, stoves, machinery. Slemp chose two old Yamaha motorcycles, their frames bent, their engines cannibalized, made a deal with the man who ran the place, and drove his Honda through the dusty yard to where the bikes lay on their crumpled sides.

He sifted out the cardboard packing boxes and, piece by piece, tossed the hand-loading equipment onto the junk mountain.

It took something out of him to do it, to trash these beautifully made tools that were now destined to be baked and peeled by the sun, ruined by the rain.

He struggled with the two wrecked motorcycles, huffed and puffed them onto the trailer, got into his car, and left.

He didn't go far, just twenty minutes along the Ting Kok Road, which skirted Tolo Harbor. He turned right onto a little peninsula, and a road that ran dead straight across the mouth of the Plover Cover reservoir, fourteen square miles of unblemished water, bright blue and pancake flat. He stopped the car, reached for the suitcase, opened it for one last look.

His hand stroked grooved cylinders and beveled sides, crosshatched grips, stippled trigger guards, and the crisply milled edges of safeties and hammers and combat sights.

He closed the suitcase, looked at the blue water, deep and waiting.

The click of the suitcase latches seemed to be a trigger too, starting off a swelling emotion that rose in his chest like something caught there at the end of a coughing fit.

No!

Not his guns.

He was damned if he was going to toss them into twenty fathoms of water to rust in the mud and silt of a Chinese reservoir.

Wrap them in an oilcloth, bury them in the backyard? If the police raided, they'd find them. They were good at things like that. Bunch of chink market gardeners, most of them.

A safe-deposit box? But they were hard to get in Hong Kong, so many people hiding money. Besides, a bank might always snoop. No, the guns had to go, but if so, why not realize some money on them?

The Pigman!

Why hadn't he thought of him before?

Sell them to the Pigman. Pawn them, really. Buy them back when Decker had been disposed of and he was sure he was in the clear. Murdoch would be furious if he found out the guns hadn't been ditched, but how would he find out? The thought of Arthur Murdoch visiting the Pigman was a rich one indeed.

Smiling at the world now, his former crushing despondence thrown off as the result of one simple bright thought, Slemp turned the car around and sped back to his house in Fo Tan.

He carried the ruined motorcycles in a wheelbarrow around to his basement, took a wrench set to them, and layered the workbenches with spark plugs, cylinder heads, a carburetor, a gunky chain, dirt-covered tires, rusted rims.

It was a travesty putting that junk on those benches, filling the basement with the alien smell of sumps and petrol tanks, like some teenager's hobby shop, but it wouldn't be for long, he reminded himself. When this affair was all over, he'd buy new equipment, get everything back the way it had been.

Slemp went upstairs, had a quick slug of Dewar's and, feeling immensely better about life, and with his precious guns beside him in the suitcase, left the house and got back into his car.

The Pigman lived over in the Walled City.

Reggie Slemp drove south.

There were many arguments about the Walled City.

Some people claimed it was out of the jurisdiction of the Hong Kong police and, therefore, unpatrolled and dangerous.

Some said it was a law unto itself because it had originally been a holiday resort for the Ch'ing emperors, and had never ever been part of the colony.

But there was one thing that was beyond argument: the Walled City, if it had ever been one, was no longer a holiday resort. It was a festering slum; one of the worst in all the Orient. And not a modern slum, an old one. The place was primitive. There were doctors there who still used blood leeches for stomachache, and herbal applications for broken bones. There were dentists who littered their shop windows with traded-in dentures, any set of which might fit a patient with a little perseverance. The Walled City had lost a lot in the last two or three hundred years, including its wall, knocked down to facilitate the building of the airport a few hundred yards away. The opium divans were gone, the brothels were gone; only poverty and mud had been left behind.

Reggie Slemp walked along a perimeter street, through the sewer stench of the Kowloon nullah, went down a short flight of broken stone steps that bordered a piece of cleared land. Ahead, a kind of tunnel led into a low mass of dwellings made of slatboard pieces, and the ubiquitous corrugated iron sheeting, cut as if it were as malleable as paper: two-story shacks that looked to have been tumbled by a severe earth tremor.

Slemp followed the only path, a muddy track just wide enough for two people to squeeze by each other. There was no piped water in the Walled City; instead, it was serviced by a central pump which, having no runoff, overflowed and turned the dirt alleyways into sticky mires. Duckboards had been put down at the worst parts of the path, the boards squishing into a gray and reeking stream as Slemp picked his way across them.

Entering the City proper, the stone walls of the houses shrank in to hug him, the path winding between little tin shacks and small shops, none of them much more than holes scooped out of the stone. Slemp stayed on the track as it curved past the iron roof of a sunken ruin. The roof, at Slemp's belt level, was plaited with garbage tossed down from the dwellings above. A large rat, undisturbed by the scattering of people walking by, nosed among the offal, ignoring also a bobtailed cat that was scavenging farther along the roof. Both animals were safe from the inhabitants, while a dog wouldn't have lasted thirty seconds.

The path broadened as it turned a bend, two women ahead standing in mud washing clothes at an open pump. Children played around their feet and sailed paper boats on a stream full of refuse and dirty gray soapsuds.

Beyond them the track became a tunnel again, burrowing under some rickety cabins, the daylight strangled here into a thick and smelly gloom.

Slemp kept moving; he knew where he was going; he'd been taken to the Pigman when he'd first come to the colony, but had found that the guns the man had to offer were standard pieces of no quality or interest. He hadn't been back since, but you couldn't get lost in the Walled City if you stayed on the main path.

The tunnel opened; daylight fought its way down again past a house made of supermarket cartons, another no bigger than a sentry box: home to a toothless old woman.

One hundred feet farther and the sharp change in the air told Slemp he was close. The fetid smell of sewage gave way to a stronger one: the unmistakable high and sour stench of hogs in mud.

The shack had been built like a kid's treehouse from uneven bits of wood torn from a packing case, the doorway a sawed gash covered by long thin strips of blue-and-white nylon fabric.

Slemp coughed and swallowed at the smell, steeled himself, then went through the blue-and-white fly curtain.

It was just one room holding a sagging rattan table, a cot, and a peeling leather trunk. A wall bench held chipped enamel mugs, a pan, a bowl, a hessian sack full of something dark and leaking. The bodies of flies stained the rough planking of the floor like a mosaic, and a hundred live ones buzzed and hummed and tried to settle on Slemp's face and hair.

From beneath the floorboard came the grunt and shuffle of the animals below, their stink like waves of heat rising in squiggly lines.

Slemp, breathing shallowly, fighting down an internal reaction, concentrated on why he was here.

"Hello? Anybody around?"

A trapdoor opened, and a man came up from below.

Slemp was well aware of the old adage that says that people sometimes take on the look of the pets or animals they're in charge of, and the Pigman was an extraordinary example of this. He had a fat, hairless body with a nose that was both wide and round, like a snout, and eyes that seemed smaller than they should have been. He wore black shorts and black rubber boots caked with mud and swill. When he saw the gweilo standing there with a suitcase in his hand, he knew he was about to do business.

The Pigman pushed at a stick which hinged open a window cut into the rear wall. It opened onto the roof of a neighbor's shack, and some fitful light struggled in. A cloud of flies grabbed their opportunity. The Pigman seemed not to notice them, nor they him; but they went at Slemp, forcing him to slap at them and wave his arms and curse.

The Pigman patted the top of the rattan table, set it under the window, and pointed to the suitcase.

Slemp opened it and, one by one, took out the guns, each one wrapped in a soft cloth duster.

He laid out his arsenal on the tabletop.

The Chinese showed no surprise, but Slemp knew the man would not have seen more than two guns for sale at one time, not in Hong Kong, where the usual way to acquire a sidearm was to knock a beat constable on the head and steal his .38. Slemp had never been quite able to understand why the colony's biggest, perhaps only, gun fence was allowed to stay in business. He assumed it was because the police, knowing who sold the guns, thereby had a measure of control. Perhaps they knew, being nothing if not realists, that somebody would sell guns if the Pigman didn't; and better the devil you know than the one you don't.

Slemp brushed at the flies, tried to ignore the smell seeping up from the pens, and said in a jovial and hearty voice, "It's your lucky day, my man. Seven guns, all personally customized, all with hand-loaded ammunition. Just look at this beauty"—Slemp didn't care for the role of salesman, but the chinks always expected a sales pitch, and were ferocious hagglers, so one had to take them on at their own game—"a Dan Wesson Model Fifteen Two. Twelve-inch bull barrel, fiberglass Sile grips, forty-six-degree hammer arc, double cylinder latches, adjustable micrometer sights."

The Pigman had no comment.

Slemp went on to his next treasure.

"A Sig-Sauer three-eighty. See? Reprofiled slide, reshaped ejector port, beveled mag well, filed hammer spur, accurized barrel."

The Pigman washed his tight little eyes over the offering and said nothing.

Slemp went through them all, lovingly showing off the guns, extolling their individual merits, proudly laying out, on the rattan table, blued steel, stainless steel, chrome and nickel, dull or gleaming; everything perfect.

The Pigman spoke at last.

"Fifteen hundred Hong Kong."

"For which one?"

"For all."

Slemp didn't get it; even when they bargained hard, the Chinese started off at something reasonable.

"You can't be serious."

The Pigman moved three guns to one side. "These good." He waved in disdain at the remainder. "These no good."

Slemp was scandalized, flabbergasted. "What?"

The Pigman nudged the Patterson Colt, pushed at the big square frame of the 1911 Belgian pistol, pushed at the Webley. "Old. No good."

"They're classics, you blithering idiot. The Patterson alone is worth two thousand U.S."

The fence prodded the .22, the Ruger. "Barrel got holes."

"Well, of *course* it's got holes. I drilled them myself. This is a silenced gun. Don't you understand? You'd pay a thousand dollars for something like this in New York."

"This Hong Kong," the fence said with a practiced cunning.

"Ten thousand Hong Kong, and not a penny less!" Slemp's flabby cheeks had become inflamed, and in spite of the fat Chinese's dreadful smell, he stood close to him and shouted in his porcine face, "Ten thousand. Take it or leave it."

The Pigman wanted the Dan Wesson, and the Casull, and the Sig-Sauer, exactly the kind of large-caliber guns a hotshot lodge kid would snap up. But nobody would want the two collector's items. And the .22 wasn't intimidating enough to be attractive to his regular customers. And the Webley only fired one shot.

"Two thousand Hong Kong. Last offer."

Blinking quickly, moisture in his eyes he was so humiliated, Slemp knew that the fence meant it. He snatched up the Ruger, plunged his hand into the suitcase, grabbed three magazines loaded with his home-made tracers, slammed the case shut, tossed it across the room. "Six pieces and ammo," he yelled at the man. "Twenty-five hundred. Pay me!"

The Pigman had never understood Big Noses, but he knew them well enough to recognize that this one was not about to bargain anymore. And twenty-five hundred was only a quarter of what he'd eventually make on the buy, so he was happy to concede the small defeat.

He disappeared through the trapdoor in the floor, returned a minute later and counted out money, which Slemp shoved into his pocket. Then the Englishman, boiling over, marched out of the reeking shack. Twenty-five hundred Hong Kong! Less than three hundred U.S.! The rogue! The rotten Chinese bandit!

Slemp fumed, wiped spittle from his mouth, stomped off down the filthy path, blaming the whole miserable experience on one man. That bloody Yank, Decker!

Oh, he was going to get his. Wasn't he, just!

And not only from a knife blade, either. Bugger Murdoch and his triad killings.

Slemp patted the Ruger tucked under his sweater. Let's see how the Yank feels with his kneecaps shattered by a couple of high-speed .22 longs. Let's see what he has to say for himself with the phosphorus of a tracer burning in his shoulder, blazing in his gut.

Slemp checked his watch in the feeble light as he emerged from a tunnel, sloshed over duckboards, splashing putrid muck onto his trouser cuffs.

That bastard was going to die the death he had coming to him.

Bumpy called just after seven-thirty, got Decker in his hotel room.

"Deck? Sorry it took so long to get back. We had to run all over Macau to find Winters."

"Was it worth the trip?"

"You betcha buns. Once he knew we hadn't come to find out Margaret Thatcher's hat size, he was happy to talk. You ready?"

"Shoot."

"Okay. The big guy from Taipei, with the apartment in Repulse Bay. He's a lieutenant general in the Taiwanese Air Force. A squadron leader, yet."

"Does he fly dope?"

"Probably, from time to time. But Winters says he's just a dabbler. He makes his real money peddling influence, helping out the big wheels like Murdoch."

"Okay. Anything on the two local guys, the businessmen?"

"Oh, yes. Just a tad. I'm still reeling from this one. Winters says they're both Shan Chus."

"You're kidding . . ."

"No, sir. I've been here five years and I didn't know that. What I wouldn't give for one hour alone with the files at Special Branch."

"Did Winters know their lodges?"

"Winters knows what time it is on Mars. S. J. Lam runs the Green Pang. Sai Ho Koo is the boss of the Yee On."

"Do tell," Decker said slowly. That was a revelation, and then some. "How about Murdoch? Anything juicy?"

"Ah," Bumpy said, sounding as if he were rubbing his hands. "It turns out that Murdoch's official history, the one you read in all those profiles on him, is just a little bit of a lie. According to Winters, Murdoch was born in a brothel in the French Concession in Shanghai. His mother was a hooker, a White Russian named Kursnetsov. She was killed in the Communist riots in thirty-seven. Murdoch was adopted by a guy named Kot Sui Wong. And even I know who Kot Sui Wong was."

"Tell me."

"He ran the Green Pang, Chiang Kai-shek's old outfit. Murdoch became his number-one son and assistant. But Winters says Murdoch has been divorced from the Pang for twenty-five years, although he's still kept up local contacts. Hence the current leader of the Pang sits at his dinner table."

"With the current leader of the Yee On," Decker said, thinking about it. "You figure those two were burning yellow paper?"

"Sure. Some kind of deal going down. Cooperation of some kind. But listen, there's more. Winters says both those guys are on their way out of the colony. They've sold up on the quiet. Going to the States, probably. He says they've already sent their sons over there."

"Because of Peking taking over?"

"Sure. Winters says the lodges know the good old days are over when the PRC gets here. He says most of the lodge biggies are virulent anti-Reds anyway and wouldn't want to live under a Peking regime. And listen to this: Winters figures Murdoch has probably sold out too. Getting out now while prices are still up."

"Uh-huh," Decker said with the phone to his head, his mind flying. "Bump, what are those two lodges into these days?"

"Lots. The Pang controls the waiters and the hotel help around Tsim Sha Tsui, the building cleaners Hong Kong-side, prostitution in Yau Ma Tei, marine-store hawkers, the mah-jongg schools. Big in narcotics. The Yee On looks after the godown coolies in Western, the firemen, dockyard painters and scrapers, some restaurants, and a whole bunch of gambling rooms. Also big in narcotics."

"All right, Bump. Good trip, kid. Hug Miriam for me."

Bumpy said he'd check with him later, then they both hung up.

Decker sat on the end of the bed and slotted what he'd just heard into what he already knew or suspected.

Arthur Murdoch, famous anti-Communist, was making plans to get out long before 1997 rolled around.

For his own safety?

Sure. The People's Security Bureau had had spies in Hong Kong for forty years; they'd know all about Murdoch, his present and his past. If he was still here in 1997, he'd be in jail a year later most probably. The Chinese had long memories; they'd go after anybody who'd been a member of the Green Pang in Shanghai, settle some old scores.

So Murdoch was getting out now at the top of the market.

Made sense.

And he'd decided, seeing he was living in one of the world's major drug centers—and seeing he had such good lodge connections—to move a little weight on his way out.

Or, more correctly, *re*move a little weight, because Decker was pretty certain that the drugs Murdoch had his eye on was the stuff coming in on the freighter tomorrow night.

Murdoch was planning to steal it from Eddie Fong and his chopper-freak pals, the Wo On Lok.

Decker tried his theory on Johnny Risotto when the big man dropped by to pick him up for dinner. He filled Johnny in on Bumpy's phone call, and gave him his reasoning.

"Let's start with Eddie's bunch, the Wo On Lok. They get this neat little idea for moving some boy into Hong Kong, stick it in a crate of fireworks that's being loaded in Kaohsiung, Taiwan. They need somebody to oversee that part of it, and come up with the lieutenant general, who, according to Winters, is no stranger to the dope biz. Check?"

"Check," said Johnny.

"Now, let's say this general," Decker continued, "also happens to be a business associate of Arthur Murdoch. He's Murdoch's Mr. Fixit in Taiwan. The general sees a way to jazz up his end of the deal with the Wo On Lok. He goes to Murdoch and lays it out for him. A straight and simple ripoff. So does Murdoch go for it?"

"Would I eat a bowl of fettuccine?"

"Okay. So Murdoch brings in another business associate, a guy who runs the Green Pang, Murdoch's old lodge, plus another locomotive from the Yee On for some backup. The leaders of the two lodges are getting out of Hong Kong anyway, so it'll be no skin off their teeth. How am I doing so far?"

"You got a three-hundred game going."

"Murdoch takes over. He's the take-charge type. He gives the thing a code name, doh mei-doh, because he wants this deal kept very secret. Okay, things start to come together, start looking good. Murdoch dictates a memo. Why does he do that?"

"Because," Johnny said, "he doesn't trust his phone, and doesn't want to meet with the principals too often. The safest way to communicate is to use the mails."

"Right. And Angela Waters was killed because of what she heard on that memo. But maybe what she heard wasn't that Taiwan is happy about CND, but that Taiwan is happy about C *and* D. The two sound pretty close."

Johnny nodded. "I'll buy it. But what's C and D mean?"

"I took a guess," Decker said. "I figured they might be the initials of two people's names. If you keep in mind that this deal involves fireworks, who would you say C and D refers to?"

"Charles and Di," Johnny said, pointing ahead of him. They were in the car, driving west on Des Voeux. The traffic was tight in Central, municipal workers setting up sawhorse barricades on the sidewalks, and men in cherry pickers stringing up huge blowups of the royal couple. The answer had been literally staring Johnny in the face.

"It also explains the code word, doh mei-doh," Decker went on. "Bumpy says it's Hakka for something like burnt ground. And burnt ground—"

Johnny spoke over him, revelation widening his mouth, "—is what you're left with when you fire off half a ton of commercial skyrockets." He thumped the horn in delight. "Ooh, isn't it nice to know something the bad guys don't, for a change."

"My feeling exactly," Decker said.

They went over it in detail at dinner, and the more they talked about it, the more it seemed to make sense; the more everything tied in. There weren't any unanswered questions; they had them all covered.

There *was* something they didn't know, however, and would have been very surprised to discover they didn't know. It was simply this: they were totally wrong.

Doh mei-doh had nothing to do with a narcotics shipment.

Doh mei-doh was something far bigger.

Doh mei-doh was huge.

14

The Jade restaurant, where Decker had an appointment at ten-thirty, is in the Edinburgh Tower, a steel-and-glass skyscraper which, together with its twin, Gloucester Tower, houses one of the city's most prestigious shopping malls, the Landmark.

At this late hour—late for Central—only the Pedder Street entrance was open, solely for the convenience of the patrons of the Jade restaurant.

Johnny Risotto guided the car in to the curb, and told Decker that he'd wait for him, if it was only going to be a fast drink.

"I'll make it quick," Decker promised, and got out of the car. He had the sidewalk practically to himself; there were no attractions on Pedder Street, few people around except for an army of cleaners on the high floors above him.

When Decker reached back into the car for the umbrella, Johnny asked a question with his eyebrows.

Decker said, "This guy Harris may be a messy drinker."

He crossed to the entrance and climbed some steep stairs wondering himself why he'd brought the umbrella: a smart restaurant in one of the city's best addresses? But hell, if he'd had a gun he'd carry it, wouldn't he?

The stairway bent into a short corridor which opened out onto a mezzanine floor and an immense atrium. Not high compared with New York standards—five stories only—but very wide: three floors encircling the base of both tower buildings, with a spectacular fountain on the lowest floor, and glittering boutiques running all the way around three levels.

During the working day thousands of people crowded the area—tourists, shoppers, office people—filling it with a bright busyness;

but now there was nobody except Decker, no sound but for the click of his shoes on the marble floors; the escalators were stopped, the pumps beneath the glass globes of the fountain switched off.

A standing sign pointed to the Jade restaurant, one floor above. Decker bounded up another flight of stairs, pushed against the restaurant's florid door.

It stayed shut.

His glance fell on the opening hours listed on the restaurant's painted wooden sign.

The place had closed half an hour ago; somebody had got their signals crossed, Decker figured.

He went back down to the mezzanine floor, then strode toward the security desk on the chance that a message had been left for him. Decker walked through the smell of freshly polished brass and marble left gleaming by the night-shift cleaners. Over the brass rail, thirty feet below, floor tiles whirled in a concentric white pattern, and broad pot plants awaited a sliver of filtered morning sun.

The security desk was a triangular steel counter built into a corner and backed by a wall of red and yellow indicator lights. There were usually two men manning the station, but it appeared to be empty now. Decker went up to its shiny counter, peered over to see if there was maybe a note there, or the promised letter, with his name on it.

The men lay on the floor.

One of them barely stirring, the other moaning and breathing heavily. Blood trailed in lacy patterns down their faces, flowing from deep gashes on their scalps, the kind of wounds the handle of a cleaver or a heavy knife might make if brought down hard by a muscular arm. Decker knew, beyond any question, that if he turned now there'd be two fighters standing there, with their right hands behind their backs.

The knowledge brought an adrenaline rush. He felt the jolt of the pump kicking in, getting his body ready.

Decker turned.

And saw that he was only partly right.

Not two men. Three men. But they did have their right hands hidden.

Eddie Fong had done a number on him again. Flipped once, flopped once. Flipped again, flopped again. Well, what could you expect?

He stayed very still, letting the adrenaline get on with its work while he assessed the situation.

Brain first, body second; that's what they'd taught him. Except, for this particular agent the caution only worked now and then.

He figured it. There was only one exit to the street, the Pedder Street entrance, the one he'd come in. And the three fighters were blocking it. He could go all the way around the level, but that would only take him in a circle, and he'd still have the knives to get past.

Run down the escalator to the bottom floor?

No way out down there.

Take an elevator up?

There'd only be one working this time of night. And on a key, not on a call button.

So if he was going to get out of there, he was going to have to get past the three fighters.

Correction. Two fighters; two 49 boys, young, enthusiastic, probably good at their work. The third man was a Red Pole; older, tougher, a lot like the one who'd tried to stare a hole in him at the meeting at the container terminal. He wore rope-soled sandals, cotton pants, a pale-colored shirt a little too tight for his thick chest.

The fighters wore younger clothes: jeans and T-shirts with animal emblems, and tennis sneakers. They chewed gum, and looked as if they wanted to get this over quickly so they could get home and watch a rerun of *Miami Vice*.

Three against one. Not good, but Decker figured he had an advantage: they'd had surprise on their side but they hadn't used it; too cocky.

Now Decker had surprise on his side.

And sweat breaking down his temples.

Holding the umbrella as he would an ordinary one, like a man out for a stroll in a rain-threatened park, he went toward the three men, who had begun to move carefully forward, the two fighters leading, the Hung Kwan at the rear.

"Hey, there's something wrong," Decker said, deepening his voice to keep the wobble out of it. "The security guards," he said, half-turning, pointing back at the desk with the umbrella.

He wondered what they had behind their backs, knives or choppers. If it was knives, they'd come at him with gut thrusts, a sharp punch forward, then an upward slash on the diagonal—the usual Hong Kong technique. If they'd chosen cleavers, there'd be no technique; they'd just go at him like men hacking their way through a dense jungle. The two fighters separated, spread apart, their hands coming into view.

Black-handled beef knives with eight-inch blades.

"Behind the desk," Decker called, pretending not to see the knives. He was still pointing with the umbrella, his right hand holding it as he had the long bamboo shinai at the dojo that morning.

The fighter to his right closed on him, accepting the inviting target, picking his spot, planning to go in just above the belt buckle, into the left side of the hit's floral shirt.

It was a fast movement the man made, but, knowing it was coming, it was like slow motion to Decker.

The umbrella flashed up and over his shoulder, his left hand grabbing the handle four inches from his right hand.

He launched himself into the blow.

The umbrella, tightly furled, hissed through the air. The attacking kiai burst from Decker's mouth on a whoosh of breath.

"Ha!"

The umbrella slashed around in a migi-do cut, the steel shaft slamming onto the fighter's right collarbone.

The cracking bone sounded like a sharp handclap, the fighter's shrill scream part of the sound.

The second man, coming in with a groin thrust, tried to check the action and duck, but he didn't succeed. Decker stepped right and back-handed a hidari-men—*"Ha ya!"*—belting the fighter on the cheek.

The man crumpled on jellied legs as his senses left him, folded onto the hard marble floor, his eyes rolling up in concussion, dull and white like boiled eggs.

The third man, the Red Pole, had sprung back and assumed a defensive position, thinking about it.

Decker shaped to slash at him, but instead swung at the first fighter again, the steel shaft thwacking into his good arm, which he still could have used. The man yelled again, and tottered away, both wings busted; out of it.

The Red Pole stood his ground.

He should have turned and run, seeing what he was up against, seeing what had happened to his two fighters, one coldcocked and stretched on the floor, the other crouching and whimpering in awful pain. Yet the man remained impassive, rooted there. He had thick eyebrows like twin S's lying on their sides, broad mouth, broad nose; no personality to his clothes or his features—all the personality belonged to the knife in his strong right hand, the blade wide and with a gentle curve to it, a good-quality, three-rivet knife. The enforcers were always finicky about their working tools.

Even though he'd witnessed the dreadful damage the steel umbrella had done, he appeared to be without fear. His hand was steady, and he didn't gulp or swallow or lick his lips, and his forehead was clear.

Decker's was bubbled with sweat, his ribs cold with moisture, his mouth gone prune-dry.

As slowly as a man in a dream, Decker raised the umbrella high overhead, began to move, left foot sliding forward, right foot up to join it. Repeated the step: left foot sliding forward, right foot up to join it. The Japanese foxtrot, somebody had once called it. It was also known as the turtle and the snake: move like a turtle, strike like a snake.

The Hung Kwan moved carefully, backing closer to the brass rail atop the balustrade.

The only sounds were the keening of the fighter crouched on the floor, the scuff of Decker's shoes, the scuff of the Hung Kwan's sandals.

Decker pushed strategy into his head past the thump of his blood, the sting of sweat in his eye. Go for a straight slash, a shomen, or fake him first? The man was holding his knife near his hip, his other hand a few inches from his body, both hands out of reach of the umbrella. He knew what he was doing, this one. He would have put in his time behind the Western fruit market settling interlodge disputes, leaving bodies ripped and dying. An experienced man like this would be expecting a feint.

So why give him one?

What would the guy do? Wait till the sweat on the gweilo's face caused him to blink, then come in fast and get under the swing?

Probably.

Decker kept moving in his slow shuffle, the umbrella directly over his head, arms high, elbows out.

The enforcer moved with him, like his partner in a dance.

Sweat trickled, broke up in the hairs of Decker's eyebrow, dribbled toward his eyelid.

He made a big movement out of blinking, jerking his head to flick it away, and the enforcer sprang forward low like a charging lineman, his right shoulder dipping, the knife beginning to travel in an upward slicing arc.

Decker bunched wrists and forearms, stomach muscles flattening. *"Ha ya!"*

The man knew he'd been tricked but knew it too late, his rush committing him. He tried to dodge and hunch his shoulder like a boxer protecting his chin.

The furled steel shaft belted into his shoulder bone, shocking him backward, the knife dropping from his paralyzed arm. He staggered, half-turned as if he'd been violently shoved, and lunged for the brass rail topping the balustrade, trying to stay on his feet.

His draining senses got it all wrong, and he missed the rail, slammed into the balustrade, and like a man clumsily climbing a low fence, toppled over it.

He fell thirty feet, crashing onto a table of a restaurant below, caromed off that into two chairs, and finished in a heap on the floor.

Decker ran to the balustrade, took a look: the enforcer had survived the fall. He was on his knees, trying to get his feet under him, and failing.

Decker spun around, checked the corners, checked the hallways leading to the exit. There was no backup; three men was standard for a rip job. The knives were all out of action.

But there was something else. Something on the other side of the atrium.

He got the impression of a stealthy movement, then a quick one, as if somebody had ducked out of sight.

He was still thinking blades, so he wasn't worried; he could easily make it to the exit ahead of whoever was across the other side. And no knifer in the world could throw a blade that far with any accuracy.

Then he caught a glint, a semiglossy reflection that wasn't stainless steel bouncing the light. It had a dull, blue quality; unbright. There'd been a rainy-day game Decker had played as a kid, known as Air Raid, played within four walls. Each wall was given a color: red, black, blue, green. When the referee called out "Green," everybody had to race for the green wall, and last to make it was out. If the referee called "Air Raid," you had to hit the floor, flat on your stomach, as fast as you could.

That's what Decker did now.

Just as if some voice from the past had roared *"Air Raid!"* he kicked his feet out and let gravity flatten him.

It took only half a second, but that was plenty of time for him to know why he'd reacted like that: the flare he'd caught was exactly the kind you got when an overhead light hit a blued gun barrel. A half-second was also plenty of time for his eye to catch a flash of white searing across the dark center of the atrium; plenty of time to recognize the bright air burn of a tracer bullet, and to know that he'd been unkind to Eddie Fong, blaming him for the setup, when it was all the work of Arthur Murdoch. And Major Reggie Slemp.

A silenced gun that fired a tracer bullet?

Who else?

The hard floor grunted breath out of him, not the only noise just then, as, concurrent with his slam to the polished marble, came the crash and splinter of glass. Like a tiny burning ax head, the beacon slug smashed into the window of a boutique and neatly drilled a mannequin modeling a black-beaded Cacharel dress. The dummy fell, a puff of white smoke issuing from between its nippleless breasts graphically illustrating the path the bullet had taken.

Decker saw all this from his position on the floor; knew the bullet would be buried in the back of the store somewhere, burning and sizzling as if furious it had missed its mark.

Decker crawled along to the shelter of a concrete flower tub, a thick and heavy stone-studded tub in which was planted some kind of showy green fern. He stayed there, hunched up, thinking strategy again, strategy against a different weapon now, and a pretty good one. Those rounds Slemp had made were like a poisonous snake: it didn't matter where it got you if one got you—with powdered phosphorus boiling in each bullet's tip, the slug, if it stayed inside a meat-and-bone target, would torture with a white-hot chemical flame that no liquid could extinguish, not even blood, until it had burned itself out.

Best move? Decker thought about it.

Slemp was diagonally opposite him, too hard to spot from this position through the smoked glass of the balustrade.

An elevator? The security men would have the keys. He could probably make it to the counter, dive up and over its protective bulk. But on the reverse run, Slemp would pick him off like a rabbit running for its burrow.

If he went left, dashed for the exit, he'd have to turn into that narrow little hall whose marble walls would ricochet bullets like stones skipping off a millpond.

Decker listened past the moans of the fighter behind him, listened for Slemp to make a move, peeped around the concrete flower tub, got a fast look at the basement floor, the barely conscious enforcer down there amidst the ruins of the table and the scattered chairs. Away to the man's right was a blue canvas awning belonging to the restaurant, set out above the tables to give the effect of a sidewalk café.

Decker thought the awing was interesting.

If he could get down to the basement floor, he'd have a chance of getting under the overhang of the mezzanine, and out of Slemp's line of fire. And that awning would be a fast way down. Forty or fifty feet Decker reckoned he'd have to cover to be over the top of it. And with another flower tub twenty-five feet away, and another the same distance beyond that one, it would be possible to make it in two goes, as long as he could beat Slemp's Ruger twice.

"Slemp," Decker called. "Let's talk."

A little distraction first.

"Put the gun up. I think we can work something out."

An answer echoed across the space, a voice pushed forward in anger.

"There's nothing to work out. Do you know what you made me do?"

Decker wasn't sure what he meant, but it didn't matter—keep the guy talking; get him concentrating on something else.

"It's what Murdoch made you do that counts. Isn't that right?"

Decker pushed himself into a crouch.

"It's your damned fault," Slemp shouted, a petulant tone now. "You butted into this thing."

"I had to. I was under orders to do—"

Decker went then, like a ballplayer stealing a base. He got a big jump on Slemp.

Again there was no sound, or maybe the slightest hiss, like the sound a door makes closing against an air-pressure device.

The dim light in the middle of the atrium was scorched by a white streak like a laser beam in a science-fiction movie: three distinct beams creasing the air, three distinct sounds of glass caving in.

Decker dived and slid on the shiny hardness of the marble floor, belly-skidded to the safety of the flower tub. He lay there breathing hard, pain in his chest from hitting the floor, pain in his right knee, which had also taken a belt. But there were no little white-hot pokers boring into his flesh; no feeling of shock or faintness, of draining, as if somebody was changing your oil, which was how it felt when you'd been shot, according to those who'd had the experience.

To his right Gucci's display window was a web of sharded glass, a display of black patent pumps strewn over the store the store's broadloom as if a playful puppy had got loose inside.

"Slemp!" Decker called, wondering if the guy had already left his position and was coming after him, circling the level. He would have seen his goons taken out by the umbrella; the question was, did he know the umbrella was back there behind the first flower tub? And why should he fear it anyway, with an eleven-shot Ruger in his hand? Seven shots now, but he'd have a couple of full mags in his pockets for sure.

"Listen to me, Slemp. Put up the gun. I walk away, you walk away. Kill me and it's all over for you."

"You bastard," Slemp called back. "I don't care if they do get me. At least I'll get you."

Why, Decker wondered, was the guy so mad? It was some kind of personal vendetta he was on. Because he'd been fooled? But he hadn't stayed fooled; he'd gone to Murdoch, and Murdoch had told him exactly who the American mechanic was, and no doubt reamed him out for being idiot enough to fall for a stranger's story.

It surprised Decker; he'd thought he'd been safe there, thought that Reggie Slemp would have kept it to himself and avoided any friction with his boss.

Live and learn.

If you can stay alive long enough to learn.

"Slemp! I'll make a deal. You give me Murdoch, you go free."

"I am free, you damn fool. But you're going to be staying here. You're going to be too dead to leave."

The voice was tight, scolding.

And it had come from a different position.

Slemp was on the move.

He was at the corner, at the turn of the balustrade, Decker judged.

Once he got around that, the guy would have a back shot. Better to give him an angle.

He'd beaten the Ruger once, twice if you figured in the first miss. Was Slemp going to be third-time lucky? It'd be like a miniature rocket torching through his flesh, setting his innards on fire. Negative thinking.

Positive thinking was the reason why he'd missed: because that drilled barrel had reduced the pistol's accuracy. And maybe Slemp wasn't such a hot shot anyway—too much time spent in his workshop, too little on the range.

Decker charged out of his crouch, head down, shoulders pumping. Glass smashed a millisecond after something tugged at his sleeve. He smelled the burning cloth even as he pitched himself into a slide and made the sheltering bulk of the third concrete tub.

He took a fast look, saw the edge of the restaurant's awning directly below, sprang up, vaulted the rail, and dropped.

Just twenty feet down, but he felt like a flushed partridge waiting for a shotshell to blow it apart; the drop seemed to take forever.

He hit the awning feet first, tucked his head, and shoulder-rolled. The canvas sagged and split under his weight, ripping at one corner, tearing from its supporting post, falling away and spilling him out. Decker landed on a table as the enforcer had, fell off onto the floor, kept rolling, using the momentum to scramble up and sprint for the café's interior.

He was aware of pain in his shoulder from the fall, a lump beginning under his eye where he'd hit a chair, but no snapped tendons, no broken bones, no smoldering holes in his body.

He heard a shout; Slemp yelling his name, furious at such evasive and unexpected acrobatics. He heard plates exploding, glasses popping, crockery shattering like a carnival shooting gallery, and knew that Slemp had to be leaning over the balustrade above, firing blindly into the restaurant. There was the briefest pause—a magazine change—then the barrage began again, the line of fire switching to the arcade beneath the mezzanine balcony, the arcade down which Decker was running.

It was as if he were breaking trip wires as he dashed past the glamorous boutique windows, triggering off explosions behind him as window after window was punctured and splintered and torn apart by the hot white lances; Slemp playing Zeus, hurling vengeful thunderbolts from his position on high.

Unable to see his quarry, he was going purely on the sound of Decker's shoes slapping down onto the basement floor, but he was way ahead of his target. Decker was actually running toward the slim white zips of heat, which, like animation, appeared suddenly twenty feet in front of him, each instant band of light accompanied by the crash of flying glass as, one after the other, the windows of Hermès, Dior, Charles Jourdan, two other stores, were split and starred by the stinging power of Slemp's fiery-headed slugs.

Decker ran for the escalators, his only way off the floor and out into Pedder Street, hearing, in between the rupture of glass and his pounding feet, the clink and bounce of cartridge shells popping like hot toast from the Ruger's ejector port, spanging off marble and brass rail.

He made the bottom step, took the steel rise of the frozen stairs two at a time, safe from Slemp for the moment, the escalators blocking the Englishman's angle.

It was down to a footrace now: Decker had to hit the top of the escalators up on the mezzanine floor, diagonally opposite from where he'd started, then go left and run for the exit corridor and the stairs that led down to Pedder Street and Johnny Risotto and the car. It would be crystal clear to Slemp what he was trying to do. Slemp would be backtracking, pushing his flabby body into an awkward trot, running to get a shot at him when he made his dash for the corridor.

Decker rushed the last two steps, bolted left, heard Slemp's wheezing breath, heard him coming around the balustrade on the other side, running to cut him off.

Decker went for it, ribs thumping, lungs burning as if one of Slemp's evil little bullets had buried its hot little head in his back. He burst around the corner into Slemp's line of fire, and Slemp, coming down at him, his gun arm pumping, tried two quick and impossible hip shots that flamed past him, finding glass again; there was nowhere else for the bullets to go—it was either into a store window or into meat and bone out here on the shopping level.

Decker charged into the corridor, belly-flopped as he heard Slemp pound around the corner, skidded like a seal over the edge of the steps and down, slugs hacking at marble a foot above his sliding body.

He somersaulted, belted into the wall, found his feet, flew down the curl of the stairs, down the second half-flight, leapt for the doorway, out into the night, breaking its hot, quiet silence.

"Johnny!"

Behind the wheel of the car, Johnny Risotto wrenched around.

Twenty-five feet away, and sprinting hard, Decker yelled a cryptic message: *"It's mud! Go! Go!"*

Johnny had the car rolling as Decker reached the rear door, burnt rubber taking it away with Decker barely inside.

"Down! He's heavy!"

Johnny hunched, flung the car into Queen's Road, heeling it into a four-wheel skid.

Decker looked back in time to see Slemp come dashing out into Pedder Street, jolting to a halt, the gun coming up in the Weaver grip.

Johnny tromped the gas pedal; the car swerved and corrected, then shot forward.

Slemp launched two narrow white bands of fire, but his target had vanished behind a line of parked cars.

The incandescent bullets hit an empty Audi, slammed into the gas tank. The fuel got one whiff of the bubbling phosphorus and ignited. The back of the Audi went up with a wommfff!, a sheet of flame billowing from its rear like a jet kicking in its afterburner.

Johnny wheeled the car into Ice House Street, took a slashing right on Des Voeux, and put distance between them and whatever had caused that explosion back there.

"What the hell happened?" He slowed the car, looking at Decker in his torn clothes, his bruised and sweaty face.

"Slemp and three knifers." Decker took big breaths, his head back, eyes closed, drained. "I handled the blades, but Slemp was something else."

Johnny's face went dark, his big jaw clamping down. "Goddammit, I should've figured a setup. I just sat in this thing like a dummy."

"If you hadn't sat in this like a dummy, I'd be in the gutter right now. Take the tunnel."

"Where we going?"

The Walled City."

"Why there?"

"Because if Slemp was mad at me before, he's positively livid now. He couldn't get a clear shot at me and kept missing, thank Christ."

"Why the Walled City?"

Decker knew Johnny had guessed the reason, and knew he didn't like it.

"He practically destroyed the place back there," Decker said, feeling at his face, his ribs, getting his breath easier. "He must've ruined a dozen store windows. Gucci, Hermès. It's a pretty classy mall, isn't it?"

"Deck . . ."

"I have to see the Pigman, Johnny."

Johnny guided the car through light late-night traffic, his silence a strong comment.

"I have to, buddy," Decker said. "Slemp's given me a choice now. I can either leave town sitting up in economy class or lying down in the baggage hold."

"It's not the way to do it, Deck. Call Arsenal Street. Have them pick him up for possession."

"That's the way I'd like to do it, but how? We tip Arsenal Street, they raid his house up in Fo Tan, they won't find a thing. He'll have gotten rid of everything. We've got to get him with that damn gun on him. Offer him a deal in exchange for a few accusations about his boss. He's dangling from Murdoch, Johnny. Flapping in the breeze. Murdoch's smooth, seamless, nothing to get your nails under. We can only get to him through Slemp."

"Sure, but in the meantime, Murdoch's getting to *you* through Slemp. You're gonna have to stay off the streets, Deck. It's the only way. Going to the Pigman's asking for trouble."

The car dipped down into the Cross Harbor Tunnel entrance, the yellow lights making Decker's wan face look malarial. He rubbed at his swelling eye, moistened his caked lips, said to Johnny, "So is being without a gun when you've got one at your back. It's either arm up, or watch from the bleachers, and I'm not gonna do that."

"You're putting yourself on the target range, Deck. He missed this time, he may get lucky next time."

"He'll have to find me first."

"He'll know where you're staying. Don't go back to the hotel."

"I'm not planning to. Tomorrow night we'll get Eddie Fong and company out of the way, get 'em behind bars. Then I'll go after Slemp. I'll reach him through Murdoch. Set him up like he did me."

Johnny Risotto knew he wasn't going to be able to talk his pal out of it, so he didn't try. He just drove. Beside him Decker moved painfully, grunted at a sharp twinge.

"How you feeling?" Johnny asked.

Decker had to think about that. The only other time he'd been shot at he'd nearly lost an eye. And that had been just the one potshot. But Reggie Slemp, largely because of an inaccurate gun and a difficult terrain, had fired a dozen shots and missed him with every one.

"A lot better than I should," Decker said.

At twenty minutes before midnight the Walled City was quiet, deserted, a locked, abandoned, buttoned-up look to it, the only sounds the trickle of water and the squelch of duckboards as Decker and Johnny crossed the reeking little stream.

The lighting was minimal; different shades of darkness fluttering over the muddy track that wound through the silent enclave. Here and there a patch of blue light, emanating from a weak fluorescent bulb, illuminated the entrance of a dead-end alley or stone steps that vanished into total blackness. The City seemed to suck in the night, section it off and drain all color from it, leaving it like a black jungle.

Decker knew how dark the place could be; he'd been here before, to the Pigman's a few years back when he'd been trying for a lead on a trafficker who he thought might have bought a gun. On that occasion the Pigman had claimed ignorance, and he always would, knowing that to do otherwise was to risk being chopped up and fed to his own hogs. Johnny had paid a similar visit only recently. They moved beneath the arch tunneled under the shacks, went through a stygian passageway to where corrugated-iron roofs began at another level below them. Claws scuttled over the ridged metal in a flash of eye and tail.

Decker, leading, stayed on the path where it forked, crossed the quagmire made by the dripping pump, the duckboards submerging under Johnny's weight.

The smell riding the dark air began to change, the pigsty stench strangling the mix of sewage and trash. It guided them, that smell, like a foul olfactory beacon to the door of the Pigman's shack, which was open to the night, the sliced strips of nylon—the absurdly inefficient fly door—the only barrier.

They entered the gagging darkness, no sounds inside except for the bump and snuffle of the hogs below, sensing the presence of strangers. For a moment that was all there was: the darkness, the squish of the pigs blundering around in their slop, and their dreadful smell rising through the floorboards. Then a cot creaked, and feet thumped on the rough planking, and a flashlight beam hit them.

Decker spoke fast Cantonese.

"We're here to buy. Let's see something."

The flashlight studied them, then moved away, illuminated a hurricane lamp and a hand striking a match. The wick caught, sending an anemic light creeping into the room, flickering thin shadows.

The Pigman was wearing dirty gray Jockey shorts and a shrunken shirt that stopped well above the folds of fat encasing his invisible belly button. He climbed into a pair of rubber boots, and took the lamp down through a trapdoor.

A weak glow filtered up through the floorboards, accompanied by the snorts of the animals excited by a visit that could mean an earlier feeding time.

Their owner reappeared with Slemp's suitcase, placed it on the rattan table, brought the lamp near.

"Your timing's good," he said, chopping his tones northern style. "Several new pieces have just come in. I bought them from a wealthy collector from New York."

He opened the suitcase, moved the lamp closer again, and Decker got a look at the Pigman's wares: a couple of Saturday Night Specials—cheap .32's assembled from poor-quality parts—a Charter Pathfinder that had seen better days, a .25 automatic with a broken handgrip, and a pellet gun posing as a Detective Snub Nose.

The rest of the weapons were the ones Reggie Slemp had so proudly showed him in the basement of his house in Fo Tan.

"So that's why he's mad at me," Decker said in English. "He had to sell his toys."

Johnny Risotto, moving in closer, immediately saw the difference in the guns, and understood what Decker was talking about.

"A classic," the Pigman said, picking up the Patterson Colt. "Hand-engraved. I had to pay five-hundred American for it. I'll let you have it for just fifty dollars more. Or," he hurried on, spotting buyer resistance, "for a more practical sidearm you couldn't do better than this." He held up the Dan Wesson 15-2. "At seven hundred U.S. it's a bargain," the Pigman said.

Decker watched the lamp's flame burnish the weapon, still thinking about Slemp having to give up his little loves. He wouldn't forgive that.

Decker went into his pants pocket for his wallet, extracted three one-hundred-dollar traveler's checks, borrowed a pen from Johnny, signed the checks, and handed them to the Pigman.

The fence's rotund face looked bemused as Decker reached for the compact little Sig-Sauer.

"Three hundred?" the Pigman moaned. "I couldn't let it go for less than six-fifty. It's factory fresh. Never been fired."

"If it's factory fresh," Decker said, dropping the magazine and showing the Pigman the empty well, "who beveled this?"

"Factory fresh, then customized," the fence said quickly, realizing he'd underestimated this customer, whom he vaguely remembered as some kind of American law enforcement, like his big friend.

"Let's see the ammo," Decker said.

The man protested about the price, shaking his head continually. "Not for three hundred. I had to pay twice that to the New York guy."

"You bought this gun from a Brit," Decker said, using the local Hong Kong term. "A Brit with a mustache. He told me what you paid him. At three hundred American you're making money. Let's see the ammo. Get it out."

The Pigman was left with no comeback. He grumpily shoved his hand into the suitcase, found a magazine that fit the gun, rammed it in, and slapped the automatic down onto the tabletop.

Decker worked the slide. The top round chambered with a silky ease: one of Slemp's lovingly made hand-loads.

"Ho ga chien," Decker said, the traditional phrase used for concluding a deal. The Pigman turned his head and spat.

Decker moved Johnny ahead of him, and they went through the fly door out into the night.

Walking back through the darkness, through the fetid smell of the open drains and the refuse, Decker was comforted by the feel of the automatic under his shirt, pressing into his side.

Slemp had a gun, now he had one too. And both weapons had been customized by the same man.

What could be fairer than that?

Johnny Risotto waited until they were in the car and driving before he spoke.

"Six of those guns back there belonged to Slemp, right?"

"Yeah."

"I wish there were seven back there that belonged to him."

Decker smiled in the dark of the car; he was a good man, Johnny Risotto. "So do I," he said.

Johnny dropped him off at Faye's apartment house. Decker went up in the elevator, let himself in with the key Faye had given him, and beat her to the punch.

"Sorry I'm late. I had to meet a guy."

Faye's face had gone white. "It looks like you met him. Are you okay?"

"Sure," Decker said, trying to bluff. "Why?"

She led him to a full-length mirror in the hallway.

Decker looked back at himself: dried sweat had stiffened his hair, and a purple bruise was blossoming on his cheekbone. His shirt was ripped down one side and scorched at one sleeve where Slemp's bullet had burnt a hole. His left knee was showing through a three-cornered tear.

"Jesus! I look like a little kid who's been in a fight."

"You look like a big kid who's been in a fight." Faye wasn't smiling. Her worried eyes took in his face. Stress had drained his natural color, and blood had dried at the corner of his mouth where he'd bitten his lip.

"Let's get you into a hot bath." She moved to take his shirt before he could stop her, and exposed the automatic stuck into his belt.

"You weren't supposed to see that," Decker said.

Faye blinked as if she'd just received some bad news. She looked at the gun, then at Decker, then started on the shirt again, but slower now, peeling it off him as if expecting to find a gaping wound. There was no real blood, but a graze the size of a dinner plate decorated his ribs.

"You have any witch hazel?"

Faye nodded.

"I'll have a double on the rocks."

She helped him with the rest of his clothes, went into the bathroom and ran a tub, sat him in it and let him soak, brought him a cold beer. She dried him, dabbed witch hazel on his cuts and bruises, and put him in her bed.

She stripped and got in beside him, held him gently, waited till he'd fallen asleep, which didn't take him very long.

He woke around six A.M.

Faye hadn't slept much; she'd lain with her head full of fears, content for the moment to be there beside him and supply him with a little simple security.

When he turned to her, the movement tightened his mouth.

"How do you feel?" she asked.

"Fine in selected parts."

He eased his body, snuggled into her softness, kissed the hollow of her neck.

Faye asked him a question. "Do you know what a financial analyst gets good at?"

"We gonna start discussing jobs at this hour?"

"Yes, as a matter of fact."

"I don't think I want to."

"Signals. Signs and the reading of."

"I had to chase a guy tonight. I fell down a couple of times. No big deal."

"Chasing or being chased?"

"It amounts to the same thing. You get out of breath whichever one you do."

"Don't try to snow me, Hugh. There's a world of difference. I know about the gun laws here. You wouldn't have got a gun if you didn't have to defend yourself. Are you going to tell me I'm wrong?"

"No, you're right. If I'm chasing a guy, and he's got a gun, I have to defend myself."

"I saw your shirt," Faye said, close to him in the dark of the bedroom. "I took a look at it while you were in the bath. There's a hole in the sleeve, and it's bigger at the front than it is at the back. So somebody chased you tonight and tried to kill you. I'm not going to ask why. I know why. You're getting too close to somebody. Probably Arthur Murdoch. But I would like to know when."

"When what?"

"When he'll try again."

"When I let him. I'm not going back to the hotel. And when I go to the office, I'll have protection."

"What kind? Who?"

"Johnny, Bumpy, Miriam . . ."

"But they don't have guns, do they? So it comes down to just you and whoever wants you dead."

"What they want is not necessarily what they're gonna get," Decker said into her hair.

She kissed his face, careful with his bruised cheek, and asked a question that sounded strange coming, as it did, in a lover's voice. "How many people have you killed, Hugh?"

"I don't know. Somewhere in the low double figures."

"How many?"

"None. But it's something you don't need much practice in if you have to do it."

Faye put a hand on his shoulder, moved him back with gentle pressure, spoke to him in a way that was calculated to impress. "You won't have to do it if you go to the police. Let them find this man. Catch him carrying a gun."

"Faye. Listen. I can't go to the police."

"Why not?"

"Because," Decker said with irrefutable logic, "I'm carrying a gun too."

IV

DOH MEI-DOH DAY

15

Reggie Slemp had a problem.

At six A.M. he too was awake and thinking, only Slemp was in a cheap hotel room up near the new bus station off Chatham Road. He hadn't dared go back to his house in case the Yank had called in the police. They wouldn't have been able to prove much, but where to hide the gun? Leave it in his car and park it somewhere out of the way? A possibility, except that, in Hong Kong, cars had a nasty habit of always being found.

He lay on the bed in the dim dreariness of the shoddy room and worried the main problem: how to find Decker.

To simply wait for him outside his office was no good—far too public a place, right there on Garden Road. And there was no guarantee the man would even go to his office anyway. Where would he have fled to last night, a hotel? And if so, could he be traced?

The room wasn't conducive to thinking; the sheets felt damp, and there was a strong sea smell rising from the stained carpet, as if a fish tank had been broken, and fish and sand and seaweed had been spilled out. In a couple of hours' time Murdoch, up there in his glass palace, would hear the news on the radio, or get a report on breakfast TV, hear about the scene at one of the city's most fashionable shopping malls: boutique windows smashed, security men knocked unconscious, another man found with multiple injuries, a man who, no doubt, would be identified as a known gang member. The other two would have staggered out of there by the time the watchmen had called the police. Murdoch would hear about all this, would wait for the mention of an American national who'd been found on the premises stabbed to death, and when that little tidbit wasn't forthcoming, he'd be furious.

Let him be.

His employ with Arthur Murdoch was clearly over anyway.

Slemp lay on the clammy sheets, sour juices stewing in his mind. That bloody Yank Decker was making him look like a fool. He'd never ever failed to put down his mark, never. And he'd never cared about them, never even known them. But this chap, this jump-off bastard, had personally put the needle into him; had had the gall to confront him, trick him, bring him down to his present wretched position—holed up in a crummy hotel room with one gun left to his name.

One good shot at him, that's all it would've taken, but the bugger had dodged and squirmed and scampered like a rat. Well, this was Hong Kong. He could run, but he couldn't hide. Not for long.

Slemp rose from the bed and crossed the smelly carpet to the window and the ineffective rumble of the air conditioner. He fiddled with the control flap, which was hanging by one hinge, turned some knobs, but they spun brokenly. The place was a dump, but the guests remained anonymous, which was the main thing for the moment.

He stayed at the window, stained scarlet by the neon sign that climbed the side of the building. Down below, the street was beginning its day—some delivery vans arriving, road sweepers, a cook in a noodle stand readying pots and pans for the breakfast rush, which would blend into the luncheon rush, and on into the dinner rush. The Chinese, Slemp thought, were forever filling their heathen faces.

He gazed down at the noodle stand, conjuring up an enjoyable little fantasy: him tailing Decker, watching Decker stop for a quick bite, sitting down at one of the tiny tables, ordering, beginning to eat. Then just walk up behind him and say, "Mr. Decker?" And as he turned, the bowl up to his face in the Chinese manner, shoot him right through the bowl, blow noodles and shards of pottery all over his face, the hand-load entering his chewing mouth on a downward angle, lodging in his neck, hissing, scorching, burning through cords and sinews. Then saying, "What's the matter, old boy? Too much hot sauce on the noodles?"

Reggie Slemp's slow smile died as a word/idea association snapped into his brain: tailing Decker . . . Murdoch would have done something about that. Absolutely! He would have had him tailed as he always did anybody who posed any kind of threat. And, Slemp realized, his excitement beginning to effervesce, he would have probably employed the same man he usually did, what's-his-name . . . it sounded like a dim sum dish . . . Cha Bau, that was it, Tommy Cha Bau, the one who drove the old green Datsun. Good God, the man just lived around the corner off Kimberley Road, near that big restaurant where the tourists went for beggar's chicken.

Slemp slapped his leg, delighted with himself and his ability to think something through; it had always been one of his strong points. At seven A.M. he threw on his blazer, picked up the Park 'n Shop plastic bag containing the Ruger, and left the room.

Less than an hour later he'd found out what he wanted to know, had crossed under the harbor, and was driving toward the Mid Levels.

Driving toward MacDonald Road.

It was amazing how things just fell into place when you built on the basis of a bright idea, Slemp thought to himself, turning off Cotton Tree Drive. A sleepy Tommy Cha Bau had been easy to bluff. "Murdoch wants to know where he can find Decker right now," was all he'd had to say, and the Chinese hadn't questioned any of it. The man had told him that the American had a girlfriend at the Cloud Regency Apartments.

The address had rung a bell.

And then he'd remembered; of course, it was where the Waters woman had lived.

Tommy Cha Bau had bribed the watchman there. The woman's name was Keeble, and she was staying in apartment 12B. That's where Decker had gone last night. Tommy Cha Bau had waited outside till two A.M., then left. He assumed the American had spent the night there.

It made sense to Slemp; he wouldn't have gone back to his hotel. He would've gone someplace he felt secure.

Only it wasn't going to be quite as secure as he thought.

Approaching the apartment house, Slemp saw with satisfaction that the street was practically deserted; nobody to see his rusty little Honda Civic and remember it; just a taxi swinging down the drive-way and, fortunately, going the other way.

He parked thirty feet up the street, walked back in the clear new morning. It was going to be another warm day.

He slipped in through the glass doors of the apartment house, hurried across the elegant lobby to the elevators. Still nobody around: fortune favors the brave, a maxim he'd always believed in. Besides, his luck was running; he was on a roll, as they said in Las Vegas. Slemp rode up in the elevator glowing with pleasant anticipation. He'd press the bell—everybody opened the door in Hong Kong, all the Westerners, anyway, because they knew they were safe—and the Yank would be standing there in his pajamas, bleary-eyed from fucking his girlfriend half the night.

Shove the Ruger in his face and say something like, "Did I wake you? Sorry. Why don't you go back to sleep?" Then pull the trigger: a pop, a hiss, the smell of scorched flesh, a slug ricocheting around in his skull, frying his brains.

Catch him as he falls, lower him without a sound, then close the door and get out of there.

Slemp began to whistle a tune, an old Sinatra thing. He liked those sixties arrangements, so much better than some of the later things he'd done, those self-congratulatory bootstrap songs.

He kept the whistle up as he walked down the corridor and stopped outside 12B. He took the Ruger out of the supermarket bag, thumbing off the safety with a practiced and natural movement.

He didn't have to check to see if it was cocked; it was always cocked. Cocked and locked.

He pushed the bell.

No response.

Then the tread of movement from inside.

The door was opened wide, just as he'd known it would be, but not by the right person.

A sexy woman in pajamas stood there, a look of expectancy on her face, as if she thought she knew who'd be ringing the bell.

The look vanished when the Ruger came up six inches from her forehead. Her eyes enlarged, and her skin blanched.

"Make a fuss and I'll kill you stone dead." Slemp nudged the gun in a little directive, and backed her into the apartment. Looked quickly right and left.

Stopped.

Listened.

Heard nothing.

He grasped the woman's arm, shoved the Ruger's drilled barrel behind her ear, took her with him on a tour.

Nobody in the living room. A quick glance out at the terrace, but there was just a slice of sun out there and empty chairs around a table. In the kitchen was the start of breakfast for one, another coffee cup in the dryer rack.

Nobody in the first bedroom, the bed made up.

Nobody in the second bedroom, but two people had slept in that bed; two rumpled pillows, double indentations on the bottom sheet.

The bathroom was empty.

"Damn!" Slemp said out loud. The man who'd been in that bed, who'd had the cup of coffee in the kitchen, had gone. Slemp damned his luck again, and wondered about that taxi he'd seen pulling away as he'd arrived.

"Where's he gone? Your boyfriend, Decker. Tell me!"

Faye gritted down on her fright and her fear; got some strength into her throat. "The airport."

"Where's he going?"

"Thailand."

"No, he isn't. If he was, you wouldn't tell me. Not without a little inducement, anyway. And we may just get around to that."

Shock began to steal over Faye, sliding in behind muscle and bone, chilling her. It had been so quick: expecting Hugh at the door, unable to find his key, come back to tell her something—and finding, instead, the man who was trying to kill him; who'd come to kill him. Lying awake in the small hours, she'd tried to imagine that person, as if by giving him form in her thoughts it would make him that much less real, more of an abstract threat. She was sure she knew his name: Slemp. Murdoch's pistolero, Hugh had told her. She hadn't imagined him as a forty-five-year-old Clubland Brit, the kind that seemed to have washed up in Hong Kong from an England that no longer existed. She'd imagined somebody small and ferret-sly, not a man like this, so distasteful-looking; his flesh had begun to bunch and hang on his face, his teeth were bad, his hair greased but unwashed, dandruff lying heavy on his rumpled blazer. His mustache was neatly clipped, as if you were supposed to focus on that feature and overlook the rest. He looked like a painting of himself that had begun to rot. His unpleasant breath came closer.

"He's running around town, isn't he? Poking his nose into places it doesn't belong. Well, we'll wait for him to return. Just you and me. I'm sure we'll find a way to amuse ourselves."

Faye shied back. He still had hold of her arm, and seemed to have recognized a new situation now: a man with a gun, a woman in pajamas, a warm, rumpled bed in front of them, the covers down.

She wrenched her arm away, backed up until she bumped against a bedside table, knew as she felt it hit her leg what was on it: a lamp, a book, the nail file she'd left there. It was a long one with a bone handle. She'd bought it on Austin Road.

Faye spun, grabbed the file—it looked like a dagger coming into her hand—spun back, and spat out tough words.

"Touch me again and you'll get this right in your balls!"

With a fast forward step and a quick movement of his left wrist, Slemp batted the file from her fingers, grabbed her elbow in a fierce grip, and shook Faye like a parent angry with a child.

"Now, look here, missy, let's get one thing straight. If there's any violence to be done, I'll do it. I'm a specialist in that area, as you'll find out if you get on the wrong side of me. We're going into the living room and sit down and wait for your boyfriend to get back. And if you have other ideas, and try to scream or get away, I'll take this pistol and knock your pretty front teeth out, throw you across the bed, and give you a little bit of what's good for you. Do you get my drift?"

Slemp shook her again to enforce his message, and liked the effect it brought. Her breasts swayed inside her loose pajama top, and her nipples, stiffened by fear, moved back and forth like twin cherries beneath the silk.

It was in his mind—she could see that, the bed right there. He was close to doing it.

She watched him swallow, stare at her pajama top, sequins of moisture breaking out on his brow. A quick surge of an unwashed smell emanated from him.

She forced thought, groped for a way to turn him off, halt the nervous, lascivious emotion that was clearly building in him. Not aggression; that was too easy for him to respond to. He'd demonstrated that. Not ridicule. A man like this, not very bright, wouldn't have the sophistication for that; he'd lash out.

Hit him with reality, then. Maybe that would work, if he recognized it. It risked getting him hurt and angry, but there was nothing as deflating as the sharp barb of a simple truth.

"You stink," Faye said, low-voiced.

"Just my normal musk, dear girl. Brought on by the sight of your nellies jumping around inside there. I'll bet they're white as milk and heavy in the hand, are they?"

Slemp shoved the gun barrel inside the top of her pajama jacket and popped a button.

Faye didn't try to restrain him. She said in the same flat tone she'd used before, "Not just your grubby person. Everything about you. You stink of death."

That stopped him. Slemp's face turned in on itself, a squeezed lemon. He didn't like the sound of that, hadn't been expecting it. He said, like somebody grasping at something, "I deal in death, girlie. It rubs off."

It was an attempt, perhaps, at wit, but he was shaken by her accusation, delivered, as it had been, in such a knowing way, as if she had a window on the future. Still talking, wanting to recover lost ground, Slemp said, with his mouth curving down, lopsided at one end, "We all die, my dear. The trick is to die later than most. And I'm personally going to see to it that your con-artist boyfriend is one of the many people who'll precede me."

The morbid subject switch did its job, broke the sexual spell Slemp had been drifting into. He jerked her roughly across the room, pushed her stumbling out the door and into the kitchen, where he rummaged around, pulling out drawers, slamming them closed, until he found the thing he was after.

Faye froze when she saw it. Given this man's kinky turn of mind, the repression he exuded, a ball of heavy twine, and its attendant possibilities, was a chilling sight.

He marched her ahead of him into the living room, shoved her into a chair, sat opposite her. "Now we wait. And if you misbehave, we'll take a little trip into the bedroom and play a variation of Sultan and Slave. Ever played that game? It's much more fun for the Sultan." He leered at her, and held the gun at his crotch, tilted upward in an obscene parody. "Six and seven-eighths inches long. You'll have an orgasm that'll take your breath away. So will I."

Faye closed her hands on the arms of the chair and slowly began to squeeze. It was something to focus on, to help keep the fear off her face. She fixed her gaze on the broadloom; a piece of fluff down there the vacuum cleaner had missed. Hugh had said he'd be back for lunch around noon. Impossible to warn him unless she could get away from Slemp. It couldn't be done by force; he was flabby but he was strong, and quick too. Go to the bathroom, yell out the window? He wouldn't let her go by herself, he'd insist on standing outside the open door; maybe inside the open door. That would be about his level.

There seemed to be only one way to do it.

Use the weapon every woman had. Get him into bed.

It wouldn't be hard to make it look like his idea: give him a glimpse of her boobs, a swaying, hippy walk to the kitchen for a glass of water, spill some down her front, get a wet-shirt effect; no problem there. The risk was what he might do to her once she got him into the bedroom.

This man just might rape her with that gun.

He was uncomfortable with women, and trying to mask it; grinning too much, being too hearty, having a great joke with that pistol. The old cliche for the male: a gun as penis. But she knew what he meant about that orgasm: it would be the gun's orgasm. When he came, he'd pull the trigger, with that dreadful barrel inside her.

In a chair opposite, a grin tugging at his lower lip, Slemp tossed the ball of twine into the air like a cricket ball, caught it, dropped his eyes to the creases her pajama pants made edging into her crotch. A door banged somewhere outside in the corridor, a burble of voices tacked onto it.

Slemp wagged the gun in a no-no gesture and kissed the Ruger's narrow muzzle.

The voices receded, and silence returned.

Faye went back to the ball of fluff on the carpet, her mind jumping ahead in time.

When Hugh got back, he'd let himself in. The first she'd know about it would be the scrape of his key in the lock. She could yell, warn him that way, but that wouldn't stop Slemp from firing at the door. She knew next to nothing about firearms but was certain that veneered plywood wouldn't stop bullets.

Then Slemp would shoot her too, and walk away.

She looked up at him. He was staring at her body, two fingers of his left hand slowly moving up and down the gun barrel.

He was getting close to making his move.

She knew she had to beat him to it if she were to have any control over what was obviously about to happen.

"Would you get me a glass of water, please?"

"Do you think I'm stupid?"

"Then I'm going to get one."

Faye got up and started toward the kitchen. Slemp let her go, but he was right behind her.

There was a tumbler on the drying rack. She filled it, fumbled it to her mouth too quickly, and spilt most of it down her front.

"Don't be nervous, dear girl." Slemp handed her a dishcloth with an overly courtly gesture.

Faye took it, wiped at her pajama top, hitched at her pajama bottoms, walked back into the living room, knowing Slemp was watching the tight silk stretch over her buttocks.

She sat down again, getting it together in her head: there were safety catches on guns. Revolvers and automatics differed there; she seemed to recall that from some cop show. Revolvers had no safeties, automatics did. Was that right? A revolver had a cylinder. The gun Slemp held didn't have one, the bullets were somewhere else. It was an automatic, then, so one of those knobs was a safety catch. Which way was on, which was off? And didn't they do something with automatics on TV? Pull at something before they fired one? But Slemp had been ready to use the gun when he'd rung the bell, so all that had undoubtedly been done.

So all she had to do was get that gun into her hand, point it at him, and pull the trigger.

She'd have to shoot him. It would be foolish to try to menace him with it while she called the police; he'd take it away from her as quickly and easily as he'd disarmed her before.

Could she do it? Wound him, maybe maim him? Perhaps kill him?

Faye looked at the man, his evil gulping leer, a sheen on his pasty skin, little flecks of spittle at the corners of his mouth.

He'd kill Hugh if he could; would have killed him already if Hugh had left a few minutes later. And he'd kill her too. So it would be one life in exchange for two.

"You're a fetching little thing, aren't you?" Slemp said. His voice was parched, and he was beginning to blink rapidly, eyes on the damp front of her pajama jacket, the outline of her left breast, the nipple clearly delineated. He had the ball of twine in his free hand and was fondling it like a furry pet, feeling its texture. The grayish tip of his tongue took several trips around his dry and fleshy lips.

When the phone rang, Faye jumped and Slemp shot to his feet, the gun swinging up as if the phone was an outside signal of rescue. An answering machine took the call, a red light blinking. Slemp heard a man's voice, an American accent. A voice he recognized.

"Hey, babe. It's me. You in the shower? Dammit, what am I doing here? Listen, I can't get free for lunch, and I have to stick around for showtime tonight. But let's have a drink if you're downtown. Six o'clock at the Bull and Bear, okay? Yours sincerely, Hugh C. Decker."

Slemp put the machine back on Answer and gave Faye another of his meant-to-be-dashing grins. "That's jolly considerate of him. Here I am wondering where he is, and where he'll be, and he phones up and tells me." He checked his watch and looked happy. "Ten minutes to nine. We have about eight and a half hours in each other's company. We can relax now that we don't have to worry about friend Decker bursting in on us. Relax and enjoy ourselves."

Slemp lost a piece of his voice on this last sentence, and covered by ending with a bright little laugh. A kind of libidinous fit was beginning to steal over him, a terrible fixed curve to his mouth. He was in an agony of discomfort.

Faye closed her eyes for several seconds, then spoke in a monotone. "I think we should get it over with."

"Get what over with?" The laugh was almost a giggle.

"Sooner or later you're going to take me into the bedroom. I'd prefer to get it over with."

Slemp's laugh came out as two spoken words. "Ha, ha. You make it sound like a visit to the dentist."

"Please," Faye said, rising from her chair. "Don't tie me up. Do anything you like, but don't tie me up."

When he heard that, a sexy young woman telling him to do anything he liked, his voice left him and he began to tremble.

Faye turned and started for the bedroom, keeping part of what she had to do away from her thinking. A horrible part: letting this awful man have her body. The other part chilled her, the shooting and possible killing. But it was what she'd decided to do, so it was what she had to concentrate on.

She'd make sure they were near the edge of the bed, maneuver him there, then, just as he climaxed, when he'd be totally inside his head, those few wrenching seconds when a man was overwhelmed by release, she'd tip him, thrust and swerve so that he'd roll and hit the floor and not know for a brief disoriented moment what had happened, and that would be all the time she'd need to reach the gun on the side table—he'd be certain to, keep it close—snatch it up and shoot him. In the arm, the shoulder, the leg if possible. Anywhere else if she had to.

Watching her walk away, watching the roll of her hips, those luscious cheeks he'd be seeing, touching very soon now, Slemp found that his knees wanted to give on him, and he had a light buzzing feeling in his tummy. The prospect of what he was about to experience danced and shimmered in his imagination, an erotic mirage that gripped and squeezed at his testicles as if he'd plunged into an icy pool. Maybe this time, he thought, maybe this time he could do it: actually screw a woman.

This was no cheap and dreary whore; this was a clean and juicy piece of tail walking toward the bedroom; American pussy. It was said to be superior stuff. But could he do it, he wondered, without the old problem occurring? PE. Premature ejaculation.

Nothing to be ashamed of, merely an overabundance of male hormones, or a highly developed libido, so he'd read somewhere. It wouldn't be easy. She'd be taking off those pajamas, letting those heavy titties out, dropping the pants down over her round ripe bum, a clump of hair guarding her coozie thick enough to plait with ribbons.

Something lunged inside Reggie Slemp's chest. He'd never ever been in a situation like this; it was fantasy stuff: a peach-skinned, wholesome woman with a centerfold body, an expensive, finely furnished apartment to be alone with her in, and she was his to do whatever he liked with: her exact words.

God, what if it did happen again? What if the sight of her thrilling nakedness sent a too-early message to his gonads, and he came while he stood there, not yet fully undressed, the stain spreading over the front of his trousers while he bent over in a half-jackknife, grunting like an invalid in the grip of a heart attack?

She'd laugh at him, sneer at him. Despise him. Not even man enough to take her.

She'd get up off the bed, get dressed, and have nothing more to do with him. And if he tried to get her back into the bedroom, she'd say: "What for? You feeling sleepy?" The same as that Jordan Road whore had said to him last week when a similar thing had happened.

No.

He couldn't have that.

He had to keep her there, keep her on that bed. Keep her naked until he was ready again. It would be okay the second time.

Reggie Slemp picked up the ball of twine and hurried after his prize. But she'd made it plain she didn't want to be tied up, and she'd resist it. And if she did, it would be damned hard to tie her arms and spread her legs and tie all four limbs to the corner bedposts. He'd have to stun her a little, just enough to make her groggy, sap her strength temporarily till he got her lashed down.

Then she'd be his.

Reggie Slemp coughed against the force of the thrill that was coursing through him, tingling the ends of his fingers, his feet; his dick already semi-tumescent.

With an easy, deft movement he reversed the Ruger in his hand, the heavy butt like a hammer, moved up fast behind Faye Feeble just as she reached the bed.

The gun, a silent weapon however used, swished quietly through the air.

Decker didn't see any reason to begin the morning any differently from the way he'd begun them for the last few days: with a workout at the dojo.

He put his body through a hard joust with the master, punishing it. It hurt, but it got out the kinks. His ribs were bruised and his eye was swollen and discolored, but he discovered, during the lesson, that his movements weren't restricted by the previous night's athletics, although stretching cost him.

He found it strange to be wielding a bamboo sword after the weight of the steel umbrella; strange also to be slashing and thrusting in mere exercise after having done it, so recently, to keep from being killed.

Now that he could look back, from a position of victory, on the fight against the three knifers, he felt great satisfaction. It would, without question, have been the first time that any of those gang members had run up against any kind of opposition when they'd been on a hit. It felt good to have literally struck a blow on behalf of all their past and future victims.

As for Reggie Slemp, he knew beyond doubt that he'd be going to the mat with the guy. Slemp wasn't about to be called off; the man was on a mission now, a vendetta. The weapons had been chosen and, seeing as how they were pistols, one of them was going to end up dead. It was a heavy thought but Decker filed it in order of priority; he had to first get Eddie Fong's pals arrested and, at the same time, stay out of the way of some marauding lodge fighters bent on larceny. Life had not been dull lately, and showed no signs of becoming any less boring.

When Decker and the pig-tailed yudansha had finished hacking at each other, and Decker was standing before him breathing hard and perspiring, the master yet again told him the story of Bokuden and Rinsai. Decker had given up wondering why the master never moved on to another anecdote, or why he never told it differently. He half-wondered if his instructor hadn't confused him with some other student, and didn't know he was repeating himself.

Sitting mokuzu, Decker found himself thinking about Bokuden, the warrior poet, what he'd looked like, what his life had been like before the fateful meeting with Rinsai. And what had happened to him after his storied triumph. He'd killed a man who'd killed his wife; not much of a trade-off. Did he conquer his grief as well? Put up his sword and perhaps remarry, and live out a fruitful life as poet and philosopher, making achingly beautiful brush drawings of willows and mountains?

Decker wondered if he was supposed to ask the master this, or conclude for himself how the great swordsman had ended his days.

He thought about it for quite a while.

He called Faye from a phone outside the dojo, got her answering machine, left a message, then called Ralph Dobrinski, gave him a rundown on the events at the Landmark shopping mall. Dobrinski told him to stay away from St. John's House in case Slemp had any ideas of laying for him there, advice which Decker was happy to take. He didn't want to get involved in any official report about an attempted murder; that would bring in Arsenal Street, and that was a complication he wanted to put off.

He spoke to Johnny Risotto, arranged to meet him downtown, then went around the corner to the Chinese Emporium and bought a new shirt and a pair of jeans to replace his torn clothes. He spent most of the morning at the teahouse with Johnny and Bumpy and Miriam, working out the best way to handle Eddie Fong's pals out on the fireworks barge that evening.

He didn't mention that he was carrying the Sig-Sauer under his new shirt; what Bumpy and Miriam didn't know couldn't hurt them.

He and Johnny went off to keep a lunch date with a man named Ramsey, a chief superintendent in Narcotics at Arsenal Street. The lunch was an easy, relaxed affair. They let Ramsey know, in the kind of veiled terms that had become standard, that there just might be a grocery delivery in the harbor that evening, something the Wo On Lok had going. And they hinted that it was possible that the Green Pang, and maybe even the Yee On as well, might try to horn in on the deal. They told Ramsey where and when all this might happen, although they weren't sure exactly when. However, if he wanted to have a couple of launches parked around, say, Lai Chi, they'd try to get a message to him on the police frequency if they heard anything more definite.

Ramsey, playing the game, told them he might just do that, and left to make some arrangements.

"It's looking good," Decker said to Johnny. "I think it's gonna work out."

Johnny, sipping at a bowl of almond soup, agreed, then added a caution." "As long as we're off that barge before the choppers come out. I don't want to lose weight that quickly."

Decker considered that last remark. "The Hong Kong Triad Diet. Lose pounds in seconds. Think it'd sell?"

"Only in California."

Over on the other side of the Peak, Arthur Murdoch had awakened early on this, for him, his day of days.

He'd canceled Valerie, the masseuse with the magic fingers, wanting to retain every ounce of his energy, but, needing action, had risen earlier than usual, grabbed his crutches, stomped into his gym, and worked out vigorously.

At seven-thirty, when his kitchen amah had brought him coffee and clicked on the morning TV news, Murdoch had learned about the events at the Landmark eight hours previously. Somebody, the newscaster said, had gone on a rampage, shooting out the windows of famous-name boutiques. A man had been found in the luxury shopping mall, a man suspected of having triad connections, who appeared to have fallen from the mezzanine balcony. He was in serious condition but expected to live. The newscaster made no mention of anybody else being found, alive or dead.

Murdoch was livid.

Slemp had done it this time. He was going to have to be put into the ground, where he couldn't make any more mistakes.

As for Decker, Murdoch realized he'd underestimated him. The guy was a survivor. Different arrangements would have to be made. But it needed some thought.

Murdoch had propelled himself into the bathroom and showered sitting in a specially constructed plastic support. He didn't bother to soap his legs; they did nothing but hang there, why should he give the fucking useless things any attention?

He'd dried himself, dressed himself, and allowed his chauffeur to drive him down to the office.

As usual, when the car reached Wanchai Gap Road and the famous vista opened up, Murdoch watched the Morse-code message flashing from the water tank of his building: A. M. A. M. A. M. But this morning he'd watched it in a different way, with a different feeling. He'd elevated his gaze over the top of the tank, up over the blue wash of the harbor, the mass of Kowloon, and the green expanse of the New Territories. It was a fine day, a ching ming day, clear and sunny, the air vacuumed by early-morning breezes.

He could see all the way to Red China.

And looking at it, Arthur Murdoch had experienced a sharp thrill of pleasant anticipation.

The day had also begun early for a man named Yung Tsin, the captain of a hundred-ton lighter, an ungainly vessel that was really nothing more than a motorized, live-on-board, high-gunwaled barge.

His contract with the Yellow Sun Company called for him to work any designated ship in the main western harbor, and this morning's job was a Filipino freighter which had arrived via Shanghai and Taiwan. Yung's lighter, snuggling up to the freighter's starboard side, received all manner of goods from the ship's hold—machine tools, canned food, clothing, shoes, small appliances—and because Yung's craft flew a dragon pennant from the TV aerial of the red-and-green living quarters, the freighter's first mate made sure that the last things lowered by the ship's sling were two wooden crates. The crates had been marked with vivid slashes of red paint and had the word "Explosives" stenciled on them in Chinese and two other languages.

With the lighter low down in the water, and moving sluggishly, Yung guided it to the western reaches of the harbor, to the fireworks barge anchored less than a mile away from the wildly overpopulated streets of Mong Kok. The barge, a floating pontoon, had a long and wide flat deck, and a steam derrick mounted at the stern. Normally it was used to transport heavy machinery, and would be towed by a tug. Now it was just a launching platform positioned so that the big skyrockets would burst and fall over the narrow part of the harbor, easily viewed from both Kowloon and Hong Kong sides.

Yung used the lighter's crane to swing the two crates off the top of his cargo pile and onto the barge. They were accepted by four men supervised by somebody whom Yung recognized as the Vanguard of his lodge. This man had quizzed him, five years ago, on the ritual questions during his initiation when he'd crawled through the Mountain of Swords.

Yung still remembered the ceremony; it had been the highlight of his life so far.

"Why do you come here?" the Vanguard had asked.

"To enlist and obtain rations," Yung had replied, coached in his lines.

"The red rice of our army contains sand and stones. Can you eat this?"

"If our brothers can eat it, so can I."

"When you see the beauty of our sworn sisters and sisters-in-law, will you have adulterous ideas?"

"No. I would not dare to."

"If offered ten thousand taels of gold to arrest your brothers, would you do so?"

"No. I would not dare to."

"If you have spoken truly, you are loyal and righteous, and may enter the lodge and protect it with your whole life and being."

He had been declared a New Brother, and had crawled back through the Mountain of Swords reborn.

Glowing with the memory of the honor accorded him, Yung backed up his cumbersome vessel and headed toward the godowns of Kennedy Town to deliver the rest of his cargo.

On the barge, the four men who'd handled the crates jimmied the tops off, then broke them down. These four were a group from a private firm that had won the contract to orchestrate the fireworks. None was a lodge member, but they'd been told that whatever happened on board the barge would be none of their business, and their cooperation in overlooking it would be appreciated. And as there were three Wo On Lok heavies also present on the barge, cooperation was, more or less, assured.

The fireworks had been packed in twenty wooden boxes about twice the size of orange crates. One of these boxes had a stencil of a tiger's head painted on it, and it was this box that the Vanguard, assisted by his three tough-looking helpers, removed to one side. After that there was nothing for them to do but watch the fireworks being set up, and wait for the evening to arrive.

* * *

For Ronald Pei, Sergeant First Class in the Royal Hong Kong Fire Brigade, the day had begun with a visit by a Straw Sandal messenger. The message the man had for the sergeant had originated with one of the guests at Arthur Murdoch's most recent dinner party, Sai Ho Koo, whom Bertie Winters in Macau had correctly identified as the leader of the Yee On lodge.

Sergeant Pei received the note, then drove his little Nissan to the North Point Control Center, made the rounds, and got the word out to the duty men of the day, ninety-five percent of whom had sworn allegiance to the Yee On. A twenty-four-hour strike was being called beginning with the evening shift, which was due in at six P.M. It would affect the three big stations that service the Central District: North Point headquarters, Harcourt Road, and the new station on Cotton Tree Drive.

Strikes, being illegal in the Crown Colony, were more in the nature of a go-slow, or a work-to-rule: members called in sick, reported late, and arrived in dribs and drabs so the stations would be undermanned and nowhere near operational. Curiously, there was usually equipment trouble occurring at the same time as a strike: pumpers that wouldn't work, engines that wouldn't start, hoses that had somehow got into a tangle.

Just why the strike was being called wasn't revealed to Sergeant Pei.

He didn't know and he didn't care.

He just followed orders.

Another of the guests at that same dinner party on Mount Cameron Drive, S. J. Lam, had also been correctly identified by Bertie Winters as a lodge leader, the lodge being the Green Pang, Arthur Murdoch's old outfit. And Winters had again been right when he'd told Bumpy that among the tradespeople the Green Pang controlled was a large proportion of the office cleaners in Central.

Doh Mei-Doh Day had started earlier for some of these people than for anybody else when they'd crossed the harbor on the five-oh-five ferry from Kowloon to run the floor polishers and vacuum cleaners in the big buildings in Central: the morning shift, getting the offices ready for the day's commerce.

Sixteen of them had been given their orders the night before, told what to do: look for a man in the underground walkway that connects Statue Square with the Star ferry terminal. This man would be wearing a Japanese headband and holding a black Samsonite suitcase. The sixteen selected menials were to identify themselves by carrying Konica-camera shopping bags which had been issued them. They'd been told that the man would give them something wrapped in butcher's paper. It would look like a morning snack. They were to unwrap the package when they got to work. Inside they'd find an electronic device, the function of which was immaterial.

All they had to remember was this: One, push the little red button on the front of the thing. Two, conceal the device about halfway up the building in an office facing the harbor.

All but one of the people chosen for this job worked in particular buildings in Central. The odd-man-out wasn't a cleaner at all.

He was a gardener.

He also worked at a particular address, but one that was on the way to the Mid Levels.

He'd been instructed to place his device in the bushes directly beneath a high balcony. A high balcony that faced the harbor. None of the cleaners, nor the gardener, had any trouble in carrying out their instructions. And by seven that morning all the little devices were in place and operating smoothly.

The third guest at the dinner party, the general, got out of bed much later than anybody else involved in the big day.

The general had got to bed rather late, having spent most of the night with a fourteen-year-old Hau Nuijai mouth girl in Taipei.

Twenty miles outside the city now, he breakfasted around eleven A.M., then put a call through to his bank in Singapore. Yes, he was told, five million dollars had arrived in his account yesterday afternoon. The general would have been surprised if it hadn't. Though he never took anything on trust—hence the phone call—he'd always found Arthur Murdoch to be a man of his word.

At noon the general held a meeting with his team, a meeting that would have appeared, to anybody just passing by, to be nothing more than just a regular briefing: the general at the blackboard, his group sitting silently, studying his instructions, checking their references, making notes—notes that would be carefully destroyed later.

He had complete confidence in his men; they were handpicked. Besides, they were all being paid two hundred thousand dollars to perform this little chore and to keep their lips buttoned afterward.

With the briefing finished, the general went out to inspect the loading arrangements. Again everybody looked normal. The loading team had got their cut too. And the two men in stores.

It would all come out eventually, of course; something this big was bound to. But the general wasn't worried; he wouldn't be around the Orient much longer anyway. He had retirement coming up soon and was bound for the U.S. West Coast, where his money would buy him some hotshot lawyers who would ridicule any subsequent accusations that might arise, turn them into vicious rumor circulated by a political Taiwanese clique hostile to their client.

He had a whole new career waiting for him in America: he'd been able to buy his way into the Chu Lien, the United Bamboo, which had carved out a nice little niche for itself in Los Angeles, specializing in murder, kidnapping, extortion, loan-sharking, and, of course, narcotics.

The general was looking forward to LA with a hungry anticipation. All that young, tanned, high-stepping, twelfth-grade cheerleader poonj.

It was going to be heaven.

16

Knowing early where the Yank would be, and when, Reggie Slemp had had a lot of time to think just how he would kill him. He was definitely not going to pot him, knock him off like a bird on a branch; the job would be done close in so the man would know he'd been defeated, know that, even though he'd won a few games, he'd lost the match.

Everything was going nicely, although he'd had a few anxious moments when he'd had trouble getting downtown. Charles and Diana had arrived on an RAF plane around five P.M., and the procession in from the airport, and the waiting crowds in Central, had choked up traffic.

Slemp had cursed the royal couple under his breath. Like a lot of Englishmen abroad, Reggie Slemp gave only lip service to the concept of a British royal family. He stood straight for toasts at the club, chatted about their latest doings, but in his heart he regarded royal-watching as a tiresome pursuit much more suited to women. As little girls, most of them had played at being princesses, and still went gaga over the Cinderella coaches, the pomp, and the pretty colors. It was all a lot of upper-class humbug whose main function, these days, was to keep the tourists and their foreign currency rolling in. The visit merely represented a delay for Reggie Slemp, but one, he was greatly relieved to find, that had not affected his game plan.

He made it downtown a few minutes before six and ensconced himself inside the window of a bookstore in the Hutchinson Building. It gave him a view across Murray Road to the Bank of America Building, and the black-and-white English Tudor facade of the Bull and Bear. It was another of the British-style pubs popular in the colony, specially with expats, and a convenient downtown meeting place. Slemp had been there many many times.

From his vantage point inside the bookstore, half-hidden behind a large-format book, *Poisonous Snakes of Southern China,* Slemp watched through the window.

Six o'clock came and went.

Then six-oh-five.

At six-oh-nine a cab pulled up and the Yank got out and went through the pub's Tudor doors.

Slemp figured to play a waiting game; he'd simply follow Decker when he came out, hopefully to someplace where he could get him by himself so they could have a little chat before he dispatched him. He'd tell the Yank what had happened to his girlfriend—Decker would adore hearing that—then riddle him, then get a taxi to the airport and the first plane out. Make a fresh start.

With one eye on the door of the pub, Slemp turned the page of his book; the green-headed pit viper, he noticed. Lots of them in the colony. Lantau Island was infested with them.

At six-twenty-five, when Faye still hadn't appeared, Decker found a pay phone at the rear of the pub and called the apartment.

All he got was the answering machine again. He assumed that Faye hadn't got his message, had gone into the office and probably got stuck in a meeting. He called her firm and got a tape telling him that the office had closed for the day.

He returned to the bar and sat over a draft ale and wondered if the pub had been such a smart idea. There were just so many spots that were popular with Westerners in Central; it wouldn't take Slemp long to make a tour of them on the off chance that the guy he was hunting had dropped in somewhere for a six-o'clock drink.

Decker stood at the bar half-turned to his right so he could watch the door. The .380 under his shirt was only an inch away from his right hand, his right arm bent casually on top of the bar.

He sipped his ale and watched the place fill up.

It filled up even more twenty minutes later when Johnny Risotto arrived, adding not just his own considerable bulk to the crowd but also that of two large metal suitcases. They had a slow drink together, making the drinks last, then Johnny glanced at his watch and said, "It's showtime, folks."

He picked up the suitcases. They left the pub, went out into the growing darkness, and got into a taxi.

* * *

Reggie Slemp didn't tell his driver to follow that cab; nothing so dramatic. He simply watched where it went and told the driver where to go.

It wasn't a long trip anyway; just down the road to Blake Pier. Slemp got out on the traffic side and took his time paying the fare, letting Decker and the big man he was with—probably another DEA agent—get a little ahead. He wondered about that big man; he was carrying two large metal suitcases. Was he going across the harbor to a hotel? Was Decker on some kind of job? If the big man was still around when Decker got to a good spot, that was just going to be his bad luck.

Slemp watched them move down to where the walla wallas were moored, the water taxis that would take you anywhere on the harbor for a price. Slemp saw them get into one as the night came on, saw the boat set out onto the harbor, and had to wonder about that: were they crossing to Kowloon, or going somewhere special?

He hurried down to the quay, stepped into a boat that had been tied to the one the two agents had taken. The walla-walla man looked as if he'd been on the harbor for years; a skinny body, and a face that had seen all kinds of weather.

Slemp handed the man some money, pointed to the stern light of the departed boat. "Those men that just left. Where did they want to go?"

"Fireworks barge."

"That's where I'm going too," Slemp said.

The taximan started the engine, a little inboard diesel, took the boat chugging away, an open boat twelve feet long with canvas-covered wooden benches.

Slemp was delighted. He'd hoped for someplace isolated, and what could be better than a barge out in the harbor? You couldn't pick up the telephone on one of those!

He patted the Ruger stuck into his belt, the long drilled barrel hugging his hip.

A breeze off the water pressed against his face, salt-fragrant and refreshing. The city slid farther and farther away, an island bejeweled with lights—pink, white, red, green—massing into a homogeneous brilliance.

Reggie Slemp felt great.

Excited.

Truly alive.

* * *

Hong Kong and Kowloon were like riverbanks on fire, the harbor a wide dark stream between them.

Dotted on the stream, like glow worms hovering just above the surface, were splotches of yellow light thrown off by ships and the lighters working them. Overhead the blaze that roared up from both banks faded gradually as it reached out over the harbor, and dyed the night sky a pale shade of crimson.

Decker and Johnny said nothing. They'd had all day to go over tactics, and knew that too much talking about a job made you start questioning earlier decisions which had been thought out with care.

They sat in the walla walla with traffic slicing around them—ferries, boats, launches—and watched the signs begin to multiply—Philips, Yashica, Aiwa, Carlsberg, GEC, Subaru, Winston—belting out into the night from atop the Ocean Terminal and the beehive shape of the Harbor Center buildings, their clashing colors spreading across the water like bright and glowing carpets.

Johnny handed Decker an item which was a curious thing for one man to give another in the middle of Hong Kong harbor: a small piece of sandpaper. Decker used it on his fingertips and thumbs. Johnny had already done the same so as to keep his prints off the two suitcases.

Five minutes later the barge they were heading for appeared, looking like a floating and dimly lit tennis court. As they drew closer, Decker saw that the illumination came from a work light mounted on the barge's crane; it was just enough to pick out several figures in the middle part of the barge busy at something, plus another group, three men, who were sitting on a box and watching the little boat approach. They got to their feet as they saw the water taxi was heading straight for them.

The driver throttled back, let the boat drift in alongside the barge.

Decker and Johnny, telling the taximan to wait, climbed out onto the barge, already in their roles of the day before: Johnny the Mafia biggie, swaggering and looking around him with heavy nodding movements, and Decker the subservient, fixer, carrying the two suitcases like a hotel bellboy.

The barge was huge, a sheet of flat metal almost as wide as it was long. Taking up most of it were rows and rows of rockets, three feet high, green-tipped, and mounted in bamboo firing racks. Behind these were cardboard bombs, long fat mortars, Roman candles,

75-mm. mines, and screecher starshells, whole phalanxes of them standing up in wooden frames. All the portfires had been linked to a wire so they could be set off by an electronic timer. The fireworks team had choreographed the display, choosing each piece for color, shape, and design, to get the maximum effect when mirrored in the water.

The colony had splurged; it had spent a fortune aiming for the most spectacular display in Hong Kong's history. To Decker's eye there appeared to be enough fireworks for a week's celebration. He followed Johnny across the clang of the metal barge, down to where the three men were standing beneath the crane: two fighters and an enforcer. Decker had met the enforcer before, recognizing him by the disalignment of his lumpy jaw: he was the one who'd watched him so closely during yesterday's lunch at the container terminal.

Only three men. That wasn't going to be enough, Decker thought; not if another lodge swooped while they were on the barge. The dope had been safe out here all day, because a marauding gang would want to grab the buyer's money as well.

Timing was still the big question; if the raid he and Johnny expected came too soon, nobody would end up in jail. There'd be a lot of bodies floating in the water.

The enforcer watched them walk toward him, looked past them, swept the harbor, very cautious, very deliberate.

"So? Where is everybody?" Johnny rumbled at Decker. "I thought we was gonna do a little bidness here."

"They'll be here just as soon as they think it's safe, Mr. Bruno."

"Safe? Two of us and six million of them, and *they're* worried?"

"I'm sure it won't be long, Mr. Bruno."

"Shit," Mr. Bruno said, sounding disgusted.

The enforcer, apparently satisfied, grunted into the walkie-talkie he held in his left hand, in touch with somebody out in the harbor. Decker knew who it would be: a scout, zipping around in a skiboat, circling the area, checking for any suspicious craft.

A few minutes later a power boat appeared out of the night, its souped-up inboard engine sounding like a float plane's. It slowed and settled forward, looped expertly past the waiting water taxi, and reversed in time to kiss the side of the barge. Four people got out of the boat, which immediately took off. Decker recognized two of the approaching men: Eddie Fong and the sallow-faced 415 man, the planner from yesterday's luncheon. The third man was a strong-looking fighter, already mean-eyed, and with a grudge against the world. The fourth man was vastly different from the other three, a fact that Johnny Risotto noticed too.

"Bingo," he said under his breath.

"You're right," Decker told him.

The man was in his fifties, and wearing a double-breasted suit. His hair was carefully barbered and had gone silver over his ears. His expression was bland but still gave the impression he didn't like being where he was. He looked like the chairman of the board, a man who belonged behind a large teak desk, some kind of topflight business executive.

They'd asked for a Sheung Fa, an assistant leader, and it looked very much like they'd gotten one. And you didn't catch one of those every day of the week.

Decker went forward to meet them, raising his chin at Eddie Fong.

"The stuff get here okay?"

"Yeah," Eddie said. "Sure it did."

Eddie Fong wore his nervousness like the bowling jacket that clung to his thin shoulders. It was understandable: in a very short while he'd be a marked man with the lodge.

He ran a hand over his mixing-bowl haircut and said, with an attempt at formality, "You remember Mr. Chu. And this is the gentleman you wanted to deal with."

Decker did his part; he nodded deferentially to the well-groomed man and half-turned toward Johnny Risotto. "Mr. Bruno from New York."

The man didn't understand English but he knew that Mr. Bruno was the buyer.

Johnny pointed a stubby finger at him. "He the boss man?"

"I would say so, Mr. Bruno," Decker answered.

"Sure he is," Eddie Fong contributed. "You wanted the boss, you got him. You got a Four Three Eight here."

The sallow-faced planner seemed to understand this. "Boss," he said, moving his head up and down.

The 438 stared at Johnny, stared at Decker, but said nothing. The young fighter had moved to his side protectively, as if the honor of the lodge were being impugned.

A little way away, the fireworks team, in their hard hats and coveralls and thick cotton gloves, were pointedly ignoring the meeting and running last-minute checks. It was coming up to seven-forty.

Johnny looked around him, raised his hands. "Okay, so where's the crap?"

The planner said something to the assistant leader, who signaled an affirmative. The planner then led the way down the barge, down to the after-section where the three heavies stood beneath the crane guarding the box with the tiger's-head mark on it.

It took them less than a minute to break the box open, pull out five fat blue plastic bags.

Decker bent to one of the metal suitcases. Like its twin, it was held closed by a padlocked wire cable; the buyers were clearly taking no chances of a suitcase springing open at the wrong time.

He took out a small commercial weighing scale, set it down on a level piece of the deck, and weighed all of the bags.

He went into the suitcase again, came up with a stiff new manila envelope caught by a rubber band. He laid out the envelope's contents: a matchstick, a plastic spoon, a roll of Scotch tape, and a small brown bottle of what looked like eye drops.

Decker took the matchstick—it was sharpened to a point—licked the end, pricked a small hole in one of the bulging bags, and worked the match through the blue plastic. He carefully withdrew the match and tapped several grains of coarse gray powder into the plastic spoon. He sealed the hole in the bag with strips of Scotch tape, then picked up the little brown bottle, unscrewed the top, squeezed the bulb, and sucked up some of the liquid inside—a marquis reagent: concentrated sulfuric acid and formaldehyde—and squeezed a drop onto the grains in the spoon.

The grains began to quickly change color, going from the color of paste to a light purple.

"It's quality stuff, Mr. Bruno," Decker said. "A fast change and a good deep shade. Handle it nice, it'll go ninety for sure."

"It will, huh?"

"Yes, sir. No question."

Johnny Risotto looked disappointed, as if he'd been hoping to get into an argument with the suppliers. "I thought that last bag looked a little light."

"They're all five keys, Mr. Bruno. I'll weigh 'em again, if you want."

"Nah," Johnny said moodily. He pointed to Eddie, jerked his head at the assistant leader, who'd watched the testing with disapproval, like a rich man forced to help his chauffeur change a flat tire. "Tell your boss we got a deal," Johnny said.

Eddie translated, but it was the planner who answered. Eddie put the response into English. "They'd like to count the money."

"When it gets here," Johnny said.

Eddie Fong looked blank for a moment, then asked for an explanation.

"I told you yesterday. I got a guy bringing it in from Manila. Flight was due in twenty minutes back. You'll have your money in . . . what?" Johnny asked Decker.

"Ten, fifteen minutes."

When Eddie Fong relayed the information, nobody looked happy. The planner glared at Eddie as if he were to blame for the hold up, and the assistant lodge leader was standing very stiffly. His eyes searched Johnny's face, looking for signs of treachery, but Johnny was a good actor and gave an excellent impression of a bored and irritable man.

"Ten, fifteen minutes, then we can all go home. Okay?"

The Chinese group backed off and muttered among themselves, the planner embarrassed and defending himself from some sharp words from his boss.

Decker knew that this was the crunch part, but the excuse was reasonable: buying dope was strictly cash-and-carry, and a large amount of money had to come from somewhere.

Ten minutes went by and brought the time that much closer to eight o'clock, which was when the fireworks display was supposed to begin.

The team had completed their final check and were standing around comparing watches.

"Hey!" Johnny said loudly to Decker. "You think that flight got held up, maybe?"

"It was on schedule when I called, Mr. Bruno."

"Then where the fuck is he?" Johnny peered into the night, shook his head, got a sudden disturbing idea. "You told him out here, the fireworks barge, right?"

Decker looked startled, then apprehensive. "I thought you told him that, Mr. Bruno."

"What? I left it to you to tell him. What the fuck did you tell him?"

"I told him Blake Pier. Then you changed it and I thought—"

"You goddamn stupe! I didn't tell him a goddamn thing. A lot of fuckin' good the money's doing us at the fuckin' pier."

"I'll go get him, Mr. Bruno."

"No you won't. I want sumpthin' done right for a change. I'll get him myself. Lock this stuff up."

Decker threw a mortified glance at the Chinese group. "They're top people, Mr. Bruno. They'll be insulted."

"I don't give a rat's what they are. You never heard of the old switcheroo? I'm making sure what I bought's what I get. Lock it up."

Decker obeyed. He worked the combination padlock on the other suitcase, opened the case, put three of the bags in it, the remaining two bags in the other case. He slammed both cases closed, threaded the wire cable around them and through their steel handles, handles that were built solidly into the steel lids.

Eddie Fong was in a heated exchange with the planner, and the enforcer looked ready to pull his knife.

Johnny ignored them. "Hook 'em up," he said to Decker.

Decker looped the cables around a steel support at the bottom of the crane, snapped the padlocks closed, and spun the combination wheels.

"Okay, then," Johnny said. He turned to the group and made an attempt at conciliation. "No hard feelings, okay? Just protecting my end. Just good bidness, that's all."

He waddled away to the side of the barge where the water taxi was waiting. It would have been too neat for them both to have gone back for the money, much too suspicious. This way the dyspeptic boss, disgusted with his subordinate, was grabbing the broom and doing the sweeping himself, a move the Chinese would understand. Johnny climbed into the walla walla, and it puttered off toward Hong Kong.

Decker apologized to the planner, apologized for the delay. The planner didn't like it, nor did his superior, but they had to go along with it. Half the arranged sales and buys never even came off, and when they did, they were usually fraught with delays, no-shows, mistrust; the Hong Kong Chinese had always felt that snafus were to be expected if you dealt with Westerners; the Big Noses had no talent for organization.

Everybody settled down to wait; nervous, ruffled.

Decker wondered how much time he had.

If the Yee On or the Green Pang was out there in the night somewhere, keeping the barge under surveillance, they probably wouldn't move until everybody appeared to be getting ready to leave.

Probably.

Decker moved closer to the edge of the barge, ready to go the moment he had to. This part of the plan was a little clunky, but it was the best they could do. Around about now Johnny would be using the walkie-talkie he'd left in the water taxi, calling Ramsey in a police launch parked behind the finger piers above Lai Chi. There'd be two or three launches; it would take about five minutes at top speed to reach the barge, and a fraction less than that for the Chinese group to realize they'd been stung. Decker could pull the Sig-Sauer and hold them off, but that would expose his presence to Ramsey, and there'd be hell to pay.

So the simplest way of making himself scarce was to jump into the harbor, hide under the lip of the barge, and wait for Johnny to come back and fish him out.

He glanced down into the water. Eighty-five thousand ships a year for the last fifteen or twenty years had left the surface thick and viscous; the harbor was home to oil slicks, ordure, garbage, and a lot worse.

He checked the time.

Eight o'clock.

Down toward the middle of the barge, the head of the fireworks team pressed a button.

Three hundred feet above the harbor a dozen four-ounce rockets blew apart at the top of their soaring arcs and trailed a thousand red ribbons across the dark of the night sky.

Red changed to orange as magnesium dragon stars popped and exploded, burnt brilliantly in their slow fall, exploded again into a silver rain, a Milky Way descending.

New rockets flew, and yellow suns and purple moons mirror-imaged in the still black water, showered down their marvelous light on the skimming harbor traffic.

Reggie Slemp had his head back, his face turned bright pink by a comet flashing through the sky. It exploded in thunder, became a dazzling supernova, then shredded into fizzing streamers that swayed together like a gorgeous curtain drawn across the dark. He wondered if it were time to make his move.

He'd seen the big man get into the walla walla and head back to the city, leaving Decker on the barge for some reason. He could make out a bunch of other men there, behind the area where the red tails of the rockets leapt into the sky. It certainly wasn't going to be a private meeting, but in the end, what would it matter? Not at all, really. Specially if those men were Chinese, and they probably were; the chinks had learned long ago to see no evil. If something didn't concern them, they kept out of it and told the police nothing.

"We'll go in now," Slemp called to the driver. "In to the barge."

They got within two hundred feet of it before a powerboat cut across the taxi's bow and slewed around them, a wheelman and a fighter on board. As Decker had correctly guessed, this was a scout boat, a lookout boat. When the fighter had seen the walla walla making for the barge, he'd radioed the enforcer, asked him if they were expecting another gweilo. If he had a bag with him, something to carry a lot of money in, was the reply.

The scout boat drew alongside the taxi for a look.

Much higher than the little craft, it was easy to see that the Big Nose carried nothing.

"Ney sow my been guo?" Who you got on board? the fighter called.

The driver called back, recognizing a command in the question.

"He's following the other two. Didn't know where they were going."

The fighter called something else, and the skiboat drew closer.

Slemp didn't understand; he didn't like it. He couldn't make head or tail of the damned singsong lingo, never could.

"What the devil's going on?"

"Mechanic." The taximan had to shout over the boom of the exploding sky. "Want spare engine part. Circle harbor. Service taxi."

The fighter was climbing on board, yellowed by the pyrotechnics bursting overhead.

"What do you mean, mechanic?"

"Work for company. Want part for boat broken down Kowloonside."

Slemp didn't think the man looked much like a mechanic, but then these chaps seldom did. They never wore the uniform of their trades; grocer, welder, cook. They all dressed in flipflop rubber sandals, short-sleeved shirt, and jeans.

The man brushed by Slemp, bent down at a locker beneath the rear seat. Slemp turned away, annoyed at the intrusion. Then a hand clamped onto his elbow, and the flat side of a cold blade put a hard pressure under his jaw.

His first thought was that he was being mugged—some new kind of mid-harbor piracy. He didn't resist, but allowed himself to be pushed down the boat. He didn't dare go for the Ruger; a flick of the wrist would turn the blade edge and slash his throat.

He let his captor force him into the skiboat, trying to brave it out. "What the hell do you think you're doing? I'm a British citizen." He was shoved roughly down onto a seat. The skiboat shot away. The walla walla turned and headed back toward Hong Kong.

Slemp began to understand: there'd been no attempt to take his wallet, and the boat was surging toward the barge. These weren't muggers, they were triad thugs. Decker, a DEA man, was out there on business, just as he'd thought. Reggie Slemp almost laughed; it was some kind of drug deal he'd blundered into.

Well, now. That changed things considerably. There'd only be triad riffraff to deal with, like this brute who had the knife under his ear.

Slemp was very antidrug; he thought of it as a filthy business and the people involved in it as little better than pederasts. So the barge wouldn't present any problems.

As they drew closer, he estimated the number of people on it to be eight or nine, not counting the hard-hatted fireworks team, who wouldn't be giving anybody any trouble.

Eight or nine plus the two men in the boat here.

The Ruger fired eleven rounds, and he had an extra magazine in his pocket.

Plenty for all.

As the distance between the skiboat and the barge narrowed, the noise increased. Thirty-millimeter Roman candles popped bright bouquets of exploding flowers straight up overhead. Scarlet serpents, thunderflashes, and repeater shells broke apart at the top of their fiery trip. Starshells banged and bombettes rose on great silver tails. And, right behind them, a row of pot mortars, like cannon defending a fort, bombarded the sky as if they meant to bring it down.

Slemp could see the people on the barge clearly now, Decker clearest of all. The Yank was standing to the right of the crane, facing toward Kowloon.

Excellent. It looked like it would be a surprise visit right up to the last moment.

The skiboat dropped its speed, the bow plunging.

Slemp got a close-up of the Chinese group as the boat bucked and settled for its run up to the barge. One, two, three, four thugs, and three other men who didn't look as if they were there for any physical reasons.

Slemp knew about the lodges, knew that their muscles seldom used firearms. The four thugs would have knives, just like the one who was getting him to his feet.

They were going to be so easy.

He felt the thrill speed through him, that tight, tingling buzz in his insides he always got when he was about to go into action.

He didn't really choose his moment; it presented itself to him. The fighter pushed him ahead, out of the boat and onto the barge, jumped out himself, and made the boat fast.

Slemp took a few steps, stopped, drew the Ruger as he revolved, and less than three feet away from the fighter, put a bullet into his forehead.

The man behind the wheel of the skiboat took two slugs in the throat.

Slemp turned; checked Decker first.

Decker hadn't moved. He seemed to be watching for something up past Stonecutters Island.

The Chinese group seemed confused, as if they didn't understand what was happening. They'd seen the fighter fall, but hadn't seen the gun, and certainly hadn't heard it.

Slemp began to stroll toward them.

He didn't get far before he saw sudden understanding stiffen the thug on the left, older than the others, heavier-built, and with a hard and ugly face. The man called out something as a knife came into his hand and he moved in front of an impressive-looking Chinese in a fine blue suit.

The three other thugs charged, beef knives appearing from shin scabbards.

Slemp shot the three fighters as they rushed him in line, mowed them down from near-point-blank range. He found it interesting that they all died in the same way, clutching at the fire inside their chests, then staggering as their legs jellied on them, then belly-flopping onto the hard metal deck, the knives bouncing away.

The ugly one with the thick shoulders stood stolidly in front of the blue-suited man, who was staring in fright like his two companions, their mouths circles of alarm.

Slemp walked forward between the twitching bodies of the fighters. The ugly man, his blade held low, jumped at him.

Slemp shot him in the chest, shot him in the stomach, and watched him crumple just like the others. Slemp was a little surprised; he'd looked a lot tougher than that. He felt a mild twinge of disappointment like a big-game hunter whose kill had proved too easy.

But he cheered up, because the real sport was yet to come: he'd kill Decker in little bits and pieces.

The man hadn't seen him, Slemp noted; he was still fascinated by something at the north end of the harbor.

Slemp walked up to the three Chinese, who saw death coming for them and were frozen by the sight. Up close Slemp confirmed his initial opinion: none of these men would carry a weapon, but they could always pick up one of the knives from the steel deck and try to sneak up on him while he was taking care of the Yank.

"Any of you speak English?" Slemp had to raise his voice over the roar of the skyrockets zooming up from their racks. There was a soft pop from high overhead and a shower of stars that turned everybody green.

Slemp watched one of the Chinese, a thin, consumptive type in a bowling jacket, nod. "If you stay exactly where you are, you'll live," Slemp told him reasonably. "If any of you move, I'll shoot you. It's as simple as that."

"Okay," the thin one said, and Slemp, sure of their acquiescence, turned and faced up the barge.

This was a wonderfully dramatic moment for him; he wanted the Yank to turn away from whatever was holding his interest on the north side of the harbor, and to look down the barge, and to see him, Major Reggie Slemp, standing there—a nemesis that had appeared out of thin air the way it happened in legends; crimsoned by the floral fountains exploding above, with perhaps some stunning silver lightning as well, accompanied by a thunderclap like God announcing his doom. It would be more than fitting, Slemp thought, seeing as how he'd once played God himself. And, all false modesty aside, played him very convincingly.

Slemp got his wish.

He laughed out loud, it was so absurd, but life could be like that —could smile and be kind and go your way for a change, as it was doing now.

Because, behind him, a dozen 14 mm. mortars had crashed out in unison, and a winter snowstorm, blindingly white, was streaming down from the hot skies, turning night into day, illuminating him like a great performer hit by a hundred spotlights.

The great boom of the display jerked Decker's head around, and Reggie Slemp experienced the finest moment of his life: Decker, that lousy, interfering, life-spoiling bastard, transfixed by the sight that met his staring, unbelieving, fireworks-dazzled gaze.

Almost lazily Slemp raised the pistol, intending only to wing him, a little appetizer before the main course.

Decker was only ninety feet away, but drilling the Ruger's barrel had destroyed the rifling, killing any chance of real accuracy, and Slemp took careful aim, not wanting to put one through his heart by mistake.

He never got to pull the trigger.

Decker, turned bright amber now by a falling, burning Niagara, had ceased to be a struck-dumb statue and was darting his hand under his shirt.

Slemp had been around guns too long not to recognize the movement. He jumped even as the shock ran through him; Decker was armed! Slemp spun, grabbed the man in the business suit, leapt behind him, swung up the Ruger, but Decker had vanished behind the massive iron base of the crane.

It looked to be a standoff, both of them protected from each other's fire, but Slemp knew he had an ace up his sleeve that would give him a heavy advantage.

He looked down the barge, picked his spot: the crane's cable cylinder. It was almost as high as a man, and ten feet across. He'd need that, because when Decker heard what he had to say, he couldn't be sure the Yank wouldn't try to kill him anyway, even with the hostage in front of him. And depending on what kind of gun, and what kind of ammo he had loaded, a bullet could pass right through the Chinese, and do for little Reggie Slemp. No, he'd talk to Decker after he got squirreled in behind that cable cylinder.

Slemp shoved the Chinese forward and, staying close behind the trembling man, began his advance toward the crane.

Decker had felt edgy and unsettled; a lot could happen in the five minutes it would take the Narcotics squad to make it. The planner and the 438 could go sour on the deal at any moment. They'd hated seeing the heroin base locked up that way. They could smash the padlocks if they really tried, wind the deal up, and put it off for a week or two.

Decker watched for the police launches, wondering how soon he'd spot them, how much warning he'd get. He knew he wouldn't hear them till the last moment; the engines would be drowned by the aerial bombardment, which was increasing in tempo. The entire night sky appeared to be aflame. It was like being under a burning building and watching huge chunks of it flake off and come tumbling down in ordered patterns.

He settled himself, stood there close to the crane, close to the edge of the barge, keeping watch.

He thought about other things: about Faye, and what he was going to do about her when his time was up in Hong Kong. He'd only known her for a few days. How long did you have to know somebody before you knew what you wanted?

He thought about her ex-roommate, and the men who'd helped kill her, Murdoch and Slemp. He thought about Slemp and his silenced pistol, and wondered how to go about finding him without becoming too much of a target.

This was the thought he was drawing out in his mind when the bank of giant mortars went off, the colossal noise swinging his head around. And astoundingly, unbelievably, Slemp stood there, like an apparition in a fairy tale, bathed in shining silver and gold, standing ninety feet away grinning at him.

For an instant Decker was seized in a clamp of inaction, as if the luminescence tumbling down from the skies were some kind of paralyzing ray.

It was too quick, too impossible—like a wizard physically assembling an image of a person through the power of his great mind—and Decker was stunned.

He blinked and broke the spell, shut out reason, blocked off questions, and went for his gun.

Slemp guessed he wasn't trying to scratch himself and did a smart thing, exposed as he was: grabbed the Sheung Fa for a shield.

Decker ducked in behind the crane and watched Slemp push the Chinese forward, coming for him.

He could see Eddie Fong and the planner standing still, helpless; see the bodies stretched out on the deck and, closer now, the terrified Chinese and Slemp's glimpsed outline, both figures stained a brilliant orange hue as a flight of cascade rockets reached the explosive apogee of their brief, spectacular lives.

Decker wanted the Sheung Fa alive, but not at the price of his own head.

He shouted out: "I'll kill him if I have to, Slemp."

"I just want to talk," Slemp called back, kept on coming, then shoved the Chinese aside and jumped behind the iron bulk of the cable cylinder.

Decker relaxed a little. Slemp was finished now; the Englishman couldn't get to him unless he charged, and he'd be dead if he did that. In three or four minutes' time the police launches would come zipping out of the night, and Slemp would be exposed on the metal deck, a man with a gun in his hand, caught by a searchlight.

They'd give him only one chance to put his hands up and Slemp wouldn't take it. He was a gunman; he'd try for a searchlight, but it wouldn't much matter whether he hit it or not.

Decker knew that all he had to do was wait.

Slemp called to him. "Decker. I told you I want to talk to you, and I do. I have something to tell you."

A barrage of rockets detonated, whooshed up from their racks with a hissing roar, and Slemp's words were hard to hear. A bright yellow waterfall appeared overhead, became a glittery golden river flowing down into the harbor, gilding the barge, gilding the top of the rusty cable wheel.

"I have something to tell you too, Slemp. You're a coldhearted fucking killer, and I don't think you're long for this world."

Slemp laughed; he didn't believe a word of it. He called an answer. "Then at least I'll die on a good day. I had a splendid morning. Care to hear about it?"

They were able to see a tiny piece of each other, but nothing that offered a suitable target. Slemp, peering through a slot in the cable drum, could see an inch of Decker's sleeve. Decker, through a joint in the crane's boom, could see the toe of Slemp's suede shoe. And there was something else Decker could see: the Hung Kwan, the big enforcer, had got up off the deck and was moving in a stumbling run, coming down the barge, bent over and with one arm across his stomach, his knife in his right hand.

"Don't say I didn't tell you," Decker called to Slemp, and wondered if it was a callous comment, or whether he'd tried to warn the son of a bitch.

Whichever it was, Slemp must have sensed something, or caught the meaning in his words.

Eddie Fong was in the best position to see. The Hung Kwan was almost on the Englishman when the guy swung around and shot the enforcer in the face.

The enforcer fell away. He wouldn't be getting up a second time.

Decker's view was blocked by the cable cylinder, but he saw the enforce stagger out from behind it and collapse. He wondered how many shots Slemp had fired since he'd boarded the barge, not that it would make much difference; the guy had either reloaded or was doing it now.

With no change in his tone, speaking as if nothing had happened to interrupt him, Slemp called out again. "I paid a little visit to your girlfriend. The one in apartment twelve B."

Behind the stanchion of the crane Decker's breath caught. His legs felt funny, as if all his strength had flowed down from his shoulders and arms into his thighs.

"Decker? Can you hear me with this infernal racket going on?" Slemp was only twisting the dagger; he knew perfectly well Decker could hear him, just as he knew he had to pry him loose from that crane he was clinging to like a barnacle, winkle him out, and, to stay with the shellfish analogy, gobble him up.

He had to get the Yank to rush him.

Then he'd shoot his teeth out.

"She's a very attractive piece of fluff, your girlfriend. Lovely little body. I'm a tit man, myself, and she really does have a splendid pair. Firm but soft to the touch."

Mortars pounded, Roman candles flashed, and bombettes and whistling mines shot into a pastel sky, popped and umbrellaed at one hundred feet, and sprinkled the harbor with rose and peach and apple-blossom fire.

"I just missed you this morning, otherwise you'd be on a slab right now. She answered the door in her pajamas. White ones with a red trim. Quite revealing. Bit brazen of her, don't you think?"

Decker was ice.

Faye had been wearing those pajamas when he'd left this morning. Slemp was telling the truth.

He couldn't swallow; his body seemed to have seized up like an engine run without oil.

"Naturally I took her straight into the bedroom. I wasn't about to look a gift horse in the face. Or should that be gift whore? She does rather flaunt it, doesn't she, old boy?"

Magnesium shells broke high above the water, metal powders igniting in paroxysms of flash and thunder. Hong Kong was ruby red, Kowloon was the color of a fabulous emerald.

"Athletic little trick, your girlfriend. Didn't want to at first, but once I was in the saddle, she took me over the jumps, I can tell you."

The sky, bathed blue, then pink, became a roaring conflagration, coming apart in a shower of scarlet. Two hundred feet beneath it, on a barge of the pink-tinged harbor, Decker felt the first hot red sparks of rage.

"Lovely little bum on her. She loves it up the shitter, doesn't she? I thought her moans would bring complaints from the neighbors."

Red sparks glowing, turning white inside him, heating his blood, boiling it through his veins, bubbling in his spleen.

"And what an eater! Very healthy appetite, that one," Slemp said, raising his voice, the Ruger up and ready, ready for the Yank to come and get him. "Gobbled the old knob like a starving dog. Took the full pint, too. Thirstiest little wench I've met in a long time."

Decker stomped on the anger, wrestled with its expanding strength, tried to shove it back into its bright red box. But it fought him, snaked out and clung to him, enveloped him in its strong and mindless coils.

"I fucked her five times, Decker. Natty little snatch on her. Plenty of gravy for the potatoes, what? I knew what she was doing, of course. I mean, nobody's that enthusiastic. She was trying to get my mind off why I'd gone up to the apartment in the first place. When I accused her of this she went all frigid on me. Closed up her slit tight as a drum. But I was just getting into my stride, so I tied her up. Strung up her wrists and ankles to the four-poster. You know the one, of course. The one with the blue quilt on top."

The heavens burst and threw down a crimson hail.

Red-hot flashes in Decker's head. A murky crimson tide flooding his vision.

"She was resisting me by then. All tuckered out, poor little dear. So I had to hit her," Slemp confessed. "But like a fool, I put too much breakfast into it. Popped the little slut's skull. Took all the fun out of fucking her, I can tell you that. Afraid she's dead, old chap."

Decker felt his muscles bunch in response to some signal from his red-fogged brain.

He was launched and on his way out from behind the protective slab of the crane, gun at his hip, finger ready to mash the trigger over and over again.

But something stopped him, brought him up like a man running into a force field.

Rockets glared red, then softened to pink, became glistening cool silver the color of ice.

He calmed. His anger diminished, curled up into a ball and faded away to nothing.

Decker spoke; heard himself saying words he didn't understand till he listened to them.

"In Japan, in the Age of War," Decker said, deepness and thrust to his voice, "one of the greatest swordsmen was a soldier poet named Bokuden."

"What?" Slemp said.

"He fought nineteen duels with the live blade, and killed nineteen men."

"What the devil are you glibbering about?"

"There is a record of a match that Bokuden fought against a famous swordsman named Rinsai."

"Have you gone mad?" Slemp shouted.

"Rinsai won his matches by enraging his opponents past the point of clear thinking. He killed Bokuden's wife, and broke the news to Bokuden before the match."

"The man's balmy," Slemp said out loud. He didn't like it. Was the Yank playing some kind of game, or had he cracked under the strain of facing the Ruger again?

Down the barge a battery of snowball rockets rose on flaming tails, burst prematurely, and unleashed a white blizzard of blazing phosphorus which fluttered down into the water and hissed like a sea of angry snakes.

It was getting to Slemp; he didn't like the noise, or the strobing light, like some infernal disco. And he didn't like what was happening to Decker. Whether by design or madness, he seemed to have whipped away the initiative. The bastard was spoiling things.

"Decker, you bloody idiot. What's the matter with you, man? You in a funk? Come out where I can see you, dammit!"

"Rinsai," Decker said, his voice coming to Slemp with a curious and upsetting clarity. "Tactics do not depend on the sudden charge or the cowardly blow. What matters is a mind kept cool as winter's snow. You have slain my wife. Pray to Buddha, Rinsai. You are about to lose your life."

"Madman!" Slemp yelled, biting into the word. "You've gone starkers."

A bank of repeater shells detonated with a thudding whomp. Slemp, unnerved, spun his head around and cursed the head-splitting noise. He checked on the three Chinese. They were still huddled together, obeying him like obedient dogs.

He focused past them, his eye caught by something on the harbor lit by a Vesuvius of shooting stars: a line of surging bow waves. Only two kinds of boats traveled that fast on the harbor: the Macau hydrofoil and police boats. And the hydrofoil had only two bow waves.

Slemp jerked around again, and spotted for the first time the two metal suitcases locked to a stanchion.

He had a hazy understanding of what was happening—Decker, a DEA man, the Chinese thugs, some kind of drug deal going on. And the police had found out.

Or Decker had brought them.

The skiboat, the one that had captured him, brought him here. He could still get away. But he wasn't leaving Decker behind to crow and jeer and scoff at the limey making a run for it. Decker was going to get his. And right now, by God!

He had a fresh mag in, and one up the spout. Eleven rounds.

Rush the crane, keeping low, lay down his own covering fire; a withering burst from the Ruger that would keep that interfering bastard pinned down. Then whip around the side of the crane and shoot him right through his addled brain. Burn a hole through his head with a couple of tracers.

"Decker," Slemp called, gathering himself. "I've got something for you, Decker. Your own little skyrocket."

He fired three times, as fast as he could pull the trigger, the bullets clanging into the iron boom of the crane, spanging away in instant ricochets. He fired right of the boom, left of the boom, right and left again, quit the safety of the cable cylinder, and charged like a soldier going over the top of a World War I trench, crouching, running, and firing at the same time.

He rushed, he sprinted, firing three more shots—ten gone now, saving the last round for Decker.

He made the crane, swung around the side of the boom.

Decker shot him twice in the chest.

Slemp tumbled, the Ruger jolted from his grip.

He crashed against machinery, slid down to a sitting position on the stamped metal deck. He would have looked like a man shaken up after a clumsy fall had it not been for the red stains spreading on his shirt.

Blue and yellow palm trees appeared in the sky, rockets splitting off from the blazing trunks to shape wavy green fronds. It was a superb effect, and the trees glowed like chandeliers hung from heaven.

The display lit up the gun in Decker's hand, and Reggie Slemp's face as recognition dawned.

"I say . . ." He sounded affronted, accusatory, as if somebody had picked up his mug of beer at the club. "That's my Sig-Sauer."

But Decker was gone.

He was running toward the cable cylinder, and the figure of the enforcer stretched out next to it. He shoved the Sig-Sauer into the dead man's still-warm fingers, fired off several shots to get blow-back particles on the man's hand, then dashed down the barge. He grabbed Eddie Fong, pulled him back with him toward the edge of the barge, pushed him into the skiboat, called to him, "Get him outta there!"

Eddie Fong pulled the dead fighter away from the wheel. Decker jerked on the boat's painter, freeing it.

The sallow-faced planner tried to brush by Decker, heading for the boat, the Sheung Fa trotting fearfully behind him.

Decker shoved the planner away, jumped for the boat.

Eddie Fong kicked over the engines. Decker snatched at the wheel, belted the throttles. The boat slewed, powered forward, swept around, then sat up on its stern, its twin Mercurys thrashing it over the water.

Decker had seen the police launches, wasn't sure if they'd seen him, the skiboat being on the Hong Kong side of the barge. He didn't much care, anyway. He was telling himself that Slemp had been lying, because if Slemp had been telling the truth, he didn't want to face it. To rape her, Slemp had had to hit her with that big-handled Ruger. And killed her.

No.

That's not what had happened. It had all been nothing but pathetic bragging. Faye would have been too smart for him. She would have found a way to talk him out of it, or make sure it wasn't worth his while. A cipher like Reggie Slemp would have been candy for Faye Keeble.

The skiboat slammed over the harbor, the scream of its engines shaded by the explosions in the sky, the route to Queen's Pier and its taxi rank a shimmering multicolored path.

Eddie Fong was pushing and tugging at the body of the dead fighter, got it leaning over the wildly bounding gunwale, levered it with a heave into the water. At the speed they were going, it hit with a mighty splash and disappeared astern in a shower of spray.

Eddie was yelling something at Decker. Decker ignored him, carved through the harbor craft in a swerving zigzag, powered past the tip of Kowloon, zipped the remaining mile with the throttles jammed forward. If there'd been any kind of sea running, the boat would have flipped.

A crowd on a ferry waved; several launches hooted at the speedsters. The smaller craft shied away from a wake like low surf.

Hong Kong widened and grew, the buildings gone red and yellow and pink. A crowd on the pier, down for the fireworks, pointed at the flying skiboat and wondered about it as it rushed toward them.

Decker left it to the last moment, killed the pace, belted into reverse. The twin engines bucked and shuddered in their housings, screeching at the too-high revs.

Eddie Fong fended off thick wooden pilings and shouted at Decker. "What do I do now?"

The boat had blood in it, and Eddie Fong's prints everywhere.

"Dump it!"

"Where?"

"Anywhere." Decker was scrambling for a ladder. "Castle Peak. Sink it in the anchorage." Then he was up the ladder and running for the cab rank.

The taxi ride was the worst time. Unable to take the wheel himself, slash the cab through the traffic, as he had in his dash across the harbor, he had to sit still in the rear seat and keep telling himself that Slemp had been living a little fantasy, taunting him with a make-believe tale dredged out of his erotic, sadistic imagination. He'd revealed himself, Slemp had; given a glimpse of a dream life in which he beat beautiful women and then snuffed them. Well, this was the real world now: a five-year-old Japanese taxi that needed work on the tappets, turning painfully slowly into MacDonald Road, a middle-aged Chinese behind the wheel who'd want money for the hack work.

Decker ran into the lobby, into the waiting elevator, which, like the cab, he was unable to drive any faster.

A passive occupant, he watched the indicator light creep toward twelve. When the doors slid back, he found that, instead of jumping out, racing down the corridor, he slowed and walked at a normal pace. He didn't question why. He admitted to no speculations other than ones that appealed. And what appealed most was that Major Reggie Slemp had been bluffing.

He dug into his zipped pants pocket. He'd put the key in a small billfold, ready to swim in the harbor. He extracted the billfold, found the key, inserted it into the lock.

The door opened on silence.

Involuntarily his nostrils tested the air, his forehead waiting for a bounce-back of some kind.

"Faye?" A normal voice, like that of a man home from a day at the office, hoping for a martini in a chilled glass, and a roast spluttering in the oven.

Dead silence.

His forehead prickled.

He crossed the living room, went past the sofa, the bergère chairs, the coffee bench with the green-edged copies of *Geo* magazine.

Down the hall to the main bedroom.

Decker stepped inside, ready for an image to register on his corneas, beam through to the retinas, be relayed to his brain.

What he saw was what he'd told himself he wouldn't see: Faye Keeble, naked, arms spread, legs spread, wrists and ankles lashed to bedposts, a gag in her mouth, a dried splotch of jism on her stomach, and blood on the pillow behind her head.

Washed of all thought, all feeling, Decker stood in the bedroom doorway and waited for shock.

And then Faye moved her head.

Her eyes were open, staring at him.

He ran to the kitchen, snatched up a knife, ran back to the bedroom, sliced the twine that bound her limbs. Immediately she curled herself into a protective ball like a released spring.

He fumbled the gag out of her mouth, unstopping a torrent of sobs. He held her, all he could get of her, wrapped up, as she was, in a snail form.

"It's okay. It's okay."

She unwound after a minute, flung her arms around him, said his name over and over.

"I thought you were dead, Hugh. I thought you were dead."

"I'm not dead. Slemp's the one that's dead."

The nightmare banished, the relief was almost as bad. She cried, wailed, her shoulders shaking.

"Faye. It's all right. It's finished."

She took great gulping breaths, calmed her sobs, tried for control. .Decker gentled her, asked her a question he had to.

"Did he rape you?"

"He couldn't. He wasn't capable."

Decker carefully parted the wet hair at the back of her scalp. Blood had dried around a wound that would need stitching. He hugged her, rocked her, held her close.

"Don't let me go," Faye said. "Don't leave me."

"I'm not going anywhere," Decker said.

17

Six jets flying in V formation.

Six McDonnell-Douglas Hornets, FA 18's, fighter attack aircraft, bearing the markings of the Taiwanese Air Force beneath the cockpit canopies and on the sleek swept-back wings.

The general, flying leader on the right, astern of the apex man, was feeling good. Happy, and more than a little contented. He loved to fly, especially at night. He loved the feeling of being snug in the white-lit glass cockpit, the pilot's canopy, surrounded by the blue-and-white electronic displays which told him everything he needed to know at a single sweeping glance: master monitor display, multifunction display, horizontal situation indicator, up-front control panel, digital engine monitor display. The works, all spelled out for you in easy-to-read numerals, symbols, illustrations. He loved this aircraft with its miracle avionics, its processors and computers, its unbeatable radar system that actually drew you a map of the terrain below.

And the variety of ordnance! Like a professional duelist, the general delighted in the choice of weapons: missiles like the Skyflash, Sparrows, Sidewinders, Walleyes, HARMs. Bombs like the Mark 82's, 83's, 84's, Mavericks, Hellfires, Hobos.

Not to forget the Paveway Two, a laser-guided smart bomb, a two thousand pound monster, four of which the general's Hornet was now carrying, as were the other five planes in the flight. Twenty-four bombs in all. Over twenty-one tons of high explosives.

Twenty-three of these bombs would be released on a north-to-south run. But before that, one would be released on a south-to-north run, this arrangement being for the simplest of reasons: the secondary target faced south, while the primary target faced north.

At a signal from the general, the flight, twenty-five miles east of Lema Island and twenty thousand feet above the South China Sea, began a smooth and graceful turn to bring the planes on course for the secondary target.

The general's target.

Arthur Murdoch's great glass house.

Balanced on his crutches, standing in front of the vast glass wall, Arthur Murdoch looked down the dark slope to the pinpoint lights of Repulse Bay and Stanley far below.

At eye level the sky was black, and above that, the clouds were too high to reflect the fiery celebrations that were lighting up the other side of the Peak.

Murdoch knew he wouldn't be able to see the Hornets, even though their course would take them quite near. Nobody would see them; not actually anyway. The fireworks had a maximum of three hundred feet, and the jets would be coming in seven hundred feet above that. They wouldn't appear on any military radar, because there was no military radar in Hong Kong; at least none that patrolled the skies.

There was civilian radar, of course—at Kai Tak—but that wouldn't be a problem tonight.

Murdoch had seen to that.

Two repairman had shut down the system just before eight P.M. It wouldn't be working again for a while, and in the meantime, traffic at the airport was on virtual hold, and the incoming flights had been spaced wide apart.

That had a double advantage: first, it made a visual sighting of the general's squadron from a commercial aircraft—a romote chance at any time—even less likely. Second, because there would be one or two such aircraft flying, the noise of the Hornets over the New Territories would be put down to a commercial flight—to most people jet noise was jet noise. Over Hong Kong and Kowloon, of course, the fireworks would drown out everything.

Murdoch dwelled for a moment on one of those commercial airliners landing at Kai Tak. What a sight those passengers would see! Sixteen of Hong Kong's finest buildings in flames.

They'd find out from the TV in their hotels tomorrow that a group known as the New Red Guards was claiming credit; the New Red Guards, holdovers from the Cultural Revolution, who disagreed violently with everything Hong Kong stood for—were dead set against the assimilation of the colony into China—and had moved, in their inimitable, fanatical way, to demonstrate that opinion.

Special Branch would voice strong doubts, claiming that no sabotage operation of such stunning size and effect could possibly have been mounted without their getting at least an inkling of it. But that would be discredited, put down to the embarrassment of a department caught napping.

The New Red Guards story would be believed; it was the kind of shocking and outrageous thing the world had become inured to. After all, what was the destruction of a mere handful of downtown buildings when, over a period of time, seventy-five percent of the city of Beirut had been destroyed?

And, as with all good terrorists, it could be pointed out that they could have struck during the day, when fifteen of those buildings would have been packed with office workers. But, being after symbols, not people, they'd timed the explosives to go off when the buildings would be empty, all but for a few custodial staff, a few cleaners. The smallest possible loss of life.

It would be believed, all right, if for no other reason than that there'd be nobody else to point to.

When an aerial bomb containing almost a ton of modern high explosive went off, the bomb's fins and casing were vaporized. And if there was, by chance, anything left, the subsequent flames would burn and bend and twist it beyond recognition.

Nobody would see the jets. Nobody would see the bombs fall. Nobody would find a sign of them afterward.

A large well-organized, totally committed group had taken a colossal amount of explosive into those buildings, perhaps only thirty minutes before detonation, and got away with it because most of Hong Kong had been watching the fireworks display.

Arthur Murdoch went over it in his mind for the hundredth time, and it still looked seamless.

Naturally, he didn't think that *nobody* would see the jets. The Red Chinese would see them on their radar for certain. The Foo Chow installation would know the moment they took off; would follow the flight on their radar as they did every military flight that left Taipei. They'd watch the flight fly southwest, then Canton would pick up the planes, verify that they were still heading in that direction, then lose interest in them as they always did, according to the general, once they knew they weren't coming their way.

The flight would double back, swing around, and fly north, back over Hong Kong island, a tight turn over the New Territories, then into its attack run, bombs away one thousand feet above Kowloon, and just keep on going, overfly Hong Kong out to sea, then turn north for home as if it were on its way back from a training exercise.

Would Peking tumble when they heard what had happened in Hong Kong? Probably. Once they checked on the New Red Guards and were told that there was such a group, but they were being sat on night and day, and that none of their members had been anywhere near Hong Kong, then they'd have to wonder about that flight that flew off Canton's radar screens.

It wouldn't make sense to them—Taiwanese jets bombing Hong Kong, their buddies and allies—but the circumstantial evidence would be very compelling.

They'd set their spies in action, Murdoch was certain of that; activate their people in the Taiwan Air Force, get them to snoop around. But by that time the general and his five most trusted pilots would have been buried with full military honors.

The general had often told him, after numerous glasses of Mou Tai wheat wine, how he and his favorite pilots would pile into an air-force van and drive from the base in Taipei for a little R&R, and get back, with sore heads and sore dicks, somewhere around dawn. Well, as everybody knew, Taipei had a traffic problem. Accidents happened all the time.

Peking would be left with nothing but strong suspicions. In fact, they'd know what had happened when five pilots and a general were killed in a car crash. But would anybody believe them, mouthing off yet again against Taiwan?

They probably wouldn't let it out anyway, preferring the value of a secret and the power that it brings.

Doh Mei-Doh Day.

Here at last.

Arthur Murdoch breathed in deeply with a fulfilling sense of accomplishment.

Burnt ground, it meant, the code word, Doh mei-doh.

Scorched earth was another interpretation.

In this case the correct one, because scorched earth was his tactic. When the foe was outside the gates, and there was no way of stopping him, a good general adopted such a policy; made the enemy's victory as pyrrhic as he could.

They'd get Hong Kong, the Reds—it was theirs on a plate—but they'd be getting damaged goods.

The Hong Kong Bank, the Hopewell Center, the Connaught Center, the Hakka's Tooth, all the stars of the show would be blackened ruins tomorrow, especially as the fire department was on a go slow, courtesy of his pal S. J. Lam, leader of the Green Pang.

They wouldn't be rebuilt, those structures; not now, with 1997 so close. And nobody would be willing to spend the millions it would cost to tear them down. So they'd just be left as they were, burnt-out wrecks scattered throughout the famous Hong Kong harbor-front: black, stumpy gaps in a Pepsodent smile. A symbol of the rot and decay that would come once the Reds took over.

He was leaving Hong Kong, had been all ready to go for quite some time; had ninety percent of his assets loose and ready to roll. But he'd come back, Murdoch had decided; come back as a visitor on the day the colony was handed over. And he'd stand way in the background, over in Kowloon somewhere, and think: Here you go, Peking. It's all yours. Sorry it's a little tarnished. And he'd be a happy man, because he'd have done something about the theft instead of just standing meekly by.

Which was what the goddamned liver-shitted British government was doing.

They'd wrapped up the colony in pretty pink paper, tied it with a bow, and pleaded with Peking to accept the humble present. So it was only fitting that the representatives of that crappy government, the once-and-future king, no less, and his trendy, delicate consort, should go up with the city that had been so gutlessly given away.

Was that a heavy load to carry? To be responsible for the demise of the next King of England?

Not really. There'd be banner headlines around the world, a zillion newspapers sold, a huge funeral covered by the world's media, and then everybody would snap back and perk up, and the tourists would come flooding in to get a look at the next King of England and his freckle-faced bride.

No, Murdoch decided, his conscience would be clear. He'd be helping a lot of people make a pisspot full of money, and what could be bad about that?

He checked the Heuer on his wrist, then hit a console switch and killed the lights. He stared through the glass wall, wondering if, after all, it might be possible to catch a glimpse of the Hornets in the southwestern sky. It was black and still beyond the glass, moonless, the few visible stars looking cold and remote. He fixed his eyes on one of those stars, hoping that he'd see it blacked out for an instant as a dark delta shape flashed across it. He thought about the general leading the flight. What a shame it was to have paid a man five million when that man would be dead within a day or two. The general was a whoremaster and a fool; screwing had turned his brains to water. But all the same, Murdoch had to wonder if the general might not have something working on the side. The man was vulnerable; he had to know that. There was no possible way any of this could be pinned on Arthur Murdoch, one of the city's biggest boosters, but if the truth ever got out—if it became known that aircraft had blown up those buildings—the experts would soon guess, by process of elimination, where those planes had come from.

From Japan? Out of the question.

From China? Absolutely not.

The Philippines? A crazy idea.

South Korea or Taiwan would be the guess, because there wasn't a product or a service or a person you couldn't buy in those two places. And of the two, Taiwan, because the royal couple had been blown away, and everybody knew there was no love lost between Taiwan and Great Britain. Taiwan was still smoldering at the way Her Majesty's government had tossed the colony to Peking, Taiwan's bitter enemy, like some old clothing it was through with.

The investigators would focus on Taiwan, on the air force, check out the officers who owned a squadron; find out who among those visited Hong Kong a lot, perhaps clandestinely. It wouldn't take them very long to shake out the general.

But the general would be safe as long as nobody talked. He'd feel safe. There were only nine other people who knew the truth: his five pilots, his bodyguard, the two lodge leaders, and himself, Arthur Murdoch.

The general would be sure of his pilots, sure of his bodyguard. And lodge leaders never talked for any price.

So that would leave only the brains of the outfit—the instigator.

And he was a gweilo   And maybe the gweilo might ask for his five million back or he'd expose the man who'd led the raid, and laugh at any counteraccusations.

You could never trust a gweilo.

So Murdoch wondered if the general wasn't planning an accident for him. Just as he himself was planning one for the general.

Balanced on his crutches in the living room, gazing through the immaculate glass at the blackness around the stars. Arthur Murdoch became convinced.

Sure, the general would have to try to kill him in order to enjoy his retirement free from worry.

How?

How would a man like the general arrange it?

That spooky bodyguard of his? Send him along with a knife in his hand? He'd have to get past the front door first, and the house had good security against unannounced visitors.

The general would know about the security, so he probably wouldn't try anything at the house. More likely on the way to the office tomorrow: two men and a submachine gun on a motorcycle, the way it was done in Taipei.

Or would the general try something cuter than that?

And sooner than that?

Murdoch remembered something then: a question the general had asked him at the dinner party a few nights ago.

And he was suddenly very glad he'd switched the house lights off.

The Hornets banked, wheeled, came round to face the northwest, then maneuvered onto their plotted course.

Such a joy to fly, the FA 18, and so easy, the general thought. Everything was done for you. He was always surprised that people thought you had to be some kind of of mental whiz to jockey a Mach 2 fighter. It wasn't true, although you did need to know, if you flew a Hornet, which of the sixty buttons to push, and when. But the plane had very forgiving avionics; if you made a mistake, no real harm was done. Nothing vital was erased from a memory; you just kept trying until the right picture came up.

The one area of expertise was learning your way around throttles and stick. Left hand on the throttle control, right hand on the stick. But as there were thirty control choices, your fingertips had to learn the geography of the buttons. It was a little like learning to drive a stick-shift car: after a while you didn't have to look at what you were doing.

All those buttons were the general's friends; he was most conversant with them. Especially the little button at top left on the stick. The A/G weapons release.

Press that and a rack beneath the wing ejected one of whatever

you were carrying; in this case, a Paveway smartie, which would find
its target all by itself, with a little bit of help.

The general checked his aids; a Litton ASN-130 inertial system
had got them where they wanted to be, and an APG-65 system
showed a profile of the terrain below, preset so there was no chance
of clipping a mountaintop. The Raid Assessment Mode used a
Doppler beam to build up a picture of the target.

The general chose the White Hot Mode, and got a magnificent
picture on the Head Up display of a white rectangle against a black
background: Arthur Murdoch's glass house.

It looked like a flash photograph that had been overdeveloped: all
light and very little detail.

But then, very little was needed—the bomb on the outer starboard rack knew where it was going.

With an easy confidence, and just a flick of his eye, the general
pressed one of the sixty buttons surrounding him in the white-lit
canopy.

The Laser Spot Tracker glowed red. Stayed red. Stayed red for
another half-mile.

Then changed to green.

The general's finger stabbed the weapon release, and the Hornet,
a sudden two thousand pounds lighter, bucked gently for a second
until its pilot brought it effortlessly back under control.

The bomb dropped down the sky slanted at an angle, the way a
thrown javelin falls. Eight plastic fins at the rear, four at the front,
the long slim body painted jet black. On its nose was a tubular laser
pod, mounted curiously off-center. Within this pod a micro processor considered the information it was receiving from the device the
general's bodyguard had planted beneath the south-facing balcony
of Arthur Murdoch's glass house.

The micro processor evaluated, computed, issued control commands. The bomb, sixteen feet of densely packed high-explosive
material, responded in the dark night.

"Where are you planning to be?" the general had asked, his
broad fleshy face breaking into a smile. "During the excitement?"

"Right here," Murdoch had answered. "Right in this house with
the Peak between me and the festivities."

Murdoch remembered the general's interest now; had thought of
it then as nothing more than a conversational question from a
mildly drunken dinner guest.

But had it been more than that? Could it have been the casual inquiry of a cunning assassin?

Murdoch was very good at hunches; it was one of the reasons for his success. And he had a hunch now. More than a hunch. He was certain the guy was planning to kill him tonight.

There was no fear, no heart-stopping seizure. Murdoch considered the problem logically, dispassionately.

The general was a military man. What would a military man use? A sniper?

Maybe.

But there was no way a sniper could get a shot at him except from the lawn at the side of the house. And even then, a gunman would still have to put a ladder against one of the side walls. Besides, as a quick glance over his shoulder told him, the master monitor light was a placid green. And nobody could get into the grounds without the security system knowing about it. A hundred thousand bucks' worth of security took some fooling.

So how would the general do it?

A military man.

An air-force man.

A flier.

Murdoch went by that last thought, but it came roaring back. *A flier!*

Then something did seize up inside him. Something ice cold dragged at him as two, three things whipped into his brain, one folding into the other in instant and stunning succession: a flier might just use the weapon he knew best, the one he had most access to: his aircraft.

And in the general's case that aircraft, which would be somewhere overhead now, was an FA 18. A Hornet.

Murdoch stared wide-eyed up at the sky; gazed up at the weak stars. And for the briefest instant something blocked out those stars, black against black; a long, sinister shape traveling at enormous speed.

Traveling *down!*

As a piece of the night rushed toward him, Arthur Murdoch, transfixed, had a third thought.

The fortune-teller at the temple all those years ago. He'd said a bee would kill him.

He'd been close.

It was a foolish and laughable action, but it was something to do in the half-second he had left. Murdoch snatched the can of bug spray from the clip on his crutches and shook it and sprayed it in one action; sprayed it in front of him at the glass wall, his finger jammed down on the valve.

The Paveway hit the house about ten feet above the laser device, and roughly thirty feet to the right. Its two thousand pounds, traveling at such tremendous speed, took it through the thick glass wall with a force that shattered the wall throughout its entire length, imploding it into a thousand jagged pieces.

A section the size of a tabletop slashed into Arthur Murdoch just above his hips, the air the bomb had pushed ahead of it hurling him back all the way to the rear wall.

The Paveway plowed through the beautifully laid floorboards, smashed through the joists and plaster of the ceiling below, and buried itself in the parquetry of the ground floor.

Just before it detonated, in a tidal wave of naked force, Arthur Murdoch's stunned brain had one last thought.

An amazingly lucid one.

He'd fetched up against a sofa lying on his side. Not far from him, half-covered by shredded chunks of glass, were his severed legs, one lying across the other, slightly bent at the knee.

A moment before the Paveway exploded, Arthur Murdoch looked at his separated limbs and spoke, although it was more in the nature of a sigh of relief.

What he said, at the end of an expelled breath, were two words. "At last."

Things happen fast in a military jet traveling at attack speed. It took the general and his men less than ten seconds to cover a mile, so they were already on the north side of the Peak when Arthur Murdoch's magnificent house dissolved in a hurtling ball of matchsticked wood and cauterized steel and powdered, pulverized glass. The general got only a brief view of the city as the flight flashed over its western reaches. The harbor was just a glistening black-and-red splotch off to the right, backed by the million lights of Kowloon and the bright clusters of apartment houses beyond Kwun Tong.

Twisting in his seat, looking back, the general caught a glimpse of Hong Kong-side: North Point, Central, and Western joined in a single sinuous strip of high-rise splendor. The general was fully aware that he could abort the mission anytime he liked. With the money safe in his Singapore bank, and Arthur Murdoch past history, there was nothing to stop him from calling off the raid. Except the idea appealed to him, piqued his fancy. And he was looking forward to wounding the British government by taking care of its most famous and illustrious couple. Also, there were his men to consider: countless missions practicing against dummy targets, it was time they had a real one. Otherwise they'd just go stale.

Besides, in three or four years' time, when it was safe to drop a few hints, and it was whispered that he, the general, was the man who'd led the daring raid, the prestige and respect that would be accorded him was delicious to contemplate.

Dwelling on this part of it, the general's mind wandered. He'd been navigating visually since he'd sighted the harbor and its brilliant canopy of fireworks, ignoring the displays that showed him his heading and his projected route to target. That route, which had been punched into the computer before takeoff, was designed to take the flight, from this point on, over Tsing Yi island, on over Tai Tau Shan, the western extremity of the New Territories, take them east in a shallow turn over Deep Bay, swing them south over Fan Ling golf course, bring them in to the east of Kowloon Peak, and over the harbor at Stonecutters Island. Weapons release would be one thousand meters beyond that point.

Every flier is strong in certain areas, weak in others, and the general's weak area was a tendency to lose concentration when he flew the Hornet. He could usually afford it because it was such a forgiving aircraft.

But he made a mistake this time that was not in the aircraft's power to forgive.

In Canton, twenty-five miles north of the Sham Chun River, the border between China and the New Territories, the flight had popped back onto the military radar shortly after the planes had turned north for the run on Arthur Murdoch's house.

Canton recognized the flight as the one that had flown off their radar a short while back when it had been heading southwest; recognized the flight as the one they'd picked up from the Foo Chew installation, the one that had taken off from Taipei.

And now it was heading north.

Right toward Canton.

And at bombing-run height and speed.

It was a classic maneuver: you faked to go one way, then came around on the blind side. The question was, was it another tiresome testing of defenses, or had Taipei something more serious in mind this time?

A duty officer picked up a phone. In Peking the call was answered. As was the duty officer's question.

Instructions were given; twice, so there'd be no chance of confusion.

The duty officer hung up and issued commands.

In an underground bunker the lights on a pair of manned control panels went from green to amber.

Just in case.

The general's men could see the mistake that was about to be made. And wondered about it.

Wondered if the general had made arrangements they weren't party to. Probably. The man could finesse anything. In any case, he was their leader, the paymaster, their protector. And where he went, they followed.

The flight flew a good two miles over Deep Bay before the general started a turn to the east.

When the flight straightened on that easterly course, it was over Kwangtung province.

It had passed the border of the Sham Chum River and was flying over China.

The general, contemplating future glory, was blithely unaware of this. And even if he had checked his display, it would have been way too late to correct anything. Because the moment the flight had passed the border, still heading for Canton, the duty officer in the underground bunker in that city had immediately followed orders.

The flight turned southeast now; about ten miles to go before Release. A scattering of lights below: the little farming villages of the Territories. Then a town of some size on the left: Fan Ling. The general smiled, remembering the lovelies in the town's gymnasium. Ahead, a rise of hills, and beyond them, to the east, the dark, red-beaconed shape of Tai Mo Shan, Kowloon Peak.

Descending now, losing altitude, coming in on an attack slope; a good, sharp angle.

Total blackness to the left—the Jubilee reservoir—tiny pinpoints of double lights to the right: car headlights negotiating the tortuous bends of the Twisk Road.

Lower now, approaching the forty-story rabbit warrens of Tsuen Wan Town, the northwestern edge of the harbor.

The general, a big man, happy in his white-lit cockpit, in his white flight suit, white helmet. He checked left, checking the flight. Good fliers all; maintaining formation, watching for his lead like musicians keeping one eye on the conductor. The Paveways under the planes looked like long dark torpedoes. They'd be reading signals any second now, riding down on beams like heavy ring bolts sliding down a taut wire; locked on, unstoppable.

One of those signals would be coming from a device hidden in a hedge beneath a white stone balcony of Government House.

The general could easily imagine the scene: the elegant furnishings of an upstairs reception room, local dignitaries, scarlet sashes and beribboned lapels, and women in silks and jewels. And out on the balcony, their royal highnesses and the governor and his lady, drinks in hand, the regal guests marveling at the splendor of Hong Kong on a hot and still night with fireworks in the air.

The jets hummed along.

A quick scuff of cloud ahead. Through it into dark clearness and the harbor below, the city in the distance.

Beautiful.

A web of cerise was hanging in the sky, breaking up and floating down like bunches of bright cherries. Looping rainbows zoomed up, blossomed into dazzling garlands of glittering flowers: asters and dahlias and flamboyant red roses. Shooting stars strained for height, blew apart, showered down silver and gold largess on a town already rich.

And the tall white buildings of Central, their windowed facades bouncing the fire of magnesium, phosphorus, lined up like tenpins in a bowling alley.

The general, lost in the loveliness, the sight of the target, was barely aware of something tweaking at the corner of his vision.

There! In the right-side mirror.

Rockets.

But not looping in graceful parabolas. Boring in at frightening, colossal speed.

On his tail. The whole flight. Missiles closing fast.

His brain flagged, unable to make a connection, but his left thumb responded in a conditioned move. It hit a button, top-right throttle: the chaff button.

The missiles were American, sold to China to help ward off the

Soviet menace. They knew all about chaff, shiny strips of aluminum that could upset a radar contact. They simply ignored it. They were the latest IR heat seekers, designed to win big. Released from the site near Canton, they'd gone after the infrared trace of the jets, their on-board computers sniffing the sky, tracking them down.

And now they'd found them.

Every fireworks display has a climax, a grand finale, and the people who'd designed the display for the royal visit had produced a beauty. Six racks of four-ounce howler rockets, six racks of screechers and whistlers, a bank of multishot mortars, ten 80 mm. glitter mines, croakers, blinkers, titanium gerbs, six spiral showers, a dozen four-break repeater shells, serpents, silver tails, flower fountains, and forty projectiles erupting from a French cock's comb.

All of it went off at one-second intervals, an incredible spectacular that left a couple of million onlookers ringing the harbor breathless with awe and wonder.

Even those who were used to celebratory fireworks, and had seen them at their best at Annecy, Monte Carlo, many parts of the world, were dazzled by the noise and color.

On the stone balcony outside the reception room at Government House, Prince Charles conveyed his thanks to the governor of the colony, and his congratulations.

"Magnificent, Sir David. Truly impressive."

As the governor was about to reply, six eye-searing flashes appeared in the sky, accompanied by concussive explosions like the bang of close thunder behind a fork of lightning. Burning pieces of stars, like huge spinning catherine wheels, spun briefly through the night, white-hot in the blackness, then splashed down, far-flung, in several areas of the harbor.

Princess Di, a soft and pretty presence, smiled at her host.

"I thought it was all over." she said.

The unintended irony of the remark, and that of the governor's answer might have amused the general, had he been around to hear it.

"So did I, Your Highness," the governor said.

Epilogue

Nobody had changed the pictures on the wall at I Street while he'd been away.

The same somber group of men still stood in front of the furnace with shovels held like shotguns, feet steady on the sack of seized contraband.

The notice board was a little different, although the owner of the 1985 Cougar with only 36,000 miles on it was still looking for a buyer.

The occupant of the corner office hadn't changed much either: Old Blood and Guns Johnson, as large and lumpy as ever, same iron-gray hair, still as short as a marine's, jacket open on a stiffly pressed shirt rumpled at the waist; the butt of an automatic peeking from a belt holster.

"Ready when you are, Sonny Jim," he called.

Decker entered his office, took a chair, the same one he'd sat in ten, eleven days back? Somewhere in there.

Paul Johnson had cleared his desk since his last visit, Decker noted; now there were only two files in front of him: a yellow-covered Case Report, and one covered in blue.

His boss picked up the CR, balanced it on his fingers as if he were trying to guess its weight.

"Hugh C. Decker. Boy agent," he said, his voice a growl, but no teeth in it this time. "Recently returned from Hong Kong, Pearl of the East." Johnson began to slowly leaf through the report, turning the pages like a fussy librarian. He wasn't seeing anything he hadn't read before; just going through the motions of a man refreshing his memory. "Well, let's take a look at the scorecard here. Names and numbers of the players. A crook named Arthur Murdoch," Johnson said, reading. "A killer named Major Reginald Slemp. And Brian Fairweather, madman. The three people responsible for the murder of Angela Waters. Murdoch is dead, because somebody put a bomb in his house. Slemp is dead, shot on a barge in Hong Kong harbor by a triad heavy. And Fairweather is on his way to an asylum for the criminally insane. Case closed. That is, as far as this department is concerned."

Paul Johnson glanced up at Decker, waiting for a comment. When none was forthcoming, he returned to the report, flipped a few pages, and summarized those.

"Eddie Fong. New York trafficker. Persuaded to cooperate, resulting in the arrest, for narcotics possession and suspected trafficking, of two native Hong Kong Chinese, one of whom Eddie Fong has identified as an assistant leader of one of the major lodges. Yeah, that counts as a battleship," Johnson said. He went on scanning the text. "Twenty-five kilos of heroin base locked up in steel suitcases so the sellers couldn't toss the stuff into the drink when they saw the law approaching. Sure, why not? Also ten thousand dollars federal money, previously appropriated by Eddie Fong, recovered in its entirety. All right. Now let's see what this says."

He reached for the second folder, propped one shoe against his desk, and squeaked the backrest of his chair, a big man who did not like sitting down.

"According to the statement made by the arrested felons on that barge, there were two Americans out there who'd agreed to buy the dope from them. They say the deal had been brought to them by an American Chinese who escaped with one of the police. They described the Americans to our local office, the police seemed to have leapt to the conclusion that the two Americans, described by the felons, were DEA agents."

"They've really got it in for us, haven't they?" Decker said.

"Never have liked us one little bit," Paul Johnson agreed. "The police claim that one description, light-colored hair, mid-thirties, well-built, fits you. And the other, late forties, big and quite fat, fits Agent John Rizzo."

Decker shook his head. "Can't be Johnny Risotto. He's not quite fat. He's very fat."

"Exactly," Paul Johnson said. "They're clearly grasping at straws." He returned to the report. "The felons say that the man later identified as Reginald Slemp boarded the barge and shot five of their associates, and was in turn shot by one of the Americans, the one the police say fits your description."

"Impossible. I wasn't anywhere near the harbor. I was at a friend's apartment watching the fireworks."

"Sounds reasonable," Johnson allowed. "However, there's a complication. According to the Hong Kong Homicide Division, specifically Chief Inspector Douglas Portloe, there is doubt that the triad heavy shot Slemp. Portloe says the guy was found lying behind Slemp. And Slemp was shot in the chest, not in the back."

"Wait up a second. I was told Slemp used a twenty-two. That right?"

"So it says here."

"Well, there's your answer. They're popguns. A guy can take a twenty-two slug and have time to go for pizza and beer before he falls over."

"Exactly. However, Portloe also claims the gun found on the heavy was put there in his hand."

Decker shrugged, said blandly, "Lucky Doug's a good man. But he has his off days like everybody else."

"Nobody's perfect," Johnson said, taking Decker's point. He frowned over the blue folder again. "But there's another glitch. The felons claim that the American answering your description was the one who shot Slemp. But if you were in your friend's apartment at the time, I frankly don't see how that could be possible, do you?"

"Only if there were two of me."

"One's plenty," Paul Johnson muttered. He flicked the folder closed, riffled the pages, said thoughtfully, "So you're saying that these two drug dealers, principals in a lodge that also specializes in kidnapping, extortion, prostitution, and loan-sharking would resort to fabrication of the truth?"

"I hate to call a man a liar," Decker said. "Especially somebody just trying to make an honest buck flogging twenty-five keys of boy. But I'm afraid they're fibbing."

"Why should they lie?"

Decker had to confess something. "I never could figure out the Oriental mind."

"Me neither," Johnson said, tossing the folder back onto his desk.

Some silence stretched between them before Decker asked a question. "Incidentally. About Eddie Fong. Where is he?"

"In the Program. New ID, new look. Sydney, Vancouver. Maybe even Shanghai. It'd be the safest place for him."

They watched each other for a long moment, a lot of unspoken things getting said. Then Paul Johnson started speaking as if the subject had been formally switched.

"You thought Murdoch was running dope, huh?"

"It looked that way. Now I think he was aiming for something bigger."

"Uh-huh." Paul Johnson took his right foot off the desk, put his left foot on. There weren't many moves allowed a big man in a small area.

He juggled the subject again. Or seemed to.

"They found some funny things floating in the harbor, day after the fireworks. You hear about that?"

"Yeah. The newspapers were pretty vague, but there were some interesting rumors running around the consulate."

"Metal junk, I heard," Paul Johnson said. "Looked like it might once have been a couple of FA Eighteens. And they say they had Taiwan markings. Blew up over Kowloon, God knows what they were doing there. Taiwan's not saying a damn thing, and neither is Special Branch."

"That's probably because they're all on Valium," Decker said, "on account of Charles and Di being around when whatever happened happened."

Johnson shook his head. "Weird stuff."

"It's a weird town. I like it."

"It ain't mutual." Johnson pointed to the blue folder. "Chief Superintendent James Crane wants your balls in a pickle jar."

Decker smiled fondly. "Dear old Waxy. What a swell time we had laughing and talking about the old days."

"So," Paul Johnson said, thinking about things for a minute, "anything you want to add to your report?"

"Nothing I can back up with facts. And you wouldn't want conjecture, would you?"

"Not in a CR, no. We'll have a beer together next time I get to New York. You can tell me your theory then."

A beer with Paul Johnson? Decker wondered if he'd heard right.

There was another long pause. The meeting, such as it was, was over. But Johnson had something else to say, and was taking his time getting to it. He came forward in his chair, picked up a pen, and began doodling on a jotter pad. It surprised Decker; he hadn't figured him out for a doodler; was sure the guy would have regarded aimless scribbling as a pursuit for trivial minds.

"How did you do it?" Johnson asked.

For a moment Decker thought he was asking for details about the shoot-out on the barge, but that didn't make sense. He wouldn't want to hear about that in the office, where it would be official.

"How did I do what?"

"Not fuck up," Johnson said, still doodling. "To beat Murdoch, and Slemp, and Eddie Fong's pals, you had to beat somebody else I could name. How did you do it?"

Decker understood. He explained it easily. "I took lessons."

Paul Johnson pinched in his face. "More Zen Buddhism?"

"Yeah, but with sticks."

Knowing there was more, it was Johnson's turn to wait.

Decker shifted in his chair; his boss certainly knew how to stare at a person. He said, "That first trip to Hong Kong, I made some mistakes. There were some things I did I shouldn't have. And some things I didn't do I should have. So this trip I tried to do it the other way around."

Johnson moved his head and grunted some kind of acceptance. Decker waited to be dismissed, but Johnson apparently hadn't finished with him yet. He started talking about a wildly different subject, about when he'd been a kid in school. Decker had a hard time imagining this fifty-five-year-old tough cookie, with a square jaw and a gun on his hip, running around a schoolyard in knee pants.

"I had a teacher in the third grade, an old battleax with a mustache. Miss Sweet, believe it or not. When you handed in your schoolwork, she graded on two standards only. It came back with one of two rubber stamps at the top of the page. A red elephant meant you'd flunked and were a dunce. A blue star meant you passed, you did okay." Paul Johnson tore off the top sheet of the jotter pad and handed it to Decker.

Decker solemnly accepted it, got up, nodded at Johnson. Johnson nodded back. Decker left the office and went down the corridor. Faye Keeble, in a plain white dress, very little makeup, and looking marvelous, turned away from the picture she'd been examining: the pen-and-ink drawing of the old DEA headquarters on Connecticut Avenue.

She took Decker's arm as they headed for the elevator.

"How did it go?" she asked. She stood close, watching the indicator light begin its climb.

"Not bad." Decker held out the piece of paper Paul Johnson had given him. "I got a blue star."

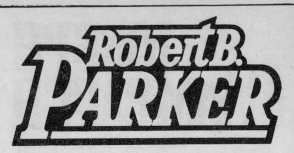